THE TWIN PANTHERS

HÉCTOR FOX

The Twin Panthers

Copyright © 2024 by Héctor Fox

Fifth Avenue Press is a locally focused and publicly owned publishing imprint of the Ann Arbor District Library. It is dedicated to supporting the local writing community by promoting the production of original fiction, nonfiction, and poetry written for children, teens, and adults.

Printed in the United States of America

First Printing 2024

Cover art by: Raúl Cruz
Editor: Gabriella Jones-Monserrate

ISBN: 978-1-956697-35-3 (Paperback); 978-1-956697-36-0 (Ebook)

Fifth Avenue Press
343 S. Fifth Ave
Ann Arbor, MI 48104
fifthavenue.press

For my mother, whose passion for storytelling and writing inspired me to craft my own worlds in my own words.

For my uncle, who gave me a copy of the Popol Wuj *as a child, a gift that undoubtedly shaped my fate.*

"*Estas son las cinco direcciones*
según los astrónomos mayas:
El rojo amanecer del día (oriente),
el negro atardecer agónico (occidente),
el blanco del norte friolento
el poder amarillo en el sur
y en el centro del mundo
el verde azul intenso del trópico."

—de *Las cinco direcciones* por Victor Montejo, 1995

"These are the five directions
according to Mayan astronomers
The red dawn of day (East).
The dying black of evening (West).
The white chilly North.
The yellow power of the South;
and in the center of the world
the intense blue-green
of the tropics."

—from The Five Directions by Victor Montejo, 1995

Author's note

THIS ISN'T WHERE IT STARTED. But we can begin here. It's kind of like a dream—except you're awake. Mostly awake. Sometimes it's just the dream. Clouds of smoke that reveal a path you've never walked.

But it's not real. It's not anybody else's story. All those academics, they wouldn't like it anyway. They think they know things. So, truth is always scary to them.

But this isn't truth.

It's just an idea. Like an old woman's smile.

Have you ever had a family? I think it would be nice to have one like this. A young girl's laugh.

Anyway, just take it in small doses. You'll do fine.

Pronunciation Guide
and Terminology

The names for people, places, social titles, etc., in this novel draw from a Mesoamerican background, and as such, include words, sounds, and spelling conventions potentially unfamiliar for an English-speaking audience. Most are adapted or derived from different Mayan languages (mostly K'iche' and 'Yucatec' Maya), but some are also modified from Nahuatl. The table below gives a pronunciation guide for the spelling of names and locations used in this book. Most importantly, though, the letter "X" is pronounced like "SH."

The letter "X" is pronounced like "SH."
The letter "X" is pronounced like "SH."
The letter "X" is pronounced like "SH."

LETTER	PRONUNCIATION	NOTES
A	ah	Never 'ey'
E	eh	Never 'ee'
I	ee	Never 'ay'
O	oh	Never 'uh'
U	oo	Never 'uh'
X	sh	As in 'fish'
Ts/Tz	ts	As in 'cats'
J	h	As in 'hole' but with the tongue farther back in the mouth than for English or Spanish
H	h	More light, breathy, and airy than an "h" in English

How do you pronounce the letter "X"?

Many words, character names, and place names in this book include sounds with what is sometimes called a "glottal stop." This is indicated by an apostrophe (') after the letter (e.g., Ts', Tz', K', T', Ch', Q', etc.). The idea with these is to pronounce the consonant but without letting air escape the throat. Think of closing your throat slightly while making the consonant sound so that no vibration in your throat can be felt for that letter when you say it.

Glottal stops can also occur between vowels. In this case, there is a pause between the two vowel sounds. The first one finishes completely, and then the second one is pronounced. In English, an example of this occurs in the pronunciation of the word "bottle," which would be written like "bo'ul" if such glottal stops were recognized in English writing. It is also present in the correct pronunciation of "Hawai'i," where there is a noticeable pause between the two 'i' sounds.

Just as in real Mayan languages, the presence of a glottal stop in this novel **can and usually does alter** the meaning of a word or name. For example, the difference between snake (kan) and yellow (k'an) is the presence of a glottal stop. Double vowels without a glottal stop are used to indicate a "long" vowel sound. This is not a distinction used in English writing conventions but can be heard in the difference of the 'a' sound between 'had' (long 'a') and 'hat' (short 'a'). This doesn't crop up too much, it's not a huge deal to miss out on it.

Finally, the people and nations centered in this novel do not all speak the same language despite sharing similar language features (like how French and German are different but share an alphabet and many similar sounds). And even the people within one kingdom vary in how they speak. So, some spelling differences exist in how names are written by different people. For instance, one character might use 'ts' while another uses 'tz.' If this seems confusing at first, consider the following spelling variation in common English names: Katelyn vs. Caitlin, Ashleigh vs. Ashlee, Nickolas vs. Nicolas, Catherine vs. Kathryn, etc.

Some examples of important words with their pronunciation:

"Ajaw" (meaning ruler or king) pronounced "*ah-how.*"

"Yaxchilan" pronounced "*yahsh-chee-lahn.*"

"Itza'" pronounced "*eats-ah.*"

"Xok" pronounced "*shoh-k.*"

"Chanil" pronounced "*chahn-eel.*"

Part One:
Panther Cubs

First Moon

Men go to war for only three reasons. Pride, wealth, or starvation. A dangerous thing happens when all three come together at once.

—Letters from A Queen in Exile

CHANIL TASTED BLOOD IN HER MOUTH. She felt the salty, copper-tasting liquid slide down her large lips and over her square chin. She spat the blood out and clenched her jaw. Her muscles ached. Sweat drenched her light, woven armor. The early morning sun peered down at her mercilessly, baking the area in a wet heat that promised it would be a humid day, indeed.

But she couldn't stop. No matter how tired she felt.

Another attack came. A horizontal strike that could decapitate a man's head. She blocked it with her shield reflexively. Such movements were ingrained in her eleven-year-old body from her endless training sessions. Nevertheless, her opponent was huge—a tall warrior woman who towered over her. The power in that woman's strikes felt like running into a ceiba tree at full sprint. The reverberations from the impact shook Chanil's arm and shoulder joint.

Another attack. And another. And another. Her opponent was relentless.

Chanil moved her body in the way she had been taught, starting from the moment she was old enough to hold a stick. She braced against her shield to block and slipped her own weapon around and under her opponent's blade to counter.

But her movements were slowing.

She was tired.

Her body hurt.

And not just from combat.

"Why do we fight, Chan?" The voice was strong. It echoed off the painted stone walls of the pyramid temple buildings surrounding the plaza where Chanil fought.

Another attack. Another block. Not as steady this time. Chanil was losing focus. The heat was bothering her.

"Why do we fight, Chan?" The woman's voice came again.

This time, Chanil answered compulsively, the words ingrained in her as much as any other technique her mentor had taught her.

"We fight to protect our people, our relatives, our land!" Chanil shouted, her voice hoarse. She needed water.

She braced herself for another attack. It didn't come.

More words echoed around her in the plaza instead. She knew they came from the warrior woman, but they seemed to fill the air like wind in a thunderstorm and whip at her from all directions.

"That's right, Chan. You must have a purpose for why you fight. You have to fight for something greater than yourself. Otherwise, when the day comes you run into something stronger and tougher than you, it will make you quit—unless you have that inner purpose that keeps you going."

"Yes, Lady Night Star." Chanil's throat managed to croak the words out. She was bathed in sweat. She huffed and gasped, trying to catch her breath. She leaned her weight against her shield. It seemed impossibly small compared to the long, full-sized weapon that Night Star wielded.

"I can keep going, my Lady," Chanil said. She clenched her jaw again. She swallowed the blood in her mouth and cast a hard look up at the tall woman.

Night Star looked down at her and smiled warmly. The older woman was tall and broad and the fierce trainer of the Yaxchilan army. She had a square jaw and hard chin that made her imposing and frightening in battle. But her eyes could be soft. And now that the lesson was over, her lighter brown irises beamed at Chanil, full of affection. The woman let her big lips spread in a wide smile. A trick of the light seemed to bounce the sun's rays off her deep brown skin, and Chanil felt, for a moment, as if she were looking at a reflection of her own face—of the woman she could be, the warrior she could become. If she kept training.

And she wanted to keep training.

Despite the pain and the sweat and the blood. Despite the aches in her muscles that would plague her every step tomorrow. Every moment spent training was one less moment spent wearing stupid, fancy clothes. Or learning how to step correctly as a royal lady. Or how to lower her voice properly for when a prince from another realm came to visit.

Training meant freedom. Training meant forgetting her duties as the heir of the largest kingdom in the east. Training meant she didn't need to remember she was destined to be a queen. She could just be what she wanted. She could just fight.

"I'm ready," Chanil said.

Night Star saw the shift in the young girl's attitude. Chanil had been uncertain for a moment. Tired. Exhausted. Then she switched. She dug deep and pulled out her resolve.

But Night Star shook her head. "We're done for today, little one." Chanil opened her mouth to object. But Night Star looked up at the sky. "You see where the sun is, yeah?"

Chanil slumped her shoulders. Another lesson, she thought grimly. They were definitely done fighting.

"Yes, Lady Night Star."

"And where is it?"

"Just past where it was last time we stopped," came the honest but reluctant reply.

Night Star nodded. "A little longer each time. That's how we improve."

Chanil nodded. Her face was squished into a disappointed look, though. Her brown eyes, lighter in color than was common in her family, were somewhat downcast. Her square jaw was held in an expression that belied the girl's insecurities.

Night Star sighed. She loved Chanil deeply. She had known the girl all of her life. She felt like she understood the heir-apparent better than most.

"Don't want to go, yeah?" Night Star asked, kneeling down and setting aside her weapons to look young Chanil in the eye.

The girl made an equivocal expression. "It's going to be such a long ceremony. And they're all . . . watching me. Makes me uncomfortable."

Night Star nodded. "You're a woman now, Chan. And the whole city is here to celebrate you and your future."

"Did the whole city celebrate the first time *you* bled?" Her question was half sass, half genuine interest.

Night Star smiled again. Her full, red lips spread wide across her face. Her expression beamed like a second sun. "Things are different where I come from. But we celebrate just as much on the Island as we do here in Yaxchilan. I got many presents. And so will you."

A sigh escaped Chanil's throat. She twirled her training weapon against the ground, looking at the patterns of dust it kicked up. "I don't want all those presents. I don't *need* all that stuff. I just want to fight—with you."

"I know, Chan. And I want that too. But maybe this will help." And then the older woman stood up suddenly.

She reached under her training armor and pulled out a small deerskin bundle. She looked at it long enough that Chanil was also forced to look. Chanil scrunched her face suspiciously, but her eyes sparkled.

Night Star shrugged casually. "—See, I was going to give this to you during the ceremony. But since now you don't want presents . . ."

"What is it??" Chanil's brown eyes went wide, and she couldn't keep the excitement out of her voice. A present from Night Star was different. That, she very much wanted.

The older woman handed Chanil the bundle with a smirk. Far above, the morning sun still baked the large plaza. Ringed around the open area, the tall pyramid temples were painted in brilliant colors and carved with glyphs and depictions of fearsome creatures and old gods, who all watched the two women below. One end of the plaza was open, and a broad avenue led out into the huge markets of Yaxchilan. Chanil wondered if this present was from those markets.

But when she opened the bundle and saw what was inside, she knew that this had come from nowhere nearby. The gift was a necklace. A simple, black cord that held a beautiful blue-purple gemstone pendant carved with an odd design.

She looked up at Night Star. "It's wonderful, my Lady. But . . . what is it?"

The laugh that came in response was long and loud. It grew from deep in Night Star's belly. "It's from the Island, from my people, the Ayiti. Think of it like a protection spell, yeah? It will keep you safe during all those deadly lessons on proper etiquette with Lady Xok."

She grinned mischievously, and Chanil smiled back with her wide mouth. Chanil had full lips, and a broad face that Night Star knew some of the other kids teased her about. But her smile brightened up Night Star's whole world. She clasped the necklace around Chanil's neck, and the girl beamed up at her. The older woman knelt again to say something else to Chanil.

But this time, the angle of their bodies stopped the sound from carrying over to the figure, that had been watching the scene unfold from the bushes at the edge of the plaza. Peering out from those bushes was a pair of dark eyes. The eyes were so dark that they looked black and glinted with a glassy texture, like obsidian stones. Wisps of strange colors danced in those cavernous irises as they stared out onto the scene with Chanil and Lady Night Star. Jade green. Lightning yellow. Sometimes, blood red.

Dark skin against dark eyes blended into the shadows under the bushes. The figure crouched like a stalking, black jaguar. She saw everything. She saw the way the two women in the plaza moved, how the younger one beamed up at the older one. But the spying figure also perceived her world in other ways. She could smell those two in the plaza. The acrid scent of their sweat. The rounded, earthy scent of the doubt and worry in the younger girl. The flint and obsidian dust on the tall, older woman's boots.

And, sometimes, if she tried hard enough, the figure with obsidian eyes thought she could almost hear their heartbeats, too. Distant thumping sounds, like two drums out of sync. And then a faint rushing, like a river that pulsed in time with the thumps. Only, not a river. It was like—

"Itza'!" The voice came from behind her. It was a low baritone, heavy and masculine. She recognized it at once.

She whirled from her hiding place and put a finger to her lips. She cast her intense, obsidian stare up at the owner of that voice. The man was grinning wolfishly down at her. He was a giant, chiseled form of dark muscles and lighter scars. His hair, a chaotic mass of light curls, fell across exactly one half of his face, exposing a long, snake-like scar along his jaw on that side.

"Shh!" Itza' insisted from her shadowy hiding place.

The man covered his grin with one massive hand. "And what are we spying on today, little one?"

Without a word, Itza' beckoned for him to come and see. Obligingly, the giant mound of muscles knelt down awkwardly beside the young girl. He didn't really fit behind the bushes like she did. But that didn't matter. It only mattered that Itza' believed they were hidden.

"Look there, Great Ajaw, my Lord 5-Thunder," Itza' said, pointing to the figures of Chanil and Night Star as though they were a pair of mysterious creatures never before seen in these lands.

The Ajaw of Yaxchilan looked at her with a wry grin. "You do know you can call me Papa, right?"

Itza' shushed him again. "And reveal our secret identities, Great Ajaw?" Clearly such a notion was preposterous.

Lord 5-Thunder opened his mouth. "Ahh, of course. Good thinking, my loyal subject."

Itza' nodded, apparently satisfied that their real identities as father and daughter were now safely hidden away.

"I have found something most troubling, my Lord," Itza' continued. "A fearsome warrior! And she appears to be training an apprentice, Great and Honored Ajaw. From the look of it, she is going to be a great warrior herself one day. They could pose considerable threat to you, my Lord."

Lord 5-Thunder scowled fiercely. His brow furrowed, and the snake scar on his jaw wriggled. He nodded, as though considering how best to deal with this threat.

"And how do you think we should proceed?" he asked. "Should we attack and destroy this up-and-coming threat?" The wolfish grin returned to his face as he imagined them launching a pretend surprise assault on Chanil and Night Star.

But little Itza' was shaking her head. "I advise not, Great Ajaw. Such violence might invite . . . reprisals later on." The complicated words sounded funny on her six-year-old lips.

Lord 5-Thunder nodded in genuine admiration this time. "Very smart thinking there, little one."

Itza' made a face, her black eyes shimmering like obsidian blades for a second, and the Ajaw felt an actual chill. "I'm not little!"

She shook her head as though exasperated. "Perhaps an act of kinship? We could offer them an alliance?"

A deep chuckle sounded from the massive being. "Good thinking, my child. Very astute."

He stood up suddenly and gently pulled the young girl from her hiding place. "Now—time for you to go get ready, yeah? Before you-know-who finds you've been spying again."

He started to say more, but a violent cough shook his body

like the tremor of an earthquake shaking a mountain. He pushed it down and smiled, then said, "I'll go offer this alliance to our friends there."

Itza' smiled. Her eyes glinted and she giggled. Despite the intensity of her eyes, her easy smiles and childlike giggles usually made people like her instantly. "Fine, Papa," she said, realizing play had to end sometime. "But then what should I say if our Glorious Queen asks where I've been?"

The Ajaw grinned again and backed up, hands in the air. "Official business for the Ajaw, of course."

Itza' giggled again and ran off for the palace. She knew there was much to do before the ceremony for her sister's first moon—whatever that meant.

Atop the Temple

Blood flows in only one direction.

—*Xelaq'am's Songs*

"OH DEAR. LOOK AT YOUR FACE, CHAN!" Lady Xok looked mortified, mouth agape. Her regal, wraparound dress danced in the breeze from the open windows. The animal figures embroidered on its shimmering strands seemed to writhe and come alive with the Queen's movements.

Chanil tried to shrug it off as she entered the stone chamber. "It's just my face, Mama."

"You're bruised!" Lady Xok's sharp tones cut into Chanil's kneecaps like the bite of the stingray needles that would prick her later in the ceremony.

Chanil took her place in the center of the open room. Xok crossed to stand in front of her, a disappointed look on her face as she assessed the dark spot on Chanil's chin from where one of Night Star's sticks had landed that morning.

"This will take a while to cover up, my dear. And we already have to rush to get you ready in time." Xok's voice was becoming sterner.

The Queen of Yaxchilan saw only the ceremony ahead and what needed to be done before it began.

Chanil just sighed in resignation and closed her eyes.

I don't really need to be here anyway, she thought as she slipped into the all too familiar role of passive participation that she always adopted while she was made ready for fancy ceremonies.

"Really, couldn't Night Star give you one day off for this? Everyone will be watching." Xok had asked a question, but Chanil knew from experience that she wasn't really looking for a response. Chanil remained silent. Then Lady Xok called the aides in.

With her eyes still closed, Chanil heard the *swish* of robes. She felt the next several moments as a blur. A swarm of young girls came and went through the room. They combed her gentle curls and twisted the strands, braiding them up into a tight ringlet around her head. They brought in makeup and paint to cover her face. Not just for the bruises, but to paint her face appropriately for the ceremony. Chanil knew she would barely recognize herself by the time they were done.

Multiple aides worked at once, moving deftly around each other and speaking in quick, short phrases that indicated their long familiarity with this work. When they had finished painting her mask, she said, "I learned a new trick today, Mom. A twisting lunge behind my shield. It was great!"

Silence. Only the whispers of the wind and the aides.

Chanil peeked her eyes open. Lady Xok had already left—the Queen was gone. Chanil sighed and looked down for a while before closing her eyes again.

And then came the clothes. The aides dressed her in a fancy headdress, but not one of the exciting ones that the warriors wore. This was a maiden's headdress. No fearsome, gaping jaguar maw or brilliant coyote in mid-strike. This was a small, dainty, simple corona of feathers atop her head, almost like a crown. As they carefully tied the small headdress in the back, the curtains at the doorway swished open, and little Itza' entered, followed by her own flock of aides.

"Hey Itz," Chanil said loudly.

"Hey Chan," the younger sibling responded with a grin. "You look great!"

Chanil grinned awkwardly. "Thanks, little one. Your turn, yeah?" Itza' nodded and sat on a tall stool several feet away. The aides went to work on her too. They pulled back her hair and began braiding it. Unlike the soft, brown curls Chanil had, Itza's hair was jet-black and pin straight. The younger girl had more of an oval face than Chanil or their father, Lord 5-Thunder. It was somewhat like Lady Xok's, but Itza' got her strong jaw from the Ajaw. Her nose bridged out and hooked down at the tip as it broadened. She looked very much like the faces of past queens carved and painted on the murals and stone monuments around Yaxchilan. Her skin was the darkest brown, and her movements were unusually fluid and pantherine for one so young.

"Hey Chan . . ." Itza' said after a while. The aides were painting spots on her arms and shoulders. When they were done, she would look like a jaguar skin had been draped over her whole body. It was the young girl's favorite look.

"Hey Itz," the older sister responded. Her own look was almost complete. Her arms and upper chest were unpainted, but she had a sinewy mat of gold and silver strands, embellished with jade and other gemstones, that sat along her clavicles, her upper chest, and wound up and around her neck. Her long wraparound dress shimmered. And the feathers in her headdress swayed in the breeze from the open windows.

"What's a first moon anyway?" Itza' asked.

Some of the aides giggled, the ones old enough to know. Chanil smirked and shook her head at her six-year-old sibling. "Trust me, little one, you're better off not knowing."

Lady Xok, the Queen of Yaxchilan, knelt in full regalia atop the giant temple in the central plaza of the city. Her dress was long and richly embroidered in patterns and glyphs depicting the story of her lineage. Her headdress was studded with gems and precious metals that glinted in the bright afternoon sun. Affixed to the headdress was a corona of macaw and quetzal feathers that danced above her head, quivering in the wind brought in at such heights. She had jeweled armbands and rings and a necklace of teardrop-shaped jade pendants that lay across her entire upper chest.

She knelt atop the temple, a stingray needle in one hand and a small bowl in the other. In front of her, the head priest of Yaxchilan—the day-keeper, Q'anchi'—stood with an incense burner affixed to a long staff. The sweet-smelling smoke of incense swirled around the two figures. Q'anchi's golden and green robes shimmered brightly under the hot sun. His fire-brown eyes gleamed with a fierce intensity as he waved the incense smoke over the Queen and prayed. His hair, salt and pepper locs, was pulled back into a loose bun atop his head. The tattoos and ritual scars that covered his entire body peeked out from under his sleeves and collar.

In the still, humid air, the pounding of the slit-drums down below reverberated throughout the entire plaza. A dozen drummers beat out the familiar rhythm for the immense crowd. Every head strained to look up the steep temple steps, and every pair of eyes watched as the Queen deftly pricked her tongue with the stingray needle and allowed a few drops of blood to fall into the bowl. The warm liquid dripped reluctantly, her body stubborn after so many years of bloodletting.

In her mouth, she felt the copper taste of blood mix with the metal bite of the gold inlays in some of her teeth. She stood up in one fluid motion while Q'anchi' continued to pray, his loud voice carrying over the sounds of the drums and settling like a gentle rain over the crowd.

From behind Lady Xok, just out of view of the immense crowd, Lady Chanil of the Sky stood waiting. Her feet shifted uncomfortably in her fancy sandals, and she swallowed nervously. She felt the tight necklace resist her throat's movements, straining against her wide neck.

Chanil was vaguely aware that her mother was speaking to the crowd now. She knew that the Queen would declare what an important day this was for the city of Yaxchilan and the whole realm. How the eldest child of Lord 5-Thunder was now a woman. And how their future was secured.

Can't our people's future be secured more . . . privately? Chanil thought, clenching her jaw as she realized it was almost time for her to step out into the light and face the giant crowd.

Almost without realizing it, one of her hands reached into her pocket and fiddled with the necklace Night Star had given her earlier. The one that wasn't fancy enough for her to wear during this ceremony. She rubbed her worries and anxiety into the blue-purple pendant and felt a strange sense of calm, as though the stone were really taking those feelings away.

"You're almost up, sis!" Itza's excited voice reminded her. Chanil's nervousness returned as nausea.

"Thanks, little one, I know," she said to the little six-year-old figure painted like a regal jaguar standing next to her in the shadows.

The drums stopped. That was Chanil's cue.

She swallowed again against the tight-fitting jeweled necklace and stepped forward. The song of seashells accompanied each of her steps from the anklets she wore. Moving from shadows into light, she was almost blinded at first. The sun was intense and hot. And humid. The rains would be coming any day now.

She regained her bearings as her eyes adjusted. In front of her: Lady Xok, smiling but waiting intently. Q'anchi', also smiling but eyes filled with warmth and admiration. To her right, Lady Night Star in a warrior's regalia. As second wife to Lord 5-Thunder, Night Star's presence was also required for these kinds of things. On Chanil's left, the Ajaw of Yaxchilan, Lord 5-Thunder, as tall and imposing as ever, with a corona of feathers that seemed to reach the sky itself and block the sun for a moment as Chanil moved forward.

Reaching the edge of the platform, Chanil tried not to look down. She didn't want to see the steep staircase that she knew would be lined with colorful banners and gifts that such-and-such prince or sajal or village leader had brought for her. She didn't want to see the swarm of faces below, an entire city watching her with rapt attention, wondering if she would be a worthy queen for them one day.

She raised her arms. That was what she was supposed to do now.

The crowd cheered and whooped. The drums slowly came back, pounding out a gentler rhythm this time.

Might as well get it over with, she thought. She hoped her mother would approve of her delivery. She swallowed again. Then she said the words that Xok had taught her—drilled into her relentlessly—day after day after day after day.

Still cloaked in shadows behind Chanil, little Itza' watched her sister intently. Itza' saw the way the light caught on her sister's dress and how bright and beautiful and strong she looked. She also saw the tension in Chanil's shoulders. She knew her sister was nervous and would need some time later to talk.

That was fine. It was just Chanil's way.

Lady Xok made a face at Itza' then, and Itza' realized she was supposed to come out too. She scurried to stand at the Queen's side. The sunlight was bright and Itza' preferred the shadows. But she stood there, listening to the poetic words Chanil recited to the crowd. Then she looked down at the crowd and down the intricately carved and painted stone steps of the pyramid. Every single step had a gift.

Itza's mouth dropped open. Whatever a first moon is, she thought, I definitely need to get one. Maybe Chan can give me one when she is queen.

The Great Army

When we count the days, we learn the future. Life plays out like a spiral, a giant cycle, coming back again and again to the same patterns and rhythms that have happened before. Pay attention to the past, and the future will be made clear. At least, that's what my teachers used to say.

—the Book of Queen Snake Lady

THE FIRST TIME ITZA' HEARD them mention the Great Army, she was almost eleven years old. She lay motionless in the rafters high above the council meeting chamber, spying on the scene below. She peered through spaces between wooden boards, dark eyes caught in shadows that rendered them nearly invisible. She couldn't see everyone in the room this way, but she could hear them. And smell them. Everyone had distinct scents, she knew. And they picked up more and more scents throughout the day, telling a story of where they had been.

"The New Alliance is spreading, my Lord." A smooth voice—feminine, strong, and confident. The person was out of view, but Itza' recognized Lady Night Star easily. Her boots smelled of flint and obsidian. "Their Great Army conquers and consumes everything as it marches."

There was a low growl in response. Deep and heavy with violence and mischief. That was the voice of Itza's father, sitting almost directly below where Itza' spied. He smelled of the blood he had given in ceremony earlier that morning. "Maybe that is what Tlapallo wants to talk about when he visits."

"Have our neighbors joined with the Great Army, then?" Itza' heard the voice of her sister, the youngest voice. Her hair smelled woody with fluted edges. She was only half visible below Itza'. Chanil was fifteen, and as the heir-apparent, she was now part of the council meetings her father had with his advisors.

Itza' had decided she should be part of these meetings then, too.

"I'll ask Tlapallo when he gets here," Lord 5-Thunder replied.

Itza' knew who Tlapallo was. This wasn't her first time eavesdropping on the council. Besides, the man had visited before. He ruled Coyolapan, the realm directly west of Yaxchilan. His people were Tlaxcala, like most of those directly west. Itza's people were the Winaq—but everyone just called them 'The People.' They ruled the lands in the east.

She didn't know who the Great Army was, though. But she had heard of the New Alliance. It was an empire that people said was far, far away in the west. But now, it sounded like maybe they weren't so far away anymore.

"If Tlapallo joins them, my Lord, we would lose a valuable trading partner." Soft words. Perfect tone and pitch. The Queen had spoken.

"And if the New Alliance is looking to spread this far, then they might come for us next." The raspy fire of Q'anchi's voice floated up to Itza's ears. She could smell the incense on him, the medicines he made to heal their people, and the cacao beans he used to see the future.

"Q'an is right. We have to do something." Chanil's voice, young and brazen, returned to the conversation.

"Such as?" Lord 5-Thunder prompted his daughter.

Chanil lifted her arms. "Maybe we stop the Army before it gets to Tlapallo's city. Or we make a deal with him to not join up with the Army."

Lady Xok shook her head. Her voice patronizing as she said, "We cannot simply launch our army against theirs, Chan. The Great Army is vast, much bigger than ours."

"I'd like to avoid open war if possible, yeah?" Lord 5-Thunder said flatly.

"But we have to do something! Don't we?" Chanil was insistent.

"We do," came Lady Night Star's calm tone.

Lord 5-Thunder leaned back in his chair, one hand half over his mouth. He spoke from behind a pair of fingers. "I've known Tlapallo a long time. We fought together. He's a good man. When he gets here, I'll ask him."

"And if he says he's joining them?" Chanil leveled her gaze squarely at her father. Her strong features had only grown stronger as an adolescent. Her chin was dimpled, her jaw sharper, and her look more confident.

"Then we find out why and try to reason with him. I'm telling you—he's a good man. He'll listen. Now—what else do we have?"

And that was that. The Ajaw had spoken. Yes, he listened to his council—which was more than some ajaw did. Yes, he listened to his wives, both Xok and Night Star. But, ultimately, Lord 5-Thunder was related to the gods, and his word was law. No one else had such authority in the realm.

Chanil could do nothing without his approval. She felt her gut twist and she clenched her jaw. She knew she was young, but she also knew you didn't just wait while an enemy got stronger and stronger. You didn't stand still while potential allies were scooped up or turned against you.

Let's see what this Tlapallo has to say, she thought, when I ask him myself.

"Chan, you have to take smaller steps. You don't want to intimidate people." Lady Xok watched Chanil try to cross the room from one end to another in proper fashion for a royal lady. Small steps, soft but not silent—utter silence would be unnerving. Back straight, chin slightly lowered. Elegant but not demanding. Poised but not cocky. It was simple.

Except it wasn't for Chanil. She either stalked like a jaguar in the hunt or strode like a warrior who had just returned from massacring an entire army on her own. Nothing in between.

Chanil turned from the far end of the room and strode back to Lady Xok. Head held high, shoulders back, small steps—

"No, now you're being *too* quiet, Chan! It's . . . well, it's unusual." Lady Xok crossed to meet Chanil in the middle of the room.

"Itza' is just as silent, Mom."

Lady Xok pursed her lips and fussed with Chanil's robes. "Believe me, I *know*," she said in a terse voice. "The Twin Panthers— did you know they call you that in the streets? Always sneaking around in silence. It's . . . not what I want my children remembered for, yeah?"

She pursed her lips again, looking Chanil over. Xok's septum piercing moved with her nose, and the jewel in her chin tilted forward as though also assessing the young lady.

"Mama, can we talk about the Great Army and Lord Tlapallo?"

Xok raised her eyebrows. "You certainly had strong opinions on *that* earlier today."

"We can't just sit back while a terrible enemy is coming."

"Your father is going to handle Lord Tlapallo. This isn't the first time an empire has risen in the west, you know." She strode back to the entryway of the room.

"Now, let's try it again. Make *some* noise, okay?"

Chanil puffed her cheeks and sighed hard. She started walking again.

It went on and on like that. First, lessons on how to walk. Then how to speak. Quiet but not too quiet. Clear but not overly aggressive. Tone and pitch must be perfect.

Chanil disappointed her mother on all counts.

Then calendar lessons—lessons on what days were good for marriage, for rest, for specific ceremonies. Lessons on their neighbors and family members—where each cousin, uncle, aunt, and other cousin lived; who ruled what kingdoms and what they believed or ate or liked to eat or dreamt or had visions about or how many unmarried sons they had or the size of their harvests, the amount of obsidian in their mines, the clothes they wore, or—

"It's time for training!" Chanil hadn't meant for her voice to sound so excited. It had been hours, and finally it was the time when Night Star trained the younger warriors. Chanil waited all day for this.

"We aren't done yet, Chan," was Xok's curt reply. She opened the book—the codex—again and pointed at the astronomical chart that Chanil was supposed to be able to read by now.

"I'm exhausted, Mama. I need a break." She stared down at the chart and felt nauseous. There were so many numbers.

"Fighting is not a break. And you won't be fighting every day as queen, yeah? But you will need to *know* this stuff. You can skip a day of smashing sticks and getting bruised to focus on the important parts of being queen."

Chanil turned to look up at Xok. "I'll need to fight if the Great Army comes, wont I?"

"Not this again, Chan."

That was how it had been all day since the council meeting. Every time Chanil tried to mention the Great Army and her thoughts, or ask a question, Xok pushed it aside in favor of the lesson of the moment. Chanil was getting irritated. She had ideas and opinions, and it seemed no one wanted to hear them.

I'm going to be queen, she thought bitterly. People would have to listen to her then.

Abruptly, she got up. "My mind is full, Mama. I need to do something with my body. I'm going to go train."

Xok huffed, but she couldn't really stop Chanil. The young woman gave her a slight bow—the wrong kind for this situation,

Xok noted but decided to keep that to herself for now—and then walked out of the room. As soon as she was outside, Chanil rushed off, taking long, heavy strides that she knew Xok would never approve of as she rushed to her room to get her training gear.

The large, open plaza where Night Star trained the younger warriors was located just off the city's central square. It was a raised field with stone steps on three of its four sides leading into the main ball-court where the ceremonial games were held and down to avenues that penetrated deep into the city. The back of a stout, terraced pyramid formed the fourth side of the plaza—a tall red wall topped by another courtyard where the politicians and noblemen sometimes watched.

By the time Chanil made it to the plaza, training had already started. There were probably more than forty or fifty children there, varied in age and skill level, finishing their warm-up drills. Nearly all were children of noble parents or businessmen. Some might even become actual warriors one day—if they could survive Night Star's lessons.

The young warriors-to-be were divided up into different groups based on age. But Chanil had already been bumped up to train with the older boys and girls. The ones who were seventeen and eighteen years old. The ones who had often already seen real battles or helped in small skirmishes. The ones who liked to train rough.

"You're with Eztli'," Night Star said as Chanil rushed up beside her. The warm-up was done. Chanil would train cold. It was the only punishment Night Star could really give her.

"Yes, Lady Night Star," Chanil said quickly, and she crossed to stand in front of the girl with a round face and wide-set eyes. Chanil nodded at Eztli'. The girl just grunted and eyed Chanil slowly, up and down.

Eztli' had a chip on her shoulder. She didn't like training with younger kids, and she didn't like Chanil. Her family wasn't the fondest of Lord 5-Thunder either, and Itza' had told Chanil that this might have something to do with the girl's attitude toward them. But Chanil didn't care. Training was training. She had waited all day for this. She had sat through the morning council where no one listened to her and plodded through the day's lessons with the Queen, and now she could, finally, hit something.

Chanil slid the light training helmet over her head. She felt the sounds around her muffle slightly, the shift in the air around her face. She twirled her training sword in her hand and lowered herself into her stance.

Night Star gave them a simple partner drill. She trained the older groups directly. The drill was a standard one. Attack-counter-deflect, then return attack, return counter, return deflection. Back and forth. Over and over. The movements became a rhythm. Chanil found herself distracted for a moment, wondering if the upcoming visit from Tlapallo would mean danger for Yaxchilan—

Smack!

Chanil growled as the flat edge of Eztli's weapon, empty of real blades but still a thin end of hardwood, slapped sharply against her elbow, sending little fires down the nerves of her arm. Eztli' grinned in sick satisfaction, her bright septum piercing coiling upward and her brown eyes ablaze.

"Come in cold, and now you're napping, big lips? Pssh." Her words dripped in venom.

Chanil said nothing. They went back to the drill. Eztli' swung her attack, a diagonal forehand maneuver meant to slice across Chanil's body. Chanil countered the way they were supposed to— high block, a step to the outside, roll the blade over to cut down toward the head or neck. Eztli's deflection was a redirection—she shoved Chanil's arm away by the tricep. But instead of returning with the same strike as they were supposed to, Eztli' turned her blade down and slapped the broad, paddle-like side of her weapon hard against the back of Chanil's thigh.

The sound echoed against the nearby stone walls. Chanil felt the sting and the promise of the bruising and welt to follow. She clenched her jaw. But she didn't cry out. She never let herself do that.

"We aren't drilling that one," she growled through clenched teeth.

Eztli' shrugged. "Real battle, you gonna say that, big lips? When the Tlaxcala come, you gonna tell them 'oh that's not what we practiced today, good sir'?"

Eztli's smile was like a mask of death. Chanil clenched her jaw harder this time. Her blood boiled, and she wanted to poke out Eztli's eyes. The girl was always making fun of how she looked.

They went into another drill. This time, they weren't going back and forth. Eztli' got to play the attacker, and Chanil had to defend. Eztli' launched toward Chanil with a flurry of heavy strikes. Chanil's only objective was to block each one. The younger girl circled, remembering not to just back up. Intuitively, Chanil knew the blocks were practice. In real fights, you didn't block the weapon, you just cut the hand or the arm. That was your block. But the motions were the same, it was just the angle that changed. So, it was safer to practice this way.

But Eztli's attacks were coming in hard. The older girl was a bit bigger and taller than Chanil, and she swung like she wanted to take Chanil's head off. Chanil could barely block the swings without Eztli's stick crashing through. She teased Chanil as she attacked, always poking fun of her face.

"You gotta block better than that, big face."

"The Tlaxcala hit harder than this, big lips!"

Chanil growled low, her back teeth glued together. She saw the wild look growing in the other girl's eye. Eztli' wasn't really playing anymore.

That was fine with Chanil. She didn't need to play either.

A mean grin forming on her face, Chanil adjusted her angle on the next block and aimed for the hand, stepping farther out so that the end of her weapon would crash into the back of Eztli's hand. It worked. Eztli's hand collided with Chanil's oncoming weapon, and she felt the wood smack into bone.

Eztli' lost her weapon as a result and gasped in pain. Before the weapon had even clanked to the ground, Eztli' was in Chanil's face. She shoved Chanil hard. "The fuck was that, you big-mouth bitch? Think you can hurt me?"

Chanil barely moved despite the shove. She grinned wildly seeing Eztli' bounce back slightly from the failed attempt to move her backwards. She felt her heart pumping and the rush in her veins that always came when any real violence started.

Suddenly, Eztli' swung a round punch at Chanil's face. Chanil ducked under it and circled Eztli', letting her weapon go as she did so. Like a jaguar in the hunt, she was behind the older girl in an instant. She wrapped her arms around Eztli's waist and pressed her hips tightly just under Eztli's, leaving no space as she violently pushed her hips forward and upward. Chanil lifted Eztli' off the ground, leaned back, and rotated as they fell—a beautiful move that slammed Eztli' hard into the rough ground of the plaza.

Chanil was on top of her in a second, raining down punches and elbows. They wouldn't all get through the training helmet, but she didn't care. She was laughing and taunting the older girl.

"Thought we were improvising, yeah? This how you fight the Tlaxcala? This what you train for?"

Her elbows slammed into Eztli's forearms to smash them out of the way so her punches could slip in. Chanil's light brown eyes blazed like a fire. She grinned like a madman. She felt the rage from being ignored, from being putdown, from being poked and prodded—she felt it all seeping out onto the bloody face of the girl who had ridiculed her for the last time.

"Stop!" Night Star's voice bellowed out across the plaza, but it reverberated in Chanil's ear. The older woman was already on top of her. She pulled Chanil away, locking her arms through the girl's shoulder pits to haul her away from Eztli', who was coughing and clutching her nose.

Night Star dragged Chanil several paces away from the other

children, but still close enough to keep an eye on everybody else. She whirled Chanil toward her. "What are you doing, Chan? You can't do that to the other kids."

Chanil's eyes were wide, and she was breathing heavily. She looked incredulous.

"She's been goading me the whole time!"

"You could kill someone, attacking like that. I've told you—you have to hold back sometimes. You're stronger than she is."

Chanil shook her head. "She's bigger! And she's older!"

Night Star clamped a hand down on Chanil's shoulder and looked her hard in the eye. "It doesn't matter. It's the same as with the kids your age, remember? You could be their leader one day. They'll remember this."

Chanil narrowed her eyes. "They better."

Then, she added, "She's been taunting me—she's always making fun of how I look."

"Aahhh." Night Star stood up tall. She raised her eyebrows pointedly as she said, "So now she's the enemy, yeah? We should kill her, yeah? That how you show your troops who the boss is?"

Chanil swallowed. She didn't know what to say. Her blood was still boiling.

"New partners! Start the drill over!" Night Star bellowed out to the group. They moved quickly.

"Not you, Chan," she said quietly, looking down again.

"I just wanted to train," Chanil whispered sullenly.

"I know," Night Star said, kneeling down in front of her. "But you will be queen one day, and these will be your warriors. You have a duty to lead—"

Chanil rolled her eyes. "Not you, too. All day, queen this, queen that. You all want me to be queen, but none of you will actually *listen* to me. We have an army marching this way, and none of you want to do anything to stop it. You're all just afraid of the west!"

"Enough, warrior," Night Star said, her voice stern and commanding. "Take a break."

"You're kicking me out?!" Chanil was furious.

"I'm saying take a minute to clear your head and focus, yeah?"

Chanil scoffed and threw up one hand. "You all just want me to do whatever you tell me to do."

She stalked off away from the plaza and down the steps, toward the broad avenue that led into the city. From one end of the plaza, Itza' saw her sister leave. She quickly ducked under the painfully slow attack of the boy she was training with, tapped his neck gently with her weapon and said, "Got ya!"

Then she snuck away quietly while the teacher wasn't looking, chasing after her sister.

Xiimbal Kaaj

We lost everything in the war. But it's the smells I miss most. The scents of the markets and the people I grew up with. Now, there are only strangers. Now, there is too much dust in the air.

—*letters from A Queen in Exile*

THE WOMAN BOWED HER HEAD LOW. "Great Lady, what a joy! My husband will never believe this when I tell him Lady Chanil herself came to my fruit stand!"

The woman smiled broadly, the sun-etched lines of her face creating new wrinkles as she did so. She spread her arms wide to indicate all the different fruits arrayed before Chanil under the canopy. The woman's arms were thin, compared to Chanil's, but long and elegant.

"Whatever the Great Lady desires." Her full lips reached from one end of her face to the other with her grin. The patterns on her simple huipil hummed in anticipation for what the royal daughter might want.

Chanil felt her stomach grumbling as she looked at all the different fruits—sweet ones and tart ones, ones with prickly coverings, and ones with gummy insides. They came from every corner of the realm. They all looked delicious.

"How would I ever choose?" she said, mostly to herself.

A young voice sounded from right next to her. "I like the pink ones, personally."

Chanil turned to see Itza' standing there, a mischievous look on her face. Her black eyes glinted in the low light of the late afternoon.

"And the Lady Itza' as well!" the shop owner gasped. "The Twin Panthers of Yaxchilan!"

Itza' giggled.

"And how is your family, Kots'ijal? Your son still playing that dice game?" Itza' gave the woman a knowing look.

The woman laughed and turned toward the young girl with a sly expression. Chanil noticed, however, that the woman could only look above or below Itza's eyes, not directly into them.

"You know how he is these days, my Lady, but—actually, he said you still owe him for that last game." She squinted her eyes playfully at Itza'.

Itza' opened her mouth in a look of pure shock. "A royal lady would never. You should be ashamed of yourself, Kots'ijal."

Smiling, Itza' turned to Chanil. "You really should get the pink ones. They're great."

Chanil opened and closed her mouth. Then she turned back to the shop owner. "Pink it is."

"We'll take two," Itza' held up some fingers for clarity. Then, tossing her head toward her older sister, she added, "And she's paying."

After they got their fruits, the sisters moved on, further along the avenue. They passed through the dense cluster of vendors that lined the market area around the city center. People there watched them intently. Whispers followed their steps. They heard them mutter, "The Twin Panthers."

That was what people called the two daughters of Yaxchilan. Chanil, the bright, smiling jaguar, and Itza', the sly, dark-eyed panther of the shadows.

As they moved farther away from the city center, though, fewer people recognized them by sight. But the people knew they were noble ladies by their clothes and their walks. The shops thinned out, and the looks were more questioning now. *What are two royal ladies doing here? And alone at that.*

Chanil was acutely aware that Lady Xok would not be happy if she heard of this. But she almost didn't care. She was tired of following everyone else's rules anyway. And shouldn't she be able to go anywhere in her own city?

"So . . . you going to tell me what's wrong?" Itza' asked after finishing her fruit.

Chanil shrugged. "Long day is all . . . I mean, a lot happened . . ."

Itza' waited in silence. She knew her sister well enough. She just had to be patient.

"Okay, well, there was this council meeting this morning," Chanil said finally. "We talked about this . . . potential problem."

"I know," came the flat reply. "The Great Army."

Chanil turned toward her little sister, a puzzled look on her face. "You didn't—did you?"

Itza' grinned smugly.

"Where were you?" Chanil laughed. She thought for a moment, then said, "Under the table?"

"The rafters." Itza' giggled again.

Chanil shook her head. "I miss being able to fit up there," she said biting into her fruit.

"It's definitely not as fun without you," Itza' said softly.

Chanil shrugged. "Too many royal duties now."

They came to a crossroads, and Itza' gestured down the smaller path with her chin. "This way. I know a spot we can play panther again—no royal duties included!"

They turned down the narrower street. Stone houses gave way to pole and thatch huts, an occasional administration building or warehouse, and one large temple in the distance.

"You've been down here before? Mom let you come here on one of the walks?"

Itza' gave her sister a look. "Who said it was with Mom?"

Chanil hadn't realized that Itza's childhood prowling had extended all the way to the city outskirts.

They came, eventually, to a small but very tall stone building surrounded by large huts. Chanil could hear fires crackling and soft voices. The light from the day was fading fast now.

"The view from the roof is great, Chan," Itza' said, indicating the tall stone building. It was a bit rundown. The paint was faded. The glyphs carved around the upper lip had vines growing in some places. But there were clearly still people awake inside. Chanil could hear them talking.

"I don't think we can sneak up there right now, Itz."

But Itza' shook her head and made a weird motion with her finger. "It's okay. This is different. Ey!"

She called the last part out loudly as they approached. A short, round man with a wide hat emerged immediately from the doorway. He shouted happily and threw his arms open when he saw Itza'.

"Saqirik, ali'," he said. His voice was smooth, like water flowing between pebbles. Then he looked at Chanil. His eyes widened. His head lowered reflexively.

"Great Lady," he breathed out.

Itza' giggled seeing Chanil's confused look. "My dear friend," Itza' said to the man, the adult words not quite fitting her eleven-year-old voice yet. Then in a soft, almost pleading whisper, she asked, "Could we go up tonight?"

He beamed at her. "Of course!" He winked and added, "My wife told me you might come tonight. She said to me, 'the little panther likes to watch the full moon.' And here you are. She even left you a snack."

Itza' giggled again. Chanil just shook her head. The man led them up to the roof.

※

"So, I guess you heard everything, then?" Chanil's voice carried out across the jungle before them. From the roof of the stone building, they could see the sky breaking into reds and oranges, with purples thrown violently across the wisps of clouds as the sun slipped slowly behind the horizon to enter the underworld and begin its nightly journey. The full moon was already high in the sky behind them, brightening as its counterpart dimmed.

Itza' nodded. "I got in before the meeting started. I couldn't even move until Mom and Dad had finished talking in private—*that* took forever."

"You really are a sneak, little one," Chanil said with a wry expression. "And where are we? How do you know these people?"

Itza' just shrugged. "I talk to everyone. It helps to know things. Actually, did you know his youngest daughter can already speak three languages? I told him, when I get old enough, I'll see if she can be one of my aides. And then the girl can learn all the languages she would ever want."

Chanil nodded. It sounded nice. Nicer than having to worry about being queen or what would happen if Yaxchilan was forced to go to war.

"So, what did you think about it, then?" Chanil asked. "About Tlapallo coming and this army?"

Itza' thought for a while. "I've seen Tlapallo—he's visited before. But the army is an unknown. And the New Alliance is a mystery to me."

Chanil sighed. Nothing then.

"But—" Itza' said softly, staring out toward the setting sun. Toward the western horizon, where their enemies lived. Toward the direction of the underworld in all their stories. "—but if it were me—I'd want to know *why* the army was coming. And why Tlapallo might be tempted to join them. Maybe then we can offer them something to change their mind, yeah?"

"Wonder what they would have done if you'd said *that* from the rafters." They both laughed.

"Well next time, you can say it for me now."

"If they'll even listen to me." Chanil twisted her lips. In her mind, she saw the face of Eztli' there on the ground, shielding her face, afraid, beaten.

That I can do, she thought. I can beat my enemy and make them fear me. But that's all I can do. What kind of queen would that make me? She was too ashamed to say any of her thoughts out loud.

"You'll make them listen, Chan. You'll say it so loud they have to hear you, yeah?"

Chanil looked out at the last bits of light from the setting sun, nodding. She loved the colors, the way the sun broke the sky into violent splashes. Chanil's name was a reference to the sky—the Lady of the Sky, they called her. It was fitting. She loved looking up.

"You're right. I'll earn my name, Itz," she said softly, her eyes never leaving the western horizon. "I'll shout it so loud it breaks the sky, and then they'll have to listen to me."

Visitors from the West

Some say we carve our fate from the air around us. Others say it is written in the stars the moment we are birthed onto this land. Of course, I was taught that the day of my birth determined my fate in this life. Truthfully, though, after all I've learned and seen and had to do, I wonder… Sometimes, I even doubt…

—letters from A Queen in Exile

LORD TLAPALLO ARRIVED A FEW DAYS LATER. He came with his son, Itzcoyotl, and a small retinue—tiny really—of a couple aides and guards. Tlapallo's headdress reached up to the sky as he entered the open courtyard where the meeting was to take place. His boots were thick. Itza' could smell the sandy earth of the western kingdom of Coyolapan on his heavy steps as he approached. He crossed toward Lord 5-Thunder, the two warrior kings each adorned in coronas of feathers, armbands, and rings. Their pierced and jeweled faces glinted in the sun.

Both men ruled large realms on opposite sides of an invisible line that divided the eastern kingdoms of the Winaq from the western lands ruled by the Tlaxcala, and beyond them, the Mixtek, and Zapotek. The two groups representing both sides of that invisible border now came together in the courtyard formed by one of the platforms of the giant terraced pyramid near Yaxchilan's city center. The pyramids were built like representations of the mountains, with terraced steps leading up to a sacred room at the pinnacle—a cave in the sky. The terraced portions of this pyramid were so large that Lord 5-Thunder could host this small meeting with some twenty or thirty people.

The Ajaw was joined in the meeting by his core group of close advisors, formed by Ladies Xok and Night Star, and Chanil now as well. Q'anchi', the highest-ranking priest in Yaxchilan, was there also. Even little Itza' had been allowed up. She stood off to one side, half hidden among the robes of tall politicians, and regional governors—called sajal—who watched over different provinces within Yaxchilan's realm.

Tlapallo's small retinue of aides and guards stood somewhat apart from their own lord, almost held back, as the two kings approached each other. Tlapallo's aides chatted casually with their counterparts from Yaxchilan or with each other. There was a relaxed air among them. The realms ruled from Yaxchilan and Coyolapan had been—well, not exactly allies—but strong trading partners, distant friends, for a long time. No one had any reason to be on guard or care too much for all the typical pomp of court.

Nevertheless, Lady Xok noticed a tension in Lord Tlapallo's shoulders as he moved. Stiffness in his back, and not just from holding up the large ceremonial headdress. There was a nervous energy to his son, Itzcoyotl, who walked beside him as well. From the crowd, Itza' sensed it too. She could smell something on the visiting royal pair that was not quite fear but not quite calm. Nervousness, perhaps? She wasn't sure. Matching scents to emotions was still a challenge for her sometimes.

"Old friend!" Lord 5-Thunder boomed out, a wolfish grin on his face as he and Tlapallo met in the center of the open area. Lord 5-Thunder pulled his own headdress off, signaling a more casual air than had been present during the normal courtly meetings earlier that morning in the main palace chamber. His chaotic, black curls fell across half his face like they always did, leaving only the side with the long snake-like scar visible. The gleam in his eyes looked as mischievous as his grin.

Tlapallo followed the Ajaw's example. He took off his own headdress and placed it absentmindedly on the ground. His son removed his as well but held the large, woven imitation of a snarling coyote under one arm.

"Old friend," Tlapallo returned the greeting. Lady Xok noted, though, that his voice was less exuberant than Lord 5-Thunder's had been.

Lord 5-Thunder then turned his head and looked young Itzcoyotl over with wide eyes. "Look how your boy has grown."

Itzcoyotl lifted his chin in pride. Tlapallo's son was probably a couple years older than Chanil. He looked like someone had tried to carve a human figure out of a mountain and hastily laid down skin and muscles over the rocky canvas. He was almost as tall as Lord 5-Thunder already.

Tlapallo grinned. "They always do. Wait, is that little Chanil?"

The trio looked over at Chanil. At almost sixteen, she was tall for her age, with broad shoulders. She came up to eye level with Tlapallo. She had her brown hair parted down the middle and braided tightly down either side. Her wide face and full lips held a smug smile as she inclined her head toward Tlapallo and his son. She wore a light, woven tunic—a warrior's armor. Heavy boots gripped her feet, and her woven shorts clung to the thick muscles of her thigh. A single blade dangled from a sheath at her waist.

Lord 5-Thunder grinned wolfishly again. "Not so little anymore."

"Last time I saw you . . ." Tlapallo trailed off, searching his memory.

"I think I had just started training with a spear," she finished for him, eyes glinting happily. Tlapallo nodded slowly. He looked at his own son again. Then he shook his head. His wide nose wrinkled, making his septum piercing dance.

Lady Xok's smooth and regal voice entered the conversation. "Perhaps our visitors would like some cacao brought to drink?"

Lord 5-Thunder laughed loudly and clapped Tlapallo hard on the shoulder. "Our illustrious lord here doesn't drink cacao!"

Itzcoyotl turned to his father with a puzzled look. This was apparently news to him. Tlapallo opened his mouth to speak, half grinning, but the Ajaw jumped in to explain. He leaned in conspiratorially, pretending to whisper while actually saying it loud enough for everyone to hear. "Bad allergies. Upsets his stomach."

The Ajaw rubbed his own stomach in sympathetic demonstration. Tlapallo chuckled. "A lie, my son. An *old* one. Got me out a perilous situation once."

The Ajaw took a couple steps back, enough to allow the conversation to include the group now. "Not so perilous," he said, teasing. "I think she would have let you go . . . eventually."

He winked at Tlapallo, who just shook his head. Itzcoyotl tried smiling. He hadn't realized his own father had known the Ajaw for so long. He also hadn't realized how beautiful his oldest daughter had become. Itzcoyotl kept looking at her. She had a powerful air to her, and her features were strong but still feminine. He found it hard to look away.

Lady Xok saw the reaction Chanil elicited from Tlapallo's son. Dozens of scenarios ran through her mind. Chanil was getting older, after all. Her marriage prospects had to be carefully considered. Still, Itzcoyotl was an heir-apparent, just like Chanil. Such matches posed extreme challenges unless the two kingdoms united—and even then, it could be hard to secure stability. Nevertheless, uniting Yaxchilan and Coyolapan might be enough to stop the advance of the Great Army . . .

All these thoughts passed through the Queen's mind in a short moment. Then her thoughts turned smoothly and just as quickly to the meeting at hand. They needed to know what had brought Tlapallo and his son here.

"We are honored by your visit, Great Lord Tlapallo," Lady Xok intoned ritualistically. It was a polite suggestion that they should consider getting down to business.

He bowed his head respectfully. The entire meeting took place in the language used in Coyolapan, the Tlaxcala tongue that Tlapallo spoke. Yaxchilan honored him by using his language. That didn't really pose any obstacles, though, since even Itza' and Chanil had been taught the languages of all their neighbors from a young age.

"We are curious to know *why* you have come as well," Chanil added. She was thinking about her conversation with Itza', how her little sister had said it was important to know the motives of those around them.

Her comment brought several stares and eye raises though. It was direct, bordering on impatient. And Lady Xok had already invited them to give their reasons in a more traditional way.

"You certainly speak your mind, Lady," Itzcoyotl said, staring at her. His voice was deep but still young. Xok couldn't tell yet if he was intrigued or annoyed at Chanil's actions.

"And why shouldn't I? The New Alliance is spreading in the west, and now, here you are. We would be fools not to wonder why."

Night Star and Xok both shot Chanil a glance that left no doubt that they wanted her to back off. Lady Xok recognized the need for information, but Chanil was going to push too far too fast. And they had no idea which way Tlapallo was leaning yet. She could end up creating a problem where there otherwise wouldn't have been one.

Itzcoyotl did not respond. He just grunted, a confident smirk on his face. But he still didn't look away.

Tlapallo and Lord 5-Thunder looked at each other. "Seems it's straight to the point," Tlapallo said.

Lord 5-Thunder nodded. "Wouldn't want to disappoint the kids." Some chuckles from around the gathered party. Itza' nodded in approval from her vantage point at the fringes. She saw how her father was trying to diffuse the tension and remind Tlapallo of their old friendship and history together.

Tlapallo lifted his dimpled chin and looked Lord 5-Thunder in the face. He seemed tense. "I came here to tell you myself, old friend. Out of respect. Coyolapan is joining the New Alliance. We are joining with the Great Army."

Lord 5-Thunder reflexively clenched his jaw in anger. Murmurs spread through the crowd. Itza' could hear the various opinions, the general tone of fatality in their assessment. People would see this as a great danger to Yaxchilan and its realm.

Lord 5-Thunder opened his mouth to speak, but a cough seized him out of nowhere. He struggled to suppress it, to catch his breath.

"You've got to be kidding," Chanil said loudly in the pause opened up by her father's coughing. "They're not your friends. We are."

"I have no choice, old friend," Tlapallo said grimly, ignoring Chanil. His eyes never left Lord 5-Thunder's, who still grunted as he tried to find his voice again amidst the cough that threatened to emerge.

"There's always a choice," Chanil kept prodding. "Did they scare you or something?"

"Chan!" Lady Xok shouted out.

Itzcoyotl fumed. "You need to watch yourself, girl." There was no mistaking the violence in his tone now.

"You've been watching me enough yourself this whole time," Chanil shot back, and Itzcoyotl's eyes went wide with rage.

"Quiet! All of you," Lord 5-Thunder croaked in a hoarse voice. Tlapallo saw the effort it took for the Ajaw to speak past whatever sickness had just gripped him. And he saw how things had shifted in the space of silence left by the king's absence.

The Ajaw growled a low, menacing sound that cleared his throat. His head was lowered slightly, and he looked at Tlapallo from just under his brow.

"Tell me, old friend, do you remember that time in the south? At the base of the mountain?" Lord 5-Thunder was getting his breath back slowly.

Tlapallo shook his head. "This is different."

But Lord 5-Thunder went on, lifting his head, getting some

of his boyish grin back. "Our backs to the impassable highlands. Caught in a deep valley with those Zapotek—"

"—Mixtek," Tlapallo corrected him, a grim smile trying not to settle on his lips.

"Right—those Mixtek raiders all around us. We were outnumbered at least, what, two to one?"

Tlapallo finally let out a small chuckle. "Three to one more like it . . . This isn't the same thing, my friend."

"Do you remember what I told you? When everyone else said we should surrender—just get captured."

Tlapallo shook his head. "It's not the same."

"Do you remember what I told you, old friend?" The Ajaw's intense gaze was wild despite the calm in his tone. His hair covered one half of his face, and the single eye on the other side bored into Tlapallo with a burning ferocity.

Tlapallo relented. "You said that if we gave in, it wouldn't just be us that suffered. They'd come for our sons and our daughters, and it would never stop. Unless we stopped them ourselves."

The Ajaw held up one finger. "Not one ear of corn to those bastards. Remember?"

"I have no choice, old friend." And he said nothing more. Silence fell over the gathered crowd. The fatality of Tlapallo's words hung in the air.

Chanil let out a growl of her own. "We could help you, you know."

Tlapallo finally turned to look at her. "And what would you do, future queen? Would you feed my people? Our harvests have not gone well, as I am sure you know. Would you buy our goods? Our wares, too? Would you bring us the wealth we need to sustain our realm? The wealth we'll lose if we side against the Great Army?"

He turned back to Lord 5-Thunder. "They cut off all trade with us, old friend. Two bad harvest seasons and more than half our trade gone—" he snapped his fingers, "—like that. People are starving. My people. My children!"

Tlapallo's voice cracked at the end of his statement. He cared for his people, and he was in an impossible situation. Everyone could see that. A small cough shook Lord 5-Thunder for a moment. Tlapallo saw it and shook his head.

"Yaxchilan is not strong enough, old friend. Not anymore. And who knows how it will fare in the future," he said, looking pointedly at Chanil. "I have to protect my own people."

"It's the wrong choice, Tlapallo. We can fight them. We will fight them." Lord 5-Thunder's voice was hoarse and low but held as much confidence and certainty as ever.

But Tlapallo didn't agree. He put out his hand, spreading his fingers wide. "The Great Army spreads like the vines of a gourd across our lands, forever growing. And once one of those vines finds you and wraps around you . . ."

He squeezed his fingers together into a tight fist. ". . . It squeezes and squeezes until you have no choice but to bend to their will. It has happened before. And it may happen to you too, old friend."

"Well, that could have gone better," Itza' said, swinging in her hammock.

Chanil paced in their small, shared room, her childhood blanket draped over her shoulders. It had been a gift from Night Star, the rich purple and blue, embroidered patterns embedded with meanings Chanil didn't know because the blanket was from the Island where some of Night Star's family came from. Nevertheless, she had been swaddled in this blanket as a baby, and she slept with it every night. It kept her safe.

"I can't believe she wanted me to marry him!" Under the blanket, Chanil's hand pressed hard against the gemstone on her simple necklace. Another gift from Night Star. This one helped with worries.

"Wait, marry—oh, you mean what she said after." Itza' was trying to keep up with the angry words spilling out of her sister. There had been a lot of discussion in the wake of Tlapallo leaving. Itza' hadn't been allowed to stay for all of it.

"Offer me? Can you believe that? She said, 'we could have offered you, Chan.' Like I'm a good from the market to be traded around!"

Itza' nodded, feet dangling over the edge of the hammock. "Definitely not the best word choice Mom's ever made."

"Or idea she's ever had," Chanil added irritably.

Itza' made a face. "I mean—but you can see where she's coming from."

Chanil's feet came to a dead stop. She turned to her little sister. "You're kidding me, right?"

"Look—I'm not saying I agree. But a marriage between you and Itzcoyotl might have been usef—okay, okay, let's say *helpful*. Their kingdom is clearly struggling and if marriage united our two lands against the New Alliance . . ."

Chanil was still angry, but she bit her lip. "I guess I didn't look at it that way."

"I'm sure that was the *only* way Mom was looking at it," Itza' replied, giving her sister a small smile.

Chanil flopped down into her own hammock facing Itza'. "Well, I guess I ruined that possibility, didn't I? You're really starting to get all this stuff, little one."

Itza' just shrugged. "Perks of not having the weight of being future queen on my shoulders all the time. I can just watch more."

But Chanil knew her sister was just trying to make her feel better. "No, little one. It's . . . you really do get this. And I . . . really don't."

"But you will! Just give it time. I think you're doing great." And Itza' smiled. She was eleven, but her smile made her look like the young, little kid who had barely been able to speak the complicated words she wanted to say as a tiny child. It was a strange contrast with the intense look of her obsidian irises.

"Thanks, Itz. At least I have you. For as long as there are days . . ."

". . . As long as there is light," Itza' finished. It was a line from a play they had seen once. It was becoming a sort of refrain between them. Then Chanil sighed. "I just don't feel like I belong. Every time I try to speak up or act on what I think, they yell at me."

"You mean Mom yells at you," Itza' said pointedly.

And Chanil realized she was right. Her father usually laughed at her outbursts and then tried to work with her to find a different solution. And Night Star—she definitely demanded excellence in training, but she always gave praise and pushed Chanil to be better. As these thoughts ran through her mind, Chanil ran her hand over the fibers of the blanket across her shoulders, gripping the edge of the fabric tightly for a moment and feeling the comfort Night Star's gift brought her. It reminded her that Night Star always gave her gifts that really meant something. Not just whatever was supposed to be given based on the occasion.

"Yeah," Chanil said nodding. "Mom makes me feel like I don't belong."

"Not just you. Honestly, sometimes I wish Night Star was our mother instead," Itza' said softly. The words shocked Chanil.

"You do?"

Itza' nodded. "She says things in a nicer way. And she lets us be ourselves. Remember when we used to stalk her in the palace? Hunt her all day like real panthers?"

Chanil nodded. Now that was a memory she hadn't thought about in a while. Her and Itza' roaming the palace halls, hiding in rafters and in shadows next to statues. All the while, circling close to grab the heels of their prey—the warrior, Lady Night Star. The woman had put up with it for a long time. Lady Xok had always tried to get them to stop.

"I miss those little hunts," Chanil said. "They were so much fun. Not like court, where everything is either stupidly boring or else you have to constantly wonder what people actually mean. Because everything real is hidden or said sideways, and you can't just speak directly . . . I miss playing panther with you, little one. Everything is so much simpler when you're hunting your prey."

New Friends

I hear the drumbeat of your heart in my ears. I feel the push of your blood in my own veins. I smell the sour taste of your fear. When my enemy is caught inside my power, I sense every part of their being within me. It fuels my anger, filling me with a terrible rage that guides the path of my blade until the razor-sharp edges find their heart and finally silence that intrusive, pounding sound.

—Xelaq'am's Songs

IF TLAPALLO'S DECISION WAS GOING to bring war to Yaxchilan, it didn't happen within the next year. The rains ended, the dry season came, and Lord 5-Thunder was no longer sick. The whole realm listened for the stomp of enemy boots, but nothing came.

"It takes time to absorb a realm as large as Tlapallo's," Lady Xok was quick to point out. "And we have other neighbors they might want to conqueror before us—the Waxtek for instance." So, the consequences of Tlapallo's decision remained to be seen. People tried to go about their normal lives. Fields were burned and dried, and things were made ready for planting in the moons ahead. Peace still existed—for now. But they knew something was changing. Trade with the western realms, Tlapallo's in particular, was dwindling.

Goods from the west were becoming rarer and more expensive. Visitors from beyond the lands of the Winaq were less frequent.

Itza's eyes were changing, too. They were becoming darker. At least, that was how she tried to say it to Chanil. She had a hard time explaining it, though. They had already been black, so how could they get darker? Yet they were.

They were deeper and more intense, the wisps of colors more fleeting. The more she studied with the priests, the day-keepers, the more she learned about their world—how to cast the beans and hear the spirits around them. The more she learned about the veils between the worlds above and below, and the gods who had shaped human beings, and how to think about the future and past together . . . the darker they got. People couldn't look her in the eye now. She was only twelve years old and grown men could barely keep her gaze in the markets.

"Do you remember that jaguar we ran into a couple years ago?" Chanil had asked one night while they were talking about Itza's eyes. They lay in their shared room, swinging gently in their separate hammocks. It had been late in the night, and the temperature had dropped suddenly. Chanil had pulled her childhood blanket tighter around her broadening shoulders.

"When Papa and I went hunting, yeah? A jaguar found the deer we had shot first."

Itza' nodded. "And you stumbled right up to it before you even knew it was there, right?" The candlelight in the room danced off her features, the broad but oval jawline—like a perfect mix of Xok and Lord 5-Thunder—the wide hooked nose, and those strange, cavernous irises.

"I didn't even realize how close I was until its head reared up. Fierce, black jaguar with shimmering spots. He stared at me. I stared back—can't turn around on those ones, yeah?"

Chanil smirked as she told the tale. She might have hated public speaking, but she was a good storyteller. "Anyway, there we were, eyes locked. My heart was pounding, and I thought I was going to shit myself!"

Itza' giggled. She locked her attention onto her big sister in adoration. She loved hearing Chanil's stories.

"It's true! I felt—panic. Like a real, deep panic right here—" she pressed her hand into her liver. "—And I realized, I knew that feeling somehow. But not from fighting. I had felt it before—from you. From how your . . . gaze feels when you lock onto me that same way the jaguar did. You can make me feel the way jaguar made me feel."

Itza' had made a face. "Great, so I make you want to poop yourself."

"That you do, little sis—definitely!" Chanil had thrown a pillow or something, and they had play fought or teased each other. Itza' couldn't remember exactly. What she did remember were Chanil's words. The fear they described.

Itza' thought back to that conversation as she stood in the shadows under an awning in the market, watching the early evening life of the common people of Yaxchilan. Shops closing. People walking home from long days at work. She thought about the way her eyes had darkened that year and how she could see the fear Chanil had described reflected on the faces of many people around her now, the awkward glances and looks away. She wasn't sure what to make of it yet. She watched for a long time. Until the streets were nearly empty. Life quieted down, settling into a predictable lull.

Then, a sudden sound caught her attention. Quick steps? She listened harder. A faint shout? She moved out from under the awning, crossed the broad avenue, and headed down a narrower street in the direction of the sound. She heard it again. Eventually she was able to name it. Fast steps. People running.

She turned a corner, and the acrid scent of fear filled her nostrils. Fear and excitement. A weird mix. Whoever was running, they had just gone through here. She followed the smell and listened to the sounds of heavy boots, letting her senses guide her along avenues and around corners in pursuit of the source.

Her eyes eventually helped too. She saw a young girl being chased by two men run into a blind alley. She felt her heart seize up in her chest for an instant when she saw them. They smelled angry. And dangerous. She was alarmed at the intensity of their movements as they disappeared down the alleyway. She swallowed hard and followed them into the shadows. She had a feeling they were up to nothing good.

The sky was dark by now, and the shadows were deep in the alleyway. Itza' clung to those shadows as she moved silently into the cul-de-sac ahead. She heard an angry yell that sounded like it came from a young girl. Itza' quickly moved forward. The alley narrowed and then widened out into a small square, where people could chat, hang out, or play card games. And apparently, where adult men could attack young girls.

Because that was what these men intended. The two of them were probably outsiders. Itza' didn't recognize the smells on their clothes or the style of their dress. The person they had chased into this alley was a young girl, looking just as young as Itza' herself. She was mostly hidden from Itza's view, though—one man loomed over her, his back toward Itza'.

The other man was facing in the direction of the shadows where Itza' lurked. He had a knife in one hand, long brown pants, and a faded shirt with light embroidering on it. His eyes were wild and dark as he squinted into the shadows. His hair had once been cut in a typical bowl, but it had since grown out. His lips were wide and thin, and he looked almost excited. Itza' couldn't tell if he could see her in the shadows or not.

"Who's that?" he shouted, pointing with the knife in Itza's direction.

Well, that answers that, she thought. She noticed the man's companion looking over his shoulder only briefly in response to the words.

Itza' stepped slowly from the shadows, cautiously moving forward. "Do you know who I am, good sir?"

She was fairly certain the men weren't from Yaxchilan now. Itza' had suspected it by their dress, and the man's accent had confirmed it for her. Still, he spoke the language. He might recognize her. And the risk of being beheaded for endangering the life of the king's daughter might be enough to scare them away.

"Get over here, girl." The man gestured again with his knife. His eyes were like crazy fires dancing below his brow.

"What are you doing?" the man's companion hissed, turning partly to face Itza' and Knife-Man.

Itza's heart was pounding, but she tried to keep her face calm. She looked past the other man to the young girl standing there. She, too, had a wild look in her eyes. She was watching intently, but she didn't look terrified. Itza' could smell fear in the air, but the girl wasn't cowering like some petrified baby. The girl just looked angry.

"You have yours, Och', I want my own," Itza' heard Knife-Man say. "Better than waiting, eh?"

The other man, the one named Och', grumbled and turned back to his victim, to the angry young girl.

"I am the daughter of the Ajaw, good sir," Itza' said calmly. She stepped forward confidently, though inside she felt the icy chill of fear in her veins. She remembered Night Star's lessons on calmness—on how fear heightened awareness but also led to panicked responses. Calm usually prevailed in a fight.

"I think you two should leave, eh?" She matched the tone and expression Knife-Man had used.

But Knife-Man just sneered, and Itza' could see spaces in his teeth that suggested he had once had jewels inlaid there. She wondered where they had gone.

"High-born, eh?" His tone was vile, and Itza' realized she might have said the wrong thing to make him desire her less. "Even better."

Knife-Man stepped forward, his eyes roaming over Itza's body as he got closer. His gaze lifted to her youthful, oval face, and then he saw her eyes. He stopped.

It was just an instant of hesitation. Just a flicker of fear. But it grew. And Itza' concentrated on that feeling. On focusing her intense stare into the man's eyes, grabbing that feeling of fear she saw there, and willing it to grow. Knife-Man swallowed hard.

And then she heard it. A distant thumping. It wasn't the first time this had happened. But she didn't know why it happened, what it meant, or how to make it happen on purpose. But she knew what it was.

She was hearing the man's heartbeat.

The thumping grew louder and louder and then faster as panic gripped Knife-Man. Itza' could feel her ears reverberating; it was so loud—as if someone were banging a drum right next to her. The man was transfixed in fear.

Silently, she reached into the hidden slit of her dress and drew the long knife she carried there.

Knife-Man's companion, Och', however, was not frozen, and he had heard Itza' say who her father was. Och'—a tall figure dressed in clothes equally as drab as the Knife-Man—whirled and snarled. "You crazy? Look what trouble you getting us already here!"

His friend did not respond. "Hey, you hearing me?"

Itza' slinked forward slightly, slipping into a fighting stance— the point of her knife toward her target, held high near her head. Och' saw the movement and growled. "Great—noble girl can fight some, too. This isn't good, cousin."

Och' took a menacing step toward Itza' and his panicked companion. His back was turned, now, toward the young girl they had been hunting. And that, Itza' soon saw, was Och's last mistake.

In an instant, a knife buried itself in his thigh, just above the knee. The man let out a sickening sound. The knife blade twisted, and the man turned with it, falling as he did so. The girl turned with him, stabbing him repeatedly in the back as he rotated and finally fell in spasms of death. Now, the young girl stood facing Itza' and Knife-Man. What remained of Och' lay convulsing in a growing pool of blood behind her.

Itza' saw the whole thing as if in slow motion. Her mind registered the death. Her eyes had seen it, and her nose was filled with the scent of blood. But it felt somewhat distant for some reason. Like it was happening in a dream.

But Knife-Man was back to his senses now that Itza's gaze was no longer locked onto him. He yelled out, "Bitch!"

Itza' saw the violence promised there and lurched forward instinctively. But a knife, a dark obsidian blade half hiding in the intermittent shadows of the alleyway, sailed expertly through the air and caught Knife-Man in the stomach. He exhaled hard and bent over. The young girl was there in a second, slicing the man's weapon hand. His knife clattered to the ground as his arm was split open. Then the girl's other knife—apparently she carried two—was in his throat. She pushed that blade up into the man's jaw and yanked her other knife out of his stomach at the same time. Then she turned toward Itza' as Knife-Man tumbled to the ground beside her.

Itza' swallowed hard. She looked at the two dead—well, dying—bodies and then at the girl. The smell of blood flooded her nostrils, and she realized she had never smelled so much of it. The metallic, warm odor was almost overwhelming. Her heart was still racing. She had trained for violence her whole life but seeing it for the first time was something else. She couldn't stop looking at the bodies. But the other girl was still looking at her and still held a knife in each of her hands.

Itza' forced herself to look away from the bodies and back at the girl. The thin, lithe figure with a long, gently swooping oval face and delicate hands. A kid, barely twelve, covered in blood. A wild look lay in her deep, brown eyes. She breathed calmly, though, as if ready for her next opponent. She stared at Itza' but didn't move to attack.

Deciding that the young girl would have already attacked if she were going to, Itza' slid her own knife back into its sheath. Pushing herself to feign a calmness she did not feel, she said, "Well, you could have just said you didn't need any help." And she tried to offer a wide grin.

The young girl smirked. She was staring at Itza's eyes. "So, the rumors are true," she muttered.

"Are you okay?" Itza' asked simply.

The girl nodded slowly. She stepped toward the exit of the alleyway and said, "I'm going to go now, eh?"

Itza' was struck by her accent and the way she ended her statement. Itza' guessed the girl had grown up near Sprouting Earth, where she knew they often concluded phrases with "eh."

"You could . . . but this isn't exactly the best spot to just leave a couple bodies. They'll be found." Itza' knew that two corpses could lead to questions, and questions might mean trouble for this girl.

The girl narrowed her eyes. "How old are you? I thought noble kids were all spoiled brats hiding in their temples."

Itza' giggled. "I could ask you the same question. But how about this instead. I help you hide these bodies, and you can tell me what rumors you were just talking about, eh? About my eyes."

The girl was still looking at her suspiciously. "They're kind of big for us to carry."

Itza' shook her head. "Don't worry. I have a friend who can help." She grinned confidently. Inside, though, she was hoping her friend would be at home. And that his wife wouldn't ask too many questions.

"They just say there's a girl with black eyes in Lord 5-Thunder's household," the young girl said between bites of her tamale. "They say they're spooky or magical sometimes. Or that you can see spirits."

Itza' nodded slowly. This was interesting. She hadn't realized such rumors existed. She knew her eyes were rare. No one in Yaxchilan that she knew of had them. But people seemed aware that one could have them—especially elder women or visitors from the southern highlands.

"Well, all of those rumors are true," Itza' said mischievously.

The other girl laughed. She hadn't said her name yet, but Itza' figured that might just take time. Even if not, she liked this girl, and she wondered what her story was.

"Right, your highness, whatever you say," the girl said sarcastically. She was testing Itza', seeing if she was the kind of noble who demanded perfect displays of respect at all times. Itza' was not.

"Hey now, my eyes spooked that one guy," Itza' teased back.

The girl scoffed. "Eh, I coulda handled him without you." And Itza' figured that was probably true.

The girl finished her tamale. They sat outside the tall, stone building where Itza' had taken Chanil—the one where her friend who knew how to hide bodies lived. The one who liked and trusted Itza' enough to keep a secret like that. Especially since Itza' had promised that his youngest daughter would have a job and always be taken care of.

The other young girl, the one who had killed the men and created the dead bodies that needed hiding, stood up. "Thanks for the food, Great Lady . . . and for coming to help."

Itza' inclined her head in response. The young girl started to move off.

"Hey, friend," Itza' called over her shoulder. "Would you like a job?"

She heard the girl scoff again. But she also heard her stop in her tracks. Itza' took that as a promising sign. She stood and crossed to the girl.

"Would you consider being one of my aides?" Itza' asked.

The girl laughed. "Me? Attending a royal lady? I don't change diapers."

Itza' gave her a look. "And I don't take in mangy strays. But these are trying times. And I'm serious. This is a real offer. I need aides who know how things work . . . outside a palace, yeah? Ones who can help me."

Itza' meant it. And she did have a feeling about this girl. But the truth was, Itza' didn't totally know why she was accumulating favors from the citizens of the city or looking for special aides or learning everything she could about the inner workings of Yaxchilan and the kingdom. It was almost just instinct, like a hunch, an idea that hadn't surfaced to the front of her mind yet. But she had spent her whole childhood spying and eavesdropping, and that had made her certain of one thing. Kingdoms rose and fell based on the secrets they kept and the ones they lost control of. She wanted to know all the secrets. And to have people around her who could help her accomplish that.

An army was marching. Who was in it? How could it be stopped? What other kingdoms would come and help them? How did people feel about the possibility of losing everything? About how her father was handling things? She had to know.

She watched as the young girl considered. "You'll never be hungry," Itza' offered. "And you'll always have a safe place to live. Do you have family? Because they'll never be hungry either, if that's what you want."

The girl squinted. "And in exchange?"

Itza' smiled. "In exchange, you have to wear silly robes and learn to read and pretend you're a doting servant girl I brought in to help me get dressed in the morning. But really, you'll be my bodyguard. And you'll help me figure out how to keep this kingdom safe. And you'll be family. My family."

Itza' hadn't been sure whether to say the last part. But watching the young girl's expression flip when she uttered the words, Itza' knew it had been the right choice. Family. The young girl wanted family.

The girl nodded. "I could do that—for a while at least. I was planning on staying anyway, until those assholes came through."

Itza' figured that was as good as she would get for now. "Then welcome to the service of the Lady Itza', my friend. So . . . what can I call you?"

The girl smiled. Her brown eyes sparkled like a wildfire. She pursed her lips. "They call me Ixcanul. Like the volcano."

A Lone Visitor from the East

My power has always scared people. They see me as a witch, a meddler, a dangerous snake lying in the ground they must avoid lest my poisonous bite take their last breath. My power scared me, too—at first. But then I learned to listen. And I heard the words of the snake echoing in my blood. Now, I simply follow its path. I can finally see where it has been leading us all these years.

—the Book of Queen Snake Lady

ITZA' WATCHED THROUGH HER SPYHOLE above and behind the throne as the visitor approached the dais. The spyhole had been specially made for her. A generous gift. One that had been given mostly, Itza' knew, because her father didn't think anything else would keep her quiet.

"Chanil sits in court, why can't I?" That had been Itza's argument. Night Star had laughed. Lady Xok had sighed, already tired of Itza's relentless sneaking and spying. Lord 5-Thunder had compromised. He had patiently explained that she was a twelve-year-old girl, and it wouldn't do for visitors to see the Ajaw of the largest kingdom in the east taking direction from his baby daughter, now, would it? And, no, it didn't matter how brilliant she might be.

He had said that she could either trust in Chanil's memory to tell her what had happened later on, or she could have a designated spot to spy from.

She had chosen the spyhole.

And it had paid off. The spyhole was built into a tiny, secret room against the back wall behind the throne, offset to one side so she could see some of her father's profile. It gave Itza' an elevated but excellent view of those who came to speak to her father and mother each day.

Today's visitor was especially intriguing. The noble woman had come alone—no guards, no aides, no husband. A solitary figure slithering deliberately toward the raised dais where Lord 5-Thunder and Lady Xok sat on their ornately carved and painted, stone benches. The crowd parted for the lone woman, yielding a space far larger than her thin, athletic figure required. In her wake, she left whispers and murmurs. Itza' could hear them through the spyhole.

"The witch queen of Sprouting Earth!"

"Why is *she* here?"

"Since when do we allow *those people* in Yaxchilan?"

"Shut up, fool! She'll turn you into a toad while you sleep!"

If the Queen of Sprouting Earth heard the whispers, she gave no indication. Her walk was slow, her pace deliberate and unhurried. Itza' was fascinated by the power in her simple movements.

Her sandals were ornate and well-fitting. The dress she wore was not a typical wraparound. Instead, it was tight. It clung to the woman's hips and thighs like a second skin. It squeezed her waist and slid gently up the curves of her torso, stopping just above her breasts. And it shimmered like the scales of a reptile.

Her skin was unpainted, the natural deep, dark-brown tones visible on her bare arms and face. She wore no headdress. Her jet-black hair was braided around her head in a complex pattern that resembled a snake. Her face held no piercings, no jewelry except for her jade earrings. But along her arms, she sported two jeweled armbands shaped like snakes. They coiled around her upper limbs, from the caps of her toned shoulders all the way down to her hands. The heads of the snakes sat atop the backs of her hands. Their mouths were open, fangs shimmering, and each had brilliant gems for eyes.

Her expression was cold, impassive. She exuded confidence as she slid up, stopping several paces from the raised dais. Itza' was aware of all of this as she stared at the woman.

She heard the courtly announcer shout out, "The Great and Honored Snake Lady, Queen of Sprouting Earth, Xajaw of the Earthen Realm!" But Itza' heard the words as though they were far away, a distant echo. Because Itza' was transfixed by something else she saw in Snake Lady.

She has my eyes! Itza' thought in wonder, her heart racing. Snake Lady's eyes were black like Itza's, but darker. No, deeper. Like caves. Inky black and carrying a strange depth that seemed impossible for objects so small. Itza' had seen only one other person in her life with eyes like hers and that had been years ago, a distant childhood memory.

Lord 5-Thunder also stared at Snake Lady, his jeweled face fixed upon the Queen of the neighboring realm to the east. His jaw clenched tightly for a moment. The long snake-like scar on his face squirmed against the bone.

"It's been a long time..." He let those words hang in the air for a prolonged moment before finishing with, "...since we had visitors from Sprouting Earth."

"We are honored by your visit, Great Queen," Lady Xok said tersely. Itza' heard the contempt in her tone.

Snake Lady did not so much as glance at Xok, however. She looked only at the Ajaw with that intense but impassive stare, like a predator deciding whether or not a potential meal was worth the effort. The sweep of her jawline was strong, but her face was not blocky. It was like a rounded rectangle with skin of the darkest brown. Her black eyes were slightly wide set, giving her an unnerving look when coupled with the intense irises. Her nose was thick and hooked, her lips full and deep red and somewhat downturned. To Itza', she looked regal and beautiful but dangerous at the same time.

"I have come with a simple message, my Lord 5-Thunder." Snake Lady's voice was surprisingly raspy and rough. Itza' had expected something smoother, more like her own mother's.

"Simple messages usually come from simple messengers, Great Queen," Xok said in a cold tone.

Still, Snake Lady did not pay her counterpart any attention. From the spyhole, Itza' watched every movement of this new person. She marveled at how Snake Lady seemed not to blink and how her breathing was so slow and shallow that Itza' could not even detect a rise in her shoulders.

The raspy voice came again. There was something oddly sensual about it, though, despite the rough edges. A low, earthy note below the actual sounds that emanated from Snake Lady's throat. "I am here so that you know the message is genuine."

She raised her arms upward. The snake armbands glinted, casting strange rainbows on the walls and the deep grooves of the faces and glyphs carved into them. The tension of the scene was so great, Itza' saw the guards around the dais twitch reactively to Snake Lady's movements as though expecting an attack.

But Snake Lady just laughed, a loud cackle. She turned in a slow circle. "Am I so frightening to the warriors of Yaxchilan, hmmmm? I am unarmed, you see? I have no guards, no weapons, no protections."

She lowered her arms slowly. The guards looked around in nervous embarrassment. Itza's mother seemed unamused. It was Lord 5-Thunder, however, who spoke.

"What need would a witch have for a sword or spear anyway?" Whispers fanned out through the gathered crowd of Yaxchilan's court. Murmurs and nervous shuffling steps. Snake Lady's eyes blazed, and she cast the Ajaw a sharp look.

Itza' heard a strange groan emanate from her father. From where the spyhole had been built, she couldn't see Lord 5-Thunder's face very well—she could only see a bit of his profile. He seemed to be suppressing a cough. His neck bulged a little as though filled with air, and she thought his skin was reddening.

Snake Lady was speaking, her voice oddly calm given the fury Itza' had just seen there. "I will not stay long, great rulers of Yaxchilan. I know you do not suffer magic . . . or those who aren't afraid of it . . . in your realm."

She spoke loudly, so everyone could hear, but Itza' had the distinct impression that her words were solely for Lord 5-Thunder. Her gaze never left his face. His breath seemed to have stopped since the weird groan had escaped his lips.

Then, Snake Lady smiled. She blinked, and Itza' was certain it was the first time she had done so since entering the chamber. At the same moment, the Ajaw's breath returned and the air in his throat exploded out like claps of thunder. The sound of his loud cough suddenly filled the chamber. Itza' saw puzzled looks in the crowd.

I missed something, Itza' thought. What just happened?

"You have a new enemy, Great Queen and King." Snake Lady's words were flat and factual. The guards stiffened, and Chanil stepped forward reflexively. Snake Lady's gaze shifted toward Chanil. She eyed the heir-apparent intensely, scanning her whole person as if deciding what to make of her.

The crowd began muttering louder.

"Is she threatening us?" someone said.

"What is this?"

"Quiet!" Lady Xok's voice trumpeted over the crowd. Silence came reluctantly.

"What are you saying, Honored Snake?" Xok asked the question directly. Itza' could see her mother's stiffness, the sidelong glances she was trying not to make in the Ajaw's direction. Lord 5-Thunder still seemed to not have gotten his voice back. But his throat no longer bulged, and his skin wasn't as red.

"Foreign mercenaries have plagued our land for several years," Snake Lady began.

"The Invaders—we know," Xok interrupted curtly.

The snake smiled, a thin spreading of her lips accompanied by an almost smug expression. "They are dying—" She held up a hand to stop the interruption coming from Lady Xok, who stiffened angrily in response.

"—We are winning our war, good Lady and Lord," Snake Lady continued. "The Invaders flee. Which means they will be on your northern border soon. They are running west."

More noise from the crowd. Shouts and yells. The Queen quieted them down. Lord 5-Thunder still seemed unable to speak.

Itza's heart was racing, her mind puzzling over the events unfolding in the room below her and the mysterious visitor.

"Why would these Invaders be running west?" Xok asked simply.

Snake Lady gave her a look that said she expected the answer to be obvious. "Why else? They are joining the Great Army. They will be your enemies now, too."

The crowd erupted again. People did not believe her. "Lies!" they shouted.

"How can we trust someone from Sprouting Earth?"

"How can we trust this . . . woman?"

"Enough!" Finally, the heavy baritone voice of the Ajaw returned. It rained down on the crowd like a thunderclap. He banged his scepter against his throne. The room quieted down quickly this time.

"So, this is why you came, good lady?" Lord 5-Thunder asked.

"Hmmmm," Snake Lady hummed in an odd way. The sounds seemed to echo in the stone chamber. "I would not want Yaxchilan to think we had sent this threat purposely. But the Invaders will undoubtedly raid along your lands as they flee."

Lord 5-Thunder clenched his jaw. He seemed even angrier than usual. "And you would help us to fend them off, then?"

At that, Snake Lady raised her eyebrows. Xok did as well. "An alliance, my Lord?" Lady Xok asked in a whisper. But it wasn't discreet enough, and many heard the question.

A loud cackle escaped Snake Lady again. "We have no wish to do your work for you, Ajaw. We simply wanted to make sure you knew of this threat. They say the Great Army has already taken the lands west of you. You are becoming surrounded."

There was an uncomfortable finality to Snake Lady's words. Lord 5-Thunder growled, saying, "We will deal with the west, make no mistake. And we will handle these raiders. With or without help from other kingdoms . . . or witches."

Itza' thought Snake Lady might be angry again, but instead, she smiled. It was a confident and intense grin that looked as though she had just won something. She inclined her head, bowing in perfect form. "I leave you then, good sir, to make whatever decisions you think best for your kingdom."

Without another word, she whirled effortlessly and strode away from the throne. The crowd parted for her. Itza' saw the looks of fear, hatred, and awe. But no one dared say anything directly to the Queen of Sprouting Earth.

Snake Lady walked away, head held high, and exited the chamber. Itza' had already left the spyhole to chase after her.

Itza' had intended to catch up to Snake Lady before the woman left the city. But as she stalked the Queen, she quickly realized that Snake Lady wasn't leaving Yaxchilan. She was going to visit someone else.

Itza' watched from a distance as Snake Lady led herself around the back of one of the priests' temples, following an old footpath there that led to a long, short, single-story building. The building was behind the temple, private and out of the way. Why is she going to Q'anchi's house? Itza' wondered.

She trailed Snake Lady distantly up the path, moving in complete silence. She saw Snake Lady go to Q'anchi's house and enter right away, but it took Itza' a while to catch up to Snake Lady.

Despite his station as the most respected and oldest priest, or day-keeper, in Yaxchilan, Q'anchi' preferred this humble dwelling. His single-story, stone building at the end of the path was just enough for one old man, and that suited him just fine. And the outside was painted in a vibrant mural, which told of one of the failed creation attempts wherein the gods endeavored to make humans. Itza' knelt near a depiction of human-like figures made from mud as she skirted along the outside wall to crouch below an open window. She hoped her own fate, in that moment, would not be as bad as that of the mud-people painted on the wall. They had all drowned in a flood.

Itza' could hear rustling inside Q'anchi's house, feet shuffling and voices. She tried standing up, body tight against the wall. She turned to peer inside with just one eye and found she could see most of what was going on in the small living area.

Q'anchi' sat opposite Snake Lady across a low, stone table. They were both sitting cross-legged, feet tucked beneath them. Snake Lady's cavernous black irises opposite Q'anchi's fiery red-brown eyes, which burned like the embers of an old campfire.

Those reddish eyes sat under thick, salt-and-pepper eyebrows and the sun-etched lines of his face. His skin was dark black, and he had a short mustache and beard of tight, black curls. He wore his hair loose at home, the mass of greying locs falling like four thousand snakes around his head. His dress was a simple grey shirt and shorts, exposing the tattoos and ritual scars that covered his entire body.

Q'anchi' watched his visitor carefully as he slid a cup across the table for her. Snake Lady took it and smiled. "Thank you, old man," came her raspy reply.

"If I had known a queen was coming to see me, I would have made something more fitting." Q'anchi's voice was smooth, with an earthy depth and overtones that sounded like wind rushing through old tree logs.

Snake Lady sipped her drink. "This will be just fine, old man."

Snake Lady wasn't young herself, probably around the same age as Lord 5-Thunder, Itza' guessed. But everyone seemed young compared to Q'anchi'. He had served Itza's family for at least three generations now. He had been present for Itza's birth, for Chanil's, and for their father's and his brother's. He was a constant in Itza's life and the closest advisor to the king. So, why was he meeting in secret with someone so obviously distrusted by her family?

Snake Lady's gaze skirted along the table between them. It held a blue bowl and plate to her left. To her right, a small bag with cacao beans. She looked up from the beans to Q'anchi'.

"Would you read for me, hmmmm?"

Q'anchi' inclined his head slightly. "I serve only the family of Yaxchilan, Great Queen. I cannot advise for another kingdom—nor would I dare to pry into the secrets of *your* future, my Lady."

A short cackle came in response. "I could divine for you, then, old man. What would the Great Viper ask, I wonder? The day of his death? No, too obvious. Ah—perhaps the fate of his king?"

Q'anchi' stiffened slightly hearing the translation of his name. But his face remained a calm mask of hospitality. Eventually, he smiled. "Perhaps. But would your reading be accurate, I wonder."

Snake Lady lifted her eyebrows at that and smiled wryly. She took another sip from her drink then reached under the table, out of view for a second. She reached into a pouch at her waist, and her hand came up with two objects. She slid them across the table. A small deerskin bundle—it would easily fit in the palm—and a folded piece of paper.

Q'anchi' looked at the bundle. "A gift," Snake Lady explained slowly, catching his glance. ". . . for *her*."

Something about Snake Lady's tone caught Itza's attention. Her? she wondered. It almost sounded like the same tone her father used when he talked about *her*—the old woman who lived at the edge of the city, in the ancient, crumbling temple that every citizen of Yaxchilan avoided even looking at. But how would Snake Lady know about *her*?

"She still won't see you, huh?" Q'anchi' said, taking the gift and placing it out of sight.

"She would see me, old man. I just have no wish to bother her, eh?" Snake Lady used that particular expression to end sentences that was common in Sprouting Earth.

"And this?" Q'anchi' asked, lifting the paper carefully, as though it might be poisoned. He did not unfold it yet.

Snake Lady just shrugged, an oddly casual gesture from her. "Information for your Ajaw. A more detailed description of the routes the Invaders are likely to take on their way out of our lands."

"Why not give it directly to Lord 5-Thunder, then?" Q'anchi' asked simply.

Between sips, she said, "Your Ajaw would never believe me anyway, eh? Better it comes from you."

This seemed to satisfy Q'anchi', though Itza' wasn't really sure why. A lot was going unsaid, she felt. The two had obviously known each other for a while.

Q'anchi' unfolded the paper and looked over the writing. He nodded. "Curious how you and your husband managed to fend off this foreign plague."

"The Great Lord Shield Skull is a fearsome warrior and brilliant king. My husband fought the Invaders well and leveraged many alliances to great effect."

Q'anchi' looked at her pointedly. "I'm sure he tells his subjects the very same. Can't have people believing that wars can be won with magic, yeah?"

Snake Lady cackled. "Whatever has been done was done to protect our people. They are safe now. So that is all that matters. Curses or not, eh?"

Q'anchi' pursed his lips in a paternal gesture. "I'm glad your kingdom is safe, then, Great Queen. And that no curses were involved. I'm sure I don't have to remind *you* that such things can have unexpected consequences."

Itza' saw Snake Lady's eyes blaze again for a second. That same furious rage that Itza' had seen when Lord 5-Thunder called her a witch. Itza' felt like so much was hidden here. Focus, Itza' chided herself. Snake Lady was speaking again.

"I saw that the Ajaw's daughter is doing well," Snake Lady mused in a casual tone. The fury in her eyes had disappeared.

"Ahhhh," came the long reply, followed by a short laugh. "So, that's why you're really here. Come to try and figure out how Lady Xok broke your curse, yeah?"

"Merely curious how such a brutish, young girl would fare as queen," Snake Lady shot back. "Rumors abound, Honored Viper. The advance of the Great Army. The sickness plaguing Yaxchilan's Ajaw. Your kingdom could be in real peril, old man."

"And if we fall, the rest of the kingdoms of the Winaq might fall as well. Only *we* stand in the way of the western kings' ambitions, eh?"

Snake Lady sipped loudly. "You—and the Red City."

She finished her drink, placing the cup gently on the table. "Thank you for delivering my gifts, old man."

She got up—a smooth movement that barely made a sound, her tight-fitting dress seeming to move with her as though sown to her skin itself. Q'anchi' also rose and bowed low.

"Great Queen," he said. Only his tone had none of the irony or contempt that Itza' had heard in her mother's voice when addressing Snake Lady earlier.

The meeting was over. Snake Lady was leaving. Itza' was gone before Snake Lady exited the building. She had changed her mind about wanting to talk to the queen. There were too many unknowns now. Her mind was racing in four thousand directions as her feet took her away from Q'anchi's house. A curse? Against Lady Xok? For what? Why? Who is this woman? And why does she have my eyes?

On the morning after Snake Lady had left, Itza' sat with her mother in a small library underneath one of the priests' temples. Lady Xok was studying a small codex. Itza' was pretending to study, but really, she was watching her mother carefully, assessing her mood. The

Queen seemed fixated on the text before her. Itza' thought her mom might be distracted enough to let something slip.

"Mom, why is there a feud between Sprouting Earth and Yaxchilan?" Itza' tried to pitch her voice in a soft and light tone. Casual. Nothing important going on here.

"Hmm?" Lady Xok didn't look up from her codex at first. "Oh— well, not a feud, really. It's not as though there's ever been war or anything."

"But people don't trust each other from the different kingdoms, yeah?"

Xok considered this. She raised her head, looking off into the distance, one hand over the page she had been reading, eyes scanning the colorful mural on the wall. "They aren't trustworthy people, Itza'. I mean, it's not everyone of course. But their rulers and politicians have always been . . . untrustworthy, that's all."

Itza' was familiar with this assessment. It was all over Yaxchilan. *That person is okay, but I knew someone else from Sprouting Earth, and they lied to me once.* Or, *no, no, no, my cousins' wife is fine, it's just the qjaw over there—he's corrupt.* And, of course, it had always been this way. But nothing in those comments ever gave a reason. And that was what Itza' searched for.

"Do we mistrust them because their queen does magic?" Itza' asked in a polite tone.

Lady Xok swallowed. She looked at her daughter. "You're wondering about the visit from Snake Lady, yeah?"

Itza' nodded honestly. "I didn't know she had my eyes. And people were whispering a lot of things about her."

Lady Xok nodded. She hadn't liked that her husband built a spyhole for their daughter to watch what went on in court. Too many things she could see or hear that weren't good for a young lady her age. But she had relented to her husband's great wisdom because she had agreed with him that Itza' would, more likely than not, find a way to spy with or without their help. At least, this way, they knew what she knew and how.

"Some people just have those eyes, my dear," Xok said with a smile. Itza' was familiar with this refrain as well.

"Now, as for Snake Lady," and Itza' could hear the bitterness in her mother's voice, even just mentioning that name. "No one knows much about her. But she certainly has a reputation."

Reputation. That word was key with her mother, Itza' knew. It meant people talked about Snake Lady. And what they said did not meet with Lady Xok's approval. Chanil and Itza' had a reputation, too. The Twin Panthers. The Queen didn't like it.

Reputation. Rumor. Nothing specific. Nothing to explain how Snake Lady knew Q'anchi' or what he had meant about her mom breaking a curse. Was it possible her mother didn't know she had been cursed? Q'anchi' said Xok had broken the curse, but could she do that without knowing what she had done?

"A reputation for doing magic, Mom?" Itza' knew better than to ask what she wanted directly. That almost never worked with her mother.

Lady Xok raised an eyebrow, but her attention was already returning to her book. "A reputation for being . . . ruthless. I'm sure the rumors are exaggerated about her powers."

Itza' wondered if her mom was playing dumb. Itza' wondered a lot of things. But it seemed like she was going to be stuck wondering unless she found a way to force someone to give her some answers.

"You have nothing to worry about, little one," Xok was saying, fingers tracing the glyphs she read. "Your eyes are just intense. Plenty of people have them, I'm sure. You are nothing like Snake Lady, my dear."

Itza' could tell she would need to find answers elsewhere. Itza's attention slowly returned to her studies. The Queen sighed. Her daughter was intelligent—secrets were hard to keep from her. But, she knew, some secrets needed to be kept.

Political Decisions

My future was written from the moment I was born. The rivers of blood and piles of ash that I left in my wake were etched into the history of the heavens before I ever took my first steps or breathed my first gulp of wet air. If only someone had known this. If only someone had told my enemies what was coming for them.

—*Xelaq'am's Songs*

IXCANUL TWIRLED IN HER FANCY ROBES. The skirt was long and embroidered with rich patterns depicting animals, mountains, valleys, rivers. It lifted slightly as she twirled in front of the polished obsidian mirror. The robes shimmered and played with the light. They were the fanciest clothes Ixcanul had ever worn. She stopped her turn to face Lady Itza', who sat cross-legged on the floor watching her new aide.

"You have got to be kidding," Ixcanul said. Then, because Itza' was looking at her pointedly, she added, "... my Lady."

Itza' giggled. "I think you look great. Besides, you have to wear it."

Next to Itza', a girl named K'utalik also smirked. Unlike Ixcanul, K'utalik was perfectly comfortable in her fancy robes. But she had also grown up very poor and sympathized with the transition

Ixcanul was making.

Ixcanul looked herself over in the mirror. She had the same face—dark skin, gently curving oval jaw, prominent nose, and pin-straight black hair—but everything else was a stranger as far as she was concerned. Headband woven with expensive strands, embroidered huipil with designs unique to Yaxchilan and the royal family, and the long skirt, tight-fitting sandals. She wondered how much all this cost.

"You know, my *Laaaady*," and she dragged out the formal title she was required to use at all times now. "You're lucky I don't just run off with all these expensive clothes. I bet I could get a moon's worth of food for this skirt alone."

K'utalik held a hand over her mouth, a slight gasp escaping between her fingers.

"Like I said—you'll never be hungry again," Itza' teased. They all laughed.

Ixcanul knew that she could, in fact, have run away. She could have decided this wasn't for her and just left. But she liked Itza'. And, the more time they spent together, the more she liked her and trusted her and wanted to—what?—at least make sure she was safe. And consistent meals and a safe place to sleep seemed a fair trade for being a royal lady's attending.

"So, what will your father do about the raiders, my Lady?" K'utalik asked, practicing the way of speaking that she would need to adopt in public. Her tone and pitch weren't perfect yet, but they were very close. K'utalik was the daughter of the man whose roof Itza' liked to sit on—the man who helped her hide the bodies that had brought Itza' and Ixcanul together.

"He's going to send warriors to stop them," Itza' said. "Probably with Lady Night Star leading them and my sister alongside her. Q'anchi' said he received information about their movements, so the warriors should be able to attack them on the road."

Ixcanul and K'utalik both looked at each other, wide-eyed. Itza's life was very different from how either of theirs had been. The Lady talked about politics and the actions of angry kings and mysterious queens. She knew brave warriors and had grown up with them. But Ixcanul was used to only thinking about her next meal, and K'utalik had never left her corner of the city. They could not imagine a war band marching in the jungle to defeat some terrifying, foreign enemy.

K'utalik wrestled with her own fingers, a nervous habit that Itza' would have to teach her to control lest she give herself away. K'utalik wasn't as street-smart or sly as Ixcanul, but her mind was as sharp as Itza's. Itza' saw a lot of potential in her as an aide.

"And your sister will go with them?" Ixcanul asked somewhat suspiciously.

Itza' shrugged. "I would imagine so. She's a great fighter!" They could hear the pride in her voice.

K'utalik shook her head. "Sounds so scary. Especially for a girl!"

Itza' felt her worries for Chanil like a deep pit in her stomach. What would it be like with her big sister gone? She wasn't used to sleeping away from Chanil. Or not having her comforting protection there. Or not seeing Chanil's face smiling down at Itza' every day. And what if something happened to her? What if she were killed or injured, or—worse—captured? Did the Invaders even take captives? Itza' didn't know.

"She'll be okay," Itza' said reassuringly. She tried to believe the words. "She's a great fighter. She'll be okay."

"What do you mean I can't go?" Chanil was genuinely shocked. "Isn't this exactly the kind of thing I train for?"

Lady Xok tilted her head slightly and ground her teeth. The visit from Snake Lady had been a difficult surprise And her husband's strange choking incident in front of everyone at court had left Xok unsettled. Now they faced potential raiders in the north, and Chanil wanted to help defend the northern border with Night Star, which made sense, but she was so young and reckless.

"You are the heir, Chan," Xok said, deliberately forcing calm into her tone even though she did not feel that way. She pressed her feet hard into the floor, feeling the solid weight of the council chamber's stones pressing back up against her. "It's too dangerous for you to go."

Chanil stared blankly at the Queen from across the stone table. She looked at her father, who sat next to Xok. "Father, weren't you fighting raiders at my age?"

He grinned and looked knowingly at his wife. "She has a point."

Xok rolled her eyes. She would never have done that in public. But the only people in the room were the Ajaw, the Queen, and Chanil. The Queen often rolled her eyes at Lord 5-Thunder in private. "You aren't helping, dear. Besides, your father wasn't the heir—his brother was. So, he sought his reputation . . . in other ways."

"Okay, but Dad leads the army. He still fights. I want to protect our kingdom, too." Chanil felt dumbfounded. Of all the things they would try to prevent her from doing, this made no sense. She trained every day with Night Star. She lived for that. And this was a chance to go into real battle, to help rid Yaxchilan of enemies. And they were trying to stop her. Again.

No, not *they*, Chanil realized. Just Mom. Just the Queen.

Lord 5-Thunder sat up straighter. "I do need you here, too, little one. We need to figure out if Tlapallo will attack us or the Waxtek to the south first. Or both."

It was a stalling tactic. A compromise. Chanil was beginning to see that was her father's usual way of operating these days. What had happened to the brazen warrior of his legend? The one who flew into battle at every opportunity. Had being crowned a king really changed him that much? If so, would it do the same to Chanil?

"Look, Q'anchi' gave us details on the routes those mercenaries would take, yeah? It's not like they'll be expecting us. And we will be expecting them. Let me go with Night Star and the other warriors.

Please. This isn't a risky mission. I have to do something useful around here."

Lady Xok actually looked compassionate for a brief second. "Oh, Chan. You are useful, my dear. It's just—all missions are risky. And you've never been in a real battle. We can't risk losing you. And there is plenty to be done here, believe me."

Chanil swallowed. She knew what that meant. More learning. More politics. More scheming and plotting and seeing Xok's face try not to show her disappointment as Chanil failed again and again at whatever task Xok sent her way.

"I'm a warrior, Mom," Chanil said flatly. "That's what I'm made for. Why can't you accept that about your daughter?"

Lord 5-Thunder sighed heavily and looked at his first wife, starting a long, silent conversation that Chanil couldn't gain access to. She couldn't piece together the unsaid things like Itza' could or pick apart tones and subtle expressions the way her mother wanted her to. She had no idea what her parents were saying to each other. But whatever it was, she had a feeling it didn't end with her joining Night Star and the other warriors to go fight off the Invaders. She felt nauseous, angry, and a little defeated. She felt like giving up.

"I do accept that, Chan," Lady Xok said, finally. "You are a great fighter already. But being a queen is more than just combat. And this realm will need you—alive and healthy, yeah?"

"Okay, Mom," Chanil said flatly. Her voice was completely unemotional. "I understand."

The Queen opened her mouth. Then closed it. She had expected the fight to keep going. Her shoulders relaxed visibly.

"You do?" The Ajaw was also surprised.

Chanil nodded. She stood up. "I still would like to be useful, though."

Lady Xok held up a finger. "Well, actually, Night Star did ask for your help. In figuring out which warriors should go. It's the kind of decision a ruler would make, and she wanted *your* help with it."

Xok clearly intended this to be an uplifting idea. Something really exciting for Chanil to do. Paperwork, Chanil thought with a mental sigh. Thrilling.

But what she said out loud was, "I can do that."

Then she inclined her head to both parents and quietly slipped out of the room. Lord 5-Thunder and Lady Xok looked at each other in surprise.

Chanil handed Lady Night Star a short piece of paper with some twenty names on it. They sat outside in the cooler, late afternoon air on some of the steps leading up to one of Yaxchilan's raised plazas. The steps themselves were rich works of art, painted and carved with enough glyphs to fill pages and pages of a codex. By chance, Chanil was sitting very close to the glyph for her own name. It was well done, but Chanil couldn't help but feel like it was incomplete somehow, like it was missing something.

Night Star carefully looked over the paper that Chanil had handed her. She nodded. "This is great, Chan," she said, smiling.

"Picking who is good in a fight? That I can do," Chanil said. But they both knew there was more to it than that. Age, experience, compatibility. Who could march for days and not complain? Who sang songs and told stories to keep morale up? But that all made sense to Chanil. It was all part of the fight—the team.

"Leave Ch'ojal here, though. He should be in charge while I'm gone. He's one of the oldest generals, knows everything backwards and forwards around here."

Chanil nodded. Night Star always made gentle corrections whenever possible. Chanil thought about the names for a second and then said, "Okay, so keep Ch'ojal here and send Nimaq instead?"

"Yeah . . . yeah, let's bring Nimaq. He's young but good. He'll probably be a general someday himself."

Chanil raised an eyebrow. "Nimaq is *young*?"

Night Star laughed, a deep rumble that grew in her belly. "Well, not like you, little one. But compared to Ch'ojal . . . he's *younger*. Less experienced but good. Fights like a wild boar."

"Hence the name," Chanil added, smiling.

Night Star saw the next name and smirked. "You think Ch'akanel should go?"

"He's good! He can improvise really well, knows multiple weapons, and he's not a brag like the other boys his age."

Ch'akanel was eighteen, only a year older than Chanil. They had been training a lot together recently, Night Star had noticed. She gave Chanil a questioning look.

"Look—he's not as good as *me*, but he's good," Chanil said, grinning.

"I'll consider it," Night Star said with a laugh. "I'd rather have you, though. I wish you were coming."

Chanil was surprised to hear that. "You do?"

The older woman nodded, her eyes softening as she looked at Chanil. "You need to learn these things," Night Star was saying. "In our world, leaders fight alongside their troops and lead them into battle. No one will follow a king or queen who can't fight."

Chanil threw up her hands. "Say *that* to my mom. She doesn't even know how good I am!"

A look of sadness passed Night Star's face. Like a shadow of grief ripped out of her, disappearing just as quickly. But Chanil saw it. "Your mother knows, little one."

Chanil was going to say 'well, then, she doesn't care,' but something about the way Night Star had said 'your mother' made her pause. *Your mother knows.*

"How did you do it, Lady Night Star?" She asked the question softly which, Night Star knew, meant the question was important to the girl.

"Do what, little one?"

Chanil shrugged. "Become the famous warrior. And still be a noble lady. The second wife to the most powerful Ajaw. *And* you command the army. You did it all. I can't even walk right, according to my mom."

That look of sadness surfaced again, but Night Star shook off the feeling. "*I* think you walk just fine, little one."

Chanil gave a half smile. "That isn't exactly an answer, though. I mean, were you always a warrior?"

Night Star nodded gravely. There was a sudden intensity in her eyes. "Always, little one. Every day. Even when I wasn't holding a weapon. Or they didn't want me to fight. I never stop being a warrior. I live for it."

Chanil realized she was holding her breath. "That's how I feel," she said with a long exhale.

"I know."

"You do? Feels like no one sees what I am."

"I see it in you every day, little one. I have since you were just a tiny, little thing. I know I'm not the only one either." The older woman smiled warmly. She remembered the sweet baby that Chanil had once been. And then the spunky toddler. And then the obnoxious four-year-old wanting to play with sticks.

Chanil felt her stomach twisting. She looked at Night Star as though the woman held all the answers. In that moment, she just wanted to bury her head in Night Star's chest and let out all the frustrations and worries and pent-up anger inside her.

But what she said was, "But *how*, Lady Night Star? How did you make it happen?"

Night Star sighed and pursed her full lips. "Okay. The truth is, I took it. No matter what they said or did or what they tried to change me into. I knew what I was, and no one was going to tell me any different, yeah? I didn't care what it cost me. I took it—I took myself, and I ran."

"Wait—like ran away from home?" Chanil was stunned. But Night Star laughed.

"No, little one, not like that. Not literally. I mean, I took hold of myself, what I was, and what I am, and I ran with it. I walked that path, head held high, and refused to let anyone take me off it."

Chanil was grinning. This was what she needed. Not being

bashed over the head with what was wrong with her. She needed someone to tell her to live her life as she was meant to.

I was ready to give in and just wilt like a dumb flower under my mom's burning sun, she thought. But now, she felt different. Night Star's words had kindled something inside her and given her hope. She couldn't just wait for the grownups to decide she was ready to be a warrior. She knew she was ready. She just had to take it. And she knew exactly how she was going to do that.

Lady Xok kissed her husband's forehead gently. Her fingers traced the line of his chiseled jaw, pausing just a second as she touched the snake-like scar there. "Finally feeling better, my love?"

He smiled. She rose from where she had been kneeling in front of him and placed the warm cloth back in the bowl. The liquid sloshed slightly, releasing a jagged, pungent odor into their bedchamber. The healing herbs were some of the fouler smelling that Q'anchi' had made. But they helped with the fevers that accompanied Lord 5-Thunder's coughs.

"I don't know if the herbs helped," he lied. "But I always feel better after time with you."

She rolled her eyes, but her lips could not fight the smile that grew there. She walked back over to him and sat in his lap. His massive arms draped around her. She found it such an odd mystery that a man so large and strong should be sick so often. There had been years without sickness. And yet, it had returned with the rains one year. And no one had any explanation of why.

"We should cherish this time, love," Xok said softly, whispering into his ear and tracing her fingers along his bare chest. "With raiders in the north and Tlapallo to the west, we may have difficult times ahead—"

He put a finger to her lips. "Then let's forget those worries, yeah?"

"Forget them?" She gave him a look.

He grinned wolfishly. "Just for now. I'm sure I can help you forget, my Lady."

He pulled her toward him and pressed his lips against hers. Their lips played together like that for a while, and Lady Xok had just begun to forget everything outside the bedchamber. Then, without so much as an announcement, the door slid open, and someone entered.

Lady Xok threw up her hands but instantly realized who it had to be. The only other person in Yaxchilan who could just walk into the Ajaw's bedroom. His second wife.

Night Star grinned. "Sorry, I should have announced myself. I can always come back. Like three minutes, yeah?"

She shot Lord 5-Thunder an evil, smug smile. He laughed, shaking his head. "And how would you know?"

Night Star lifted one eyebrow. "It was a once in a lifetime experience. How could I forget?"

"We really should get a lock installed," Lord 5-Thunder said to Lady Xok.

Xok was still embarrassed, though. She stood up awkwardly. "I'm sorry, Night Star. I should have left the sign . . ."

But Night Star was shaking her head. "Don't be silly, friend. I'm the one who forgot."

Xok nodded, pulling herself back into her usual regal control.

"I just came to say that Chanil and I finished our work," Night Star said. "The warriors are assembling, and we should be ready to head out day after tomorrow I expect."

Lord 5-Thunder nodded. "Who are you leaving in charge?"

"Ch'ojal," Night Star said flatly. The Ajaw and Queen both approved. "But I'll be taking Nimaq—he's less experienced but promising. It will be good for him to get used to command. And Ch'akanel."

The Ajaw squinted. He didn't remember who Ch'akanel was. Lady Xok did, however. She remembered everyone and everything.

Her mind pulled up an image of the young boy, and the mental appraisal of his lineage was quick. "The merchant's son? Isn't he *too* young? He's practically Chanil's age."

"No younger than I was when I started fighting off raiders," Lord 5-Thunder said.

It was not lost on Xok that Chanil had made that same argument in favor of them letting her go earlier.

"I would have liked to take Chanil," Night Star said, also thinking of Chanil's potential as a warrior. "She's the best. But you two seemed adamant about her staying."

Xok nodded, and her eyes widened. "Very adamant. I don't want Chanil anywhere near a battle yet. She's far too young."

Chanil tied the necklace that Night Star had given her tightly. She looped it so that it wouldn't swing or make noise that might give her away. She wanted it with her. She checked the knots on her traveling sack. She didn't want anything slipping out onto the road. She had already double-checked her supplies. Armor, some food, fire starters, hammock. Her weapons would be slung on her shoulder. She wouldn't have a shield, but that didn't matter. Night Star and the other warriors would have several surplus shields just in case.

She had to hurry. Her palms were sweaty, and her heart was racing. But she had to focus. The warriors would leave in the morning. She had to sneak out before that. She needed to be on the road before sunrise. Then she could track the warriors after they went by. She would stay out of sight the first day. Maybe the next, too. Long enough so that they would be too far from Yaxchilan to turn back when she revealed herself.

She finished the letter she was writing. Hastily scribbled. But Itza' knew her handwriting and would be able to read it. Chanil left it in her little sister's hammock. She might show it to their parents. Chanil wasn't sure. But she couldn't do anything about that either way. She tucked the letter in tight before she left. It was dark already, but Itza' was studying late with the priests. Chanil would be outside the city by the time Itza' found the letter.

Campfires

Everything is connected for us. The weather, the stars, the words we speak, the time we plant, the ceremonies we hold, the measurements we make to keep track of the time. The fate of our cities and people. All is connected in a delicate web that our ancestors have tried to help us understand how to walk without breaking. Any misstep we make reverberates through the entire web.

—*letters from A Queen in Exile*

CHANIL SAID A SHORT PRAYER before she dipped her hands into the river. The cool current gave her a chill in the pre-dawn air. She splashed her face—a sharp wake up call.

She filled her drinking gourd. The water in the river came down from the mountains to the far south, kept clean by the rocks themselves and a subtle network of wetlands tracing across the area. It would keep her alive while she was away from the city.

Chanil heard the sounds of the birds around her, the scamper of insects and mice on the ground. The louder movements of deer and monkeys nearby. She had laid some traps the night before. After she drank and washed up, she went around to check the traps. A rabbit and an agouti. She thanked their spirits the way her father had taught her as a little girl. They had spent time in the jungle before. He had shown her how to live here. She skinned each carcass quickly and efficiently, leaving a certain piece behind as a gift in each spot.

As she moved on to gather the plants she would need for food and medicine, she realized that, although she and her father had done things like this, she had never been alone like this before. She had never walked out so far from Yaxchilan by herself. She felt a twinge of nervousness but tried to push it down. Warriors went out into the jungle all the time. They slept out here, marching and camping. She tried not to think of the fact that when warriors marched, they did so in large groups that included hunters, gatherers, and servants. Going alone into the jungle was different. But the pilgrims and farmers did that, so she could, too.

Besides, she told herself, she wasn't really alone. Night Star and other warriors would be leaving Yaxchilan around now. Chanil knew they would take the main road north and have to cross the river to reach the northern border of their realm. All she had to do was stay somewhat close to where they would cross and then follow them—from a distance—the rest of the day. Simple. Easy. She just had to wait.

She walked in a large circle around her makeshift camp. The sun still had not risen, but the sky was lightening. This was the worst time for most people to see. But not Chanil. She had good night vision—not as good as Itza', who seemed like she could see in total blackness—but better than most. Chanil liked this time. It was the prelude to her favorite moment—when the sun broke above the horizon and the sky shattered into different colors and patterns. Each day the sunrise was different, a new beginning. And this was certainly a new beginning for—

She felt the thing before she heard it.

A quiet thump.

A wet smell. Warm and earthy.

Chanil's knife was in her hand before she faced the source of the sound. She whirled around quickly. She stood tall.

The jaguar before her crouched low. Its fur was bright and brilliant, even in the low light, and its yellow eyes seemed like twin suns shining out of its massive, blocky head. Chanil could tell it was an older one, wide-set face and alert eyes. Thick muscles and a stocky build. It stared at her, licking its lips.

Chanil raised her arms, making herself as big and tall as she could. The yellow jaguar was several paces away. It just stared at her, but she saw it flinch as she made herself larger. Its massive shoulder muscles twitched, and the panther took one step forward.

"No! Get back!" Chanil spoke loudly and clearly. Her heart was thumping, and she felt every muscle in her body scream at her to run away. But she knew that could bring death. Never turn your back on a panther, her father had said. Never run. The knife she held would do little, she knew. The best idea was to make sure the jaguar knew she was too large and challenging to be a suitable meal.

"Ey!" she shouted again. The yellow eyes of the old jaguar watched her intently, pupils widening slightly. Chanil felt panic in her blood.

Then the jaguar tilted its head and made a soft sound, like a deep snuffle or hiccup. It turned away from her and bounded off, powerful claws digging into the earth as it climbed a hill and then disappeared.

Chanil laughed as soon as it was gone. Her shoulders slumped, and she couldn't stop laughing for a while. All the nervousness and panic had vanished with the jaguar's disappearance, leaving an empty space in her gut where a crazy sense of relief and adrenaline could take up space. She had encountered a jaguar up close and lived.

She laughed again, then headed back to her camp. It was just a little pit for a fire and a hammock strung up between the tall, buttressed walls of roots formed by a large tree. The sky was just brightening as she got back. Chanil knew she had a bit of time before she should move closer to the main road and the spot where the warriors would cross the river.

She made some food. She cooked the rabbit and agouti meat she had caught. She wouldn't have time to do much with the pelts, so she had decided to set those aside. She boiled some roots and vegetables to make a stew.

While she ate, she thought about the jaguar she had seen. Its fur had been so bright and its eyes even brighter. They usually didn't come this close to a main road, Chanil knew.

Was that a sign? she wondered. She knew what people called her and Itza'. 'The Twin Panthers.' Itza', the sly, dark jaguar lurking in shadows. Which made Chanil the bright, smiling, yellow jaguar. A balance of opposing forces. Was that how Chanil saw herself though? She wasn't sure.

The jaguar was an important creature. He ruled the underworld, and many of the Winaq rulers were guided by a pantherine spirit. When Chanil became queen, she knew she would have to undergo a special ritual that would reveal to her which spirit would guide her rule. She would become something more than human when that happened. She would be connected to the gods who were her ancestors, and whatever spirit came to her would bury itself deep inside her, and the two would rule together.

At least, that was how it had always been explained to her. The ruler merged with a spirit. And usually took a new name connected to that spirit. It wasn't always an animal. Her father was guided by thunder and lightning. Hence, he took that name into his regal title.

Maybe the jaguar would reveal itself to her when she was seated on the throne. Maybe it would be her connection to the gods and her true power.

Was that jaguar a guide, then? Had he been telling me something? She hadn't heard the animal say anything, but she knew it didn't always work that way. She thought about the encounter again. The jaguar had crouched but not approached. It had licked its lips.

It turned north when it ran away, she thought. She smirked. She decided that was a good sign. She was heading north. The jaguar had gone north. She was on the right path.

The sky was getting bright by the time she finished eating. She cleaned her supplies and started to pack up. Day was fully underway by the time she folded up her hammock and finished packing her supplies. She needed to hurry now. She needed to get to the main road and the spot where the warriors would cross.

Chanil watched from the jungle as the large group crossed the bridge leading over the river. She counted heads. Probably fifty warriors or so. She smirked in the shadows seeing that Night Star had followed her suggestions on who should come in almost every case. Accompanying the warriors were servants, aides and assistants, and some medicine men and women—plenty of folks to carry supplies. Probably a hundred people or more in total, and Chanil knew their numbers would only grow as they marched.

As people saw and heard Night Star lead her warriors to victory over the mercenaries raiding their lands, men and women would be inspired to join the cause and put their own lives on the line to defend the realm. Of course, most of those that joined would never fight. The fifty or so trained fighters—handpicked by Night Star—would be the ones risking their lives in each battle. But the more people that joined, the larger the force looked, and that could sometimes be enough.

Chanil watched them pass—men and women she had trained with, warriors she had heard about but maybe only saw in passing. Her heart thumped with excitement. She saw their colorful, woven armor, the different helmets they brought, the weapons they carried, and their painted shields. Practically, Chanil knew that marching was long and boring, and you had to ration your food and sleep outside. But in her heart, she had never felt so close to something she wanted so badly. Even just camping overnight on her own in the jungle had been exciting. She felt more alive out here than she ever did back in the city.

The war band moved slowly. She had to wait a long time for them to pass. Even longer so she would be sufficiently far enough behind them so that no one would see her or recognize her. Ultimately, she decided to stay within ear shot but not close enough to actually see them. A band that big—there was no silencing their approach. The group walked along the white roads that linked cities and villages in the eastern lands. The roads were stuccoed with limestone, which gave them their white color. So that was what they were called—Sak Be'ob, the White Roads.

They walked until the sun was low in the sky, moving ever northward. Chanil knew what Night Star's strategy would be—she would have known it even if they hadn't talked it over before she left. Night Star would lead the war band to the westernmost area where she was certain the Invaders could not have gotten to yet. Then she would work backwards, moving east along the route the Invaders would be likely to take. That way, they were sure to find them. Night Star wouldn't chance not encountering them, she would make sure the fight happened.

She could have fragmented her group, sent some to different spots. But they didn't know how the Invaders travelled—in one large group or many small ones. If she split up the warriors, there was a chance that the Yaxchilan parties would be overwhelmed. Instead, she brought the full force to bear on each Invader group, hoping to overwhelm any smaller raiding bands they found. It would be slower, and the Invaders might raid more villages this way, but Night Star would be sure to find them. And then she would destroy them. The fight was coming. Chanil just had to be patient.

The crackling of the campfires mixed with the voices of the war camp—loud, confident laughter, songs being sung, servants giggling as they prepared meals or cleaned supplies. It was nighttime now.

The warriors had made camp and were settling in. Hammocks had been strung up and so had a spacious tent for Lady Night Star as their warrior general and commander. Chanil watched from a distance behind a large tree trunk, straining to hear voices she recognized. Her figure was covered in a dull, grey cloak, hood thrown up. Her own camp was a bit away, beyond the area where warriors might go to the bathroom. She knew she should be winding down herself, checking her pack and her food. But she hadn't been able to stay still, she was so excited. She would take just one look, she told herself. Just stay hidden and have a quick look. That had been over an hour ago.

The warriors' camp was not a long-term one, so they hadn't bothered to dig a ditch. And they were still in friendly lands, so there was only a hastily constructed defensive wall of poles and trunks. Mostly, there were a few guards stationed in a wide circle around an inner clustering of hammocks and lean-tos, supplies at one end, weapons kept under watchful eye, and several small fires as people clustered together with the ones they knew. The whole place would disappear in the morning, she knew. But for tonight, it was enough to keep them safe.

Truthfully, Chanil couldn't see much, but it made her feel like she was part of the group.

And that was worth it to—

Chanil stiffened suddenly. Something rustled nearby.

"Who's there?" A young voice. Masculine, woody. She cringed.

Ch'akanel! she thought. He must have gone to the bathroom nearby, and she hadn't seen him or heard him.

She turned slowly. Her hood was up, and the shadows were deep. He stood several paces away, looking at her. His eyes were blazing and on guard—as he should be. Chanil slowly put up her hands and started to back away.

"Hey! Stop!" He lunged forward, closing the distance. "Hey! Over here!" He shouted out. That was smart. No one should engage a potential enemy alone. But Chanil needed him to shut up.

"Shh! It's me!" But it was too late—he closed in, weapon drawn. "Over here!" he shouted again.

Chanil's heart raced. She hadn't considered this. She had no time to think, though, Ch'akanel was moving fast, knife aimed at her arms. She moved quickly and fluidly to one side, deflecting his arm as he slashed. His aim had been slightly off, and she guessed he couldn't see very well at the moment. But he kept slashing. She blocked another strike, slamming hard into his forearm and twisting his wrist. The knife started to fall.

She grabbed the handle and scooped up the weapon gracefully. She pulled him in hard by the arm and placed the blade against his throat. Then she threw back her hood quickly before he could try anything.

"It's me! Chanil!" she whispered intently. Ch'akanel's eyes went wide.

"Chan?" He grinned excitedly as his eyes slowly adjusted. She could see the mix of surprise and joy in his face. Chanil smiled back. She liked his grin, the way it spread and made his whole face sparkle. He was growing his hair out too, and his short, tight locs swayed to one side. Chanil liked that as well.

"You aren't supposed to call me that, remember?" she teased back. She was Lady Chanil to everyone in Yaxchilan. Except to her family and then, only in private. With them, she was Chan—just Chan. Just Sky.

He held up his free hand slowly. "Hey, I forgot—no need to kill me, yeah?"

She laughed and let him go. He straightened, rubbing his wrist where she had twisted his grip loose. He was still grinning at her.

"So, what are you doing here, Chan?" Ch'akanel said smugly.

She gave him a fierce look and shook her head. She pointed the knife blade at him. "Teaching you how to guard your weapon better—like always."

Then she looked back at the camp. She could hear sounds— rushed, fervent maybe. Then rustling in the jungle around them.

Multiple footsteps. Ch'akanel's eyes went wide as he realized people were coming. He gave Chanil a sorrowful look. *Sorry*, his expression said.

She puffed out her cheeks and exhaled loudly. "It's me! Don't attack!"

"It's Chanil, guys!" Ch'akanel added, just as a half dozen warriors emerged from around trees and shadows. They all had weapons drawn. But as they heard the words and saw her face, some started to grin, a few laughed, and some shook their heads. A thick-set man with wide eyes and a bulbous nose approached confidently.

"What are you doing here, my Lady?"

Chanil shrugged. "Just out for a stroll, Nimaq. Beautiful night, don't you think?"

Some of the warriors chuckled. Nimaq shot them a stern glance to quiet them down. Chanil tried to read the expression in Nimaq's eyes to gauge whether or not he approved of her being there, but she couldn't tell. She heard the warriors whispering around her.

"That big lips?"

"Thought she couldn't come?"

"She snuck off to fight with us!"

"Good—we could use her."

"We don't need some baby getting in the way."

Nimaq pursed his lips and looked at Ch'akanel. The younger warrior's face probably would have been red, but the shadows and his dark skin hid any embarrassment. He just threw up his hands. "Hey, don't look at me—I saw her when I was taking a piss, sir."

Nimaq shook his head and growled. His growls weren't always bad, though, Chanil knew. That was just how he talked sometimes. Low, throaty mutterings. Like a private conversation between his head and his stomach. He nodded again.

"You're not supposed to be here, my Lady . . . Guess we better tell Night Star, yeah? See what the old lady wants to do with you."

More than a few warriors let out quiet cheers. Some groaned in disappointment. Nimaq hushed them and made them march at the rear of the group. Then he pushed Chanil forward gently but firmly by one arm. He walked side by side with her into the camp.

Night Star stood in front of her tent, arms crossed in front of her chest. Her long hair was pulled back into a single braid running down her spine. Her large, full lips were pulled into a hard expression as she watched the young figure approach, flanked by some of her best warriors. Nearby, other warriors peeked out from their hammocks or from over their bowls to watch the scene unfold.

Nimaq made Chanil stop a few paces away from the commander, then he stepped back. Chanil looked across the space toward Night Star. Her head was held high enough to look Night Star in the eye. Chanil's long hair was pulled back into two braids on either side of her head. She tried to keep a blank expression on her face. She really wasn't sure how Night Star would react.

Nimaq and the others gave space for Chanil to feel isolated, there, under the watchful gaze of the commander. But not so much space that they were separating themselves from her completely, Night Star noted. They formed a small circle around Chanil, looking as much at her as at Night Star, and Night Star saw a mixture of expressions on their faces. Some looked cheerful, hopeful—like Ch'akanel. Others, like Nimaq, seemed protective but ambivalent. And still, others looked at Chanil with undisguised animosity. They clearly didn't want another young one here.

"Report," Night Star said, looking sharply at Nimaq.

"Heard the young one shout," Nimaq began. Then, realizing there were now two young ones, he pointed with his chin at Ch'akanel, opposite him in the circle. "That young one. We came out, and there *she* was . . . With his knife."

A few snickers and suppressed laughs at that. Nimaq's report was technically all business. But his comment, while true, certainly suggested Chanil had disarmed Ch'akanel. And if she could do that—

maybe she belonged here. At least some of the warriors seemed to think so.

Night Star kept her face stern and serious, ignoring the whims of those around her. She turned to Ch'akanel with a questioning look. He nodded.

"I thought she was a spy. We fought—she got my knife, my Lady." More whispers and reactions.

Finally, Night Star looked at the future queen of Yaxchilan. The girl's light brown eyes stared up at her more or less calmly. She didn't look defiant per se, but her expression said she wasn't sorry. She knew the risks.

"You do know, my Lady, that disobeying your Ajaw is punishable by death, yeah?" Night Star said grimly.

Chanil twisted her face for a second then said, "Can't the heir just take a walk around her future kingdom, Lady Night Star?"

Night Star shook her head. She moved forward, standing over Chanil, and placed her heavy hands on the girl's shoulders. Chanil had felt the weight of those hands many times. She could feel the callouses there, the roughened skin, the strength. And the warmth.

Lady Night Star leaned in close and whispered in her ear, quiet so that only Chanil could hear her. "Couldn't you have stayed hidden just another day or so? We're not *that* far away from the city yet, you know."

Then she pulled back and walked toward her tent again. "You've put me in a difficult position, Lady Chanil."

She turned back to the crowd. They were holding their breath. Every pair of eyes was fixed on Night Star to see what she would do. Chanil took a deep breath. She knew Night Star was going to send her home. This had all been for nothing because Chanil was stupid enough to have wanted to play warrior and see the camp. And stupid for letting herself get caught up in that moment, letting Ch'akanel find her.

"Your presence here is not authorized by Lady Xok," Night Star said formally. "Therefore, I cannot approve of you being here."

Chanil's heart fell. Whispers ran like waves through the crowd. Warriors let out different hushed reactions. Chanil looked at Ch'akanel, a sadness in her eyes. He looked back at her with another sorrowful glance. His dark brown eyes whispered to her across the distance. *I'm sorry, Chan*, they said.

But it was Nimaq who spoke. "My Lady, should we send some warriors to—"

"Not now, Nimaq," Night Star said sternly. It was her voice of command and it silenced everyone. Chanil swallowed. Even Night Star wasn't going to stop her mother from getting in the way of Chanil's destiny.

"I cannot approve of you being here, Lady Chanil," Night Star repeated. "These are dangerous times. We have enemies marching on the road. Therefore, I cannot allow you to travel back to Yaxchilan unaccompanied, my Lady."

Chanil nodded. She was going to have warriors walk back with her to make sure Chanil did as she was told this time.

But Night Star wasn't finished. "And, unfortunately, I also cannot spare anyone to accompany you back."

"What?" Chanil hadn't meant to say that out loud. More than a few of the warriors also looked at Night Star with some shocked expressions on their faces.

Night Star was nodding, and now, Chanil thought she saw a hint of mischief in her eyes. "We cannot spare a single warrior. Isn't that right, Nimaq?"

Another grumble, this one decidedly with a hint of surprise. "Yes—Yes, my Lady. They are all . . . busy."

Chanil felt a warm spot opening in her gut.

"So, Lady Chanil," Night Star said. "We cannot let you go home alone, and we cannot spare anyone to accompany you. I guess you'll have to stay here under watch until we return to Yaxchilan."

A warrior behind Chanil whooped. And then another. Ch'akanel gave her a long hug. Nimaq just shook his head and walked away.

Chanil was smiling so hard her cheeks hurt. Her heart was full and light for the first time in forever. She looked through the crowd of brothers and sisters in arm around her and up at Lady Night Star. The older warrior just looked back at her, that warm, loving smile on her face. She was going to let Chanil stay. Which meant Chanil was going to fight.

Northern Border

Vengeance catches up with all of us.
And if someone should escape its watchful eye . . .
Well, that's where I come in.

—*Xelaq'am's Songs*

FINDING THE INVADERS WASN'T A PROBLEM. They just had to follow the screams. Or, really, ask the villagers they met on the road. The ones fleeing their homes in terror. It was the same story on every person's lips. Homes ransacked. Fields burned. Children and elders cut down if they couldn't move fast enough. Chanil felt her blood boiling.

Her people were being murdered.

If she'd had any lingering doubts about whether or not she had been right to run away from home to fight, they disappeared with the arrival of the refugees. Any reservations she might still have had vanished the night that she wrapped her childhood blanket around the shoulders of an old woman who had lost both her children in the vicious raid on her village. The woman shook, even in the warm night air, even with the blanket and the campfire. Chanil had brought her soup. But the woman's hands trembled, and Chanil decided it would be a safer bet to just feed the woman herself so she didn't spill all her food.

The woman's dark eyes never left the fire in front of her. She stared at it as though trying to conjure the spirits of her dead children out of its flames.

"Here, Grandmother," Chanil said softly. The woman was not related to Chanil, that was just how the Winaq referred to elders or showed respect.

She lifted the spoon to the woman's lips. It had taken a while to get the woman to eat anything, and Chanil didn't want to lose the momentum of that small victory now.

"I can't look at you, child," the woman said. Her lips were unsteady. She should have addressed a noble-born, like Chanil, differently, but Chanil didn't care about the rules of pompous nobility. Especially out here. Nevertheless, something about the woman's tone struck Chanil as filled with meaning.

"It's okay, Grandmother. Just have some soup, yeah?" Chanil tried again.

The woman shook her head. "You look like her. My eldest." The woman's eyes remained fixed on the flames. "My baby girl . . ." She trailed off, sobbing. Chanil put the spoon down then. She wrapped her arms around the woman and held her until her sobs faded and the woman drifted off into a semblance of sleep.

Eventually, Ch'akanel emerged from the shadows and beckoned to Chanil. His face was grim. She nodded. She gently laid the old woman on some furs, tucking her into the thick, purple weaving that had held Chanil since she was a baby. Chanil wondered if that would comfort the old woman. She had said Chanil looked like her daughter. Maybe she had wrapped her own daughter up in a similar blanket.

Chanil got up, then, and crossed to Ch'akanel. She stepped carefully over sleeping warriors and over villagers who had stayed with the warriors to feel some sense of protection or to join them.

Or villagers who stayed because the warriors had promised food, and many had not eaten in some time. A pair of young boys looked up at Chanil as she passed their hammock. They looked at her with something like the admiration Chanil often saw in Itza's eyes. Chanil swallowed. Would she be able to live up to their expectations when the fighting started? She wasn't sure. But she was determined to try.

She joined Ch'akanel, and he led her away from the campfires where villagers slept.

"We should kill every last invader on our lands," Chanil seethed as they walked. "Do you see what they've done?"

Ch'akanel nodded. "You'll get your chance soon enough, Chan."

They came, then, to a small meeting in the jungle near where folks were sleeping. A handful of figures around a gentle fire set in a shallow hole near the giant buttressed walls of a ceiba tree. Night Star stood there with Nimaq and a few others. Night Star inclined her head as Chanil entered the circle. Nimaq growled in her direction.

"I sent for you, my Lady," Night Star said. Even though she commanded the troops, she was still technically required to refer to Lady Chanil, heir to the kingdom, appropriately.

"I'm here, my Lady." Chanil replied simply. She couldn't quite adopt the other warriors' habit of calling Night Star 'old woman' yet. That was something the older warriors did. Chanil and Ch'akanel were still young. Night Star had trained them both since childhood. She was like a mother figure.

"Our scouts here have returned with news," Night Star said, gesturing for one of the men there to speak.

Chanil could tell he was a scout immediately. His dress was lighter armor, half covered by a longer cloak. He was thinner than most of the warriors, less muscled but still athletic. Chanil knew scouts needed to be fast—and sneaky. They went ahead and found traps or enemies, sometimes food, or water sources. Itza' would probably make a great scout.

"There is a band of Invaders nearby. Less than a day's walk." The scout's voice was smooth and nasal. His nose and chin were long, wide-set eyes, drooping earlobes.

Chanil felt a hunger growing in her ankles. The enemy was near! Excitedly, she asked, "How many?"

"Perhaps twenty, my Lady," he said, bowing his head.

Chanil's hunger grew up to her calves. She smirked. They would outnumber them, more than two to one. It would be easy.

"When do we leave?" She threw the question out to the group.

But the scout was shaking his head. "The enemy is well-positioned, good sirs and ladies. They can only be approached from one side, and the path narrows significantly there."

Nimaq grumbled—this one decidedly negative. "Smart. Our numbers might not overwhelm them, then."

The scout nodded. He gestured to include himself and his companion. "We had the distinct impression they are waiting for reinforcements."

Chanil looked up at Night Star. "We can't let that stop us!"

Night Star chuckled. Their commander had a plan already, of course. But Night Star was never one to let a teaching moment go to waste.

"Well then, Honored Lady, what would you suggest?" The question was legitimate, and Chanil knew it. The message was also clear. *You wanted us to fight, you ran away from home to be in the fight, so what would you have us do now that we are here?*

The group was silent, waiting for Chanil's answer. She was the youngest warrior there, untested, unproven in many ways. But she was also the heir, the eldest daughter of Lord 5-Thunder. She would have to get used to making decisions if she was to rule Yaxchilan and its realm. Chanil felt the weight of the silence, of everyone's expectations. She felt like everything she did here was being used to judge whether or not she would be, or could be, a worthy queen for these men and women later on.

She swallowed. Her stomach threatened her with a violent kick of nausea. Don't you dare, she growled angrily at her stomach. But only in her mind. Outwardly, she looked over each warrior in turn and the pair of scouts, before replying.

"If we had more time, we could wait them out," she began and held up a hand as Nimaq's grumble started to protest. "But the real problem, either way, is their position. So—we need to get them to move. If we can't wait for them to do so—then we force them to. Before their friends arrive to join them."

Night Star nodded, a confident look on her face. "Agreed. So—how do we get them to abandon a superior position before their reinforcements arrive to even the odds?"

The question wasn't directed at Chanil alone anymore, it was open to the group. Chanil had correctly identified the problem, but she wouldn't be expected to come up with all the answers alone. That was Night Star's leadership style—everyone had a voice.

"Do we have any idea how far away the rest of them are?" Ch'akanel's question.

The scouts shook their heads. "A day or two would be my guess," said the younger one. He was just a boy, really. Chanil knew scouts were also often just locals who knew the area very well and were able to hide away if things went badly.

"Wouldn't want to be fighting them still when their friends show up and find ourselves surrounded," Nimaq growled.

Chanil narrowed her eyes. "Exactly how is their camp set up?"

The taller scout shrugged and then knelt. He used a stick to draw things out. "The ground raises up behind them and then falls off steeply here. And this is where the river is—at their back. Then this path leads into the camp. It is fairly narrow, and they have it guarded. They have no ditch, but something of a wall around here. That's why we didn't think they are planning on being there long."

Chanil nodded. A plan was forming in her mind already.

"What do you see, my Lady?" asked Night Star.

"It's a good design for the location," Chanil said honestly. "They have enough room from the entrance to the river to fall back if needed."

The scout was nodding. He looked up at Chanil directly. "They have canoes, my Lady. Moored here, outside the camp. There might be a path down to them."

"This is where they plan on rowing west to join the Great Army then," Ch'akanel added. The others nodded in agreement. It seemed possible.

"Can't row without boats," Chanil said simply. She smirked and looked at Night Star, who gave her a quick wink.

"Go on," the older woman said.

Chanil was excited now. She thought she had an idea that could work. "If we could cut the canoes loose—or burn them I guess— then they're stranded. Some might even rush out of the camp or come down to see what is happening. At the same time, a couple warriors climb up along the backside of the camp and start making a distraction. When they're distracted, the main force comes pouring through the front."

Ch'akanel made a low whistling sound. His expression either said Chanil's idea was brave or insane. "It's risky. But if we wait for the reinforcements to arrive, we might have too large an enemy to fight."

"Agreed," Nimaq said. "And if we can take the camp before their friends get here, we can hold them off from there."

Night Star pursed her lips. "Then we go with the noble Lady's suggestion. Burn the canoes. That will draw some of them away. It will put them on notice, but when the attack inside the camp starts, they'll think that's the way we are coming at them."

"My Lady," Chanil said quickly. "I'd like to be in the front line when we meet them inside the camp."

Night Star was already shaking her head. "You haven't been in a real shield wall yet. I need my most experienced up in front this time."

What had Chanil really expected? That Night Star would put her front and center in the shield wall for her very first battle? That Night Star would choose her over warriors who had fought together and bled together in that tight formation, countless times over the years, and knew how to move as one unit? But that was fine; she'd volunteered. At least she had given it a try.

"Then I volunteer to sneak into the camp, my Lady." Her words were flat, tone respectful but assertive.

Night Star looked at her for a moment. Just long enough.

"Chanil and I are the quickest, my Lady," Ch'akanel jumped in. "It should be us."

Night Star sighed. "You would be surrounded inside the camp."

"Then you and Nimaq will have to make sure you get there on time—otherwise we may have to finish them all off ourselves." Chanil grinned. She wasn't sure she felt as confident as she sounded. But it really didn't matter. She would find out whether or not she was ready soon enough.

Chanil's face was painted black. Her hair was pulled up and braided tight against her head under the woven helmet. Her woven armor was darkly colored, too. Not the bright, shimmering battle dress that characterized the giant clashes of armies. She was dressed for shadow work. She carried two knives in waist sheaths on either side and a single-handed, obsidian-bladed sword slung on her back. She crouched under the cover of bushes and understory plants next to Ch'akanel. He was similarly painted and dressed to hide in the shadows. She could hear his breathing. And she knew she could see in the dim light better than her comrade.

Chanil watched the gentle bobbing of three midsized canoes. The crafts were tied to wooden poles shoved into the riverbank. A few feet from the riverbank, the ground shot up vertically, forming a bluff—a tangled web of vines and roots and black dirt. At the top of the bluff, overlooking the river, lay the enemy's camp—just as the scouts had reported it.

Chanil and Ch'akanel had to untie those canoes, light them on fire, and then move past the makeshift dock to where they would climb their way up the wall of dirt and vines to begin their attack on the camp itself. They had to do that while Night Star and the other warriors got into position to assault the front of the camp.

They had to be quick and quiet. At least, until the destruction began.

No one was guarding the canoes as far as Chanil and Ch'akanel could see. But they had heard voices above them, suggesting there were some Invaders up there looking over at the canoes occasionally. But the shadows were deep. The moon was hidden that night, its silver face turned elsewhere. She did not see what the humans below were doing. The patrolling guards might not see them either.

"A couple sacks in each canoe," Ch'akanel whispered. "Then cut them loose and toss in the fire, yeah?"

Chanil was thinking. How long would it take from when the fires caught to when people started shouting? What if the Invaders checked the side where she and Ch'akanel would be climbing?

She shook her head. "We shouldn't light them until we get to the top. In case the climb is long, or they see us."

"That wasn't the plan, Chan," he said, smiling.

She winked at him. "I'm improvising. Besides, we didn't know how high the bank is. We drop the sacks now, climb up, then circle the edge of the camp and toss in the fire."

"And if we can't get a good shot? Or we miss?" Ch'akanel asked.

Chanil made a face. "Okay, so screw the fire, then. It's annoying anyway. Just cut the canoes loose. They'll notice. And then we save the fire for up there."

They both agreed and went to work. This plan was easier to execute anyway. The two warriors clung to the wall of the bank, sliding closer to the poles that anchored the boats. When they were as close as they could get while still in shadow, they looked up. A few flickers suggested torches up there. They heard some gruff whispers, too. They waited. The flickers moved. The whispers faded into silence.

Chanil and Ch'akanel emerged from the shadows. Each had knives drawn. Chanil slit through the rope of the nearest canoe. The craft began to move with the current. The next canoe was moored onto the bank more, and she had to shove pretty hard to get it to catch in the current. She heard a soft grunt and saw Ch'akanel was doing the same to his canoe. Within moments, all three crafts were being dragged to the west, away from the camp.

Chanil turned right and moved along the wall of dirt and vines, skirting the thin edge of the riverbank as she moved to get on the other side of the large jutting of land that protruded out toward the river and formed the area where their enemies had made camp. Ch'akanel followed her smoothly in the shadows.

She sheathed her knife and grabbed a large root. She pulled on it, testing. It held. She pulled herself up, digging her thick boots into dirt and propping herself up on branches, rocks, and roots. The air was cool at this hour, and that felt good. But it also meant that dew formation was possible, and she had to be careful to test things before putting her whole weight on them. Her heart started to pound, and her mind raced, wondering what they would find at the top.

About halfway up, she heard Ch'akanel slip slightly. She heard a sharp exhale as his face smacked sideways into loose dirt. But he managed to catch himself on a vine before he fell further. He grinned, looking up at her reassuringly. She shook her head at him but smiled. She was glad he had saved himself. There'd be no way for her to help if he had fallen.

They were almost at the top when they heard the Invaders' voices above—a couple grunts, maybe. Then some quick shouts. She climbed a bit more. Then more shouting, this time prolonged and somewhat agitated—but not panicked. Not an alarm—not yet. Chanil guessed they had seen that the boats were drifting away. She couldn't understand anything she heard. As far as she knew, no one even knew what language the Invaders spoke. It certainly didn't sound anything like the Nahuatl languages in the west.

Chanil slowed her pace as she reached the top. She tried to catch her breath, feeling the adrenaline and excitement pulsing through her veins. This was her moment. The years of training—and climbing trees and stone walls with Itza', thankfully—had all led to this. Ch'akanel slowly lifted himself to her height. She put a finger to her lips. They listened.

There was definitely movement. Angry talking and some shouting. But it was farther away, coming from the other side of the small bluff on which they hung. Looking up, Chanil couldn't see any flickers that suggested torches nearby. She looked at Ch'akanel and shrugged. *Might as well*, her expression said. He nodded in agreement. They climbed up the last bit to the edge and reached over, pulling themselves up to peer over the edge.

Chanil saw some crates nearby and a bunch of men at the other edge of the bluff looking down into the river. They were pointing and talking emphatically. She pulled herself up and over and rolled onto her stomach. Crouching low, she made for the pile of crates. Ch'akanel was right behind her.

They peeked over the top of the crates toward the center of the camp. Most of the ground between them and the camp center held supplies, benches, and random wares. Then, beyond that, there were a few scattered tents and several makeshift lean-tos. It seemed like most of their enemies were still sleeping.

Chanil saw some moving torches farther away, beyond the camping ground. She guessed there were guards stationed there, and that was where the entrance to the camp lay.

She knew she should be nervous. That she should be scared—of death, of letting everyone down. But, instead, she felt almost calm. No, not quite calm. It was too intense a feeling to be labelled as calmness. Whatever it was, it gave her clarity and made her muscles feel light, and her body tingled in anticipation of what would happen next.

She looked back at the men arguing about the canoes. There were three of them. Chanil decided abruptly and turned to Ch'akanel.

"We kill those ones first. Silently if we can. Then light something on fire around here, yeah?"

Ch'akanel looked at the three men standing near the edge. One looked over the edge, the other two faced each other, arguing and gesturing towards the water. Some trees lined the edge of the small bluff for most of its length. He pointed at them to Chanil. She nodded. Then she pointed to the supplies strewn about.

"You shadow the trees—I'll go that way. We take whoever is turned away from us and then dispatch the third however we can." This could work.

They moved in unison. Chanil and Ch'akanel trained together often. They were friends, and they were used to reading each other's body language. Chanil realized it had been smart for him to volunteer to go with her. One of the other older warriors might not have been able to communicate with Chanil with so few words.

She stayed crouched low, slinking around the crates and hugging shadows as she moved to another pile of crates. Then another. There weren't any torches in this part of the camp, and the moon wasn't visible. The hour was very late, and the sky would brighten soon, but for now, it was still dark. She stalked her prey like a hungry jaguar, moving closer and closer to the edge where the three men stood. She stopped behind a short pile of heavy sacks. She was probably a handful of paces from the closest enemy now.

The men were cloaked in shadows themselves, but Chanil had good night vision. She could see the back of the closest man clearly. He had pale skin that peeked out from the collar of his shirt and below his shorts. He wasn't wearing any armor as far as she could tell. Nor was the man he spoke to. But the third man, who was turning now from where he had been looking over the edge onto the water, had light, woven armor. Chanil recognized it as a western style armor, but not one he would have gotten from Tlapallo in Coyolapan. Nevertheless, the third man wasn't wearing a helmet.

A bird chirped from the trees. The trio of men ignored it. Birds were waking now anyway. But Chanil knew what that sound meant. Ch'akanel was in position. His imitation birdcall was good, but she had expected it, and she knew what his sounded like. She watched the shadows crinkle in the trees and knew he would be coming forward.

It was time for Chanil to come forward too.

Her blood thudded loudly in her ears. But that strange sense of focused clarity permeated everything. She felt a deep, wet heat in her stomach. Her pupils were open wide, and she thought she could see the sweat beads on the foreheads of the men in front of her as she stepped forward and drew her knife.

In a moment, she was at the man's back. His smell flooded her nostrils—a strange, decaying odor, as though his spirit had left his body behind to rot. But she ignored that. In one move, she kicked his knees out from behind him, pulled his head back hard by his coarse hair, and plunged her knife into the space behind his collar bone. She twisted it hard then yanked it out, letting his body fall to the ground.

A flash of metal glinted up toward her face. She jumped back, feeling the swish of air as the blade sailed past her. The third man was swinging wildly in her direction. Behind him, his other companion lay dead on the ground, a pool of blood flowing from where Ch'akanel had slit his throat.

The third man opened his mouth to shout, but he coughed. And gagged. His eyes went wide, and he looked at Chanil with an expression of pure horror, as though staring at a monster. Chanil found herself shocked by the man's face for an instant. It was wrinkled and grey—as though his skin had been mummified. His beard was long and graying, too—cut so that it tapered to a point. And his eyes looked like clouds after a rainstorm, grey and wispy. He sagged forward, catching himself by stabbing his weapon into the ground.

It was an odd weapon. A single piece of long, curving, grey metal that came to a sharp, stabbing point. Chanil thought it was like a really long knife, except that the long curve would make it a formidable weapon if it were sturdy. And it looked sturdy, as it held up the man's entire weight as he gagged, blood running out of his mouth. Chanil was transfixed for some reason. She felt like a living skeleton were looking at her—a horrible monster from the underworld.

And yet, the man was looking at her as though *she* were the monster. She hesitated, on the verge of trying to ask the man where he came from. But it would do no good. She couldn't speak his language. They couldn't talk, even if he weren't already dying from the knife Ch'akanel had buried in his back. Quickly, Ch'akanel released the man's spirit by slicing his throat. He covered the man's mouth and turned it away from Chanil as the spirit left. She was only a pace or two away from the man.

"You okay?" Ch'akanel asked.

Chanil nodded. She realized she was holding her breath. She tried to relax. The man's face still lingered in her mind. Those terrified, grey eyes.

"I'm good, just never seen these people before," she said slowly. Then she gestured at how Ch'akanel was still holding the man's face away. "Thanks. Definitely wouldn't want *his* spirit trying to hide inside me."

Ch'akanel dumped the body aside. "Thought you might've gotten spooked there for a second."

Chanil's expression was hard to read beneath the dark paint and the shadows. "I'm okay," she said, sheathing her knife. "But we aren't done here."

They moved back toward the area with supplies and crates to hide behind. Chanil wanted to use the oil-soaked sacks they had brought to fire the canoes to, instead, fire the camp itself. They had left them behind an open crate filled with long spears and short arrows.

But they wouldn't get a chance to try out her plan.

A gruff voice yelled out to them. A figure approached, a man with a torch in one hand and sword in the other. His boots were thick, and his armor was well fitting. He sported no helmet, but he didn't seem to care about that. He was coming straight for them, yelling loudly. His voice carried, and it was clear to Chanil that he would wake the whole camp before they had a chance to get started lighting fires.

Almost without thinking, Chanil grabbed one of the spears in the nearby crate. She hefted it—it was only slightly different than the ones she had trained with. The tip was metal instead of flint, but the balance was similar. She took a step back, aimed, and let it fly. The sky was lightening, but the area was still dim. The spear sailed under cover of wild shadows toward the yelling man's head.

Too late, he realized what was happening and tried to rotate his body. An instant later, the long metal tip of the weapon cut deeply along the side of his neck. Blood rushed out, and he dropped his torch and weapon to grab futilely at his throat. He sagged to the ground and fell over, a hoarse, demonic shout crawling out of his neck.

But the man's shouts had already been heard. A commotion was beginning in the camp. Chanil and Ch'akanel heard other shouts, orders being given. A pair of men rushed out from a makeshift hut, swords and shields in hand. They moved quickly toward Chanil. She pulled out her own sword from the sheath at her back and charged forward.

Chanil heard a soft grunt, a wisp of air, and then a spear was buried in the chest of the closest of Chanil's attackers. The man's armor blunted some of the damage done by Ch'akanel's throw, but it was enough to knock the man back and make him fall to one knee. Chanil rushed forward, catching the edge of the man's shield against the obsidian blades of her own weapon, and turned the shield out and away. Then she turned her weapon over and cut a diagonal slice across the man's face and neck.

Out of the corner of her eye, she heard the familiar sound of Ch'akanel grunting. She heard his weapon slamming against a shield and knew he must be facing his own attacker now. But Chanil couldn't help him, because the other man who had been coming for her was on top of her now, swinging his curved, metal sword in beautiful arcs through the air.

She dodged the strikes, moving around the body of the man she had just killed, keeping the convulsing corpse-to-be between her and her attacker. Her heart was pounding, and she felt sweat dripping down her skin beneath her woven armor. She wasn't panicked exactly, but the reality of the situation was sinking in. The very real danger all around her as she moved just to stay alive. The commotion in the camp was growing, and she wondered how long until Night Star and the other warriors would start their attack.

She forced herself to breathe deep and focus on the present moment. It didn't matter what the others were doing. The only important thing, right then and there, was the man in front of her trying to kill her. This is what she had wanted—real battle. And she knew she was deadly in a fight. She just had to let it out.

Chanil's attacker fumbled for a second, slipping on the wet blood that soaked the ground around the corpse of his companion, and Chanil gave him a smug look, her confidence growing. The man's eyes blazed with a furious rage as he looked at the painted face of the young warrior opposite him. She used that moment to reach down and pick up the shield of his fallen comrade.

She took a couple steps back, moving away from the fallen body. She felt the air getting hotter as the sun prepared to break through the deep blue of the twilight sky above. She beckoned for her attacker to approach.

The man shouted something at her, but she couldn't understand it. A curse? An insult? It didn't matter. He charged at her, all the same. He swung for her head, and she raised her shield to block the blow.

The impact was jarring—the metal sword hit her foreign shield differently than the obsidian-bladed weapons she was used to. But the man was accustomed to this, and using the impact, he smoothly changed the direction of his strike. Chanil followed the curve of his blade as he turned it over, though, and sliced her obsidian-bladed sword into his ankles from beneath her shield as she crouched low under his strike.

He yelled out in pain, and she saw his ankles buckle slightly. She felt him shove against her shield with his own, pushing her back. The man was strong—far stronger than she had anticipated. In the instant of her backing up, he swung down hard with his sword. She brought hers up to block, but the force of his downward strike was so great it smashed her shield straight down into the ground while she continued to grasp it. The attack got her shield out of the way, and she felt the metal blade of his weapon grab her armor at the shoulder and bite. A sharp, hot pain radiated from her left shoulder as the blade cut through her armor and into her skin. Then another sickening sensation as he pulled the blade down and back, opening the cut even more.

Chanil roared, half in pain and half in fury. She felt her body shift then. Her eyes widened, and she felt a fierce rage cover her whole being, like the pelt of a jaguar enveloping her and demanding she push forward to maul this creature who had just harmed her.

She saw the deadly point of the man's weapon then. She knew that he was pulling it back so he could thrust that sharp, metal end into her chest. She yanked her shield up, pushing it toward the incoming point, and sidestepped to the left. She pushed against the point, letting the shield ride upward with the flow of the man's attack. At the same time, she brought her own weapon up under the cover of her shield. The full force of the blunt, rounded, axe-like head of her weapon caught the man hard between his legs. She saw his whole body lift, and his eyes glazed over for a second.

But Chanil wasn't done. She turned her weapon over and punched the rounded head of it into his face. Blood poured from his nose, and his eyes turned from glazed to panicked. Another turn of her wrist, and this time, she caught his exposed neck with her sword's razor-sharp blades. She kicked forward, knocking the man to the ground and stood over him—a pale, blood-stained pile, gurgling and choking. She stomped his face, and he went limp.

Then she looked up. Ch'akanel was sliding up sideways next to her. He looked forward—not at her, but in the direction of the center of the enemies' camp. She followed his gaze and then swallowed hard.

A wall of shields faced them, six men across and two rows deep.

As the sky finally broke from the edge of the sun slipping over the horizon, the wall of shields stepped toward them.

Wall of Shields

The Great Army was feared for so many years before it finally arrived. It grew and grew, and the empire of the New Alliance expanded without end. How much blood was spilled to try and stop it? How many sons and daughters lost their lives in service of its great ambitions? I cannot answer those questions. I can only count the bodies around me.

—collected writings of The Occupation

"COME ON, YOU DOGS!" Chanil roared at the wall of swords and shields. She banged her weapon against her shield, and Ch'akanel joined in.

"Come and fight us, cowards! You scared of some kids, big men?" Her voice did not tremble. In fact, she heard it echo off in the distance. She took a deep breath and hurled another round of insults at them. She also counted mentally. Ch'akanel had killed the Invader who attacked him, and Chanil had two dead nearby. That, plus the three they had killed silently by the bluff's edge—six. The scouts had said that about twenty Invaders were camped here. Chanil saw fifteen men in front of them now. This was probably the whole force then. No one would be guarding the entrance to the camp.

She heard shouts from behind the shields—angry and gruff voices. Jeering and laughing. No doubt they were hurling their own insults. That was how it worked. Each side pretended not to be afraid.

Only, Chanil knew they must be at least a little afraid. Else, why would fifteen men hesitate to attack two young warriors?

Because they saw us kill their friends. And we made it look easy, she thought. They're wondering how many more of us might be waiting.

Chanil hoped the rest of the warriors would attack soon. Her arm ached from where it had been cut, and she felt blood caked there on her shoulder. The wound stung, and she didn't know how deep it was. She could still hold her shield up, but it wasn't as easy as before.

There was some hushed conversation with the ranks of the Invaders. Then, the wall parted slightly, and a single man stepped forward into the gap. He lifted something up in his hand. In the light of the early dawn, Chanil saw a metal cylinder and a wooden handle. She wondered if it was a projectile of some kind. She tensed herself as the object made a clicking sound.

The bang that followed was loud. So loud that Chanil thought there must have been a thunder strike for a second. A crate behind Chanil erupted, sending wooden pieces into the air in an impressive display. A cloud of smoke that smelled like fire and flint and strange oils billowed through the air around the projectile weapon.

Chanil laughed. A sharp, jagged exhale torn out of her as she realized that whatever that thing the man held was, whatever projectile it threw, it had come so fast she hadn't been able to see it. But, fortunately for her, it had missed. And it was probably good that it had, or Chanil guessed that her organs would look like the ruins of that crate. She grinned, her big lips spreading that grin from ear to ear.

"You missed, asshole!" she shouted, knowing they could not understand her. And she laughed again.

The wall of men moved forward again. Angry shouts. They seemed upset at their comrade with the projectile thrower. Chanil and Ch'akanel looked at each other—should they run or fight?

Chanil was feeling good. She had killed some of the enemy and drawn the whole camp out into one place. And their shooter had missed. She took that as a good sign. She was following the jaguar's path, and it would protect her. She clenched her jaw, lifting her shield and sword. She moved to stand next to Ch'akanel. They would fight.

He exhaled hard and pinned his shield against hers. "You do know you're crazy, right, Chan?"

She grinned. "Don't worry, little one. It's just a show. We'll break around them at the last second and move to the front of the camp or dive into the river, yeah?"

"Of course—I'm sure you had that planned the whole time."

Chanil laughed again. Planning was not always her strong suit. And, despite her confidence that she was following the right path, she felt her knees start to shake. Her stomach was growing a pit of cold nausea, and she suddenly wanted to vomit.

The wall of more than a dozen men stepped forward. Five paces away. Chanil felt her shoulder sag slightly in pain. Suddenly, she wanted to run. But her feet were stuck in place. She was practically frozen in terror. She was grateful for the mask of black paint to hide her features.

The wall moved again. Four paces away. Her knees shook one last time, asking permission for her body to flee. She ignored them.

Three paces. One more, and then Chanil would run—

A loud, whooping yell filled the air. And then another. And another. The wall of shields stopped. The ground rumbled beneath them. And Chanil knew, without even being able to see over the shoulders of the tall men before her, that Night Star was here. The warriors of Yaxchilan had arrived.

And the enemy knew it too. Their formation hesitated, wavered. Some in the back turned to face the oncoming rush of fifty or more warriors charging at their back. Their commander was shouting orders, barking commands that could barely be heard over the din of the yells and roars of Night Star's troops descending upon them.

A warrior in front of Chanil dared to turn his head to see what the rank behind him was doing. Stupid mistake. Chanil chopped his knees out from behind him, and Ch'akanel stabbed him with his knife as the man fell.

"The supplies!" Ch'akanel shouted, and he and Chanil hurried backwards, shields still tight as they moved to where the crates of weapons were. No one followed them. The formation was breaking. Chanil saw the tall figure of Lady Night Star cutting through the enemy Invaders. They crashed against her shield like waves against a cliff, and she beat them back just as easily.

Chanil stopped in her tracks seeing Night Star fight—really fight, not just training. Beside Chanil, Ch'akanel was doing something with the supplies. Maybe grabbing a bow and arrow or more spears? But Chanil didn't bother to look. She just watched her mentor in action, moving like a thunderstorm, constantly changing direction, fluid, powerful, deadly.

The Invader formation had broken and now it was just the killing of the enemy as they scattered. The Yaxchilan warriors had them closed in, preventing them from being able to flee. And Night Star was carving those mercenaries into bloody pieces.

"Want one?" Ch'akanel pushed a spear in her direction. She took it absentmindedly. But it didn't matter. The battle was already over, really. A handful of Invaders remained—a terrified circle of silver swords surrounded by a small army. It didn't take long for them to realize their fate. They surrendered quickly, dropping their weapons. Night Star ordered her warriors to tie them up and take them captive. Chanil knew those men might have valuable information, but she didn't know if anyone from Yaxchilan could even speak to them.

Across the distance, Chanil caught Night Star staring at her. At Night Star's feet, a bloody trail told the story of how many warriors had fallen under her blades. The older woman removed her helmet, a well-fitting, woven mask of death that resembled one of the underworld gods. Her eyes blazed with an intensity Chanil had never seen, but she had heard the other warriors speak of their commander's fearsome battle frenzy. Chanil could see it now, the change in Night Star, the hunter in motion.

That is what I want, Chanil thought as she and Night Star locked eyes across the blood-soaked ground. I want to be like Lady Night Star.

By sunset, they had completely taken over the camp. During the day, bodies had been buried while captives were interrogated. The Yaxchilan warriors knew more Invaders would be coming, probably expecting to rest at this very campsite before getting into the canoes that Chanil and Ch'akanel had disposed of and heading west into the lands protected by the Great Army. But when would those other Invaders come? And how many were there? And what was the state of their forces? It would be helpful for the Yaxchilan warriors to know these things in advance. So, Night Star and some of the other older folks who were part of the warband worked to get the information from the captives.

Chanil couldn't speak the language of the Invaders, so Night Star hadn't seen what use she would be in trying to ask them questions. Instead, Night Star ordered Chanil to spend that day being bandaged up by one of the medicine men and some of the other healers. Chanil was the heir, and there was no way she was going to get anything less than the best healers. Luckily, her cut wasn't too bad. It stung and had to be cleaned with an herbal paste, but she would survive, they said. The herbs would help prevent a fever as well. Most likely.

By the time Chanil left the medical area, it was getting dark. She walked around the camp for a bit. The perimeter had been fortified with more poles and a small ditch. There was a secondary ditch now, too. People were sharpening more poles, knapping new blades, checking armor and shields. Everything was being made ready for more battle. The air was charged with a tense energy.

Chanil felt it, too. She had survived her first real taste of combat. Her body ached, and she was hungry and tired. But she had survived. More than that, she had helped her people be victorious. And that meant more to her than any lesson with Lady Xok or training session she'd ever had.

"There you are, little one." A soft voice filled with authority sounded behind her. She recognized Night Star at once. Chanil turned, smiling. She threw up her hands.

"I'm here. Right where I should be." Her meaning was clear.

Night Star chuckled. "So that little scratch—" she pointed at the bandage around Chanil's bare shoulder. "—didn't change your mind about having come out here?"

Chanil shook her head. "You were right, my Lady. This is where I'm meant to be."

A funny look played at the edges of Night Star's expression. Her eyes glinted in mischief. "That so? . . . Then come with me."

Chanil gave her a curious look, but Night Star said nothing more. The older woman turned and walked toward the camp's exit. She didn't even look back to see if Chanil was coming.

Chanil watched for a second, then she hurried to catch up. Night Star walked in complete silence until they left the camp and were beyond the protective perimeter.

"The interrogations were helpful, my Lady," she said casually as they walked off the road and into the jungle.

"Oh?" Chanil was more curious about where they were going and what they were doing. But obviously she wasn't going to get any information on that.

Night Star nodded. "The rest of their company should be here soon—tomorrow, maybe the next day. Around fifty warriors, according to the captives."

So, the battle would be larger, and the enemy would have more even numbers. Chanil wondered what strategy Night Star had planned. But she also had another question. "How do we know what the captives said? I didn't think anyone could speak their language."

"So far, we can't, though I'm sure some in the west can. But one of them could speak some broken Nahuatl. So, we went with that."

Chanil nodded. It made sense that the Invaders would have to learn how to get by with their western allies. Though it sounded like their language skills were still poor.

Up ahead, Chanil caught a sharp, familiar smell. Incense burning. She heard the crackle of a large fire, and as they approached a small clearing, she heard voices and saw the swirling smoke of the resin incense the Winaq burned.

She looked at Night Star, who gave her a sidelong glance, smirking. They entered the clearing. Chanil smiled wide. Many of the warriors were gathered there in a big circle around the fire. It wasn't every warrior, some were still guarding camp, but it was a large group. Nimaq was there and Ch'akanel. The younger warriors, too. They were still older than Chanil, but they had seen her train for years in the younger groups. And she had seen them, too. Models for her future glory.

The air carried the dense smoke of the incense, and its sharp smell permeated everything. It wrapped itself around Chanil like a blanket. A heavy hand fell on Chanil's shoulder, and she felt the familiar, calloused weight of Night Star's strong grip. The old woman pushed her forward, a friendly but uncompromising push into the center of the circle. Chanil heard a small drum being beat then. Everyone was looking at her. Their eyes showed excitement and mischief. Ch'akanel gave her a little wink, and she grinned at him.

"Lady Chanil of the Sky!" Night Star boomed out, and the drumbeat stopped.

Chanil turned toward her commander. The woman seemed to tower over her, though in reality, Chanil was tall for age and could see over most of the boys she knew. Night Star's face was partially hidden in the dense smoke of the incense, and the fire played with the shadows on her face, giving her square features an almost skeletal appearance.

"The youngest of us," Night Star spoke to the whole group, but she looked only at Chanil. "The bravest of us."

Night Star smiled then, and Chanil felt her own cheeks widening as well.

"They call the royal daughters the 'Twin Panthers' in the city," she went on. "Chanil—the bright yellow jaguar, smiling, shimmering, fangs glinting in the hunt."

Chanil heard murmurs of approval in the group, whispers of excitement. She felt goosebumps radiate along her arms and legs. Her heart began pounding as the drum returned, and she found its rhythm matched her own, the blood coursing through her veins seeming to be pushed by that relentless and powerful rhythm.

"She went after the enemy," Night Star was saying, the pace of her words matching the beating of the drum nearby.

"She did not wait for them to come to her. She went to them! She clawed their eyes and broke their bones. She stood her ground as they charged and shot and cursed at her, Lady Chanil of the Sky!"

As Chanil watched Night Star speak, she felt something growing in her heart that she hadn't known could grow there. She felt a deep sense of elation and excitement hearing the story of her own deeds, told in the way she had heard her father sing of his own battle deeds from atop the great temple in the city. At the same time, Chanil also felt something like sadness. No, that wasn't quite it. But it was close.

Night Star wasn't just telling the story, the older woman was also letting her own grief and worry and fear for Chanil's safety out through the words. Night Star had been worried for Chanil, had feared she might get injured or die. But she couldn't say that as commander. Leaders had to be willing to send their warriors into danger, to ask them to risk everything. But Night Star had known Chanil since—well, since she was born. She had helped raise her. Of course, she had been worried, Chanil realized. But she had known Chanil had to carve her own path. And now, Night Star could let those feelings of potential loss go. She could release them into her words, into the smoke-filled air, into the rhythm of the group's shared heartbeat being guided by the drum.

That was the other feeling Chanil was picking up on. Not quite grief, not quite sadness. A letting go process. A release of the fear of what might have been, in celebration of what had actually happened instead.

Night Star raised her arms, and the smoke seemed to wrap around her muscles, surfing around the edges of her armbands and jewels. "Lady Chanil, the little jaguar, struck first!"

"She struck first!" the crowd seemed to shout all at once.

"This young puma . . . strikes first!" Night Star shouted the words out, and the crowd grabbed them.

"Puma strikes first!" It became a chant. "Puma strikes first!" Then a merging of sounds to create linkages between the words— the forming of a title. "Puma-Strikes-First!"

Night Star dropped her hands. The drum ceased. The other warriors held their breaths in utter silence.

"Let that be your name now, young warrior," Night Star said quietly. The words were almost a hoarse whisper. "Puma-Strikes-First."

The older woman's voice was low and soft. She stepped forward and placed both hands on Chanil's shoulders. Chanil saw tears peeking out from the woman's brown eyes as she leaned forward to touch her forehead against Chanil's. Night Star closed her eyes, and Chanil felt their breath being shared.

Then Night Star said something Chanil didn't understand. It was in the language spoken on the Island, that much Chanil could tell. But it was so fast and Night Star's voice so quiet, Chanil couldn't make out the words to try and translate them.

As soon as the words were spoken, Night Star lifted her head and opened her eyes. She gazed down proudly at Chanil and shouted, "Now, welcome your new sister! Give welcome to Puma-Strikes-First!"

The crowd whooped, and everyone cheered. Night Star clapped Chanil hard on the arms and laughed joyously. Chanil was grinning ear to ear. Then one by one, every warrior there came and greeted her by her new name. They shook her hand or patted her shoulder. Ch'akanel's hug was deep and just a bit longer than anyone else's. Chanil couldn't help it; she felt her tears drop. She was smiling and laughing and crying.

Ch'iin Tok' Tuunich

A thing will always find its place.
Our fates cannot be unmade.

—collected sayings from the Book of Itza'

CHANIL WOKE TO SHOUTING AND YELLING. "They're here!" Again and again, the scouts shouted the words. She was up in an instant, heart racing. A quick look at the sky—just before dawn. Had she slept in? A little. She was tired and drained by the excitement of her first battle, her injury, and then her indoctrination ceremony. She had fallen into a deep sleep. Too deep.

She checked her armor. Like all the other warriors in the camp, she had slept in it, just in case. She double and triple checked the fittings and then checked her boots. She slipped on her helmet, feeling the sounds around her shift as the woven jaguar maw covered her ears.

She grabbed her weapons. A single-handed blade, etched with fearsome creatures to protect its user. A short knife in its thigh sheath—just in case things got really bad. A long knife sheathed at her waist in case she fought in the tight shield wall. And her shield.

Not the strange, foreign one she had taken from the men they had killed last night but a proper one, painted with the designs and colors of a Yaxchilan warrior, bright and shining like the old jaguar that had visited her before all this began.

"They're here! Get up, you dogs! They're here!" More shouting. The rushing sound of boots hitting the ground as warriors scrambled past the lean-to that sheltered her hammock. She was out from under the thin roof in a second and joined them. The warriors were all running toward the entrance to the camp. Looking past the men and woman jogging beside her, Chanil could see Night Star's large and bright headdress near the camp entrance. The commander was shouting orders, forming up ranks to fill the narrow gap made by the defensive wall around the camp.

Beyond Night Star, Chanil could see a large mass of warriors approaching. They wore the woven armor of the western armies, but Chanil knew they weren't from these lands. Those were the foreign Invaders, the mercenaries who had come to avenge those that Chanil and the other Yaxchilan warriors had massacred last night. They moved differently than Tlaxcala—like Tlapallo—or like the Mixtek warriors Chanil had seen once on a visit to the west.

These Invaders moved like demons. Snarling, angry beasts. But they also moved uncomfortably, as if their armor did not fit quite right. Chanil wondered if maybe they were more accustomed to wearing a different type of armor. But what that might be, she could not guess, and she had no time to think about it now. The enemy was here.

The gap in the defensive wall that led into the camp was wide enough that it took ten of the Yaxchilan warriors to fill the space. This meant the warriors could form up with over five rows of men and women in their ranks. Chanil knew that the ranks behind those in the front served many purposes. They helped to push their comrades forward and keep them upright and prevent them from losing ground. They also helped to cycle out the ranks as warriors got tired or were injured during the battle. Chanil doubted Night Star would let her be in the first rank, the one that actually engaged the enemy, but Chanil was determined to make her way as close to the front as she could get.

She pushed past bodies, sliding and stalking her way through the growing crush of shoulders and shields as the warriors formed the wall within the narrower gap of the camp entrance. Chanil heard mutterings and whispers as it became clear to everyone that the young warrior was trying to make her way to the front.

"Puma's going up there," one voice beside her whispered to his friend.

"We're with you, Puma," came another voice and a sharp clap on her back.

"She's brave!"

"She's stupid, she doesn't know how to fight in the front. She'll get herself killed."

"Puma-Strikes-First now, remember? She has to go."

Some of the words encouraged her. People knew her name already. They called her Puma. She had a reputation. Some of the words felt like a kick to the gut. But she resolved to get as close as she could. And when everyone saw her fight, she knew they would respect her and believe in her.

She felt her heart starting to beat in time to the war drums being played nearby. She felt her ankles tingle and her pupils dilate and the adrenaline come coursing through her veins as she made her way forward to the front lines. The ranks got tighter as she moved up the lines. She pushed all the way to the second rank and then—a hard hand on her chest stopped her.

"That's far enough, Puma," Nimaq growled. His eyes bore into her, and his lips were held tight.

Beyond the shoulders of the man in front of her, Chanil could see the wall of Invaders approaching. She could hear them yelling and throwing curses in their strange language. Chanil smirked, though, because she could also see and hear the arrows and spears being launched at them from the jungle off the road. There were scouts there, and villagers who had decided to join in the fight.

They weren't warriors, but they still had to be useful—throwing spears and launching arrows helped keep the enemy's heads down. Thrown rocks might not kill a man but they certainly made him nervous. And spears could sometimes get through armor even if thrown by a farmer.

Nimaq and Night Star shouted out orders and moved along the front line to make sure everyone was in their proper position. Then Nimaq took a position in the center. Night Star walked by where Chanil was standing. Their eyes locked for a moment, and Chanil saw Night Star nod slowly to herself. Would she pull Chanil out of line? The warriors were already crushing in together, the formation was getting tight.

Night Star lifted her head. "Shield wall!" The command was so loud it echoed in Chanil's ears even through the cover of her woven helmet. Then Night Star moved to the center of the front line and joined Nimaq there.

"Close!" Night Star's voice called out. Every warrior under her command knew that order. Almost without thinking, their shields raised and locked together. The wooden boards *clanked* in near-perfect unison as the warriors crushed in. Chanil was almost overwhelmed with the heavy push forward and the tight crushing of warriors pressing together, shoulder to shoulder. She could hear the breathing of the men on either side of her. She could smell their sweat. And, in her heightened state of alertness, she realized she could hear more than just breathing.

The sound of heartbeats. So faint. But when all were put together, it was like a far-off landslide echoing off distant mountains. And she could smell their fear, their anxiety. She knew someone in the rank behind her had peed himself. She could smell Night Star's sweat—so familiar from years and years of being around her. She could smell Ch'akanel's excitement—something she had begun to pick up on as they trained more together. She couldn't see him, but the scent was so close. He had to be nearby.

And then, as the Invaders' own shield wall closed within a

few paces from theirs, she realized she could smell them too. The rotting spirit smell she had found so repulsive the night before when she and Ch'akanel helped take the camp. And metal, the cold, wet bite of the scent of their swords. Those glinting metal weapons were close now. Chanil could see the oddly pale skin of the Invaders beneath their borrowed, woven helmets. She saw anger and hatred in their eyes, and heard the almost deafening roar of their murderous chants.

And then the walls met. Chanil felt the weight of the Invaders' fifty or more slam into the front line of Yaxchilan warriors. She dug her feet into the ground and braced the back of the man in front of her. By his armor, she guessed it was the young man called Red-Feet. He was probably in the middle of his second decade. Chanil knew he had gotten married recently and that his family was not very wealthy. His wife made weavings for ceremonies—

"Push!" The call came from somewhere in the middle of the second rank. There was yelling all around Chanil now. Grunts and swearing. Taunting and jeering.

"Is that all they have for us?" Nimaq's low voice bellowed into the air. He hacked and slashed at metal swords and knives stabbing in his direction. In front of Chanil, Red-Feet shoved an attacker back with his shield. In the moment that the enemy stumbled backwards, the warrior to Red-Feet's left stabbed at the enemy's groin with a long knife, and then Red-Feet finished him with a slash to the face.

Chanil heard the man gurgling and choking on his own blood. She watched him fall, and the smell of the red rivers pouring from his neck reached her nostrils and overwhelmed her senses. Her heart was pounding like crazy now. She felt sweat drench her neck, her forehead. Every joint in her body strained, and her muscles screamed as she shoved Red-Feet forward. She couldn't let him fall or be pushed back. The survival of the whole formation depended on preserving the close, crushingly tight wall. No gap could be allowed that would let the enemy make a hole and slaughter them.

"Push!" The call came again, and Chanil felt the ranks behind her shove her forward. She nearly tripped over the boots of the woman behind her, but Chanil was caught almost immediately.

"Steady, Puma." The woman's voice sounded in her ears as the hands helped her right herself back up.

A loud scream filled the air. And then another. Chanil heard the heavy laugh of Night Star somewhere to her right. Long, razor-sharp metal points flicked and danced in Chanil's direction. She had to move her head and shoulders to dodge along with Red-Feet as the Invaders tried to stab at them.

Chanil felt a moment of panic as she remembered the ache in her shoulder, the way it had felt when one of those silver blades had caught in her skin and sliced along her shoulder. She didn't want to feel that again. She realized her knees were shaking. Fear was taking over, and she felt a powerful impulse to scream or run. Men surrounded her. Shouting, violent chaos. Grunts, sweat, the smell of blood, the crush of shoulders pushing her so tightly.

Was coming here a mistake? It was the first time the question ran through her mind. She didn't feel the strange, focused calm like she had the night before. Now, she felt only a growing terror under the oppressive crush of the warriors around her.

Should she have stayed at home with Itza' and her mother? Suddenly, Red-Feet let out a horrifying sound, and Chanil's eyes went wide.

"No!" The word was torn from her as she saw the blood-covered, metal tip of an Invader's sword sticking out from between Red-Feet's helmet and his chest. He had been stabbed in the neck. Beyond him, Chanil saw the evil glint of satisfaction in the Invader's eyes. The sadistic joy swam in those grey irises like a shark circling in water, looking for more prey to kill. Chanil had a sudden flash of the old woman from the other night—the one who had lost her children in these Invaders' raids, the one who had sobbed and sobbed in Chanil's arms. And then she saw the look of the two young boys Chanil had passed in their hammock—the ones who had looked at her with hope . . . too much hope.

Red-Feet's body slumped forward as the sword was pulled from his neck. Chanil felt a deep rage explode inside her at that moment, and all thought of self-preservation vanished. Any thoughts of running back home like a scared little princess to go hide in her stone palace while real men and women fought and died to protect her lands disappeared as she launched herself forward into the gap left by Red-Feet's absence. She pushed Red-Feet's corpse forward as it fell, using it to hide her advance. Then she stabbed downward at the boots of the Invader in front of her. The long blade of her flint knife pierced his boots. And she heard him howl in pain.

But before Chanil could even finish standing upright, the man's screams were cut off by a quick death given to him by the warrior on Chanil's left. Chanil let out a loud roar then. Her rage and her adrenaline poured out through her voice. She locked shields with the warriors on either side of her, and she screamed out at the wall of enemies in front of her.

"Come on! I dare you, bastards! Come on!" She banged her shield once with her weapon.

Chaos engulfed her then.

And muscle memory.

An enemy approached, leaping into the gap left by his dead comrade. Chanil earned her Puma-Strikes-First title once again as she stabbed into the man's groin before he had even entered the gap. Then she saw the light catch on a blade, a glinting swish of death that told her a strike was coming. She raised her shield just in time. The impact reverberated down her arm, and her shoulder screamed in pain.

She stabbed around her shield, half-blind, hacking and blocking. When the man on her right managed to drop his enemies' shield a hair's breadth too low, Chanil's blade was there to catch the enemy's look of surprise with the sharp point of her long knife. On and on it went. Chanil started to find a rhythm. She felt her breathing slow, and she took comfort in the bracing push behind her. She didn't count how many she killed, but she knew it was more than she and Ch'akanel had dispatched the night before certainly.

She smirked. She caught the eyes of individual Invaders and goaded them, cackled at them, or cursed them. When a young man tried to stab down at her boots, she actually laughed, a hideous, maniacal laugh, as she slammed her shield down on his weapon, pinning it long enough to take his eyes with her blade. She took two more, and her laugh filled the air around them. The other warriors in the front started to laugh with her, and she felt the comfort of their shared insanity.

Until the pain came. She didn't even see it. But her shoulder suddenly screamed. And then Chanil screamed and roared with it. She felt hot blood running down her left arm. Her shield was suddenly very heavy.

She slashed out reflexively, and feeling her blade catch on something, she pulled back hard. A satisfying shriek of pain told her she had found the one who hurt her. But the shield was getting heavier.

Smack!

She wasn't there anymore. Just for an instant. Nothing went black, but just a moment was lost. She knew that feeling. She had been knocked out before while standing up in training. But this was worse. Her vision wasn't all the way back. The images were blurry—grey maybe? No, just blurry. She tried to slash out again. This time nothing caught.

Smack!

Another hit. A dull echo of pain in her shoulder. She tasted blood. Or was she smelling it? She stumbled and felt her body going limp. Strong arms grabbed at her, pulled at her, dragging her. But whether they were friend or foe, she couldn't tell anymore.

The jaguar had left deep footprints in the mud. Far above, the blood-red moon was full and bright. It cast jagged shadows on the jungle floor as Chanil tracked the footprints left by the huge cat. She could smell it still—the wet, earthy scent tinged with blood. She knew she was going in the right direction. The rain was fading, but the ground was still soft, and she had to step carefully to avoid being stuck. The path curved downward steeply. Chanil didn't want to lose her footing and slip.

In the distance, she heard the grunting and deep, rumbling hoots of howler monkeys. But she paid them no mind. She kept her attention focused on her steps and retracing where the jaguar had gone. She had to find it.

She slipped. She caught herself, landing on all fours. Her unbound hair fell down in front of her face, and she breathed heavily. She saw little droplets of blood fall into the mud. She was bleeding still; she could tell.

Get up! Her mind screamed at her. Her shoulder ached, and her head throbbed. But she had to keep going. She had to catch up to that panther. Where had it gone?

Chanil shot up suddenly, gasping. The light from four hundred candles seemed to assail her eyes all at once, and she squeezed them closed. Then she felt the pain in her shoulder. And her head. And four thousand other places she didn't know could hurt like that.

"Easy, little one," said a woman's voice. Then came a soft hand on her shoulder—the good one, the one without pain. "You should lie down, yeah? Do your eyes hurt?"

Chanil leaned back to lay on the cot. She realized she was still squeezing her eyelids closed. Slowly, she took a deep breath. She was alive. She let herself lean into the touch of the woman's hand and cautiously opened her eyes. It wasn't as bright this time. In fact, once her eyes adjusted, she saw that it was nighttime outside.

She had the strange sensation of missing time. She remembered being in the jungle, the sound of rain, and the feel of blood along her face. Or had that been a dream? She had been chasing something . . . footprints in the mud . . . what was it?

"You had a rough time for a while there, little one." The woman's voice. The sound was familiar, but Chanil couldn't place it yet. Her head was consumed by a low, dull pressure that distracted her. She had to think for a second before she turned to look at the source of the voice.

It was the old woman from the campfire. The one who had lost her children and said Chanil looked like her own daughter. She was smiling at Chanil. Sun-etched wrinkles ran outward from her eyelids and the corners of her mouth. Her thin lips were cracked but pulled up into an expression of pure joy. Her eyes were warm and soft, but still tinged with sadness. Considering what she had gone through, Chanil doubted that sadness would ever go away completely.

What about what I have been through? Chanil thought. What happened?

Abruptly, images returned to Chanil's mind. Memories of yells and shouts. Men and women sweating. Ground covered in blood. Then a very clear image of Red-Feet's neck cut through with a sword.

"The battle! What's happening?" She tried to sit up again, but the old woman shook her head and gently pushed her back down.

"Everything is fine, little one. We won!" She smiled. "Well, you all won. I didn't really do much myself." The old woman let out a half-hearted laugh.

Chanil exhaled hard, feeling relief wash over her. She was alive. They had beaten the Invaders. Chanil had other questions, but those two simple facts were enough for the moment. She started to regain her senses, the strange dream of the jungle fading in her memory.

Chanil looked at the old woman. "What are you doing here? Where am I?"

The old woman laughed again. She looked around. "Oh, you're still in the camp, little one. Can't move the army while the heir to the kingdom is lying in bed with a nasty cut, yeah?"

She gestured at Chanil's shoulder—the bad one, the one that still hurt. Chanil turned her head and saw her arm: bare up to the shoulder and then covered in a bandage. Beneath it, she knew there would be special medicine. She hoped the wound wouldn't fester. So far, at least, she had no fever.

Then Chanil felt the old woman stand up. She turned toward the old, wrinkled face. The woman patted the blanket covering Chanil. "As for me, little one, I just had to make sure this blanket got returned to its rightful owner."

Chanil looked down and realized the old woman had covered her with her childhood blanket, just as Chanil had done for her. Chanil felt her eyes tear up. For some reason, she wanted nothing more than to wrap herself up in that blanket and sleep for days on end. She gripped it tightly for a moment, feeling the familiar texture of its heavy threads, and then she pulled it up against her breast.

"Thank you, Grandmother," Chanil said.

The old woman nodded. "The least I could do for such a brave, young warrior, yeah?"

Then she leaned over Chanil and kissed her forehead. Pulling back, Chanil saw tears in the old woman's eyes.

"How's our brave Puma doing, Grandmother?" Chanil heard the familiar tones of Night Star as the older warrior strode up to the cot where Chanil lay.

"Oh, troublesome as ever, I'm afraid, my Lady," the old woman said slyly, giving Chanil a wink.

Night Star sat down on the cot next to Chanil but continued to ignore her. "So that bump on her head didn't fix things, eh?"

Chanil rolled her eyes. The old woman laughed.

"I'll leave you to judge that for yourself, my Lady," the elder said, bowing low and stepping backwards. Then she turned to Chanil. "Your mother is only joking, little one. I know she worries for you!"

Night Star's mouth opened and then closed. Chanil just laughed. "Oh, she's not my mom—just my excellent commander, yeah?"

The old lady looked at Chanil a second, then at Night Star, and then back to Chanil. She shrugged and gave them a quizzical look. "Humph! Well, you two must be sisters, then!"

And she walked off, laughing.

Before Chanil could say anything, she felt Night Star's hand on hers.

"How are you feeling, Chan?"

The care and worry in her voice was clear. Chanil swallowed. "I think I'm okay. I mean, my head hurts . . . and my shoulder *hurts*. But I'm alive . . . Did we really win? What happened? How did we—"

Night Star put up a hand to stem the flood of questions. She laughed and shook her head. "Yeah, you're fine."

Then, more seriously, she said, "We won. The wall held, and we managed to break them down until they surrendered. We took a few leaders captive and . . ."

She made a gesture with her hand to indicate the rest were killed. "We lost two. Red-Feet and Nimaq's cousin, the older one. I was worried we had lost you too for a minute."

Chanil rubbed her head gingerly where it was bandaged. "I don't remember what happened."

Night Star made an ambivalent expression. "I didn't see it. But Ixta' said you got hit with an axe head. And that knocked you out. She and a couple others had to drag you away before the enemy finished you off. You'll be okay, just don't jump around for a while, yeah?"

"Jumping sounds like the last thing I want. I feel like I could sleep for days." They both laughed.

Then Night Star got up. She leaned over and held Chanil's face in her hand for a second. Chanil saw the glint of tears there. "I'm proud of you, Chan. You had me worried sick, and you're a stubborn pain in my ass. But, you did well, little one, and I'm so proud of you."

She leaned in again, and Chanil thought she was going to kiss her forehead like the old woman had. But instead, Night Star touched her forehead to hers and spoke softly. The words were in the language spoken on the Island, but this time they were loud enough and slow enough for Chanil to catch the gist, though some parts still didn't make sense to her.

"Catch the winds, my shining star, and may the ocean's breath heal your ..."

Something stirred inside Chanil, hearing those words, even though she still couldn't translate the last part. It was almost like a memory. But she couldn't place it. Rather, it just felt like she had heard them some other time in her life. Maybe Night Star had said it to her before?

Then the old warrior stood up tall. Her square face looked down on Chanil, and the young woman thought Night Star looked like a hero right out of the old stories. "I should check on the others, make sure all the wounded get to see their commander. It's important."

Chanil nodded. She knew Night Star was explaining what Chanil should do if and when she ever led the Yaxchilan army herself. But before she left, Chanil called out to her.

"My Lady," she said, and Night Star turned to face her. "Do we really look that much like sisters?"

Night Star laughed and gave her an evil grin. "No way, Puma! I'm way too pretty to be mistaken for any sister of yours."

Chanil grinned and rolled her eyes as Night Star left to check on the other wounded.

Family Matters

The greatest pain is being torn from your family.

—*letters from A Queen in Exile*

CHANIL HAD SEEN WARRIORS being welcomed back home after they returned from battle before. But seeing it from the outside could never have prepared her for what it felt like to actually *be* one of those warriors. The streets were crowded, packed full of onlookers. They cheered and whooped and celebrated Night Star and her warriors as the small army marched through the broad avenues that led to the center of the city of Yaxchilan. And the people looked at Chanil in a new way now, too. She heard whispers follow her everywhere. She had women reach out to touch her hair or her armor. She had merchants offer to sell her weapon for unimaginable riches—for a respectable fee, of course, for their trouble.

Everyone looked in awe at the young girl who walked with the tall commander of the Yaxchilan army. Night Star had explained that Chanil had to walk side by side with her as they returned. It would not make sense for the royal daughter to be in the middle of the ranks. She had to stride out in the open, right there next to Night

Star, at the head of the retinue where the heir belonged.

"You're famous now, Puma," Ch'akanel shouted from a couple rows back. Chanil could hear the grin on his face even across the distance separating them. She said nothing. She just laughed. And looked around at the faces of people who cheered for her or threw flowers over them or offered her their eldest son's hand in marriage. She felt light in her heart. Despite the pain in her shoulder and the sling around her arm to help keep the limb in a comfortable place while they walked. Despite the occasional headache that still came—though luckily faded fast. Despite the fact that she was bruised and hungry, and her body had cuts from unnoticed slashes that would certainly turn to scars. She felt—happy.

Chanil was a warrior at last. She had risked everything by running away. And now, everyone in Yaxchilan saw her as she wanted them to. And everyone accepted her for who she was. The people wanted a hero. And they saw one in Chanil. And that filled Chanil's heart almost as much as battle itself.

The war band turned a corner and started the long walk up to the central plaza where the giant temple of Yaxchilan stood. The white road beneath them led straight up to the giant, imposing, red pyramid. Chanil could see that the crowd extended all the way to the temple. She saw banners whipping in the breeze all up the stairs of the temple, and she remembered when each of those steps had been covered in gifts for her first moon.

And Chanil could see the small group that awaited them at the base of the temple steps. The tall corona of feathers signaled her father's giant headdress. The glinting of jewels and shimmering strands told her that Lady Xok was there next to him. And, of course, a smaller figure equally jeweled and painted. Her little sister, Itza', waiting patiently beside their parents.

And now the real battle begins, Chanil thought, swallowing. What would her parents do? More to the point, what would Lady Xok do? Chanil had disobeyed her parents, an act that technically could warrant death. But she was the heir, so she figured a beheading was unlikely. Still, Chanil knew Lady Xok would not be pleased.

"Keep going, Puma," Night Star said, noting Chanil's pace had slowed slightly upon seeing the Ajaw and Queen. "Stay by my side and follow my lead, okay?"

Chanil nodded but found she had no words. She almost would have preferred going back into the shield wall than facing her parents after running away. The scouts would have arrived a day or two beforehand to tell everyone the warriors were returning. Chanil's deeds and the fact that she was still alive would have been reported at least to some extent. And, of course, the small matter of their victory over the Invaders and protection of the kingdom. So, it wouldn't be a surprise, per se, to see Chanil alive.

But that might just mean they'd had time to think of her punishment.

They were getting closer now, striding through the plaza and toward the base of the temple steps where the royal family waited. Drums beat around them, and trumpets blared to announce their entrance. From where she walked, Chanil could see Itza's big smile on her painted face. She could just make out the fire in her father's eyes—but a good fire, she hoped, one filled with joy at seeing his daughter again. Lady Xok's expression was unreadable, a perfect regal mask of contentment and austerity. But her eyes never left Chanil, except to glance at the sling around her arm.

"Do you remember your bows, Chan?" Night Star whispered as they crossed the open area. People stood on either side, a wide gap given to the approaching war band of heroes.

"Do I ever?" Chanil replied flatly.

"The princely one. The one that says, 'I'm the heir, but I respect the king.' Do that one," Night Star muttered quickly.

Then she slowed her steps, and the whole war band came to a halt with her. They had stopped so that the back of the war band stood at about the center of the great plaza. Chanil and Night Star were about ten paces from the king and queen. Lord 5-Thunder raised his hand, and the drums stopped. A semblance of quiet spread outward from his raised hand.

Night Star whispered to Chanil, "Step with me." Then the old warrior moved forward. Chanil followed a beat behind. Night Star stepped forward several paces and then came down to one knee and bowed low.

"Do the bow," she whispered hurriedly to Chanil. The young warrior did her best attempt—hands reaching outward slightly, head inclined low, slight bend at the waist. She heard the whole war band falling into deep bows behind her.

"We welcome you," Lord 5-Thunder's deep voice echoed around the plaza, bouncing off painted stone walls of the tall buildings that formed the plaza square. "We welcome these heroes of Yaxchilan!"

The crowd erupted hearing his last words. The sound was deafening. The drums resumed, and trumpets blared out. Night Star rose and stood tall. Chanil followed suit, coming out of her inclined posture. She caught Itza's eyes first and couldn't help but smile. Her sister was giving her the biggest grin. Then she saw Lady Xok's eyes and swallowed hard. The Queen might have been smiling, but her eyes were serious and cold. But when Chanil saw her father's face, she grinned again. The Ajaw winked at her.

"Now what?" Chanil whispered to Night Star.

"Wait," was the only reply. An instant later, Lord 5-Thunder and Lady Xok stepped forward. They crossed to stand just a couple paces before Night Star and Chanil. Itza' crossed too, but not formally. She didn't care, in that moment, about the social rules. Her big sister was back. Chanil was alive. Within seconds, she had her arms wrapped around Chanil's neck and was hugging her tightly.

"You're back, Chan!" She heard the whisper in her ear. The familiar voice of her little sister, musical but somewhat raspy for one so young. She smelled the incense on Itza's skin and felt her sister's strong heartbeat pushing against the rhythm of her own as they embraced.

"I'm back, Itz," she replied, the sounds muffled into Itza's shoulder.

Lady Xok cleared her throat pointedly, and the two sisters

disengaged. Itza's eyes were wild and mischievous as she pulled back to join their parents. "For as long as there are days . . ." Itza' whispered.

As long as there is light, Chanil finished the refrain mentally.

But the Ajaw was speaking. "My two bravest fighters," he said, looking right at Chanil. She thought his eyes had never looked prouder.

"You should know, my Lord," Night Star said, "that Chanil's actions helped to bring us victory."

Lord 5-Thunder grinned, his boyish smile lighting up his face as he looked down at his eldest daughter. Lady Xok sighed heavily, but Chanil felt like there was more sadness there than anger.

"We're just glad you made it back, Chan," the Queen said softly. Then, in a sterner tone, she said to Night Star, "I can't believe you let her fight."

Night Star lowered her head in deference to the Queen. "We were already engaged in our plans when the Lady revealed herself. I saw no alternative safer than to give her weapons and cover."

Lady Xok opened her mouth to speak, but the Ajaw interjected quickly. "What is done is done. We can resolve this in private—later."

Chanil breathed out in relief. She would not be decapitated— for now at least.

"You should also know, Great Lord and Lady," Night Star continued, "that Lady Chanil is a true warrior now. She has proven herself in the shield wall and killed enemies."

Lord 5-Thunder nodded in approval. Lady Xok turned to Night Star, an oddly intense look in her eyes. "We need to talk."

She motioned for Night Star to walk with her, and her attitude made it clear this was not a suggestion. Night Star followed with a quick, "Yes, Great Queen."

They walked off toward the family's palace, leaving Lord 5-Thunder with his two daughters. He gestured at Chanil's shoulder, the bandages there. "Forget to lift your shield, little one?"

Chanil pursed her lips. "He crashed through . . . my Lord."

The Ajaw chuckled. Then he leaned in close to his daughter. She saw the snake-like scar on his jaw squirm.

"I can't wait to hear you tell the whole city the tale," he said with an evil grin.

Chanil went wide-eyed. Night Star had led the troops. She was normally the one to address the crowd and tell them all what had happened. Chanil felt her stomach turn over. She hated public speaking. Shouldn't a more experienced warrior do this? Chanil wondered if Nimaq would feel slighted if Chanil spoke instead of him.

But the Ajaw was already backing away to address the crowd. He lifted his arms and bellowed out, "Our great hero!"

The crowd cheered. The king continued. "She has returned victorious, my children. She has cut down the enemy. Her arm may be bloody, but she is alive! Our newest warrior!"

More cheering. Drums began beating, and Lord 5-Thunder had a look of sadistic satisfaction on his face as he said, "And now, great citizens, my children, people of Yaxchilan, hear the story for yourselves. Hear it straight from the Puma's mouth!"

The crowd erupted. Chanil stared at her father for a second. The scouts even told him about my battle name? she realized. She looked back at the war band. Most were looking at her excitedly, expectantly. She caught Ch'akanel's eyes and saw that his expression mirrored the evil grin on Chanil's father. Ch'akanel knew how much Chanil hated public speaking, too. Apparently, so did Nimaq. The old warrior was giving her a very satisfied and amused look. He pointed with his chin for her to step forward.

"Puma! Puma!" Nimaq, himself, started the chant, and soon all the warriors had joined in. Spears slammed into the ground, and swords beat on shields. The loud chorus would continue until Chanil stepped forward and gave her speech. Her stomach did backflips in her abdomen.

"Guess you are getting punished after all, sis," Itza's soft voice reached Chanil's ears as she stepped forward to address the crowd. She wanted to vomit. She had absolutely no idea what she would say.

"We have to tell her," she said tersely. It clearly wasn't a suggestion.

"Okay, sure," Lord 5-Thunder said. "It was never meant to be a permanent secret, but why now?"

"She needs to know. If she's going to rule—"

"I agree. I think it's time. All I could think the whole time was, what if my daughter dies in battle without knowing the truth?"

"Don't look at me," the Ajaw said flatly. "I never wanted to have this a secret in the first place."

"Then we're agreed?"

"Let me do it. The truth should come from me."

"We're all responsible. We should do this together."

"Decide quickly, ladies," Lord 5-Thunder said quickly. "They're coming."

They could all hear the footsteps down the hall. The girls would be there soon.

"I should be the one to say it," his wife said. "But we should all be there."

Chanil and Itza' stepped into the stone chamber. It was a small meeting room set atop a small hill overlooking the city. It had windows on two sides with beautiful woven draperies that were currently pulled aside. The walls were painted with intricate murals. One of them depicted a famous story of how the Hero Twins had traveled to the Underworld to trick the lords of death in a fantastical ball game.

In the center of the room, arrayed in a circle, were six reed mats, well cared for, plush, and comfortable. Four of those mats were occupied. Lord 5-Thunder, Ladies Xok and Night Star, and Q'anchi'. The remaining two mats, presumably, were for Itza' and Chanil.

Something about this whole meeting seemed off to Itza' immediately. Why this building? The sisters had been summoned here—which itself was a bit odd, more formal than their family usually treated them. And the place was private, far away from the central pyramid temple or the family palace. That made Itza' believe this meeting was important. But she couldn't think of what they would need to talk about.

And why now? Was Chanil to be scolded at last for running away? But the warriors had returned days ago. Chanil had even received a piercing in honor of her bravery and her injuries in service to her people.

Itza' couldn't figure out what this meeting could be about. Possibilities ran through her mind. Had the Invaders attacked somewhere? Was Tlapallo moving against them or the Waxtek? Had Snake Lady sent more information? Everything seemed possible, but nothing seemed to explain a secret family meeting out here. There weren't even any aides present, and the girls had been forbidden to bring any of their own in the summons.

"Please, girls, sit," Lady Xok said, indicating the empty reed mats. The girls inclined their heads and obeyed. Q'anchi' stood then and lit some incense. He carried a short staff that had a burner at one end, and he wafted the sweet-smelling resin over the group as he walked the circle. When he was done, he brought some cups forward and carefully poured a beverage for everyone there, including himself.

Chanil watched the movements around her with suspicion. She wondered if she was going to be punished finally for having run away. She scrunched her nose in nervousness, still getting used to the large jade carving there. It ran along almost the entire length of her nose, carved with glyphs and a design unique to Yaxchilan. She took a long sip of her drink, letting the familiar, bittersweet taste comfort her as Q'anchi' settled back down onto his mat.

The adults all seemed nervous. Chanil and Itza' exchanged a glance, but neither one had any answers to offer the other. Chanil decided to just get it over with.

"Look, I'm sorry I ran away. But I'm not sorry for fighting."

The Ajaw looked at both his wives. But Chanil went on. "I have to learn to lead. And fight—in real battles. And I did *good*! So—whatever you're going to do to me—just remember that we won, and I'm not going to stop being a warrior, no matter what."

She nodded, more to herself than anyone else in the room. Then she exhaled hard and puffed her cheeks. Then, to her surprise, Lord 5-Thunder laughed.

"We aren't going to punish you, Chan," he said flatly. It was the tone he had when a decision was made, and nothing would change it.

Lady Xok spoke next. "Chan, my dear, we know you aren't going to stop. And I realize I was... Well, I shouldn't have tried to stop you from becoming the warrior you want to be."

The sisters looked at each other. *Did she just apologize?* Their look said. *I mean, as close as we're ever going to get, yeah?*

"You were right, little one," the Ajaw said slowly. "I don't like you making us worried, but you are right that you need to learn how to do these things."

Chanil felt butterflies in her stomach. Were they really starting to accept her then? To finally see her the way that she saw herself?

"And actually," Lady Xok chimed in, "the fact that we realize you aren't going to stop risking your life is why we wanted to talk to you today."

Here it comes, the two sisters thought. Itza' wondered what it would be. She wondered a lot of things. Why had she been summoned here along with Chanil? And why weren't Night Star or Q'anchi' speaking?

"What is it, Mom?" Chanil's voice betrayed her anxiety. She just wanted to know what they were going to do to her.

A long look passed between Lady Xok and Lady Night Star. Then the Queen said, "It's actually not my place to say, Chan."

That was weird. What would the Queen not be able to say? And since when had Xok ever placed herself below someone else's authority?

"It's my fault, Chan," Night Star said suddenly, and Chanil turned toward her slowly. "It's my fault, and I should be the one to tell you."

"It's all our faults," Lord 5-Thunder cut in and Xok nodded.

"It's not just on you, old friend," the Queen said to Night Star.

Chanil was looking around frantically now. "What is it? Just tell us already!"

Night Star sighed, a heavy and weary sound that betrayed an exhaustion the woman rarely showed. "Do you remember the old woman? The one you gave your blanket to?"

Chanil nodded. She remembered the old lady but had no idea what she had to do with anything.

"Remember what she said about us looking alike?" Night Star was speaking slowly and deliberately, as though every syllable were a painful weight that she was handing off to Chanil.

Again, Chanil nodded. She felt like Night Star was trying to get her to figure something out herself, but she couldn't see what it was.

Itza', on the other hand, felt like a boulder had just slammed into her chest. She gasped involuntarily, and her hand went to her mouth. Her eyes went wide, and she looked at Chanil with those black irises that held a mix of shock and sadness.

"What? What is it?" Chanil said loudly. She was getting frustrated now. It seemed like everyone knew something she didn't, and that just made her feel small and stupid. But Itza' seemed dumbfounded and incapable of speaking.

"Mom?" Chanil turned to Lady Xok for answers. But Xok just sat there, mouth open, something clearly holding her back.

"She's not your mom, Chan." Night Star's voice. Soft, but factual. Strained, but trying to be strong.

Chanil's eyes opened wide. She looked at Xok, who swallowed. Then she looked at Itza', who nodded. Then, finally, at Night Star, who had tears in her eyes.

"She's not your mother," Night Star repeated. A pause, a quick intake of breath, and then, "I am, Chan."

Chanil felt her stomach roll over, and nausea gripped her. Then she felt her heart starting to race. Emotions shot off inside her like fireworks. Anger, excitement, rage, sadness, confusion, more nausea—it went on and on. But she just stared at Night Star. She clenched her jaw, and her eyes narrowed. She took a deep breath.

Then she whirled on Lady Xok. "Did you do this?" She shot the question out angrily. "Did you just want to control the future queen?"

"Chan!" the Ajaw shouted out in anger.

Chanil was on her feet suddenly. "You did, didn't you? You wanted to be able to say your child was on the throne!"

Night Star stood up, too. "Puma!" her voice bellowed out, and the tone caught Chanil.

"Look at me, Chan," Night Star said. Slowly, Chanil turned to face her. "I'm sorry that we lied. But we didn't think we had a choice at the time. Xok never wanted to manipulate you."

"But that's what she did!" Chanil shouted. Her whole life had just been turned upside down. And, inside, she was raging even more at all the stupid lessons Xok had forced on her.

"All the time spent teaching me how to act like some pompous, noble princess. Acting like she was just being the guiding mother when—when—she isn't even my mom!"

"You were the first born, Chan." Itza's soft and calm voice cut through the emotional tension building as Chanil faced off against the adults.

Chanil looked down at her little sister, who was getting to her feet. Apparently, everyone was going to have this conversation standing now.

Itza' looked at Chanil. Her black eyes had a calculating intensity about them. "You were the first born. And Night Star has family on the Island."

Chanil narrowed her eyes, not totally following her younger sister's meaning. But Xok did, and was nodding, a look of pride in her eyes as she saw that Itza' was figuring it out.

The little sister went on, "Our people might not have accepted you as heir—if your mother wasn't one of the Winaq."

Chanil turned to Night Star. "But I thought your family on the

Island was distant? Like just some far away cousin or something."

"Must not be, yeah?" Itza' was talking more to herself now. Her mind was flowing like a river down a mountain, carrying pieces of information she had gathered over the years and piling them all together into a giant torrent that started to paint a picture of the complex choices and decisions being made around her.

"My uncle was the Cacique when I was born there," Night Star said. A cacique was like an ajaw to the Ayiti on the Island. The cacique was a king.

And Itza' remembered how the Ayiti inherited things. Not through their parents, not often, but through their uncles and aunts. The implication was clear.

"So, you would have been the one to inherit his kingdom?" Itza' asked.

Night Star nodded. "And he preferred his son inherit." She said it simply and factually.

"And then to protect Chanil," Itza' said, picking up the clues, "you decided to hide the truth? So, she would be accepted here more easily."

"And so my uncle and his son would have no reason to target her as they had me," Night Star finished the thought for Itza'.

Chanil swallowed. "You did it to protect me?" She was mostly following the jumps Itza' was making. But to her, the more important part was that her mother—her real mother—had loved her so much she had been willing to give her up to keep her safe.

Night Star crossed over to Chanil and put her hand on her daughter's uninjured shoulder. "I'd do anything to protect you, Chan."

Chanil felt her heart aching. But then, more anger gripped her as more thoughts rushed in. "Is that even my name? Is that—"

The hand on her good shoulder squeezed hard. "Yes, Chan. I named you. I just did it in the language of my father's side instead of my mother's. All the women in our family have names related to the heavens. It's our tradition."

Chanil nodded, feeling better. She couldn't help it. Night Star's looks always filled her with love. She hated being lied to, and her belly still boiled in anger. But she was seeing things differently now. The blanket Night Star had given her as a baby. The necklace she had gifted Chanil on her first moon. The special attention in training. All those odd phrasings over the years.

Your mother knows, Night Star had said. Because it was true. She had been telling Chanil the truth the whole time—in her own way.

"I want to know everything, then," Chanil said flatly. "About you, our family. All of it. Why you lied, why you couldn't just be my mom."

Then Chanil turned toward Lady Xok and the Ajaw. "You should have told me."

Lord 5-Thunder nodded. "You're right. We should have. No more secrets then, yeah?"

Lady Xok gave him a quick look. Then, to Chanil, she said, "I do love you, Chan. That was never a lie. I know you hate learning how to be a queen, but you would have had those lessons with me regardless."

Chanil realized that was probably true. Sure, the emotional aspect would have felt different, and for that, she was still angry. But the lessons themselves—those were unavoidable. She threw up her hands.

"So, what now?"

Lord 5-Thunder chuckled. "Keep it a secret. We'll decide together—all of us—what to do with it when the time comes for you to be queen, yeah?"

"And, in the meantime, I can tell you more about your family—our family," Night Star said, smiling.

"Fine," Chanil said. She was tapped out. Her shoulder ached; her stomach was a wreck. She had fought in her first battle and then come home to find out her whole life had been a lie. Okay, maybe not her whole life. But, still, it was a lot to deal with at once. "But first, I just want to sleep."

Chanil left the room to head back to the palace. Itza' watched her go and then looked back at the adults. She knew they expected her to go and follow her older sister. But she didn't. Not right away.

Because Itza' had figured out more than she had said out loud. Before this meeting started, she'd had one very important piece of information that Chanil didn't have. Itza' knew about Snake Lady. She remembered the conversation she had overheard between Snake Lady and Q'anchi'. The one where she had learned Snake Lady cursed her mother once.

And now she knew why.

Snake Lady cursed my mother to stop her having children, Itza' realized. That's why my father needed a second wife.

Clearly, Xok had broken the curse at some point because Itza' was here alongside Chanil. But it meant that had happened after Chanil was born. After the lie had been told to secure an heir for the kingdom and protect Chanil's identity from her dangerous cousin on the Island.

And it meant more than that, Itza' could see. It meant Snake Lady had shaped the day of Itza's birth—which, for the Winaq, meant that Snake Lady had, perhaps unknowingly, helped to shape Itza's destiny in this life. This fact made Itza' all the more certain she had to find this Snake Lady one day and get the full story.

Because it was clear that the adults hadn't told them everything. They'd planned on Night Star having a child, so why hide that? Or had that been the plan all along? And why had Snake Lady not wanted Xok to get pregnant in the first place? Why hadn't she cursed Night Star as well? There was clearly more going on here.

And Itza' was determined to figure it out.

Part Two:
Puma Strikes First

Xunan Kab

Power comes from connection, from life, from being able to listen and being able to speak. When the day-keeper is chosen, power is involved. For those children who should have been chosen but weren't ... that power can bring terrible pain. That pain is the last sign that the child is one of the powerful ones. One of the ajk'ij, the day-keepers who see the truth most clearly.

—the Book of Queen Snake Lady

ITZA' LIKED COMING TO THE APIARIES to think. The royal family had many such bee houses kept in the outskirts of the city. The hives were built from special pottery vessels sealed at each end with perfectly circular stones. The flat stones had a small hole right in the center, just big enough for the bees to come and go. The hives were kept safe under thatched roof areas that shielded them from the rains and the excessive heat. Itza' enjoyed taking the long walk out to where the apiaries were kept, to stand in the center of the buzzing and humming of the stingless bees as they went about their work to bring their offerings to the queen. There were flower fields nearby, and she could smell the different types of pollen there—just waiting for the worker bees to come and grab some.

Itza' stood in the open area, surrounded by small, thatched huts, and closed her eyes. She let her ears and nose take over and describe the world to her. The bees buzzing. The flowers in the field swaying in the gentle breeze. She could smell the familiar scents of Ixcanul and K'utalik standing under the shade of the overhang of the stone building behind her.

It was calming out here. Being here helped her to relax and think. And these days, she had a lot to think about for a thirteen-year-old girl. Behind closed eyes, she heard one of her aides approaching. By the gentle tempo of the footsteps, she could tell it was K'utalik.

"Enjoying yourself, my Lady?"

Itza' smiled hearing K'utalik's sweet voice. She could imagine the girl's face without having to open her eyes and turn around. Gentle smile, wide, curving jawline with broad cheeks and rounded nose. Her hair parted down the middle and twisted into braids running down over her chest.

"This place has been here since before I was born," Itza' replied. "With everything changing around us these days, I guess I like the reminder that some things remain the same."

K'utalik moved forward to stand next to Itza'. "Don't worry, my Lady. Your sister will return safely. She always does."

Itza' heard the movement and opened her eyes. She glanced over at K'utalik, who smiled gently.

"It's not just that," Itza' said, looking away from her aide and off into the distance. "Chanil's a warrior now. It's good she's on patrol with Lady Night Star. We certainly need her out there now."

K'utalik nodded. "Lord Tlapallo's raids are relentless these days."

Itza' sighed heavily. In the many moons since their family had revealed the truth about Chanil's lineage, things had changed a lot. Chanil was a warrior. Even at that moment, she was off patrolling the realm with Lady Night Star—with her real mother. And the patrols were sorely needed. The Great Army seemed to have finished absorbing Tlapallo's kingdom. Coyolapan was now a vine of the great, spreading gourd that was the New Alliance. They had begun raiding their neighbors—Yaxchilan and the Waxtek. Everyone but the Red City. Lord Jaguar Paw seemed to have managed to avoid their attacks by promising some sort of neutrality. It wasn't totally clear how that worked and Itza' was suspicious.

"Are you worried about the war then, my Lady?" K'utalik asked simply.

Itza' didn't reply at first. She kept looking off into the distance. From where she stood in the apiaries, she could see the ancient temple of Yaxchilan reaching high above the trees. It was the oldest and tallest pyramid temple in the city, built so long ago that no one was even certain who had built it. And though it was not as broad and imposing as the newer ones, like the great pyramid in the center of the city, the ancient temple was far taller, seeming to reach all the way to sky. But it was also the most run-down of any pyramid. It was ancient, and parts of it were crumbling. And that was because no one used it anymore.

No one except the ancient witch who was said to live there. Itza' had never seen her, but she knew many people feared her . . .

Her, that was what everyone called her. No name, no title, just *her*. Sometimes as a curse, sometimes in awe. Never in the familiar.

Except Snake Lady, Itza' thought, remembering how the woman had given Q'anchi' a gift. A gift for *her*. And she had said the word with the same tone that Itza' heard in everyone else's voice, except it was almost friendly, almost familiar.

She realized K'utalik was still waiting for an answer. She gestured at the distant temple with her chin. "Have you ever seen *her*?"

K'utalik shuddered and shook her head. She wrestled anxiously with her fingers. "No, my Lady. And I'm fortunate for that."

Itza' nodded. That was the refrain every time from everyone in the city. K'utalik shook her head again. "My father said his brother forgot to pay for some food once in the market. That very night, *she* came. Transformed into a little bat and bit my uncle all over his face!"

She was blamed for many things in Yaxchilan. Stolen property, cheating spouses, bad weather. Everyone grew up hearing about the evil magic that the woman who lived in the ancient temple could do, and would do, most certainly, if you didn't behave.

Itza' wondered, though. "But who has really seen *her*?" she asked, and K'utalik looked as though Itza' had said an earthquake was coming. "I'm just wondering, who is *she*, you know?"

"Best not to find out, my Lady, if you ask me."

But Itza' wanted to find out. Very badly. Because whoever *she* was, *she* knew Snake Lady. And that might mean *she* knew why Snake Lady had cursed Itza's mother. The world was changing around Itza', and she needed to understand the truth about her past. Chanil and Night Star were mending the bond between them. The one that had been broken by the lie concerning Chanil's birth. But Itza' wanted to know the reason for Xok's lie, for Snake Lady's curse, for all the things the adults around them were very much still hiding. And it was possible, just possible, that *she* might know something.

Itza' could hear her father coughing before she even got to the doorway of his private bedroom. The king had the special privilege of a large bed chamber with a specially made door that could lock if he so desired. But as Itza' neared the doorway, she could see that the large, wooden door was open, and the Ajaw's deep cough could be heard all the way down the palace hall. It was early evening, and Lord 5-Thunder hadn't seemed sick earlier in court that morning. But the noises Itza' was hearing now sounded pretty bad.

She stepped into the doorway and peered inside. Her father was sitting on a thick mat. Her mother, Lady Xok, was leaning over him, patting his face with a wet towel. Itza' could smell the herbal medicine on that towel from the doorway. She tapped lightly on the doorframe.

"Come in, Itz," Lady Xok said, glancing at her daughter with a small smile.

Itza' stepped into the room. It was a spacious, stone-walled chamber jammed full of things. Lord 5-Thunder had a couple of hammocks hung up on the walls and a wide, fur-draped mattress against one wall that slid into a wooden frame. He had bookshelves stacked with codices and a long desk littered with papers and writing supplies. The walls were painted with murals, and one large window looked out over the main ball-court where ceremonial and professional games were played.

"You okay, Papa?" Itza' asked. Her father flashed his boyish, wolf-like grin.

"Talk to politicians all day and see if you don't get a headache, too, little one."

Itza' smiled at the jest. But she doubted that was what was really going on.

"I heard you coughing down the hall," she offered. She knew her father coughed sometimes, usually when the rains had started. But he never seemed truly sick, and it never lasted.

Xok and 5-Thunder looked at each other for a second. The king just shrugged. "Just need some water, I guess. Would you grab me that gourd, little one?"

His daughter walked over to a small table below the window. It had a large drinking gourd on it and some smaller cups. She filled a cup and brought it over to her father. He took it and smiled at her. Seated on the floor, there in just his grey tunic and shorts, he seemed like a smaller man for a second. Not the giant pile of muscles and growls he normally was, but like a faded version of her childhood memories.

But as she stepped back to sit on the floor next to him, he grew larger and larger, and soon, he was back to being the unimaginably high mountain that had held her in his massive arms as a baby.

5-Thunder took a long drink from the cup and then said, "So what can we do for you, Great Lady?"

Xok rolled her eyes at her husband's constant teasing and sat on the fur-covered mattress. It put her slightly above them, looking down on the giant man and the small girl.

"Since when do I need a reason to come visit the Great rulers of Yaxchilan?"

Lady Xok gave her husband a knowing look. Things were sure to be interesting if Itza' started a conversation like that. But really, Itza' was stalling. She wanted to know more about *her*, about the woman who lived in the old temple. But she hadn't yet figured out how to approach that topic by the time she'd heard her father coughing, so now she was forced to improvise.

"I guess . . . I was worried when I heard you coughing." Itza' figured the doting, loving daughter routine might help. And, in truth, she was a bit worried.

Lady Xok took the bait. "Oh, my sweet little one, don't worry. Your father is as strong and healthy as ever."

Which, since Itza' hadn't exactly said what she was worried about, she realized probably meant her father was neither of those things. She silently added her father's illness to the list of secrets around her. She would have to figure out a way to figure out what was wrong with him.

Outwardly, though, she smiled, painting the mask of a relieved child on her face. A path to probing for the information she wanted was revealing itself to her. "You always tell me to go and see Q'anchi' when I'm sick. Did he help you, too?"

Lady Xok nodded. "Exactly, little one."

Lord 5-Thunder, however, was shaking his head, an amused smile on his face. He looked up at his wife with a strange look.

Itza' ignored the look and took the next step toward her goal. "How did he help, Papa?"

In response, her father tossed the sharp-smelling towel from his forehead onto hers. It covered her whole face and she giggled. "With that!" He laughed.

"Maybe we should give this one the smelly medicines he has me taking and see if it helps cure mischief, too?" Lord 5-Thunder was saying as Itza' slowly pulled the towel from off her face. She gave her father a sour look.

"You know, if Q'anchi' can't help you, maybe there's someone else you should see . . ." She let her voice fade out, her intense eyes held wide.

Lady Xok looked at her daughter with narrowed eyes for a moment, wondering what the little girl was up to. The Queen was becoming more and more aware, lately, of how Itza' often leaned into the guise of a young, innocent girl when it suited her plans.

Lord 5-Thunder, however, didn't seem to notice. He just raised his eyebrows and said, "Oh and who might that be?"

Itza' looked down at her hands. She twisted her fingers innocently and pursed her lips before saying, "Well isn't that one old woman a powerful curer or something?"

Her father's face changed in an instant. His eyes flashed over with an intense rage, and a low growl escaped his throat. "What old woman?"

Itza' just shrugged and smiled. "The one in the old temple. I don't remember her name."

"*Her* . . ." And Lord 5-Thunder's voice was filled with a venomous hatred that Itza' had only ever heard him use to describe the most reviled enemies in battle. "That witch doesn't deserve a name."

"My love," Lady Xok said quickly. "The *elder* is not as bad as people say."

5-Thunder clenched his jaw and ground his teeth. "She's worse than what they say."

Then he stood up and crossed to the window. The sun was falling quickly now, and the sounds of the markets below faded as people returned home for the evening. Xok rolled her eyes and looked at Itza'.

In a very quiet voice, she said, "Men often distrust women with power, my dear."

Itza' nodded. From the window, her father growled again. "That woman is a dangerous witch, Itza'. An enemy of our family. I would never go to her."

And with that, Itza' saw another chance to pry a bit. She remembered how Snake Lady had seemed to know *her*, maybe even regard her as a friend. And Snake Lady was not loved by either of her parents. Casting her voice in a soft tone filled with genuine curiosity and maybe just a tinge of fear, Itza' said, "Even more dangerous than that Snake Lady?"

From the way both her parents went rigid for a second, Itza' knew she had hit exactly the right nerve. She watched her father's back as he continued to stare out the window. His shoulders were tense, and as he turned his head slightly, she saw the angry expression on his profile.

"Another witch," he muttered. The Ajaw turned and crossed to stand over his daughter. His intense eyes looked down on her. "We don't need women like that, you understand? They poison everything they touch."

Itza' swallowed. Her father was an intense and violent figure, and though she had never had a reason to fear him personally, she still felt very small in that moment with the large warrior towering over her.

"I have to check on some things," 5-Thunder said abruptly, and he walked briskly out of the room.

When they were alone, Itza' got up and crossed to sit next to her mother on the mattress.

"Is the old woman really that bad?" she asked.

Lady Xok shook her head and fussed with Itza's robes. "Not at all, my dear. You father—his family just doesn't trust magic. But *she* is just a *Grandmother*. It's not her fault people in the city blame her for everything."

Xok had used the honorific term for elders but had added an accent to it, elevating the old woman even further, perhaps implying she was unique . . . special among grandmothers.

"You know her, don't you, Mom?" Itza' figured the jump wasn't too great to arouse any suspicions.

Lady Xok nodded. "I do, my dear. She's . . . an old friend. And, despite what your father might think, she's done more for this family than we could ever repay."

Itza' nodded. She could see pieces linking together. As Itza' changed subjects and chatted with her mom about things she'd observed in court that day, she became more and more certain of her decision. Itza' would go and visit the old woman herself. Maybe then she would get some answers about the past.

The Obsidian Coyote

The Great Army was like a shadow haunting our dreams. Until we woke one day and found the shadow had blanketed the entire world around us.

—collected writings of *The Occupation*

CHANIL LET HIM PUSH HER against the wall. She felt his hips press hard against hers, and he opened her mouth with his tongue. She laughed lightly.

"That's not how you're supposed to do it," she teased.

"And how would you know?" he teased back.

She pulled him in tight by his belt and kissed his lips. Then she showed him how she liked to have his tongue against hers. "Like that, see?"

He grinned. "Naw, I didn't catch that. Do it again."

She bit his lip instead. "Well, if you can't follow that—" She looked down and slid off his belt.

"—I don't know how you're going to manage the harder stuff with me."

Then she gasped as he lifted both her arms up and pinned them against the wall. "Same way I managed last time, my Lady."

She laughed and smiled. And he showed her exactly what he meant.

When they were done, Chanil was still breathing heavy as Ch'akanel slipped his pants back on. She grinned watching him. His hair had grown out fast over the past year and so had his muscles. He caught her staring at him and laughed.

"You gonna just watch or help me out, Chan?"

She winked. "Definitely going to watch. Definitely not going to help."

She dangled his belt in front of his face as she stepped out of the narrow tunnel they had used.

"Let me know if you need anything, Ch'ak," she said, still holding the belt as she walked off to find a place to pee.

"Where have you been, Puma?" Night Star asked as Chanil sat down opposite her at the fire. The warriors were camped on the road near the southern border of Yaxchilan's realm, half a day's walk from the next town.

"Just checking on supplies," Chanil said quickly, a blank look on her face. Night Star saw Ch'akanel join the group a moment later. He pointedly sat down far away from Chanil. The warriors sitting around the fire made room for him. Night Star eyed him for a moment and then looked back at Chanil, who swallowed hard.

"All filled up then?" Night Star asked her.

"What?" Chanil said, her face red.

"The supplies, Puma. Are they all filled?" Night Star raised her eyebrows, a knowing look on her face.

"Yes, my Lady," was the quick response, eyes downcast.

Night Star shook her head. To the group, she said, "Everyone should turn in early and get some sleep tonight. We head out first thing. Then we'll see just how much damage Tlapallo's raiders are causing."

"I can't believe they would attack a sacred site," Q'anchi' said softly. He pulled at the greying curls of his beard, a grim look on his face.

"They're part of the Alliance now," said Nimaq. "Those bastards don't care about anything sacred."

"They're Tlaxcala," said another warrior. "Half of them have family over here."

"And our family over on their side, too," chimed in another. "Doesn't change the fact they're raiding us."

"Not just us," said Chanil. "The Waxtek, too. They're trying to surround us."

Murmurs of agreement went around the warriors. Night Star looked at Q'anchi'. The old man didn't usually travel with the warriors on patrols, but there were reports Tlapallo had sent a raid against one of the pilgrimage sites in Yaxchilan's realm, and Q'anchi' had insisted on coming along.

"We'll see for ourselves soon enough, old man," Night Star said to him. "And we'll make them pay for whatever they've done."

The old man's eyes lifted from the fire to Night Star's face. His red-brown irises glinted with heavy sadness. "More death won't change the damage they've done."

"If we don't push them back, they'll just keep coming, though," Chanil replied. Many of the warriors seemed to agree with her. Night Star had noticed how popular Chanil was becoming among the warriors since officially joining their ranks. But Q'anchi' was not a warrior, and he had seen kingdoms rise and fall many times in his life. He looked at the young girl.

"I'm not against violence, little one. But our plans must reach beyond simple vengeance to truly bring a stop to the bloodshed."

Chanil nodded but wasn't sure what to say in response. Night Star hoped Chanil would listen to the old man's words, though. She would need a balanced perspective as queen one day.

"For now, we rest," Night Star commanded. "The war will still be there waiting for us in the morning."

In all her eighteen years, Chanil had never seen the body of someone that had been burned alive before. And she had definitely never smelled one either. It had reminded her of the smell of burnt hair at first, before she saw the bodies. But as she had neared the remnants of the small town, the smell had twisted and amplified. It had become like the smell of rotting meat. But like someone had slapped that rotting flesh onto a dried animal hide and then lit the whole thing on fire. Her sense of smell had been overwhelmed by the pervasive stench that hung in the dry, hot air, refusing to move and refusing to settle. It had clung like a fog to the wide avenue as the warriors walked into the town.

Chanil knelt over one of the bodies in the street. Flies buzzed in the air, and her stomach threatened to vomit out the large meal she'd had early that morning before the patrol had got onto the road. But she didn't care. Chanil stared down at the small, contorted pile of charred humanity. It was barely recognizable as a child anymore. Exposed, pink flesh poked out in erratic patterns of brightness beneath blackened, crisped skin. The joints had seized up and torn at strange angles. A thigh bone protruded, and one of the arm bones.

A hand rested on Chanil's shoulder. Strong and calloused, but gentle. "Get up," Night Star said.

But Chanil couldn't move. "Up, Puma," the voice of her commander repeated.

Chanil turned her head to look up at her mother. The tall figure of the warrior towered over her, and Chanil felt like a small little child again. Probably the same age as the dead child at her feet. Chanil's eyes glistened with tears, though she held them back as she turned her face toward her mother. Four thousand questions that she couldn't give voice to reflected in her brown eyes at that moment.

Night Star nodded, knowingly, compassionately. She had been where Chanil was many times. "Get up, right now. Or you never will."

Chanil swallowed. She turned back to the burnt body and then forced herself up to her feet to look away finally. As she did so, the whole scene around her started to come into focus. The town was small, mostly pole and thatch huts. A few scattered stone buildings. But off in the distance, down the main road and towering over the short buildings where people had lived and worked with their friends and families, a large pyramid temple stood.

Around Chanil, warriors checked the huts, calling out for survivors. Bodies were strewn along the road, some hanging out of the broken-down remnants of the huts that had been set on fire. But the bodies weren't hot anymore. Warm, maybe, and Chanil could smell the smoke still. But the ground was cool, the burnt-down houses were safe to walk through. The fires had died out long ago.

The warriors had arrived too late. The town was lost.

They took the main road to get to the temple. The pyramid stood tall and silent, seeming to watch the band of twenty or so warriors approaching with quiet apprehension. The jungle curved over the road on either side. Even under her large, puma-shaped warrior's helmet, Chanil felt the heat of the sun above poking through gaps in the canopy. But, under the shade of the long branches that hung over the road, it wasn't too hot.

"Looks okay from here," Ch'akanel said, walking beside Chanil. She nodded. The bright red color of the building looked intact, as brilliant as the day it had been painted. The glyphs were clear—she could read them from here.

"Don't be fooled, little one," Q'anchi's deep voice said from the front. He walked next to Night Star, his eyes glued to the sacred temple. "They probably looted the inside."

Whispers and angry murmurs rippled through the group. Some people cursed; others vowed revenge. Night Star hushed them quickly.

"Ears up, and open your eyes," she commanded. "They might still be here."

The warriors gritted their teeth and squeezed their lips together. But it didn't change the rage they all felt inside. Chanil listened to the jungle for signs of the enemy, of an ambush. Truthfully, she hoped they were still nearby. Then she could punish Tlapallo's cowardly raiders, and maybe the spirits of the burned children back in the village could rest a bit knowing the same thing wouldn't happen to other children.

But so far, all she heard was birdsong and deer tracks. She smelled the sweat of the other Yaxchilan warriors, the tinge of excitement mixed with fear. But no strange smells from the jungle. So far.

When they got to the temple, Night Star had them set up a perimeter while she went inside with Q'anchi' and a pair of warriors to see if there was damage to the temple's sacred inner chambers. Chanil remembered that this particular temple had been built over a ts'onot. The giant underground lake probably connected to the maze of underground rivers that flowed below some of Yaxchilan's realm.

Chanil stood at the edge of the jungle, her eyes scanning while the other warriors took up their posts, handed out water to each other, or patrolled around the temple. Birds chirped, and a large beetle buzzed loudly as it passed in front of her. She sniffed the air and looked up and to her left. A pair of small monkeys sat on a branch, watching her. She checked their hands for waste, just in case. Nothing would be more embarrassing than for the heir of the kingdom to have to explain why she smelled like monkey shit.

"Don't worry," she heard Ch'akanel say as he came to stand by her. "Those ones don't toss their poop. Usually."

He grinned at her. "And how would you know?" she said teasingly, eyes still scanning the jungle.

"My father grew up near a whole family of them," Ch'akanel said. "We used to play with them as kids, actually."

Chanil raised her eyebrows at him. "You're not supposed to torture monkeys, Ch'ak."

"They tortured us! They beat all the kids at the dice game. I'm not kidding—stop laughing. I was young, okay."

Chanil smiled wide, trying to hold back her laughter as she imagined a little Ch'akanel running after some monkeys, shaking his fist angrily. Ch'akanel was still giving her a menacing look in jest—when she smelled it.

Smoke, she thought. No, that wasn't quite it. It was too sour. Flint—maybe sparks of it?

She stopped giggling and looked at Ch'akanel. Then she tapped her nose. He looked at her quizzically.

"I—I smell something," she said quietly. She looked carefully into the dense jungle, trying to catch the smell again. Or hear a branch breaking or see something. But everything was still, except the movements of animals. The monkeys in the branch watched her calmly.

She had almost given up when she smelled it again. Fainter, this time, but coming from directly in front of her. She took a step forward.

"What are you doing, Puma?" Ch'akanel whispered roughly.

"Stay here," she said without looking back. "I'm just going to check it out."

"Check out what? A smell?" He knew Chanil had an unusually good sense of smell. But he had no idea what she could possibly have smelled that would warrant stepping out into the jungle alone.

Chanil didn't respond. She crouched low and moved forward toward the smell. She couldn't really have explained it anyway. Flint meant people. But there was more to it than that. The flint had smelled . . . different somehow.

She tried to think of what that difference was, exactly, as she moved quietly through the jungle. Her shield was around her back, and she had to step carefully to avoid it making any noise as she pushed past branches and vines. Another whiff of the flint smell floated across her nostrils, and she turned toward it.

She stopped for a moment to listen. There was another sound, wasn't there? She couldn't be sure. It had almost sounded like foot-steps—maybe.

She drew her knife. The long, flint blade slid smoothly out of its sheath without a sound. The weapon was familiar to Chanil—it was her favorite weapon for fighting in close combat. The handle was carved with glyphs and images, specially done so as to improve her grip. She knew the weight of the knife, the feel of the swell in the handle, the smell of the blade—

That was it, she realized as she crouched behind a tall tree. Beyond the tree, the jungle thinned out slightly, and she thought she heard a grunt from behind a wide tree trunk nearby. But her mind had finally realized why the smell of flint had seemed differ-ent to her. The flint she had smelled wasn't flint she was used to. It smelled different from the flint that formed the blades in Yaxchilan.

Was it flint from a blade knapped far away? she wondered. Possibly a flint that came farther west?

She peeked around the tree and into the sparser area. She saw nothing, but she could definitely hear someone moving about behind the wide tree several paces in front of her. She came out from the cover of her tree and quickly moved toward the wide tree ahead. She circled the giant, thick tree trunk, moving deftly over roots that ran along the ground like the fingers of some ancient giant.

Peering around to the other side of the tree, she saw the source of the sounds and the smells. A young man dressed in bright, woven armor. Chanil recognized at once the patterns of Coyolapan. This man was one of Tlapallo's warriors. This was one of the people who had burned the village and probably looted the temple. The man was knapping the blade of a short spear. His shield lay propped against a tall root beside him. There didn't seem to be anyone else around. But his back was to the tree trunk, his profile visible to Chanil.

There wasn't a way for her to sneak up behind him. She slid her knife back in its sheath and retreated a couple steps. Then she pulled out her larger weapon, the one-handed, obsidian-bladed sword that was used all over the east and the west. The blades were razor sharp and glued firmly into the narrow grooves that ran along each thin side of the weapon.

She stepped forward again, bracing herself to swing around the tree and surprise her enemy as best as she could. But just as she started to step around, a loud call sounded directly above. The familiar *owowow-owwwww* of a howler monkey bellowing from somewhere high above them. Chanil froze for a second, but it was too late.

The young man had seen her. In a flash, he took off running, grabbing his spear and sprinting off deeper into the jungle.

"Over here!" Chanil shouted. "Here!"

Then she took off running after her prey. She thought she heard someone shout out "Puma!" in the distance, but all her senses were focused forward now. Her feet thudded against the ground as she pushed herself forward, faster and faster. She could see the man up ahead. His athletic figure dodged left and right between trees and over shrubs, and Chanil ran to stay with him.

The young man was fast.

But Puma was faster.

The jungle thinned again. A small stream. Chanil leaped over it easily. The ground sloped; the jungle thinned some more. But still, trees dotted the landscape and hid many things.

Chanil didn't see the other warrior at first. The warrior watched his companion sail by with some words Chanil didn't catch. Then the warrior, decorated in a fierce eagle headdress, looked Chanil's way. His body tensed, and he drew his weapon and lifted his shield.

Chanil didn't stop. In one smooth motion, she flipped her shield from around her back and slid it onto her left arm. She leapt into the air toward him, an attacking puma, cast in alternating light and shadow from the canopy gaps above.

The Eagle-Warrior turned his body just as Chanil crashed into him. Her weapon's blades caught his woven armor at the neck. The fibers tore. Chanil yanked down and back. Eagle screamed, and his body twisted. He leapt upward, swinging his blade like an uppercut. Chanil hid behind her shield, pushing forward and moving around the Eagle-Warrior. She smashed the broad, paddle-like face of her weapon against his head, then twisted it over to slice along his neck.

Eagle croaked in a failed scream, and blood splattered out over his armor and across Chanil's chest. But she had no time to relish her revenge on the Eagle warrior for whatever part he had played in the raids. She heard loud footsteps and turned to see another warrior, tall and thin, charging at her. He swung his giant, two-handed weapon at her like a battering ram.

The impact of his strikes shook her joints behind her shield. She stabbed down at his feet and felt her weapon catch the skin of his boots and rip them. Blood came out of the tear. Suddenly, she caught movement out of the corner of one eye. A third warrior was charging in.

She didn't wait for this new one to get close. She leapt at him, smashing down on his shield with punishing blows that drove him backwards with a chaotic brutality. She turned back to Tall-Man, dodging his long slice by leaping out at an angle.

Now partly behind him, she launched forward to slice her weapon up and along his back. His armor deflected the edges this time; he didn't get cut. But the impact slammed into his spine and shoved him forward.

Chanil leapt forward again to press her attack, laughing at the curses her victims threw at her. But then she felt her legs swept out from under her, and she was on her back. She leapt to her feet, almost before she had even registered how hard the ground had felt. A fourth warrior faced her, shield up. No, a fourth and a fifth. And now Tall-Man was turning, regaining his balance.

As Chanil took on the remaining four attackers, wounding them and giving them cut after cut, she saw another figure emerging from the jungle. A massive shadow that seemed to appear from nowhere. As the large figure moved forward, small rays of light from the canopy gaps illuminated parts of him. Bright green wrist guards. Massive shoulders beneath his woven armor. Thick boots reinforced with metal plates to prevent low ankle strikes in the shield wall. And then, as the figure stepped closer to the young girl, the light streaming through the trees revealed a large helmet shaped into the gaping maw of a fierce coyote.

Itzcoyotl's eyes blazed beneath the cover of his helmet as he watched Chanil fighting his men. He knew, at once, who she was. The warrior daughter of Lord 5-Thunder had been mentioned to him time and again by his warriors, by his father, by everyone. The girl who fights like a king, they all said.

And now, here she was, slowly cutting down each of his best fighters in turn. Itzcoyotl felt his anger and excitement mix as he watched the Yaxchilan warrior with a puma-shaped helmet pull off a complicated disarm that left one warrior completely defenseless. And then, in her arrogant way, she used the moment of surprise to kill off a different enemy before finally giving the disarmed man the honorable death he deserved.

Her movements were like a brutal but beautiful dance to Itzcoyotl. He felt his heart squeeze and relax in time to every swing of her blade. When he saw her smash her sword down onto the last of his warriors, so hard that it broke through the man's collarbone and became lodged in his chest, Itzcoyotl felt the same intoxicated feeling he'd had the first time he saw Chanil as a woman.

But then he remembered the way she had insulted him and his father. The way she had shamed him by mocking his attraction to her and calling his father a fool and a coward. They'd had no choice but to join the Great Army, then. Chanil's words had made sure of that. Itzcoyotl felt his chest tighten as Chanil turned toward him, the blood-soaked bodies of his warriors at her feet. He would be sad to kill this one.

"Puma of Yaxchilan!" Chanil heard the deep basso voice that rumbled out from behind the coyote helmet. The face under that helmet was painted black. But she knew that voice. It sent a chill down to her bones, and her blood ran cold as she realized who stood opposite her. The mountain of a man. The son of Tlapallo himself. Itzcoyotl—the Obsidian Coyote.

Chanil hadn't known Tlapallo was sending his own son to lead the raids. That Tlapallo sent his *own son* to butcher her people and burn children until their own parents wouldn't have been able to recognize them. Despite everything she had seen, she hadn't really realized the depth of her feeling of betrayal until that moment.

Breathing heavy, she called out to him. "So, it's you, Great Itzcoyotl, heir to Coyolapan. The Great Obsidian Coyote. The fearsome warrior prince . . . Butcher of small children. A great man."

He smiled proudly until he heard her final words. Then he snarled. Itzcoyotl stepped forward. Chanil circled instinctively before he was in weapon range. He circled as well. Coyote chasing Puma. Puma stalking Coyote.

"You haven't changed, Great Warrior. Still the girl who doesn't know when to keep her mouth shut."

The two warriors carved out their circle there in the jungle. They stepped over bodies, staring at each other, muscles tuned to that coiled, whiplash tension—relaxed but capable of lashing out in an instant.

"If you don't like what I have to say, you should just stay in your palace, little coyote. Where it's safe."

Itzcoyotl laughed a deep bellow, like a volcano erupting in the distance. "You think it's safe for you out here, Puma?"

Chanil gestured at the dead bodies around them. "I didn't seem to have any trouble with those ones. Maybe you should train your warriors for something other than killing children, yeah?"

"Like you're so innocent? Why do you think we're out here killing you, eh? Because you forced us to join this side."

Chanil laughed. "No one in Yaxchilan forced you to do anything, little coyote."

Itzcoyotl stopped circling and shook his head at her. "You really don't get it, do you? It wasn't anyone in Yaxchilan, girl. It was you."

And he pointed the head of his weapon right at her. "My father came there that day to see if we could find a different path. Maybe even arrange an alliance. But you just couldn't keep your damned mouth shut. Your whole family saw it. They knew we could have found a way. But you just had to shame us. Stupid girl."

Chanil swallowed. Her anger started to fade, and her stomach twisted in her abdomen. Was this true? Had Tlapallo been hoping her family would offer an alliance, after all? Or a marriage? She remembered Itza' saying that a marriage between them could have suggested an alliance as an alternative to war, but she didn't think Tlapallo had actually wanted that. And if he *had* really been hoping her family would have offered marriage—why hadn't they just said so? Why hadn't they pushed for it? Had Chanil's brash words closed that possibility before it could even be spoken? Was this whole war her fault?

She felt nausea creeping up to her throat at the thought. No, this was just Itzcoyotl trying to mess with her. He wanted her off guard so he could kill her because he was afraid of the warrior who had just taken four of his men to their graves at once.

She raised her own weapon and pointed it at Itzcoyotl. "We don't ally with murderers in Yaxchilan. Or cowards who can only sneak around burning farmers and children. You were a horny little boy when I saw you last. And now—now you're just a scared little doggy who's angry I didn't want you in my pants."

Itzcoyotl's eyes raged again, and he moved forward suddenly. His weapon slashed down at her, but Chanil wasn't there. She leapt to one side and smacked the back of his thigh hard with the paddle-end of her weapon. It was an insulting strike, the kind of thing a master might do to their student. Itzcoyotl yelled out in rage and whirled on her, swinging his weapon out in a long arc. She raised her shield.

The impact felt like falling face first into an earthquake. Her whole shoulder shook, and she had to brace with both arms. Chanil felt the wind pushed out of her. Itzcoyotl swung again. She slammed into the strike with her shield this time, hoping to pre-empt the shock. She dug her heels into the ground, but still, it knocked her back.

She heard him laugh. "Come on, warrior! Thought you were the best, girl!"

She gritted her teeth. Fear gripped her knees, but she forced them to be quiet. In her head, she remembered Night Star's lessons. *Never meet force with force. Flow with your enemy, don't try to dam the river. Use their flow against them.*

Itzcoyotl came at her again with a long diagonal slash. She moved toward and under the strike, using her shield to help her slide around it. She launched herself into Itzcoyotl, shield forward. She managed to pin his elbow against his body. She punched out with her fist, knocking his head back and forcing him to move backwards this time. In the space created, she slashed upward toward his face.

He managed to dodge out of the way. The air in front of his face rippled with the passage of Chanil's sword. His own weapon followed right after, and Chanil jumped back.

The two stared at each other for a moment, eyes locked. Itzcoyotl's eyes blazed with rage. Chanil felt her lips turn upward in a snarl and tightened her grip on her weapon. Her thighs tensed, and she pressed her feet into the ground to launch forward.

But just then, she heard a low whistling sound as something tore through the air at high speed. She whipped her head toward the sound and saw the spear sailing right for Itzcoyotl.

The giant man managed to leap back at the last second. As he turned toward the jungle where the spear had come from, the tall figure of Lady Night Star rushed forward. He raised his shield just as her leg shot out. Night Star kicked him down like a royal guard kicking down a door.

Itzcoyotl hit the ground hard, grunting loudly. Then he rolled to his feet and lifted his shield as Night Star's weapon came crashing down hard. The force of Night Star's strike splintered his shield, and he dropped the ruined mass of wood and glue. She twisted her weapon toward him for another strike, but Itzcoyotl ducked under it. At the same moment, he pulled a long knife out from a sheath at his thigh.

Night Star didn't see the new weapon, but Chanil did. She

pounced forward with a loud roar just as Itzcoyotl stabbed the long knife up toward Night Star's abdomen. Chanil tackled him, sweeping both his feet out from under him as she slammed her shield into him.

They crashed on the ground together. Their bodies flipped and twisted. She felt her shield and sword wrenched out of her hands and a painful twisting in her wrists as she and Itzcoyotl rolled on the ground. For a second, she was on top, her head spinning. But she wasted no time. She rained down fists and elbows.

Then, he bucked hard with his hips. Chanil felt her head slam into the ground as their positions reversed. She looked up at him and saw that his weapons were gone too. But that didn't mean she was safe. The first punch was like being hit with a boulder. Then he was slamming his elbows toward her face, trying to break her skull or cut her above the eyes. His body weighed so much, she could barely keep her hips from being pinned flat against the ground. She had no hope of bucking him off.

She heard a shout, and Itzcoyotl looked to one side. His eyes went wide, and he leapt up to his feet. Chanil rolled herself up immediately to face him. He reached down and pulled out a small knife from a hidden sheath at his ankle. But his eyes were chaotic now, and he wasn't looking just at Chanil, but at something behind her. Did she dare look?

She risked a quick glance and saw a handful of the Yaxchilan warriors moving forward toward him. Chanil whirled back toward Itzcoyotl, a smug grin on her face.

Then they heard it. The sound of half a dozen spears being thrown toward her and the other oncoming Yaxchilan warriors. Chanil had an instant to see the bright colors of Itzcoyotl's warriors. Then everything disappeared behind the veil of a shield as someone grabbed her and pressed her under cover. The air filled with loud *thunks* as spears hit shields or dug into the ground.

The cover lifted, and Chanil stood up to see Itzcoyotl's back. He ran over to a handful of his warriors lined up in the jungle. As soon as he reached them, he gave a shout, and the raiders turned and fled.

Chanil moved forward. She wanted to pursue them. But a hand on her shoulder stopped her. The other warriors called out insults at the fleeing enemies. In one of the pauses between taunts, Chanil roared out, "Run home, little doggy, run home!"

When they had vanished, she turned around to see Nimaq looking down at her with a grim expression. He turned and walked away from her. She followed him to where several warriors were gathered in a circle around Night Star, who lay on the ground.

Chanil went wide-eyed. Night Star's leg was being bandaged quickly, and she winced as they cinched the wrap tight. After a moment, the warriors helped their commander to her feet. Nimaq let her lean against him to steady herself. He held a long knife in one hand and showed it to Night Star.

She grunted. It was Itzcoyotl's knife. Chanil saw the blood on it and guessed it was Night Star's. His strike had gotten through after all—not as bad as he had intended because Chanil had tackled him, but still. He had managed to hurt Night Star. Because Night Star had come to Chanil's aide.

Chanil felt an immense sense of guilt welling up inside her. Maybe Itzcoyotl was right after all. Maybe all of Chanil's actions just ended up getting other people hurt—or killed.

Grandmother

Where does this world end and the next begin? Who can say? With every crossing, the barrier at that place between worlds thins and thins. Sometimes, it thins so much we have to move on and let that temple go. Other times ... well, some gateways can be useful.

—*collected sayings from the Book of Itza'*

ITZA' CHASED THE RISING MOON, moving eastward along the avenues of Yaxchilan as she crossed from the dense city center toward the sparse outskirts. Urban metropolis graded into a mingling of buildings, huts, and jungle as she moved farther and farther away from the family palace. Her world became fewer buildings and more trees. She passed the area with the apiaries, saying a silent hello to the worker bees sleeping safely in their painted hives. Then she moved along the wide road that led out of Yaxchilan. Only, instead of taking it all the way out of the city, she turned at one point and took the smaller footpath that led into dense jungle. In the distance, she could see the single ancient temple peeking through gaps in the canopy, towering over the trees as she walked the footpath that led toward the pyramid's steps.

Itza' could see the moon rising over the temple, casting the room at the top in a silvery light. She felt a twinge of excitement run along her fingertips. She didn't know what to expect up there. A sleeping old woman? A fearsome monster that would try to devour Itza'? Probably not, but one never knew.

Even from this distance, Itza' could smell a strong scent of incense floating down from the temple. It permeated the jungle around her and mixed with other scents—deer nearby, some monkeys. Flowers growing along the path that the people of Yaxchilan used for different drinks and medicines. Every scent seemed sharper than usual, more intense, closer perhaps.

She felt like she was passing through an invisible threshold. Every step she took toward the ancient temple took her farther from the normal world she was used to and set her down into a new world where things were heightened, twisted, altered slightly. A sudden rustling to her right, and she saw a long snake cross the path in front of her. She stopped dead in her tracks.

The moon was bright, but the trees hid much of the light. Nevertheless, Itza' had always had great night vision—even better than her sister—and she could see as clearly as if it were midday in the market. She saw the snake as it emerged from the leaf litter covering the jungle floor. It was long and bright green with a scary pattern of black diamonds outlined in yellow scales along its entire back. Itza' breathed in deeply. She had seen snakes like this before; they were poisonous and came from the mountains. They didn't usually come down into the city.

The snake slithered across the path, disappearing into the jungle on the other side. Itza' listened for the rustle of its passage, but the sounds vanished the instant the snake was out of view. Cautiously, she moved forward, stalking quickly down the foot path away from the snake.

The moon was directly behind the top of the temple when Itza' reached the base of the long staircase that led up to the chamber at the top. The night was deep, and the sounds of insects filled the air around her. She looked up that long staircase. The building was immensely tall—far taller than the great pyramid in Yaxchilan's central plaza. The steps were steep and run-down, and the once vibrant red paint had faded, revealing the rough stone surface beneath. A graveyard of shattered pottery surrounded the base of the steps where people had broken burned vases and bowls many years ago here.

Itza' cinched her thin cloak tight at the waist and exhaled sharply. I can do this, she told herself. She stepped up onto the first stone. It was covered in vines and moss, and the paint was completely gone at this level of the steps. Even the glyphs were faded, the carved shapes chipped and crumbling in sections. She moved onto the next step and the next and the next.

She slipped.

Her sandal caught in a crack, and her foot twisted, and she fell hard to her knees. She yelped out in pain. She bit her lip and wiggled her foot to get it out of the crack. On all fours, she looked up and saw the impossibly large number of steps remaining. It looked like there were more than when she had started.

I can do this, she repeated to herself, forcing herself to get up. She felt her kneecap; it burned, and she could smell the blood there. She would have to figure out how to explain the scrape to her mother. Could that happen in training? Probably, she decided.

She took the steps slower now, testing each one before putting her whole weight on it. Whoever had come up with the idea that an old woman was climbing up and down these each night to punish children who hadn't done their chores had clearly never actually tried climbing up to the top. Itza' looked up occasionally to measure her progress but decided it was too disheartening. She didn't seem to be getting any closer.

About halfway up, the steps were completely crumbled. It was just jagged rock. Itza' frowned. Now what? she thought.

She leaned her whole body against the rough surface. She reached upward, as though climbing a mountain, finding a small handhold. She tested it, seeing if it would hold her weight. She pulled against it and searched for a foothold. The first one crumbled. The next one held, though. She pulled herself up and found another handhold. Slowly, she scaled the jagged, crumbling surface. Her face was right against the rock. She felt a large spider glide over her thigh, its soft footsteps tickling her. She forced herself not to laugh or react in any way.

Finally, she pulled herself past the jagged area and back onto the steps. These ones were in better condition. The moss was gone and the paint, though faded, was still clearly visible. The carvings were clean, too, and they stuck out enough that she could use them for purchase to haul herself up and away from the crumbling portion of the staircase.

She still moved cautiously, but now it was more like the steps she was used to from the other pyramids in the city, and she could move more quickly. The smell of incense was stronger now, too. She could hear a fire crackling above. Looking up, she saw that she was almost at the top now. She could see the square outline of the walls of the chamber at the top of the temple. She could see the flickers that told her a fire was burning inside.

She kept climbing. Her heart thudded in her chest. She wondered what she would see. What—who—would be waiting up there for her?

She took the last step.

The stone chamber had a large doorway. It was like a giant cube placed atop the pyramid. The outside walls were all painted and carved with glyphs and depictions of monsters and gods, of ancient kings and queens. Most were faded, but there was still a lot of color there. And through the large doorway, Itza' saw a big room with a circle carved into the center and a long worktable beyond it.

She stepped cautiously into the room.

It was bright. Candles and torches were everywhere, and she smelled a cooking fire somewhere. Just inside the doorway, her feet were only a few paces away from the giant circle carved into the center. To her right, a large window overlooking the jungle. To her left, bookshelves, pottery, mats, hammocks, and four thousand other supplies. In front of her, the giant circle and, beyond that, the long worktable. With a single old figure bent over it, hands working hard at something.

Around the circle, large incense burners were arrayed at each of the four directions. They had been lit recently, Itza' could tell, and the smoke was swirling intently around the room, casting everything in a grey-black haze. The smell was intoxicating, and Itza' took a deep breath, inhaling the sweet and familiar odor, letting it wrap around her like a second skin.

"Well, are you going to come in or not, little one?" An old, raspy voice called out from the worktable. It was kinder than Itza' would have expected. Itza' took a couple steps forward.

"Are you . . ." she trailed off, uncertain how to address the woman.

The old woman stopped working on whatever it was she was doing. She turned slowly, and Itza' could see an ancient face through the incense smoke. Her deep, brown skin was wrinkled, and her eyes narrowed to mere slits as she let out a giant grin that seemed to beam like sunlight through the grey haze.

"I am, little one," the old woman said with a chuckle. Then she stepped forward. Itza' heard her mutter something as she crossed into the circle, but Itza' couldn't make out the words. The old woman walked all the way up to Itza', looking at her with an expression that contained more love and amusement than Itza' had ever seen in someone's gaze.

The old woman was just a bit taller than Itza'. Her clothes were a simple huipil and skirt, embroidered with designs that seemed familiar. She hummed to herself as she looked Itza' over.

The old woman tilted her head. "Beautiful eyes, little one. Where'd you get them?" Then she laughed and whirled around, leaving Itza' with her mouth agape. The old woman crossed back over to the worktable. Over her shoulder, she said, "Grab some mats, eh? I'll bring us a drink!"

Itza' saw some mats rolled up on the floor to her left. She grabbed them quickly and stepped into the circle. She placed the mats on the floor and sat facing the long worktable. The incense smoke was thick now, and she couldn't really see what the old woman was doing until she had re-entered the circle with a pair of cups. She handed one to Itza', then sat down facing the girl.

The old woman took a sip and eyed Itza' over the brim. Her dark, brown eyes glinted with mischief.

"So, what can I do for the Great Lady Itza'?"

Itza' laughed. "You know who I am?"

"And who does not know the mysterious daughter of our Great and Honored Ajaw? The black jaguar with obsidian eyes."

The old woman was not at all what Itza' had expected. She seemed relaxed, unfazed by this strange visit from the royal child. And yet, she also seemed to be in control, as if everything that was happening was no surprise.

Trying out a regal tone, Itza' said, "You have me at a disadvantage, then, good lady. You know me, and yet, I don't even know how to address you properly."

The old woman scrunched her face into a smile. The corners of her eyes wrinkled, and her eyeballs disappeared completely behind the smile. "Oh, how cute. You came all the way up here and don't even know who I am, eh?"

Her words dripped in sarcasm, but they held no malice. Itza' felt her cheeks redden slightly. "Well, I mean . . . I've *heard* of you, but . . ."

The old woman put a finger to her chin and leaned forward. "You want to know something, Great Lady?"

Before Itza' could even respond, the old woman said, "I'm not getting any younger."

Another laugh and the old woman sipped her drink again. Itza' took a deep breath. She wasn't used to adults acting like this around her.

Itza' sighed loudly and straightened her posture. "I . . . I wanted to meet you."

The old woman nodded, eyes widening. Her expression was welcoming but blank. She looked at Itza' but said nothing.

"Eh . . . well . . ." Itza' couldn't explain why she was holding back. She wasn't used to this. She dealt in secrets, in subtle tones. She read between the lines of people's words and eavesdropped on conversations or spied from behind walls and up in the rafters. She hadn't ever really considered . . . just asking for what she wanted directly.

But the old lady just kept staring, letting the young girl's excitement and nervousness sort themselves out. Despite her claim to not be getting any younger, the old woman seemed in no rush. After an awkward silence, Itza' finally gave in.

"You know my mother, don't you?" It wasn't exactly what Itza' wanted to know, but it was as close as she could get at the moment.

The old woman scrunched her brow and nodded gravely. "I do, little one. Your mother is a sweet woman. Calls me Grandmother, eh?"

"And does she tell you things, Grandmother? About herself?" Itza' asked. She decided to use the same honorific with the old woman. She figured it couldn't hurt.

Grandmother smirked. "Something you want to know, little one?"

Itza' opened and closed her mouth a couple times. Could she really just ask? And, if she could, should she?

Grandmother gestured at the cup Itza' was holding. "Well at least tell me if you like the drink, little one. It's a new recipe."

Itza' took a sip. It was very sweet. Some sort of tea with honey, but she'd never had anything like it before.

"It's great!" Itza' said simply. She was feeling more relaxed already. Her shoulders dropped, and she had a sudden memory of sitting in her mother's lap as a young child. Her mom had been braiding her hair, or maybe unbraiding it; she couldn't quite remember. But either way, Itza' had felt so relaxed and calm, and she had just talked and talked and talked . . .

"I want to know about my past, Grandmother," Itza' found herself saying. The words seemed to tumble out before she really had time to think them through.

"Ah," the old woman sighed understandingly. "All the compli-cated family dynamics are a bit confusing, eh?"

Itza' squinted her eyes. Does she know about Night Star? Itza' wondered. And as soon as the thought had struck her, more words tumbled out of Itza's mouth. "Why did you ask where I got my eyes? Is that because they look like Snake Lady's eyes?"

Itza' put a hand over her mouth, the movement spilling some of her tea. She definitely hadn't meant to ask that. What was going on?

She wiped her cloak intently where the liquid had fallen, trying to clean up the spill. Grandmother watched her closely, nodding slowly. "It is only tea, little one. Sometimes it has to spill. Life has to be messy like that sometimes."

Something about Grandmother's words caught Itza's attention, and she looked back at the old woman. Her warm brown eyes had an intensity to them that hadn't been there before. Itza' sighed and gave up on cleaning the spill. She took another sip. It tasted even sweeter this time. It really was a yummy drink.

Itza's mouth opened before she realized it was even happening. "I was just wondering about Snake Lady because she came here one time. And I saw she has my eyes. And my parents don't seem to like her, but I don't get why."

The words were tumbling out now. Faster and faster, like spilled beans scattered all over the floor, and Itza' couldn't hope to pick them all up and shove them back in their bag.

"I mean, I know my dad hates magic, but is that really just it? I mean, her eyes are just like mine! So—I followed her. Yeah, I know. I just wanted to talk, really! I've never met someone with my eyes—and my mom says 'oh it just happens sometimes,' but I mean, come on. Really? Anyway, so I followed Snake Lady. I did. And that's when I heard her say she cursed my mom. Well, *she* didn't say it. Q'anchi' said it. I mean he implied it. But when I found out Night Star is Chanil's real mother, I got it, you know? Snake Lady cursed my mom so she couldn't have kids. But—for what reason? And I thought you might have the answers because Snake Lady gave Q'anchi' a gift for you—did I say that already? Anyway, I figured maybe you would know since Snake Lady knows you, and my mom knows you—she really likes you, by the way."

Itza's eyes went wide, and she stared at Grandmother as she realized everything that had just come out of her mouth. Then she looked down at the cup in her hand.

"What exactly is in this drink?"

Grandmother's old hand deftly plucked the cup, still mostly full, from Itza' small hands. She had a look of embarrassment on her face. "Might be a bit strong for you, my dear. Not used to getting visits from kids, eh?"

Itza' swallowed in her dry throat. Grandmother was looking at her carefully, an appraising look in her eyes. "Well, you certainly have been busy, little one."

Itza' could only nod at first, but then, as it dawned on her what had happened, she gave the old woman a menacing look. "Did you really just drug a noble child?"

The old woman pursed her lips, the mischief in her eyes never leaving. "Did you really eavesdrop on the conversation of a queen of a neighboring realm, uncover an old curse against your own queen, and are now poking around everywhere you can to try and find out what happened years ago when you weren't even born yet?"

Itza' scrunched her face. "Okay . . . That's a valid point. But you still can't go around drugging children!"

The old woman put up her hands. "Like I said, it's a new recipe."

Itza' just shook her head. But she couldn't help but smile. She really did like the old woman.

Grandmother slapped her thighs suddenly. "But if you know all that already, my dear, I'm not sure what more I can do for you. You seem to have all the answers already."

Itza' sighed loudly. "But why did Snake Lady curse my mother? And why do I have these eyes? And how do you know Snake Lady? Or my mom? Or Lady Night Star? And why does my father hate you? And why—"

Itza' slapped her hands over her mouth. The tea was clearly not done with her yet. Grandmother laughed. A cute, innocent-sounding laugh that wrinkled her face and made her eyes vanish.

"Sounds like you had better stay silent for a while, little one. Let's see? What can I say? How do I know Snake Lady? She gave me flowers once." The old woman smiled broadly at that and gestured with her chin over Itza's shoulder. Turning, Itza' saw a plant hanging in a large pot through the haze of the incense smoke. It had beautiful, light blue flowers, each with five petals. Itza' recognized them at once. They were poisonous.

"And as for your father—well for that, I blame your grandfather. Filling his head with nonsense over a simple misunderstanding."

The old woman stood up then. She got to her feet lightly despite her age, grabbed both cups, and walked them back over to the worktable. Itza' heard her muttering something about fixing the recipe for next time.

"And as for Lady Night Star—now, that's a good one. Seeing as how you already know so much, I can't see any harm in telling you about the night I met the night star." Itza' heard the old woman laugh at her own wordplay before the incense smoke seemed to intensify and swirl around the room, suddenly hiding everything from view.

Snakes

History is a poor judge of character. Anytime I read of a king adored for all of time, I am certain he must have been a horrible man. And anytime I read of a queen reviled for her merciless choices, I know instantly—that was a woman who knew how to rule.

—the Book of Queen Snake Lady

"A thick and violent rain bombarded the ground the night that the two women made their way along the winding footpath that led to the ancient temple on the outskirts of Yaxchilan," Grandmother said, smiling at Itza' in the haze of the incense smoke. Her voice came out in a quiet rasp that clung to the thick air.

"The heavy rain turned the small path to mud and muck, and the winds whipped around violently, tugging at the thick cloaks of the two figures. A nearby snake felt the approach of the women as their footsteps vibrated through the ground around him. He kept a safe distance, relying more on touch and smell than vision or hearing to relay the information of their passage. He knew the two women were from the city long before he could see them. He smelled the notes of flint and stonework carried on their clothes and boots.

"Even with his poor eyesight, the snake could see that one of the *women was noticeably taller than the other as they passed. The tall one had a broad frame. Even under the thick cloak, he saw that her frame was athletic and muscular. She moved with a hunting power. The second figure was leaner and shorter, and where the taller woman moved confidently through the muck despite the hindrance, the slenderer woman's movements were somewhat awkward, as though she were not used to the challenges posed by the weather and terrain. After they passed, the snake moved on into the night. He knew other animals would be watching the two human figures on their journey to the ancient temple and its sole inhabitant . . ."*

"Come in, my children," the old woman beckoned for the two hooded figures, soaked by the night's rain, to enter the stone chamber on top of the ancient temple.

"Yes, Grandmother," replied one of the women. Despite being shorter than the other, she carried a regal air about her as she stepped forward. The second woman followed a moment behind.

The room atop the temple was lit by candles arranged throughout. In the room's center, a large circle was carved out on the floor. Opposite the entryway the two women had used, but outside that circle, was a long wooden table that carried a dizzying array of items: bright blue-green cups and plates, mixing bowls and an assortment of pottery; papers and codices; candles; bags bulging or overflowing with cacao beans, salt, dried corn kernels, other seeds, and herbs. The old woman was moving around the room, muttering to herself, lighting several incense burners. She had not yet looked at the visitors.

The old woman worked to get the smoke billowing. "No need to hide your faces," she said, referring to the fact that they had not yet pulled back their hoods. "I cannot help but recognize my Queen."

"Yes, Grandmother," the shorter woman said, pulling back her hood. A moment later, the taller woman did the same. The old woman finished getting the incense burners going and came up to her two visitors, registering each one in turn.

"So . . . two royal ladies visit me this night," the old woman said, flashing a large and toothy smile. "You must be cold, my children. Give me your cloaks, I will dry them, and . . . I have gifts for you."

"Gifts?" the taller woman asked suspiciously. The Queen shot her a disapproving glance.

"Thank you, Grandmother," the Queen said. She pulled off her cloak and gestured intently with her eyes for her companion to do the same.

The older woman took the drenched clothing from her visitors and handed them two folded bundles in exchange. She retreated back to the long worktable, went around it, and laid the cloaks somewhere out of sight. When she returned, she had three small stools. She set the seats in a triangle in the center of the circle.

"Please, my children, sit. You have traveled far." She gestured for the women to take their seats.

"If you are Lady Xok," the old woman mused as the women sat down. "Then you, noble warrior, must be the Lady Night Star."

"I am," Night Star said, then, because Xok was eyeing her expectantly, added, ". . . Grandmother."

The old woman chuckled. "Then I am visited by the two most powerful women in Yaxchilan," she said. There was a hint of mischief in her tone, and her eyes sparkled. "What could such powerful Ladies possibly need from a simple woman like me to merit such a long walk in the rain?"

Xok did not answer immediately. Her fingers nervously traced the edges of the bundle the old woman had handed her. Night Star wanted to speak but felt it was not her place. After all, it was for Xok that she had come here to speak with the older woman.

Looking down at her own gift bundle, Night Star studied it with some apprehension. She knew the reputation of the one they were visiting. She knew many people regarded her as an evil witch. They said that her spirit traveled at night to curse those in the city who had displeased her. The old woman was the reputed cause of all manner of adulteries, bad luck, fights, missing items, and anything else that needed blaming or explanation. Night Star figured that such rumors were exaggerations and the typical fear that powerful woman engendered. At the same time, however, she was cautious by nature, and the reasons for their visit were quite delicate. She wanted to make sure this woman could be trusted with certain information.

But as Night Star continued to examine the gift bundle that the old woman had given her, all other thoughts vanished from her mind. She noticed that the bundle was a large weaving, folded up to fit perfectly in her lap. It had been made of thick strands and was suitable for a blanket. But the patterns were what stuck out to Night Star most.

At first, she couldn't believe it. She had not seen patterns like this since she was a little girl, when she had lived far away on the Island. That had been another life, a simpler one spent near the waters of the Sea. In that far away kingdom, her grandmother had made her a blanket once—with patterns just like the ones that she saw on the weaving in her lap.

"How . . ." Night Star began, but as she looked into the old woman's eyes, something stopped her just short of giving voice to the question. Instead, she felt a sudden and powerful warmth welling up inside her. The old woman smiled that loving and hope-lessly sincere smile that grandmothers are able to give to their granddaughters. In that moment, Night Star felt she was caught up in something larger than herself, something that reached across the space between her and the old woman and extended far, far out into the world they lived in. As her eyes met those of the older woman, she could feel a distant rhythmic swaying that slowly evolved into a faint sound of waves lapping against the beach. The sound of those waves reminded Night Star of her childhood life and the sounds of the ocean. In that moment, she felt the whisper of her ancestors at her back.

Accept this gift, they said to her.

And so, she did.

"Thank you, Grandmother," Night Star said, and the words felt genuine on her lips.

Beside her, Lady Xok smiled and visibly relaxed. Xok unfolded her own gift bundle then and looked at it. A long, sleeveless, wraparound dress. The fabric was thin and elegant, brightly colored and fit for a queen. The patterns were complex and beautiful depictions of the history of Lady Xok's lineage. Xok's eyes lingered on the glyphs that told of her mother, of her own birth.

Slowly, she pulled out a deerskin bundle from the belt around her waist and handed it to the older woman. It bulged slightly, and the old woman took it carefully, feeling the weight of its contents. The old woman placed it in her lap, smiling. She had no need to unwrap it yet. She waited until the Queen was ready to speak.

"I . . . wish to have a child, Grandmother," Lady Xok said softly, fingers tracing over the glyphs on her dress.

"Aaahhh," the old woman breathed out, ". . . *another* child?" The question hung in the air in the silence that followed.

Xok and Night Star looked at each other, and Night Star opened her mouth as if to speak. But then she closed it again and gripped the blanket in her hands. In the heavy silence, the three women could hear the rains falling against jungle leaves outside. The wind had subsided, and instead of a raging tempest, there was simply a never-ending cascade of gentle but heavy water falling from the sky. Abruptly, the old woman slapped the side of her thigh.

"Some food!" she said and got up. She stepped out of the circle, placed Lady Xok's gift bundle to one side, and began working at the table. With the winds gone, the incense smoke lingered in slow and relaxed movements across the room. It partially obscured the ability of the two Ladies to see what the old woman was doing.

"In the city, they say that the Great Lord 5-Thunder already has a child with the Queen," the old woman called from over her shoulder. Xok and Night Star traded glances again.

"Maybe she's right," Xok said to Night Star.

"Right about what?" Night Star asked confused.

"That there is already an heir—Chanil. I don't need to have a child anymore . . ." There was a deep sadness in the Queen's voice as she finished the thought. But Night Star disagreed. They had already discussed this at length many times over the past couple years, across many nights when the two ladies hid themselves away from prying eyes so that Night Star could nurse Chanil or simply be with her.

"Chanil is precisely why you must have a child," Night Star insisted. "If the truth of Chanil's lineage is ever discovered, it could jeopardize her ability to rule. A child of yours would ensure that Yaxchilan will have an heir no matter what."

The old woman stopped her work at the table and turned to face the two women. She looked them hard in the eyes for a moment.

"I suspected . . . But!—" and now she turned away again and resumed her work, "—such are the pains and burdens of royal service."

"Grandmother," Night Star began somewhat awkwardly. "Look, can you help my friend?"

The rustling and clanging of cookware at the large wooden table ended as suddenly as it had begun. The old woman whirled, and they could see she was holding a small plate. On top of the plate sat a circular mass of corn dough sprinkled with spices. The dough seemed to have some fruits or nuts mixed in with it. The whole mixture was steaming.

The old woman stepped forward, approaching the circle. At the same moment, the wind picked up, lifting the incense smoke and throwing it into a chaotic dance that temporarily hid the figure of the old woman as she crossed into the circle. Then, just as abruptly, the wind died down again, retreating to where it had originated. The old woman was in the circle now and stood before Lady Xok. She offered a cooked dish to the Queen. It was a small, rounded tortilla stuffed with the fruits or nuts that they had seen mixed in with the dough earlier.

Night Star blinked several times, trying to reconcile what she had just seen. She could have sworn the plate held a mixture of uncooked dough moments before. But Lady Xok seemed not to notice—or, if she did, it did not strike her as odd.

The old woman still stood before Xok, offering the plate. The Queen swallowed nervously. She stood and placed her gift bundle on the stool.

"The whole thing?" she asked.

"All of it," the old woman replied, an odd intensity in her tone. "And quickly."

Night Star was about to speak, but in one fluid and graceful motion, Lady Xok grabbed the stuffed tortilla and bit into it. She chewed quickly.

"You must finish it, little one!" the old woman said, a growing sense of urgency in her voice. Lady Xok swallowed the first portion and stuffed the rest in her mouth. She finished it as quickly as she could.

"You have been cursed, my Queen," the old woman said flatly.

Night Star rose up suddenly, hand on the blade she carried in a sheath at her belt. But the old woman held up a hand.

"You will see, noble warrior." The old woman's voice carried a sense of deep power that had not been there before. Night Star hesitated.

Lady Xok wanted to respond and tell her friend that everything was going to be okay. But she could not. She found herself unable to say anything at all. Her head was starting to spin, and she felt like her throat was beginning to squeeze shut. She reached out to steady herself against the stool, but a sudden flash of pain tore through her stomach, and she dropped to her knees. Flashes of agonizing pain shot up her body, like lightning trying to claw its way out through her skin. Night Star moved to rush forward, to help her friend, but the old woman, again, held up her hand.

"She must release it first!"

"What?!" Night Star exclaimed. On the floor, Lady Xok's world was becoming nothing but pain. Her stomach spasmed, her throat opened and closed involuntarily. Her vision blurred from the lack of oxygen, and she felt death calling out to her. Stabbing pains gripped her ankles and back, and she convulsed repeatedly. She felt her skin soaked with sweat in the cold air. She wanted to scream, to cry out in anger and rage. But her throat was closed off, and no sound could emerge.

And then things got worse.

A deep swelling sensation accompanied by an intense and raw heat. It started in her abdomen. The pain pushed out against her stomach, worse than anything she had ever felt before, and the burning heat radiated in all directions. Tears welled up and then fell from her eyes. She felt like her stomach might burst at any moment. She tried, in vain, to scream against the agony, but her throat was still closed, and all she could do was beg for death in her mind. Anything to end the sharp and unrelenting pain.

And then, suddenly, her throat opened.

She gasped and screamed. Her screams of pain, now free, would not stop. She let out a piercing cry that filled the room. A cry that echoed off the stone walls and carried out into the jungle. It drowned out the rain.

That cry made Night Star want to pull out her blade and kill the old woman for what she was causing her friend to go through.

"Not yet, noble warrior!" the old woman shouted, as if sensing Night Star's thoughts. But the old woman's eyes never left Lady Xok's crumpled and writhing form on the floor. Night Star saw a coiled tension in the old woman's stance. Her experience as a warrior helped her recognize it immediately. Grandmother was waiting for something.

But Night Star didn't care. Her friend was dying in agony. She had to do something.

"There!" the old woman cried out.

The Queen suddenly rose to a kneeling position, her movements jerky and erratic as if she did not have control over her own body. Her head tilted violently upward as if she wanted to vomit. And then, she did. Or, at least, she heaved and she gagged. Her muscles pulled and pulled, and the terrible source of the pain and agony was pushed farther and farther up her throat. Her neck began to bulge as her body tried to vomit out the thing inside her.

"Help me steady her," the old woman yelled at Night Star. Finally free to act, Night Star rushed forward with the old woman, and together, they held the Queen upright as her torso convulsed in spasms and heaving motions.

Before Night Star's eyes, Lady Xok's mouth began to open wider and wider. Her head tilted backward, her mouth agape toward the sky. And then—Night Star heard it, the unmistakable *hiss* of a snake nearby.

"Keep holding her!" the old woman shouted as Night Star's grip faltered while she looked around for the snake she had heard. Then the hiss came again, louder and longer than before. It was coming from inside the Queen.

Just then, a creature began emerging from Lady Xok's throat, its flickering tongue smelling the air before its head was revealed. As it squirmed upward, Xok's violent muscle spasms pushing it out of her body, Night Star could see that the snake was covered in bright, almost iridescent scales. As the head continued to emerge, Night Star saw brilliant eyes, like gems or jewels on fire. A cold shiver ran along the old warrior's spine. The creature turned to look at Night Star. It twisted its scaly head toward her as soon as it had enough room to do so.

But the old woman was ready for such things. The instant she saw the creature turn and expose its neck, she reached out and seized its long body with a fierce grip. The creature hissed and screamed, but the old woman would not let go. She squeezed the neck hard and pulled at its body as Lady Xok's last spasms finally expelled the curse that had plagued her for so many years.

Night Star did not know whether to stay with her friend or pull out her blade and gut this monstrous snake. But the old woman was not done. She took the snake to the table and began to work even more furiously and quickly than she had before. Night Star stayed with Xok. She didn't understand what was going on. But she at least figured Xok was better off with that thing not inside her anymore.

"Can you breathe?" Night Star asked.

Xok nodded; her body was doubled over. Her torso expanded and contracted deeply, and she felt like she could not get enough air if she breathed again for four thousand years. And yet, even as she worked to catch her breath, she realized she could feel something again that she had not remembered losing. Slowly, she sat back, kneeling on the floor with Night Star, and then, unexpectedly, she laughed. Night Star was stunned into silence for a moment. Then she laughed, too.

"It is done," the old woman said over her shoulder from where she still stood, leaning over the table. Her arms stretched something out on the top of the table.

"I can tell, Grandmother," Lady Xok said. Her voice was surprisingly light. "We must repay her with something," Xok said quietly to Night Star, the euphoria of being free from such prolonged pain giving an absent-minded quality to her words.

"Oh, don't trouble yourself, little one," the old woman said, chuckling. She turned, then, to face the two Ladies. She held up two sparkling gems. Night Star recognized them as the eyes she had seen on the snake.

"I have my payment right here," the old woman laughed.

"And . . . this means she can have kids now?" Night Star asked, bewildered at the whole experience.

But Lady Xok did not give her friend time to receive a reply. She rose up awkwardly, her legs shaky but determined. Her face, which had been so joyous moments before, was now set in a deep rage. Still regaining her balance, she half staggered over to the old woman, stopping just short of leaving the circle.

"Where did you get those?" she demanded, pointing at the jewels. The old woman did not respond right away. She gazed pensively at the Queen.

"Hmm . . . something familiar, little one?"

"They were the eyes of the snake," Night Star offered.

"Do you want them back, my Queen?" the old woman asked, pushing them forward. Lady Xok shook her head, a look of disgust crossing her face.

"Never. Keep them. Do anything you want with them. They were never mine to begin with . . ."

She whirled, a storm still raging across her face, her being filled with a sudden determination to leave. She knelt over the stool she had toppled during her fall and picked up the wraparound dress the old woman had gifted her. She went toward the room's exit, intending to leave right there and go . . . do what, exactly? she wondered to herself, stopping in her tracks as she realized the potential dangers of any impulsive response.

"You know who did this, don't you?" Night Star asked.

Lady Xok nodded slowly, feeling her anger seething. She took a deep breath, lifted her head, and composed her features once more. There were more important things than simple revenge.

"It doesn't matter. It's over with. Isn't it, Grandmother?" Lady Xok asked. The two women turned in anticipation of the elder's response.

"The curse is broken, little one," she said, smiling warmly, her voice calm and her eyes soft again. "But your story, my Queen, is far from over."

Grandmother disappeared behind the long worktable. After a few moments, Night Star heard the crackling of a cooking fire. Xok led her outside the giant circle carved in the floor and over to a back corner of the room. There, they saw Grandmother sitting before a small fire where several thin tortillas were crisping lightly on the clay skillet atop the flames.

Xok and Night Star sat down beside her. The old woman passed them both some warm drinks. They sat in silence for a while. The gentle crackle of the fire intermingled with the gently fading sounds of the rain outside, which was finally dying down.

"There's something I still don't understand," Night Star said eventually, taking a long sip of the frothed cacao drink.

"Only one thing?" Xok said smiling, her eyes bright with mischief as she looked at her friend. Lady Xok was older than Night Star, but when she got that mischievous look in her eyes, Night Star could swear she was a child again.

The old woman also chuckled lightly as she flipped the tortillas. "Don't be embarrassed, little one," she said to Night Star. "Your Queen was once just as confused . . . when she first came to visit me."

Night Star raised her eyebrows quizzically.

"We will be here all night if we start down that road," she said. "And we have a young one to get back to."

She was referring to Chanil, of course. The girl was three and a half and already quite the handful. She was currently being watched by a pair of the Queen's most trusted aides—ones who knew and could keep the secret about the girl's true lineage.

"What confuses me," Night Star said, "is why only Lady Xok was cursed? Wouldn't our enemies have wanted neither wife to bear children—I'm assuming their goal was to weaken Yaxchilan by denying the Ajaw an heir . . ."

"Ah!" The old woman's voice was full of raspy humor grating against the ancient knowledge she possessed. She finished another round of tortillas and handed each woman a plate with food.

"But!" She raised one crooked finger abruptly after handing off the dishes. "An effective curse requires *special knowledge.*" She took care to overemphasize the words and let the implication hang in the air.

Lady Xok's eyes went wide. She understood immediately. She was, after all, a queen, and her knowledge and abilities ran in the same directions as the priests and day-keepers. Lady Night Star, on the other hand, was not so sure she understood. And, ironically, the reasons for her confusion were the very same ones that answered her question.

"I'm not sure I follow, Grandmother," Night Star replied.

"Your ancestors protected you, little one," the old woman said, patting the blanket draped over Night Star's legs. Eyeing the blanket and having noticed its effect on Night Star, Lady Xok asked, "What are those patterns, my friend?"

Night Star smiled, happy to share. "They tell of how the Island came forth from the Sea." Her eyes beamed with joy as she thought about the stories there in the weaving. "My grandmother made me a blanket just like this when I was a little girl—back when I lived with her still. Simpler times, I guess. Before all the violence. Before all the secrets—"

The understanding started to sink in. Her eyes went wide just as Lady Xok's had earlier when she realized the same thing. "Grandmother, are you saying the ones who cursed Xok couldn't curse me because I come from the Island?"

The old woman was chewing intently, staring into the fire. She did not respond. Lady Xok jumped in to explain.

"To do these kinds of curses, you need to know the lineage of the one you're cursing," she said. "I bet they tried to curse you too—"

"Ha! Of course she did!" the old woman interrupted suddenly and laughed at the thought of the impotent attempt from Lady Xok's enemy.

"—But it didn't catch," Lady Xok finished.

"Because they wouldn't have known who my family on the Island is . . ." Night Star whispered, more to herself than anyone else. Another thought struck her. "Then Chanil is safe as well!"

"Hmmm . . ." the old woman muttered, picking something from her teeth.

Again, Lady Xok elaborated. "There are many curses. And Chanil's secrets might not stay hidden forever. We will have to be careful."

Night Star swallowed hard, realizing the complex path the family was trying to navigate. She also realized, suddenly, how hungry she was. Her stomach jumped around angrily in her belly.

"What about the one who cursed you?" Night Star asked of Lady

Xok as she finally bit into the food the old woman had made for them. "What will you do about them?"

"Her . . ." Lady Xok said intently. "It is an old feud with a nearby kingdom. But . . . the demands of the present take precedence." Then she added abruptly, "We should be getting back. Before the Ajaw notices."

Night Star noticed her friend had successfully evaded the question.

"Take some food with you," the old lady said, smiling as she handed them another round of dishes, this time folded up into small travel bundles. They thanked the elder, offering her many gifts of appreciation for all that she had done for them that night. She refused them all.

"I ask only one small favor, my Queen," the old woman said as she led them to the doorway.

"Anything, Grandmother," Xok said earnestly.

The old woman placed the tip of one finger gently on Lady Xok's belly, right there against the place where the umbilical cord grows. Lady Xok felt a strange chill run along her back—it pulsed like lightning for a moment and then vanished just as suddenly.

"Whenever you are blessed with a child, my Lady," the old woman said, never taking her finger off Lady Xok's stomach, "tell the little one to call me Grandmother when she stops by."

Then the old lady smiled, turned her back to the younger women, and faded into the haze of the incense still floating throughout the room.

Itza' felt goosebumps on her arms and legs as Grandmother finished the story. It was the first time anyone had just told her the information she wanted to know. She found it refreshing to have some definitive answers. But those answers had only given rise to more confusion.

"Okay, I have a question," Itza' said carefully, slowly.

Grandmother smirked. "Would you like some more tea?"

Itza' shot her a menacing look. "So, you knew Snake Lady had cast this curse. And you knew about Night Star."

"Is that a question, my dear?"

Itza' scrunched up her face. "But do you know *why* Snake Lady cursed my mother?"

"Does it matter?" The words were flat and factual. Itza' was unprepared for them. She always considered people's motivations. She couldn't even process how to understand the curse without thinking about what could possibly motivate Snake Lady to want Xok not to have children.

She thought for a moment. It was possible it didn't matter since the curse was broken, and Itza' was alive because of that. Certainly, Itza' could imagine Chanil looking at it that way.

"But doesn't this curse mean Snake Lady is responsible for the day of my birth?" Itza' asked. She had been studying with the priests for a long time now and knew that the day of one's birth was very important. It shaped their fate in this life.

Grandmother nodded. "You are the child born of a broken curse." The words sounded almost ritualistic.

"So, Snake Lady is kind of like my magical mother in a way."

At that, Grandmother laughed. She let out a long exhale. "I've never thought of it like that, little one. But I guess you have a point."

Itza' wondered if that explained something else then. "So, is that why I have these eyes, Grandmother? Because Snake Lady cursed my mother?"

The old woman rested her chin on one hand. Itza' thought there was something almost sad in her eyes. "It is part of why, yes."

"And the other part?" Itza' felt her heart racing. She felt like the answers were so close.

But Grandmother shook her head. The sad look in her eyes was unmistakable now. "That's all I can say, little one, I'm sorry."

Itza' furrowed her brow. "But why? Why won't anyone tell me?"

A long and heavy sigh escaped Grandmother then, and the

sadness in her eyes grew deeper. She looked at Itza' lovingly and tried to smile. "Because, my dear, you're going to meet Snake Lady one day and have the chance to talk to her about everything. And when you do, you'll think back to this night and our conversation. And when that happens, you'll either believe me when I say I care for you deeply, little one . . ."

"Or?" Itza' felt her stomach twist as the answers seemed to recede even farther away.

"Or you might decide you hate me as much as your father does after all."

Koeia

The heavens guide our whole lives. The stars tell us when to plant and when to harvest. The moon constructs the rhythms and shows us the omens of good and bad times. The roads above teach us about the roads we walk here and those other roads in the worlds below. The cycles of our lives are written in the stars. Without knowing or understanding their movements, we cannot hope to understand ourselves.

—letters from A Queen in Exile

CHANIL PLACED A SMALL CARVING next to Night Star's cot where the commander slept. The figurine was a stone jaguar. An artist in the city had made it for Chanil as a gift for her first battle. Q'anchi', himself, had blessed the item in ceremony and said it would help protect Chanil's dreams from witchcraft or evil spirits. Chanil wanted to make sure her commander, her mother, had good dreams while she healed from her wound.

Night Star breathed in deep as Chanil started to stand up. "Stay, Chan," the commander said softly. Her warm, brown eyes opened, and she gave Chanil a big smile.

"Didn't mean to wake you, Mother," Chanil whispered. Here, in Night Star's private tent where only the two could hear, she could risk addressing her biological mother that way.

"I wasn't really sleeping," Night Star said. "Meditating. You have no idea how boring it is to be injured."

"Actually, I do," Chanil said and grinned. She remembered the endless days of lying in a medical cot after her first battle in the shield wall.

Night Star nodded. "Do me a favor and light some more candles, yeah? They're over there. I'm sure *you* don't have a problem seeing them. But I'm half-blind in here."

She was right. Chanil could see well enough in the dim light from the dying candle in the corner. She went to a low desk in the tent and grabbed a few more candles, putting them around the room and lighting them carefully.

"Guess I got my night vision from the Ajaw," Chanil said absent-mindedly as she lit the candles.

"It certainly wasn't me," Night Star said, sitting up, wincing slightly as she lifted her tall figure with her arms.

Chanil sat down next to her mom and looked at the thick bandage on her leg. "Is it bad, my Lady?"

Night Star's face twisted in a dismissive expression. "Naw, I've had worse. Just stings. I think he dips his blade in a poison."

"Poison?" Chanil went wide-eyed. "Poison sounds bad, Mom."

Night Star chuckled and patted Chanil's arm. "If there's one thing we know in Yaxchilan, it's medicines. I'll be fine, little one."

Chanil nodded but she felt awful. She lowered her head. She felt heavy with guilt. What if Night Star had been killed? Why did Chanil rush off like she had? Why did she try to take on Itzcoyotl on her own? She hadn't even considered the possibility of a poisoned blade.

"It's you I'm worried about, Chan. You've been quiet since fighting Itzcoyotl."

Chanil shrugged. What could she say? "I'm okay. Just tired."

Night Star gave her a skeptical look. "It's just us here."

Looking into her mother's eyes, Chanil was torn. Sometimes she was still angry for the lies about Night Star not being her mom. But most of the time, that was because she loved Night Star so much and wished she had just been able to grow up as her daughter instead of the heir to a large kingdom. Chanil wanted to reach out and tell her mom what she felt, but she wasn't always sure if she could trust someone who had lied to her for so long. But if not Night Star, then who? Certainly no one else in her family understood her as easily. Except Itza', sometimes.

"He said something to me," Chanil finally said.

Night Star nodded. "A lot is said in combat. Not all of it is true. Did he get in your head?"

Chanil nodded. "A little maybe."

A long pause while Night Star waited for Chanil to continue. Eventually, she added, "He said this was all my fault. That me shaming him is what pushed him and Lord Tlapallo to join our enemies."

"They had decided what they were going to do long before they came to tell us," Night Star said.

"But what if Tlapallo came hoping we would offer him an alternative? You saw how Itzcoyotl looked at me. I know Lady Xok saw it. She even told me we could have arranged a marriage, and that might have changed the way things went."

Night Star wrapped her daughter's hand in both of her own. "Yes, he looked at you in some way. But that doesn't obligate you to him. Your words might have hurt his pride, but maybe his pride is simply too easy to hurt. He and his father are killing our children, Chan. That's no one's fault but theirs. They chose to invade our lands."

"But what if I hadn't opened my big mouth? What if I could have just kept silent? Maybe things would have gone better, and our people wouldn't be dying. And you wouldn't be hurt right now."

Now Night Star understood. She nodded, seeing the weight of the whole kingdom starting to settle on Chanil's shoulders.

"And how do you know things wouldn't have been even worse if you had stayed silent? Or that marrying Itzcoyotl would have changed anything? You think he would have let you be a warrior?"

Chanil's blood boiled the instant she heard her mother's phrasing. Let me? Her mind screamed. Let me? But that was Night Star's point. After speaking to Itzcoyotl, Chanil was certain that was exactly how he would have said it. She had a sudden flash of some alternate life where she had married him, and he towered over her, telling her there was no way he would allow her to fight. What would Chanil have done then? Certainly nothing that would have provoked him less than what she had already done.

Night Star watched her daughter, seeing her mind process the words and the implications. A rustling at the tent's entrance caught both their attention, and they turned to see Q'anchi' poking his head gently through the tent's doorway curtain.

"Medicines, my Lady," he said softly. Night Star gestured for him to enter. He carried a large bowl that sloshed with a liquid Chanil could smell before he even got close. The smell recalled all sorts of memories. Cuts, scrapes, bruises. She knew the bowl held a towel as well. She was very familiar with this process.

Q'anchi' sat on the cot next to Night Star, on the opposite side as Chanil. He busied himself tending to the Lady's leg, checking her bandage, asking her if she felt any pain or fever. But Night Star was strong, and she seemed unfazed by the wound.

"You are who you are, Chan," Night Star to her daughter. "You didn't make the Great Army attack Coyolapan. You didn't force Tlapallo to join them. And you certainly aren't responsible for the bruised ego of a young boy who wanted to bed you."

Q'anchi' chuckled hearing the last part and added, "Itzcoyotl has always been quick to anger, my Lady. His mother was the same way."

"I just didn't think his anger at me would end up hurting others, yeah? Maybe I should think more before I open my big mouth."

"Being a queen does involve some introspection, little one," Q'anchi' hummed casually.

"But being filled with self-doubt is something no queen can afford," Night Star countered. Then she looked at Q'anchi' intently and smiled. "Do you remember Koeia, old friend?"

Q'anchi' stopped his work and looked pointedly at Night Star.

He smiled mischievously. His red-brown eyes glinted in the candle-light. "How could I forget, my Lady?"

Chanil narrowed her eyes. "Who is Koeia?"

Night Star smiled warmly at Chanil and squeezed her hands. "I am, Chan. I'm Koeia."

Chanil sat up straight and heard the quick *whoosh* of a pipe being lit. She looked over and saw Q'anchi' exhaling a cloud of smoke from a tobacco pipe that had appeared in his hands. He gave the pipe to Night Star, who took a long drag.

"I think it's best if I start this story, my Lady," Q'anchi' said. His eyes glinted like embers as he stared deep into Chanil's.

"Unlike you, little one," Q'anchi' said as he exhaled the smoke from his pipe, "your mother was born on the Island, in the lands of the Ayiti.

"In those days, however, she had not yet received the royal title of Lady Night Star. Her birth name meant something like 'shining star,' so many on the Island just called her Koeia. She lived on the Island in the house of her grandmother, the very same one who made that blanket you've been wrapping around yourself since you were a little girl. Her parents—your grandparents—however, lived on the Continent in her father's kingdom on the Eastern Coasts. They had wanted young Lady Night Star to grow up as her mother had, learning the ways of the Ayiti and training with them so she would never forget her kinship there and the alliances between both sides of her family.

"But, here is the thing. Her mother—your grandmother—was the younger sister of a prominent king on the Island or, what they call, a cacique. This was the problem. You see, the Ayiti pass things across generations differently than we do in Yaxchilan. Nieces and nephews are more likely than sons and daughters to inherit houses and kingdoms. The Cacique knew this. And it angered him. He had no desire to lose his power and every desire for his own son to inherit the kingdom. And that meant he saw threats everywhere—including

in your mother, Koeia, the girl who would become Lady Night Star.

"It didn't help matters with her uncle that the young Lady Night Star was quickly becoming a great fighter. By the time your mother was thirteen, she towered over most boys, and the stories say she had already fought in many battles—though perhaps these stories have been exaggerated with time. Nevertheless, she was charming and good at helping the other warriors. Because of that, much to her uncle's continuing aggravation, she was loved by almost everyone in the kingdom. The ultimate insult to the Cacique, however, was that young Lady Night Star was also blunt—perhaps even more blunt than you, little one. She never hesitated to tell her uncle when she thought he made a mistake or could have done more for his people.

"The Cacique did not appreciate his niece's criticisms, and he grew to believe she would pose a serious threat to his rule if he continued to let her train as a warrior in his lands. The ability to leverage the warrior class can be a compelling tool to gain political power. Fearing for her safety, the young Lady Night Star was sent back to her parents at fifteen to live on the Eastern Coasts of the Continent in her father's kingdom.

"In those days, the Eastern Coasts were still recovering from a long and bloody war that had ravaged the lands for many years. So, when your grandparents learned that the Ajaw of Yaxchilan was seeking a second wife, they recognized a chance to place their daughter in a more secure position while also gaining a potential new ally with many resources and much wealth. Night Star's parents still feared how far her uncle would go to make sure Night Star never gained power on the Island, and they worried they would not be able to protect their daughter enough while also rebuilding a kingdom recovering from years of war. They wasted no time in sending an offer of marriage to Yaxchilan.

"And so it happened, that by her seventeenth birthday, I myself recommended to my Ajaw, the Lord 5-Thunder, that he consider marrying your mother, the brave warrior princess from the Eastern Coasts, as his second wife... "

"Wait, wait wait," Chanil held up her hands to interrupt Q'anchi's story. The old man smiled.

"So, not only is my mother royalty on the Island—" Chanil said, wide-eyed. She turned to Night Star, who had a smug look on her face. "—but you also stood to inherit the kingdom there?"

Night Star nodded slowly and Q'anchi' laughed. "That's right, little one," Night Star said.

Chanil was intrigued now. "But why give that all up, then? And why did Dad even *want* a second wife?"

Q'anchi' took a long drag from his pipe and exhaled slowly. He twisted his lips and his throat as he did so, and the smoke shaped itself into a passable imitation of a snake as it emerged.

"Those all sound like questions that might be answered by letting me continue . . ." he said teasingly.

Chanil rolled her eyes in response. "Fine, old man, I'll try to keep my mouth shut. But, honestly, I'm kind of surprised my mom would be okay with just being traded around like some goods at the market to be sold. I mean, did she even know my dad at this point?"

Q'anchi' stared calmly—but silently—at Chanil. Eventually, the young woman clapped her lips together and gestured for her storyteller to continue. Q'anchi' exhaled a cloud of smoke from his pipe and resumed his story.

"It is safe to say your mother was not amenable to the idea at first . . ."

"I won't marry him!" The young woman, about seventeen years old, paced the room intently, refusing to sit on the reed mats her parents had laid out for this discussion. The young woman's tall frame and broad shoulders were made even more intimidating by the shawl draped over her torso. The stone room where she paced lay atop the central, flat-roofed building in the city. It had large doorways that let in the cool ocean breeze from the waters just below the edge of the city. On colder days, young Night Star used the shawl to shield herself from the chill.

"I heard he's a brute! I can't believe you sent an offer without telling me." She stopped pacing to look down angrily at the two other figures in the room. Her square face and strong chin heightened her intense glare. Her parents returned her look calmly. The pair were seated, cross-legged, on their mats in the center of the room.

"The offer had to reach Yaxchilan on the right day, my shining star," her father, the Ajaw, said coolly. The corona of macaw feathers on his headdress danced slightly with the chilly ocean breeze coming through the open doorways. In one hand, he held an ornate scepter, marking his status as king. It was carved into the shape of a fierce creature from the mythology of the Winaq. Scars, young and old, radiated away from the hand that held the scepter, littering his wrist and forearm, as if the power of his kingship itself had carved those wounds into his flesh. His voice was calm but powerful. His eyes were an intense, light yellow-brown that always reminded Night Star of the sunset.

"No insult was meant, my dear," Night Star's mother added. Her face was painted in black and red using a style common for warrior women on the Island, where she was from. "This marriage could be a path to safety for you, away from my brother."

Night Star laughed—a loud chuckle that emanated from deep in her belly. "If my uncle is so intent on getting rid of me, then let him challenge me. He can face me directly, and we'll see who wins *that* contest!"

The Ajaw smiled but the Queen shook her head. "If I thought he would come at you that way, Koeia, I wouldn't be concerned. But my brother has grown treacherous. Poison is more his style these days . . . and assassination."

Night Star scrunched her face. "I'm not afraid of assassins or my uncle. And I won't be traded off to be some whore for a king who wants more than he's getting from his wife!"

"That is not what we are doing!" the Ajaw bellowed. His voice echoed off the stone walls and reverberated through the air. Night Star knew that voice well. It was the battle roar her father used to shout orders across the bloody fields where his warriors cut their enemies to pieces. She respected it. But she did not fear her father.

"I have no desire to be a queen either," Night Star shot back. "I'm a warrior. That is my fate. And I'm good at it."

The Ajaw wrung his hands angrily, but the Queen interjected to diffuse the moment. "You would not be Queen of Yaxchilan. The first wife, Lady Xok, keeps that title. You would be the second wife. Yaxchilan could be a powerful ally for us, my dear, and give our daughter better protection than we can provide—with how the war has left us."

"And why would this wealthy, generous Ajaw want a second wife, then?" Night Star let the question hang in the air.

Her father made an ambiguous gesture. "Lord 5-Thunder is getting old, and he is still without an heir. If you ask me, he is looking to secure his line."

Night Star made a face. "So, I am to be a whore after all? And isn't it ironic—I'm marrying one man to help him secure his line so I can avoid the wrath of another man trying to do the same thing!"

The Queen worried her husband might explode again, but he didn't. Instead, the Ajaw stood up slowly and crossed over to his daughter. He left his manikin scepter on the reed mat behind him.

Night Star was only seventeen, but she was almost as tall as the King. The two stood face-to-face just inside the doorway of the room that looked down on the expanse of the Ajaw's city. The sounds of the market blended with the sound of waves crashing against the rocks below the building as ocean and land collided in their eternal handshake.

The Ajaw lifted his hands and placed his heavy palms on Night Star's shoulders. His yellow-brown eyes glinted in the sunlight streaming through the doorways, and he managed a half smile at his daughter.

"You know that I love you, shining star," he said earnestly. "You will never—ever—be anyone's whore. And I pity the man who ever makes the mistake of trying to test your boundaries. But war forces difficult decisions on us. Yes, your fate is being shaped by the ambitions of powerful men—but you also shape their fates. Lead the Yaxchilan army, and you will influence the whole kingdom. Bear the child who comes to rule Yaxchilan, and you will steer the course of history, my dear."

The young woman pursed her lips and nodded. I could live with that, she thought.

"And if their ajaw is as much of a brute as they say?" She raised her eyebrows intently.

"Then I will enjoy watching you put him in his place, my shining star." The Ajaw's laugh was long and loud.

"Shortly after we received the offer of marriage, I made the long journey to the Eastern Coasts myself. After walking through the jungle for many, many days, I finally arrived at the city ruled by your grandfather, Chanil. The city that stood watch over the waters at the edge of the Continent. It was beautiful, little one! Ringed on all sides by a tall defensive wall. Inside, buildings painted in every color. Not just red but greens and blues and yellows. And large marketplaces with more types of fish and shells than I had ever seen in my life. Entire buildings dedicated to murals and artwork. And a giant library—that I was never allowed unsupervised access to. Too many secrets, eh?

"And there, in the shadow of the great palace, with the sounds of the ocean swirling around its giant, painted stone edifice, with the echoes of seabirds' songs reverberating off the ornate walls—there, I met, for the first time, your grandparents. The Ajaw, Lord Kan Bel Ha', adorned in resplendent quetzal feathers and mounds of jade and gold and silver. The Queen, Uk'ak'alek', your grandmother, whose

reputation as a brilliant queen and powerful seer was known from the Island all the way to Yaxchilan and the Red City. They stood atop the steps of the palace and looked down on me and my humble group from Yaxchilan.

"Stop looking at me like that, little one. Can't an old man just enjoy telling this story? This is why we priests, and not rambunctious warriors like you, write the chronicles.

"Anyway, as I was saying . . .

"And there, standing tall next to her father, clad in shining, woven armor and a headdress with a corona of macaw and eagle feathers, with armbands and jewels along the length of her arms, with thick boots that warriors wear, with an ornate shawl draped over her broad shoulders, and a tall obsidian-tipped spear in one hand, there stood the young Lady Night Star. Your mother, just a little younger than you are now, little one, watched me with a look of confident defiance that I have never forgotten.

"Your family greeted me well, and I set about working with their day-keepers to assess the potential compatibility between our Lord 5-Thunder and the Lady Night Star. Of course, the two were an excellent match. And I gathered that a healthy relationship between our two kingdoms would only be beneficial for us all. When I returned home, I gave my official endorsement of the proposed marriage. Less than a year later, the young Lady Night Star traveled with her closest aides, a handful of bodyguards, a marriage broker, and a trusted day-keeper, to visit Yaxchilan. The marriage was moving forward— and quickly. But negotiations still had to take place. And your mother refused to make any decisions before looking her potential husband in his eye . . ."

"These are the amounts of jade, of quetzal feathers, of cacao and pataxte, and some other items, that the Great and Honored Lord Kan Bel Ha', Ajaw of The Dawning City, offers to you, Great Lord and

Lady of Yaxchilan, to marry his most beloved and cherished daughter."

The marriage broker spoke formally, bowing low as he handed a large piece of paper to Lady Xok, the new Queen of Yaxchilan. The young queen, barely twenty, took the paper quietly, never removing her eyes from the tall and imposing figure of young Lady Night Star standing on the opposite side of the ornate wooden table. Queen Xok stood next to her husband, the king of Yaxchilan, Lord 5-Thunder. Opposite them stood Lady Night Star and the marriage broker. Between the two groups, Q'anchi' and his counterpart from The Dawning City stood on opposite sides of the rectangular table.

All four sides of the table were occupied. Each party was equally represented. The marriage negotiation could proceed.

And Lady Xok already had objections. She looked over the offer from Night Star's father and pursed her lips.

"I have heard the last two growing seasons went quite well on the Coasts, good sir," she said softly to the marriage broker. "I am surprised to see so few measures of corn being offered by Lord Kan Bel Ha'."

Lady Xok lifted her face to look at the man. Her expression was a perfect mask of regal innocence. Her tone had been light and airy, as if she were truly caught off guard by the inexplicably low amount of corn being offered. Though, of course, she knew perfectly well exactly how much the Dawning City had harvested recently. Because she had sent people there to find out many moons ago.

Nevertheless, her expression feigned complete ignorance. The wraparound dress she wore swayed slightly in the hot breeze from the open windows of the large meeting chamber that sat atop one of Yaxchilan's main temple buildings. The images woven into the dress ebbed and flowed as they eagerly awaited the marriage broker's reply. Lady Xok's oval face remained calm as she eyed the man. The lift of her eyebrows drew his eyes down the steep slant of her nose, over the curve of her septum piercing, and down to the perfectly nonchalant line of her full lips. She seemed every bit the demure and polite wife of a king.

"Ah, Great Queen," the marriage broker began. He was a round-faced man with wide-set eyes and a small nose. His skin was dark but seemed untouched by the sun, and his hands were smooth, uncalloused, the nails rounded perfectly.

"Everyone knows of Yaxchilan's great cornfields, Good Lord and Lady. We, perhaps, assumed corn would carry less value for you. I am sure we can negotiate a reasonable amount now that we know your concerns."

Night Star watched the man squirming beside her as he gave his response to the Queen. She had disliked him immediately. Everything about his movements suggested he had never worked the fields or lifted a weapon or done anything that Night Star thought of as real work. Watching him contort his words and his body, she fiddled nervously with the purple-blue pendant on her necklace as the marriage broker searched for the best way to secure a good price for her marriage to the brute king of Yaxchilan. The necklace had been given to her by her mother on the day of Night Star's first menstrual cycle, the day she had become a woman. And Night Star knew she would do the same for her own daughter.

I guess that daughter will be this man's daughter too, she thought bitterly, lifting her eyes to look over the Ajaw of Yaxchilan, the supposedly invincible Lord 5-Thunder. The Ajaw was looking back at her. And neither looked away.

"Very good," Lady Xok was saying. "Now this item here—the pataxte beans—acceptable . . . I suppose. But what I don't see is any offer of obsidian. The Dawning City still controls many mines, yes? I assume they are still being used?"

The marriage broker squirmed again. "Ah, well, yes, you see, my Lady—Great Queen—and King—the price of obsidian has risen since . . ."

Night Star did her best to tune the man's words out. Marriage negotiations took forever, and royal ones were even more tedious. Why I am even here? she thought. These two can argue all day over my supposed worth and never even miss my actual presence.

Lord 5-Thunder stared at Night Star as those thoughts ran through her mind. The Ajaw felt like he could almost hear the girl's impatience. Despite her youth, she towered over the marriage broker. Her retinue had tried their hardest to make her appear more demure.

Probably to make her seem more appealing as a bride, he thought. In spite of how she had been dressed, Lord 5-Thunder could see the girl was more a fighter than a princess. Her shoulders were broad, and her arms were toned, becoming muscular already. Her stance was powerful and spoke of time spent fighting, not time spent practicing how to walk correctly. She had managed to allow her makeup artists to adorn her in some jeweled armbands, and Lord 5-Thunder recognized immediately that they were the type won in battles, not the type that young maidens typically wore to emphasize social status. Her neck was unadorned, which was unusual, except for a relatively simple purple-blue pendant that carried a design the Ajaw had never seen before. A slight bulge at one hip also told the Ajaw that the young lady had probably snuck a weapon into the room.

Smart, he thought. But also, a terrible risk if I were to see it and be offended—or worse. The fact that she was willing to take that risk told Lord 5-Thunder two things about this potential bride. First, she didn't feel safe in his kingdom, which the Ajaw understood but wanted to change. Second, she preferred to ensure her own safety herself, no matter the potential cost of such an action.

"You're a warrior," the Ajaw said flatly. His deep and raspy voice cut through whatever debate about the price of a bride the marriage broker and Lady Xok had been having. The room fell into a deep quiet following the Ajaw's interruption. His words were unusual. It was not uncommon for the potential bride and groom to not even speak at all during such negotiations, let alone have a direct conversation together.

Night Star met Lord 5-Thunder's gaze without blinking or flinching. The man had a fierce look in his eyes and an odd snake-like scar that cut across his entire jaw on one side. He wore his hair free, and the mass of loose, jet-black curls fell chaotically around his chiseled features, half-hiding the jewels that adorned his face. He was tall—taller than Night Star by at least a head—and thickly muscled. He wore a relatively simple chest tunic, which left his arms and much of his torso exposed. Night Star could see the mix of scars and muscles that defined his physique.

"I'm not just a warrior, my Lord. I'm the best in my lands." Her statement was a fact. Her eyes glinted proudly, and her lips curled in an almost smug smile.

"And—and . . . *and*, my Lady is also many *other* things. She is a skilled . . . um, weaver . . . and, oh yes, she speaks several languages—also—" the marriage broker was quick to interject.

"—And I heard you're a brute . . . my Lord," Night Star said, sliding the words across the table with her smooth voice the same way the paper containing her father's opening offer had been slid across the table to Lady Xok.

The marriage broker opened his mouth wide. His jaw fell to the floor, and his spirit looked ready to leave his body and find a safer home elsewhere on the Continent. Lady Xok's eyes blazed, and she leaned forward.

"How dare you!" she shouted.

But Lord 5-Thunder laughed. He put his hand over his chin as a boyish, wolfish grin stretched from one ear to the other. His chuckles piled up on the table in front of him.

"Is that what they say?" he said, grinning. He lifted one finger off his chin as he spoke. "A brute. I like that." He grinned brazenly at Lady Xok, who rolled her eyes.

"Well, I heard," he said conspiratorially as he leaned forward across the table toward his potential new bride, "that your father annihilates his enemies without mercy and that he does so with some sort of fiery-tipped, magical weapon."

Night Star pursed her lips and narrowed her eyes. She had heard this claim before, knew its source and the mistranslation that had given rise to it. But all she said was, "That's not true. It's just some ridiculous rumor his enemies started."

Lord 5-Thunder raised his eyebrows. "Oh, really? You mean to tell me not everything you hear about a king is accurate? You don't say?"

His wolfish grin remained, and despite the intensity of his eyes, Night Star could tell he was teasing. She nodded slowly.

"Alright. I get your meaning," she said slowly. "But why do you really want a second wife? I'm not going to be your little plaything."

Another round of looks bounced from the marriage broker to Lady Xok, even to the day-keeper Night Star had brought. Q'anchi' alone seemed unfazed. He simply smoked his pipe and watched. Things were playing out mostly as he had expected.

Lady Xok leaned over to her husband and whispered something in his ear. He nodded quickly and put up a hand gently to signal she could stop.

"I need an heir," the Ajaw said truthfully. "I'm getting old—for a king, eh? And I need to make sure my line is secure."

Night Star nodded. She could see Lord 5-Thunder was not an old man in absolute terms. But approaching his third decade, he needed to make sure he had an heir. "I'm not going to spend my life pushing out babies, good sir."

"You are a Lady—" the Queen began, but her husband raised his hand gently again to try and bring the tension in the room down.

"What do you want, Great Lady Koeia?" Lord 5-Thunder asked.

The marriage broker jumped in. "I believe the Queen was just advising us of—"

"I'm not asking you," the Ajaw said, and the rumble of his deep voice held notes of violence that intrigued Night Star and quickly quieted the marriage broker.

"But the bride price—" Lady Xok began.

"—Will be just fine, whatever we settle on," Lord 5-Thunder finished for her. Then he turned to Night Star. "Now, I've told you what I want. It's your turn. What is your price, Good Lady?"

Night Star narrowed her eyes suspiciously at the man. She

swallowed. On the one hand, she hated the situation. On the other hand, she was starting to like Lord 5-Thunder. He didn't care about the ridiculous bargaining of beans and corn and jewels. And he was offering her a chance to set her own terms.

Would he let me refuse him a child though? she wondered. Would he lie and then force himself on me later? She had complete confidence in her skills as a warrior, but looking at the Ajaw, she knew it would not be easy to take him in a fight. Still, what sort of tyrant would ask a seventeen-year-old girl to name her price? Maybe he isn't a brute, just a warrior with enemies who start rumors—just like they did with my father.

The room waited in silence for the young woman's reply. In typical teenager fashion, she decided to set her price ridiculously high.

"I want to command your warriors, my Lord. I want to lead Yaxchilan's army." She said the words loud and slow, so her meaning could not be mistaken by anyone in the room.

"Why don't we just give you the whole kingdom while we're at it?" Lady Xok scoffed.

"That's my price, take it or leave it," Night Star said, doubling down.

Lord 5-Thunder looked the girl over again, still smiling. "I lead my army. And I have many generals. With far more experience than a seventeen-year-old girl."

"You could line up every warrior from here to the golden cities in the west, good sir, and never find a better warrior than the woman in front of you right now," Night Star said, leaning over the table toward the Ajaw. A long pause followed. Lady Xok squirmed, clearly wanting to speak.

"Then you'll have the time to prove it," he said finally.

"What?" It seemed to come from multiple voices around the table at once.

"It's customary for the betrothed to live in the groom's lands before marriage anyway, yeah?" the Ajaw said, looking at each person in the room in turn. "Stay here in Yaxchilan for a year. You train with our warriors. *If* you earn it, you'll lead them. And, in that time, you will have my protection and my word that no one will touch you."

"And if I decide I won't marry you after the year is over?" She was suspicious, but the thought of being a leader of warriors was exciting.

The Ajaw shrugged. "Then you don't marry me."

Lady Xok threw up her hands. The marriage broker looked in bewilderment at the day-keeper he had come with. The other man had no more answers than anybody else. Across the table, Q'anchi' stared absentmindedly out the window, a knowing look painted on his face.

Night Star smiled. "Agreed," she said simply. "Now can we drink or what?"

Lord 5-Thunder grinned wolfishly and ordered for the drinks to be brought in so the group could finally sit down together.

Chanil laughed. She hadn't meant to, but once she started, she couldn't stop. Her belly shook, and she kept looking back and forth from Q'anchi' to her mother. The two adults were looking at each other knowingly. As her laughter subsided, Chanil realized she also felt lighter than she had before the story. Before Q'anchi' had begun, she felt heavy with nauseating guilt.

But now, she felt almost joyful. Certainly, the story was entertaining. But more than that, it gave her answers and direction. Not just the factual answers about what had happened to bring her mother to Yaxchilan. But also, a window into who her mother had been as a young woman. Chanil had only ever really known Night Star as the commander of the army, the great warrior who trained other warriors. Respected, feared, loved.

But now, she knew something of Koeia, the arrogant, reckless, and younger version of her mother who didn't fear her own power and didn't let others forget it either. Chanil felt a sense of loss then, too. Would she have been a stronger woman had Night Star been able to raise her as her own daughter? Would that have changed the self-doubts that plagued Chanil? She guessed there was no way she would ever know.

"So, then what happened?" she asked simply.

Night Star smiled at Chanil, her big lips spreading open to light up her whole face. "Then I got the army," she said, laughing. Q'anchi' grinned.

"But I never stopped being myself, Chan," Night Star added. "That's the point. And you can't stop either. It doesn't matter if men like Itzcoyotl get offended or decide to take their insecurities out on the innocent. You aren't responsible for their actions. It isn't your fault that someone else is weaker than you and angry about that."

"But what if we lose, Mom? What if my big mouth costs us everything?" Chanil felt her stomach calming down as she leaned into the possibility of turning to Night Star as a mother, finally.

"First of all, my dear, wars aren't decided by the words of one person. Whether we win or lose—that won't come down to just one thing. And secondly—and far more importantly—we aren't going to lose. I promise you that."

Chanil shrugged, feeling powerless. "How do you know that though?"

"Why do we fight, Chan?" Night Star said the words, and Chanil heard the echo of all the times, over the many years of training, that Night Star had given her that lesson. Only now, she gave it as a mother as well as a commander.

"We fight to protect our people, our relatives . . . our land." The words flowed out of Chanil reflexively, automatically.

"Exactly, Chan. We fight for something bigger than ourselves. When you went after Itzcoyotl today, was it just to hurt him?"

Chanil shook her head. "I wanted revenge."

"For what?"

She bit her lip. "For those kids in the village. For the houses that they burned. For every time they came here and hurt our people."

Night Star nodded. "You were fighting to protect something bigger than just you or your own glory. And that, my little girl, will always be stronger than a desire for conquest alone. That is how I know that, in the end, we will win."

The Waxtek

They chipped away at us, slowly taking pieces of the world we knew, one by one, until nothing remained but a distant memory, a dream, of what the young people now call, 'ancient history.'

—*collected writings of The Occupation*

CHANIL AND NIGHT STAR RETURNED near the end of the dry season to report on all they had seen during their patrols. Through them, the family learned of Itzcoyotl leading the raids. They learned of the strategies their enemies employed and the villages and towns they were targeting. They learned of how Chanil had fought Itzcoyotl and how they had managed to drive him and the other raiders off their lands for the rest of the year.

But the raiders would be back. Everyone knew it. Once the rains died down again and the plants were harvested and warriors took their shields and swords off the racks, Tlapallo would send his greetings once more to Yaxchilan. The next year's dry season would be another bloodbath.

And not just for Yaxchilan, but also for the Waxtek kingdom that lay between them and Tlapallo. So, it was no surprise when the lord of the Waxtek lands came to Yaxchilan to ask for help.

His name was Lord Chehn. And Chehn looked down his nose with utter disgust at the small, lithe figure of the thirteen-year-old girl who had just spoken to him. He shook his head and raised his eyes toward Lady Xok, who sat opposite him at the large, round table in the meeting chamber of the Great Temple of Yaxchilan.

"Where is Lord 5-Thunder, Great Queen?" Chehn's voice had a sour tone and sounded to Itza' like someone was straining the man's vowels through dry corn kernels before they left his throat.

Itza' turned her gaze toward her mother sitting next to her at the table. "Lord Chehn, as I said, the Ajaw was called away to the front lines and—"

He banged his fist on the table and shouted, "We *are* the front lines!"

The noise was so loud and his voice so angry that the guards outside started to come in before Xok gestured them away with a flick of her wrist. Itza' saw Ixcanul, who was standing behind her, move in closer. The girl had a mask of demure innocence on her face, but Itza' saw the coiled tension, the latent violence that Ixcanul held in her body anytime she saw a potential threat.

Itza' cleared her throat and said, "Perhaps some cacao?"

The servants moved quickly to bring forth the drinks. Others pulled back the draperies covering the windows to let in some of the cool breeze that had followed the rains earlier that morning. Ixcanul traded a quick look with Itza'. Although drinks might actually help the situation, Itza's suggestion had really been a coded message to Ixcanul. *No danger*, the coded reference to cacao said. Ixcanul tried to force herself to relax.

Lord Chehn, however, was anything but calm. "We are the front lines," he repeated through gritted teeth as a servant poured him a cup of frothed cacao.

"Whose lands lie in the path of the Great Tlapallo's new friends?" Chehn growled. "Ours, Queen Xok. It is us that the Great Army ravages with their constant raids and those pale mercenaries they've hired. So, Great Queen, if your husband has gone to fight, then where could he have gone but to *our* very border?"

Itza' knew their visitor had a point. In fact, Itza' herself had suggested not saying that her father was on the front lines but rather that he was negotiating with potential new friends or even peace talks with members of the New Alliance. But her mother had gone a different direction.

In a way, Itza' knew, it didn't matter. It was a lie no matter what. Her father wasn't away fighting or negotiating or even outside of the city. He was with Q'anchi', probably lying down on a cot, sicker than Itza' had ever seen him. Which left Queen Xok to deal with the visitor from their small, neighboring realm. The one who was, understandably, very angry about the way Tlapallo was constantly attacking him.

"I assure you, good sir, my mother is perfectly capable of speaking for Yaxchilan," Itza' said. Her Waxtek was not perfect, but it was more than sufficient for this conversation. It didn't seem to matter. Lord Chehn did not so much as look at her.

"We are ravaged by this New Alliance," Chehn said. His eyes were locked on Xok. His dark features carried a desperate, wild look. "They don't think us even worth negotiating with, we are so small to them. They just attack."

Itza' felt her heart break hearing that. She knew that the Waxtek lands were important trading partners for Yaxchilan. Lord Chehn's realm controlled many mines to the south, which supplied them with obsidian for making weapons—among other things. While it was true that the Waxtek realm was relatively small, Itza' guessed it was that precious obsidian that really compelled Tlapallo to want to take their lands. It would hamper Yaxchilan's ability to make weapons against them.

"We will help you in whatever we can, Lord Chehn. But Tlapallo and his allies attack us as well, as I am sure you know, good sir," Lady Xok said.

Chehn practically curled his lips in response. "And as I am sure you know, Great Queen, if we fall, you will have nothing between you and the full force of the Great Army."

Itza's mind was racing. She agreed with Lord Chehn. Not only did the Waxtek supply Yaxchilan with precious obsidian, but the small realm also effectively buffered them from the west. If Tlapallo managed to take over their kingdom, or worse, turn them, then Yaxchilan's entire western border would be exposed.

She had to stop that from happening.

Itza' leaned in close to her mother's ear and whispered, "We can't afford to let the Waxtek lands fall into enemy hands. Or to lose trade access to the Waxtek mines."

"I know, Itza'," her mother said in a strained tone. "But what do you suggest? We can't spare our entire army to guard their realm."

"What are you two talking about?" Lord Chehn's voice cut through their private conversation.

Itza' smiled. "Good sir," she began, "Your people have always been great friends and neighbors to us. We do not wish to see your lands become part of the strangling vines of the Great Army."

Chehn pursed his lips but did not meet Itza's gaze. He seemed intent on ignoring her. How she must have appeared to him—small, young, and a girl. The worst possible combination for getting the respect of a man like Lord Chehn.

But what Itza' lacked in size, she definitely made up for in intelligence. She knew everything there was to know about the Waxtek. She had studied all of Yaxchilan's neighbors. She had been taught all of their languages. And she had eavesdropped on many of their politicians' secret conversations when they had visited her city over the years. Lord Chehn, however, knew none of this. He only knew what his eyes saw, and they didn't see much since he refused to even look at her.

She had to make him see her. That was something her older sister, Chanil, never had to work at. With how tall and strong she looked, people always saw her. Itza' was still a petite, young woman to most people.

"The Waxtek are more powerful than they might seem, good sir," Itza' began slowly. "I think it is often easy for powerful kings to underestimate something so small—or someone."

"We do not need the ramblings of child—" Lord Chehn began, finally turning toward Itza'. But he stopped mid-sentence. Because now he saw her. He saw Itza's terrifying eyes.

Itza' heard the thumping of the man's heartbeat almost immediately. Her obsidian-black irises locked onto his, and she poured every ounce of feral intensity that she could into her expression. Apparently, it worked, because the heartbeat pounding in her ears seemed to quicken.

"How—" Chehn's voice was oddly quiet, as though he suddenly had trouble speaking. Itza' picked up a new scent then, too. Sharp, acrid, pungent. The smell she knew as panic.

She forced herself not to smile as her gaze took hold of Lord Chehn. She fixed a mask of perfect impassivity on her face. She thought about the cold, detached expression she had seen on Snake Lady during her visit and tried to mimic that as best she could.

The heartbeat was loud now. So loud, she wondered if anyone else in the room could hear it. But she didn't look away. Lord Chehn seemed incapable of speech, and his eyes twitched as though he felt an actual pain.

That was odd. Itza' had never seen that happen before. For a second, she remembered Snake Lady's visit and how her father had seemed to be in pain right when Snake Lady was staring at him, right before he had started coughing. Itza' decided to look away.

She heard a sharp inhale of breath from Lord Chehn. Before he could speak, she said, "You know, there is a river that runs along your western border, my Lord. I bet Tlapallo crosses it each time he wants to attack."

Chehn rubbed his chest and twisted his neck as though trying to get rid of a strange kink in his muscles. He curled his lips angrily and said, "Of course he does."

Itza' noticed with satisfaction that the man seemed to see her perfectly well now. But he still had no respect for her. "We cannot guard a whole river. We don't have the manpower . . . unless Yaxchilan would help, eh?"

Lady Xok lifted her chin and said, "We can send *some* warriors, but I do not think it will be enough."

Inside, though, Xok felt her heart racing. What had just happened? What had Itza' done? And how? She felt a chill in her bones as she wondered about the power in Itza's eyes, about where it likely came from. She didn't want her daughter learning to use it like that.

Lord Chehn scoffed at Xok's words. "Of course you cannot," he said grimly.

Itza' wasn't done. "But we can send workers."

Both adults looked at her, perplexed expressions on their faces. "You have the warriors, Lord Chehn, we have the builders. Suppose we sent you workers and timber? Enough to build fortifications along your river."

The Waxtek king looked at Itza' again, a somewhat less disgusted look on his face this time. "Fortifications require less men to run them," he said.

"Exactly, good sir," Itza' let her face twist into a confident smile. She noticed her mother looking at her approvingly as well.

Lord Chehn waved his hand abruptly. "It might not be enough. They could still cross into our lands from the south."

Now, Itza's eyes sparkled with mischief, and she couldn't keep the childlike enthusiasm out of her voice. "Ah—but! In the south, there are the mountains. The paths there are tricky, and you could block the routes—force them to go where you want them."

Lord Chehn nodded, a look of violence blazing in his eyes. "And cut them down in those rocky cliffs."

He clearly liked the idea. He turned toward Lady Xok. "And you would agree to this, Queen Xok?"

Xok looked from Chehn to her daughter. She smiled. Workers were easier to spare than warriors. Inclining her head, she said, "Provided we can work out the details, I think it's certainly a workable plan."

Five Years Later

No one fights during the rainy season. The sky opens up, and water pours down on the land. Streets flood, crops are nourished or drowned. The ground becomes a deadly trap of mud. No army can march in that. But when it is dry, things change. Then comes the sun to bake the land. The roads are clear, and the war drums beat once more. The stormy season gives way to another kind of storm, and the streets are flooded with rivers of blood instead of water.

—*Xelaq'am's Songs*

"THAT WON'T WORK, ITZ!" Chanil practically yelled the words. Her hands gripped the edge of the ancient, painted stone table, and her knuckles paled under the vice-like grip. That stone table had sat in their family's strategy room for many generations. It had seen the rulers of Yaxchilan argue and fight over strategy and tactics many times. Chanil felt the weight of that history push back into her palm as she gripped the table, anger coursing through her.

Itza' shook her head at her twenty-three-year-old sister. She saw the tiredness in Chanil's expression, the wrinkles at the corners of her eyes. She saw the scars that littered Chanil's bare arms and legs. And the long one—a deep wound where one of those strange Invaders had cut a deep groove over her collarbone and neck two years ago. Chanil stared at Itza' with a fiery intensity. Her jeweled teeth and pierced chin gave her square features a powerful appearance, and Itza' could see why, after five years of war, so many feared the Great Puma-Strikes-First now.

But to Itza', this was just her big sister. And she clearly wasn't understanding what Itza' was trying to do. Itza' shook her head again and pointed at the sketch she had placed on the table between them.

"Just look at the map, Chan. Lord Tlapallo has been raiding all the major crop fields along the south of the Waxtek lands. Here—" she put her fingertip on a specific spot on the map. "—Here is their next target. I'm sure of it."

Chanil looked down at the sketch. Next to her, her father sat on the edge of the table, looking out of one of the broad windows. He glanced over his shoulder as Chanil leaned forward. He had already heard Itza's argument. Chanil shrugged. The map didn't make much sense to her. But she knew where Itza' was talking about.

"I don't doubt that, Itz," she said. "But what you're suggesting— trying to block the road before they get there. It won't work."

Itza' looked at her father for help, but his back was to them. She turned to her mother, Lady Xok, who stood between her and Chanil. Xok pursed her lips.

"Why won't it work, Chan?" the Queen asked. Years ago, before the war, she might not have given space for Chanil's advice. But now, after five years of protracted warfare in the Waxtek lands, Chanil was the Hero of Yaxchilan. The invincible Puma-Strikes-First, the warrior princess who beheaded enemies in her sleep and whose battle roar alone could capsize canoes—at least according to the drunken rumors of her warriors in the taverns.

"They walk too fast." Chanil's answer was simple and direct. Typical.

Seeing the looks from her sister and the Queen, Chanil explained. "For a raid like that, Tlapallo will use the Invaders. He'll send one of his light groups. The bastards move fast. They'll be there before us, and all they have to do is light the fire. We won't be able to block the road in time. Probably wouldn't stop them anyway."

Itza' considered that for a moment. "What if we send an advance group then?"

Chanil pursed her lips. She felt the smooth, jeweled surfaces of her teeth slide along the inside of her full lips. "If we know where they'll be, just send a full force. We'll cut them down."

Itza' sighed. "It's not that simple, Chan. We don't know the size of the force Tlapallo is sending or what road they'll take. Or if they're hunting along the way or carrying supplies."

Chanil shook her head. "That's war, Itz."

"I'd like to think we understand our enemy better than this after five years," Itza' countered.

"We know they're animals," Chanil growled. "That's all we need to know."

Itza' sighed again, looking at her older sister. She tried to remember the young girl who had played panther with her in the palace hallways when they were kids. But now, she could see only the famous Puma.

"It's your call, Itza'." The rumbling voice of Lord 5-Thunder entered the conversation. He turned to face the group. He looked each person in turn, the intense violence in his eyes quieting any possibility of a rebuke.

Except from Chanil. "She doesn't even fight yet, Dad," Chanil said quietly.

"She's been helping plan our strategies for a while now," the Ajaw countered. "Time for her to make the decision."

Then, he looked Chanil right in her eye. "Sometimes we older folks have to let the young ones do what they were meant to do, yeah?"

Chanil clenched her jaw, a mannerism she had inherited from her father. She didn't like Itza's strategy, but she also knew her father had a point. At some point, a child had to grow up. Chanil herself had taught the family that.

She turned to her younger sister. "What do you want us to do then, Itz?"

Itza' nodded. "Take a contingent immediately. I can send scouts ahead to gather workers to block the road."

Lady Xok looked at Chanil. "Does that meet with the heir's approval?"

It was a not-so-subtle reminder that Chanil's words and decisions came before Itza's. Technically.

"We will march," Chanil said flatly. "But things might not go as you plan, sis. Send your scouts."

The swish of Itza's robes caught Chanil's attention as her little sister slid up beside her in the palace hall. Chanil saw the shimmering strands of the wraparound dress Itza' wore, the way they reflected the light. It was a strong contrast to the woven armor that Chanil wore.

"Hey, little one," Chanil said lightly as Itza' walked beside her. Itza' had grown over the past few years. She was certainly a woman now, and at eighteen years of age, Chanil had no doubt the family would be thinking of who a suitable marriage partner for their youngest daughter might be.

"You're mad," Itza' said quietly. Chanil stopped walking, and the two faced each other. Chanil, tall and broad, adorned with piercings and jewels from her years of fighting and capturing enemies. Itza', athletic and slight of frame, with those fearsome penetrating eyes that contrasted with the almost innocent, childlike curve of her face.

Chanil clapped her hand down on Itza's shoulder. "I'm not mad, little one. I just don't think it will work. But we will see, yeah?"

Looking up at her older sister, Itza' had a sudden urge to wrap her arms around Chanil and squeeze her tight like they used to. But Itza' knew that Chanil didn't really like being touched like that. So, instead, Itza' gave her a small smile and said, "Either way, I know you'll beat them, Chan. You're the best! I'm just trying to help."

Chanil nodded. She felt some of her frustration from earlier subsiding as she looked at her baby sister. She couldn't really stay mad at Itza' for long. "You've been strategizing for a while now. Who knows, maybe you've seen something I don't."

"You could have overruled me, you know. You are the heir."

At that, Chanil made a face and then kept walking. Itza' followed. "It's true! I'm sworn to obey the future Queen of Yaxchilan!" Itza' laughed, trying to make a joke out of it. But Chanil seemed uncomfortable.

"What is it, Chan?" Itza' asked.

Chanil shook her head. "Just tired."

Itza' put a hand on her sister's arm. "If you think it's a bad plan, we can change it. You'll be the queen and—"

"Stop saying that!" Chanil had not meant her words to be so loud. She looked around and saw a couple of the guards quickly lowering their heads.

In a whisper, she said to Itza', "I trust your strategy, okay?"

She started to walk off, but Itza' wasn't letting up. She followed her sister intently, moving her legs fast to keep up with her sister's longer stride. "What is going on?"

Chanil said nothing until they were out of the hallways. She had taken them out onto one of the large patios formed by the terraced structure of the large temple. There, outside with no one to listen in, she turned to Itza'.

"I know I'm the heir, okay? I don't need that to determine everything."

Her tone was tense and filled with frustration. She took a deep breath and added, "Look, Itz, everyone is good at different things, yeah? So, a queen has to listen to people for what they're good at, yeah? And you—"

She raised her hands and gestured in a way that encompassed all of the city center. "—You are good at this."

Itza' narrowed her eyes in puzzlement. "Good at what, Chan?"

"Forget it," came the curt reply.

But Itza' was a little sister, and they don't give up easily. "Come on. You've been in a mood ever since you came back from the south. Was it the last battle?"

Chanil looked off into the distance. Her lips curled up as she thought about her last days on patrol. She could still smell the burnt bodies. She could hear the screams. She saw the old man shaking and convulsing as the medicine men tried to close the wound. But his whole leg had been cut clean off by the Invader's blade—what could they really do?

She shook her head to clear the images away. "Tlapallo and Itzcoyotl are ruthless, Itz. Just remember that, okay? You make sure you think about that when you come up with the tactics."

Itza' listened to the tone in her sister's words.

"The way you talk," Itza' began. "It's like you only see yourself as a warrior."

"It's what I am, little one." Chanil still looked out into the distance, eyes focused west toward where their enemies came from.

"But you're more than that, Chan. You're the daughter of the king. You'll be our ruler one day. Our tactics will be your tactics."

Chanil shook her head. "Will I? Look around you, Itz. Who spends time getting to know the politicians? Who goes out and bleeds the enemy dry? Who makes our strategies? And who carries them out?"

Itza' opened her mouth but found herself without words for once.

"You know it's true, Itz. I'm a killer, little one. That's what I am good at. It's in my blood. I'm—I'm the daughter of a warrior. You, baby sis. You are the daughter of a queen."

Goosebumps rippled up along Itza's arms. "Chan, are you saying—"

Chanil clapped both hands on Itza's shoulder. The gesture reminded Itza' of Night Star doing the same thing to her many times in training. "I'm saying, little one, that when you finally see what everyone else sees and realize who really ought to be queen, I won't stand in the way. Fuck, I'll be your biggest supporter."

Chanil smiled then, her face lighting up and brightening like the sun. The rays from that sunlight shone down on Itza', but she felt like she could never fill the shoes of someone so great and brave and powerful. Itza' felt herself cloaked in a deep shadow, a creature of the night who spied and eavesdropped and snuck around in the streets to learn everyone's secrets.

How could Chanil possibly think Itza' would make a better queen than the Hero of Yaxchilan?

Improvising

Like the jaguar, I hunt my enemies. I can leap from the shadows. I can climb walls. I can appear in the mist and the fog. Some say to always keep one eye open, to never sleep when I might be around. It doesn't matter. I can find you in your dreams just as easily.

—Xelaq'am's Songs

AN ANCIENT TREE HAD FALLEN, and the remnants of its once-tall trunk lay across the jungle floor, providing a cover for Chanil and the other three warriors as they watched the enemy camp in the late afternoon light. The sun made its way lower and lower, crawling ever closer to the entrance to the underworld. Bushes and shrubs grew around the carcass of the ancient tree. Vines wrapped around it and hung across their view, hiding them from sight. As Chanil sighed heavily, a large lizard scampered across the log in front of her. She barely noticed it. She was too frustrated.

"What you think, big lips?" Eztli' whispered from beside Chanil. On the other side of Chanil, Ch'akanel and Nimaq exchanged a glance. Chanil pursed her big lips, her eyes never leaving the enemy camp.

"I think I'll beat your ass after I'm through with these Invaders, you call me that again." Chanil was only half joking. Most of the warriors called Chanil by her warrior name, Puma-Strikes-First. But she and Eztli' had a long history. They had beaten each other up more than once as kids coming up through the ranks. But as adults, they had become something approaching friends—or at least as close as they could be. They were both proud, arrogant warrior women. Chanil knew Eztli's teasing came out of respect now. Even though it hadn't been that way when they were younger.

"Just tell me when you're done with them, big lips," Eztli' teased. "I'll be waiting."

Chanil grinned. Nimaq grumbled, as usual. "They beat us here. Just like you said they would, Puma."

She nodded and sighed again. "My sister's plan was a good one— in the mind. But out here, things are different."

"I count twenty," Ch'akanel's smooth voice entered the conversation. "Maybe more on the other side of that tent. Can't tell."

Chanil had brought about half that. Sure, a bunch of workers and servants were back at the camp. But in total, she only had thirteen warriors. They were supposed to be the advance unit. Sent to guard the workers whose job was to help block the roads and prevent the enemy from marching and setting up camp exactly where they were now—already inside Waxtek territory. Within striking distance of the large cornfields nearby and the farmers and villagers who tended them.

"The other Yaxchilan warriors won't get here in time," Chanil said bitterly. "These guys will attack and be gone before they even get close, yeah?"

Chanil needed a new plan. Reinforcements from Yaxchilan were on their way, but it would be another day or two before they got here, she estimated. Itza's plan had been to block the road in advance of Tlapallo's strike. Then to have a contingent of Yaxchilan warriors surprise the enemy and kill them easily. That whole plan was moot now.

Chanil watched the enemy camp closely. It had been constructed well. A couple of low ditches all the way around. A sturdy, wooden wall with pikes sticking out. Centrally located supplies. They had chosen their spot carefully and were guarding it well. She knew they could launch their raids from here and return whenever possible.

Eztli' saw that, too. They all did. "We wait them out maybe," she offered. "When they go raid, we attack their back."

"They'll leave some behind," Nimaq pointed out. "These Invaders are ugly, not stupid."

They laughed lightly. But Nimaq was right. The foreign mercenaries were good fighters. And Tlapallo was using them intelligently. Instead of risking his own troops to take the Waxtek, he was relying more and more on the foreigners. He used them like expendable shock troops to create chaos, raid villages, and hold important locations. They were brutal and vicious. And they fought for money, so no one really cared what happened to them.

"It's getting late," Ch'akanel pointed out. They could hear fires crackling in the camp. Darkness would blanket the jungle soon.

"Look," Eztli' said, pointing with her chin. The group turned their attention in that direction. Chanil saw three or four women being led through the camp by a couple of Invaders who were dressed in woven armor that carried Tlapallo's colors and patterns. One of the women was tall, very thin, and walked more like a noble than a servant. Nevertheless, all the women had lowered heads and looked defeated.

Their captors walked them into the camp a little ways, and then a large, burly man approach the group. He was pale with a long, ruddy beard that had been cut to a sharp point. He fingered that long beard while he looked at the group of women being brought in. Chanil and her group could hear distant conversation, but they couldn't make out any words. It probably wouldn't have mattered anyway—no one in the group could speak the Invaders' language.

"They look like Waxtek," Nimaq said, referring to the captives. Chanil nodded. The tall woman at the center did have embroidered designs on her clothes that resembled those used by Lord Chehn and the other Waxtek nobles.

A few more moments of rough conversation in the camp followed. The captive women exchanged glances, long looks that Chanil thought must hold entire unspoken conversations. Then, the women were split up. A couple of them had their wrists tied as they were moved to another part of the camp beyond where Chanil and her group could see.

"They're taking slaves now, great." Eztli's voice was unmistakably bitter. "Got to watch out for those now when we attack."

Chanil bit her lip. Captive allies, a well-guarded camp that had twice as many warriors as she did. And limited information. She didn't like the situation. Part of her wanted to retreat, to come up with a new plan. But she knew by the time they did that, the Invaders would have raided the nearby cornfields already. Villagers and farmers would be slaughtered, the food would be stolen, and it would be Chanil's fault for not doing something, for not having been able to come up with something to mess up their enemy's plans.

Ch'akanel saw Chanil's expression and knew what she was thinking. He knew Chanil better than most. He had seen that look many times. During late night talks when Chanil spoke of her guilt over the war or after having lost a battle or when she didn't get somewhere soon enough. He knew the guilt in her eyes would change to steely resolve, and her mind would jump at the first solution she came up with, and then Chanil would leave, the Puma would emerge, and she would—

"We're going to attack." Chanil's words were flat and factual. They were the Puma's words.

"My Lady, we don't know how many of them there are," Nimaq began.

"I know. But we are going to attack." Puma had spoken. It was the same tone her father used when his mind was made up. And no one could argue. Chanil was in charge of the group. She had earned her reputation over the years, and Night Star had made her a general. The Hero of Yaxchilan was subject only to the rule of the Ajaw and Night Star herself now.

"And how are we gonna take them, big lips? We just ask them to lie down?" Eztli's voice dripped with sarcasm.

But Chanil nodded and grinned. "Exactly."

Then she looked at Nimaq. "You go back to camp and get all the warriors ready."

To Ch'akanel and Eztli', she said, "You two will wait in the jungle by the road. Where it dips steeply? Go there and wait for it, yeah?"

Ch'akanel and Eztli' gave each other puzzled looks. Meanwhile, Chanil was untying her armor, stripping off the thick warrior shorts and slipping off her belt and weapons.

"Uh, big lips—" Eztli' began.

"Help me out of this shirt, Ch'ak," Chanil said as she struggled to get the woven tunic off. Then, in a vicious tone, she added, "Don't act like you've never wanted to get my clothes off anyway."

Eztli' rolled her eyes and said, "You know he's way too cute for you, big lips."

Chanil was stripped down to just her simple shirt and grey shorts now. Just the same type of humble clothing a disgraced captive or slave might wear. She couldn't hide the placeholders for her piercings or the jewelry in her teeth. But she could keep her mouth shut, and captive nobles often had such remnants anyway—for a while.

"What are you doing?" Ch'akanel asked, taking the pile of armor Chanil handed him.

"We need to know how many," Chanil said, casting a look at the camp. "I'll go ask them, yeah? And when they come pouring out after me, that's when Nimaq and the other warriors sneak in, make a mess of the camp, kill whoever stays behind."

"And me and Ch'akanel?" Eztli' asked, clearly not wanting to be left out of the fight.

"I'll lure them to the jungle. It'll be dark soon. The three of us will be waiting there, yeah?"

Eztli's expression turned from suspicion to excitement, and she grinned, a terrifying mask of death. "We hunt them like jaguars in the night, big lips."

Chanil slid her short knife into a sheath that she could conceal at her waist under the grey tunic. Then she patted some dirt on her arms and legs and over parts of her face to make herself look dirty and disheveled. She winked at them and headed off to the road that would take her into the enemy's camp.

Chanil walked toward the camp with her head down. She tried to look as timid and shaken as the tall woman they had seen taken captive. But her eyes were alert. And her ears heard everything. She saw the lazy way the guards at the entrance looked her over. One of them waved her through with an absentminded gesture, his eyes already moving on to something else more interesting. As she passed them, Chanil could smell their sweat and practically hear the lice crawling in the beard of one of the men.

Slowly, with short steps that Lady Xok might almost have approved of, she stepped through the gate, past the makeshift defensive wall, and into the heart of the camp. The crackle of fires reached her ears as she stepped into the enemy area. Light was fading fast now, dusk approached, and she knew a fierce blackness would follow.

A narrow avenue running through the camp had been created by the deliberate absence of anything placed there. Tracks of boots and sandals had already worn down the footpath a bit, and Chanil wondered how long the men had been camped here. Chanil looked around as she walked. Men lay in hammocks within their lean-tos or sat on stools on the ground, playing games, drinking, laughing, and speaking in a tongue Chanil couldn't understand but recognized now as the language of the Invaders.

Servants, almost all women, moved about the camp, too. They were dressed simply, like Chanil, or in even more ragged clothing. And they all smelled of fear. Chanil tried to imitate their halting steps, their frightened glances. She wasn't sure she pulled it off well.

From the patterns on the clothes of many of the servants, she saw they were a mix of girls from the west and from the east. Some were Waxtek, some from Coyolapan or elsewhere in the west.

Men pursued some of the captive girls, and Chanil heard shrieks in one corner of the camp. Her blood boiled, and anger threatened to consume her. She tried to push down the impulse to find the source of those shrieks.

There will be payback soon enough, she reminded herself as she kept walking.

Chanil walked carefully down the main avenue, casting discreet glances at the groups of men clustered together, or into tents where the openings were drawn back enough to reveal the inside. She heard women talking—those were more familiar languages to her—and she saw a makeshift cooking area down a small side path. She recognized the foods being prepared from their smells. They were some of the only familiar things in the camp to her.

Looking at the Invaders around her, Chanil was struck, as always, by their strangeness, their distinctly foreign nature. She could hear their strange tongue all around her, and the rotting spirit stench of their bodies hung in the air like the smell of decay. Many were unusually pale by Chanil's standards, though some had brown skin, and a few were even as dark as Ch'akanel or Q'anchi'.

And even though the men clearly used the woven armor they had gotten from Tlapallo or other western realms, Chanil could see that they didn't know what to do with it. They wore it incorrectly. And they threw the armor on the ground or used it to drape their seats when they weren't wearing it. The tough, tight fabrics were unwashed and mistreated. Some even had frayed edges that Chanil knew could mean death against a skilled opponent.

She kept moving down the main avenue, and eventually, she saw a group at its center. About five or six men were seated around a fire, chatting loudly. Chanil recognized the burly man—who had taken in the captives earlier—by his long, ruddy beard. She guessed he was the leader here, and certainly, all the men in the circle seemed to be following his lead. They laughed when he laughed and nodded in an exaggerated fashion when he spoke.

Chanil thought back to what she had seen so far. There were definitely more than twenty Invaders here but not too many more. Probably closer to twenty-five, maybe thirty. Though she knew it was possible that some were still away hunting right now. Nevertheless, Chanil's forces were definitely outnumbered. She felt a pit in her stomach as she tried to think of a way her paltry force of thirteen could defeat twice that number.

As she walked cautiously around the central group with Burly-Beard and his followers, she felt eyes on her. She looked at the group and saw that one man was staring at her. She looked away quickly. He was different than the others. He looked like he came from the west, maybe Coyolapan. Would he recognize her? She could feel him watching her for a while before he finally looked away. Her stomach relaxed a bit. Still, it made her nervous.

But then she realized that maybe this man provided her with exactly the opportunity she needed to create some chaos and turn this small army's attention on her.

She had originally intended to keep walking, to go from one end of the camp to the other, appraise their numbers, and then decide what to do. But she had already seen pretty much everything. At least, enough to know they were painfully outnumbered. There was little chance Chanil's warriors could win in a fair fight. They would have to change the situation somehow. Chanil needed to do something to make their enemies afraid and uncertain. To make them angry and stupid.

So, instead of continuing her stroll behind enemy lines, she kept walking in her circle around the group surrounding Burly-Beard. She walked until she was near the man who had stared at her. He had an embroidered shirt with patterns that Chanil recognized as coming from Coyolapan, confirming her suspicions of his origins. She walked close to him, and in the language spoken in Tlapallo's realm, she said, "I assume you can understand me."

She circled around his back as she spoke, and he had to turn his head to catch her on the other side. His dark brown eyes watched her carefully. Chanil stepped right up to him and bent forward the way a servant would if speaking to a nobleman. "You are Tlaxcala, yeah?"

He nodded but said nothing. His face was set in a cautious expression, and his eyes never left hers. A couple of the others in the circle saw their interaction but none seemed able to understand them. Or if they did, they showed no signs of caring about what was being said.

"Good," Chanil said simply. Then she stood up tall and stepped into the circle. She walked into the group of men and turned to stand about three paces in front of Burly-Beard. She looked down at him. His large form sat on a wooden stool that seemed barely able to support him. He had been engaged in conversation with the men next to him, but his attention was slowly turning toward Chanil.

Chanil's heart thumped in her chest. She felt nervous. But she also felt angry. She had no respect for the Invader mercenaries, and five years of seeing what the Great Army did to its enemies had left her with nothing but murderous rage for anyone who sided with them. She felt that anger cover her body like the warm pelt of a jaguar, soaking into her muscles and filling her heart with a powerful anger.

"Tell him to stand up and face me," Chanil said to her appointed translator.

The man said nothing. Burly-Beard was giving her an odd look now, and a couple of the others around her had started to speak in hushed tones.

"Tell him to face me, or I'll cut off his balls and cook them for my dinner," Chanil said the words calmly and deliberately.

Burly-Beard said something to Translator; it sounded angry to Chanil. "You're going to get yourself killed, girl," Translator said to Chanil.

"Tell him."

The two men exchanged some words. Burly-Beard whipped

his head up at her. His grey eyes blazed, and Chanil figured her message had finally been delivered. The other men were looking at her too, now. She stood calmly, hands at her sides. Her eyes bored down Burly-Beard. He smiled, a cocky grin on his face as he said something. Many of the men around him laughed. Chanil couldn't understand a word. But she noticed the man's strange accent. It almost sounded like he had a lisp.

"He's describing something else you can do with his balls," Translator said.

Chanil spoke directly to Burly-Beard. "Tell your men to go home, and I will only kill you."

Translator delivered her words immediately this time. Burly-Beard stopped grinning. His eyes burned with murderous anger, and he stood up slowly. At a gesture from Burly-Beard, the man on his left also rose.

Chanil could see that man's attack coming before he had even finished rising to his feet. He launched one arm out to stab her with a knife that had seemed to suddenly materialize in his hands. Before anyone could even react, Chanil had slipped around the oncoming blade, brought out her own knife, and sliced the man's exposed throat so fast that no one had even been able to tell what had happened at first.

As his blood spurted out and he clutched his neck reflexively, Chanil calmly wiped her blade on her grey shorts and folded her hands in front of her. She had barely even looked away from Burly-Beard.

Her attacker collapsed on the ground, his body twitching and squirming as his spirit left his body. Every man in the circle stood up, suddenly, but Burly-Beard yelled something and held up a hand. He looked down at his comrade and then at Chanil. She returned his stare with a forced calmness, not even bothering to look down at the man she had butchered.

Burly-Beard spoke. "He asks what you want," Translator explained.

"I want to kill him. In exchange, the rest can leave and return to Coyolapan."

A pause while Translator spoke. Then some chuckles. Burly-Beard seemed half amused and half enraged. Voice smooth with the strange lisp, he began to speak. Mid-sentence, he stepped forward.

Chanil didn't wait for Translator. She grabbed Burly-Beard's tricep and pulled him in close, turning him at the same time. In an instant, her knife was at his neck, the blade pressing hard into the skin above his jugular. She kicked his knees out from under him, so he was leaning back on her, off balance. Her other hand had a powerful grip on his arm, and she twisted it behind his back. He winced in pain.

His comrades surged forward, but a yell from Burly-Beard held them at bay.

"Tell them I'll kill him!" Chanil roared at Translator. She heard him speaking as she continued, "Tell them to back off and drop their weapons! And you come with me!"

She said the last part to Translator. She was backing up. Her blade caught in Burly-Beard's neck, enough to draw a bit of blood, as she called out orders and dragged the enemy commander with her. She made Translator walk in front, and she had to turn constantly to keep anyone who wanted to try and be a hero at bay. She shouted at them to back off, to drop their weapons. She cut Burly-Beard more than once to show them she had no problem hurting him. They cursed at her—at least, she assumed their angry words were curses.

As quickly as she could manage, she brought them to the camp entrance and stepped out of the camp and onto the road. She stood just outside the entrance now, still pressing her blade into Burly-Beard's neck. A swarm of angry Invaders marched toward her, many with weapons, all growling and snarling like angry monsters. She turned to face them all, still holding the knife to their commander's throat. There looked to be about fifteen or twenty of them there, emerging out of the camp.

"They're going to kill you, girl!" Translator shouted at her.

Chanil grinned. She had to act fast before they tried to surround her. Suddenly, she stabbed Burly-Beard in the shoulder. He yelled in pain as she sliced through the joint, and his arm went limp. Then she pulled him back by his hair and stabbed violently up into his groin, once, twice, over and over. He screamed, a long and loud release of agony. Then Chanil sliced his throat and shoved him forward into Translator's arms, and the only sounds were Burly-Beard's gurgling as he choked on his own blood.

The Invader mob yelled and cursed and charged forward. They were an angry stampede now, all ready to butcher the young girl who had killed their commander. Chanil let out a loud roar, turned, and ran down the road. She could hear the pounding of footsteps behind her as the Invader forces poured out of the camp and pursued her.

She sprinted as fast as she could, her thick, muscular thighs propelling her forward over the rise and fall of the road. She was moving so fast that when the road dipped down steeply, as she knew it would, she almost slipped. She let gravity pull her down the steep slope, and then she leapt into the jungle.

The instant her body landed, everything about her movements changed. She stepped softly now, moving surprisingly fast for how little noise she made. She watched the ground, careful to step over leaves that might give her away and over fallen branches that might snap and break.

The light from the sun was gone, and a hazy darkness engulfed the world around her. But Chanil could still see. It wasn't the way Itza' could see. Chanil recalled her sister once describing a mural while they had sat in near total darkness. But Chanil could see well enough. She heard the angry mob behind her as she melted into the jungle. She heard their curses and yells. She smelled their confidence and their rage. It was like soured fruit mixed with burnt fat.

A bird whistled. Chanil grinned. That was Ch'akanel's call. He was nearby and had seen her. That meant Eztli' would be nearby as well.

"You scared, big men?" Chanil threw her taunt into the night air. "You scared of a little girl!"

Chanil heard the men yelling. She circled around a tree and peered out at the road. It was less than twenty paces away from her. She saw a man in the group grab Translator roughly by his shoulder and shove him toward the jungle.

It was clear the Invaders expected Translator to lead them into the darkness. One of the Invaders pressed a sword into Translator's back. The man had no choice. He walked into the darkness, and some of the foreign mercenaries followed him.

Chanil crouched and watched as the men crossed over into the deep blackness. Their steps were loud, and their eyes betrayed even more fear than she had expected. A group of about ten of them walked toward her, though she was certain that none of them could actually see her.

Six men remained on the road, clearly not wanting to risk the jungle but not wanting to leave their friends either. They wanted to be able to say they had been part of the group that had killed the murderous Yaxchilan warrior.

No, Chanil realized. That probably wasn't how they would see her. That was how Tlapallo's warriors would see her. But the Invaders weren't like Tlapallo or the other Tlaxcala. They moved with fright in the jungle as though they had never seen anything like it. They fought as mercenaries instead of true warriors. Wherever they came from, their rules of warfare seemed slightly different from the ones Chanil was used to. And their lands must have different plants and weather, too.

Chanil wondered if they just saw her as a bandit then. But it didn't matter; she would kill them all the same.

The group of ten Invaders crashed noisily through the jungle. Chanil let them pass her. One even walked right by her, and it was clear he saw nothing. She trailed the man who was last in line. She stalked him close, stepping in time with him. She felt her blade growing hungry.

In one fluid motion, she covered the man's mouth and sliced his throat. She gripped him tightly, stabbing repeatedly as she lowered him onto the jungle floor. She felt her heart race and her bones tingle. She dropped his dying form and jogged off in a new direction. In her wake, she heard whispers. Then the shouts as his comrades found the body.

Then more shouts in the distance. A loud bang, like a volcano erupting, and Chanil knew that at least one of the Invaders had tried to use the explosive weaponry they sometimes carried. The sounds were distant—she figured Nimaq and the others were attacking the camp.

The men in the jungle grew angry. Their shouts became louder and louder as they realized their comrades back at camp were being attacked. Chanil saw a couple of them go one way, breaking away from the group and trying to head directly toward the source of the sounds and where they thought their camp was. Chanil saw a shadowy figure trailing them and recognized Ch'akanel. She didn't expect that the Invaders would make it back to their camp.

The group of seven men in front of Chanil turned in different directions. They weren't sure which direction the road was in. Translator said something to them, pointing in a direction that was almost the right way back to the road. They followed him. Chanil moved in a gentle circle around them, heading toward their rear.

The men had learned something, though, and were walking in pairs now. She saw the way the last two in line looked around, eyes darting fearfully. They tried to stay close together, but it was getting hard to see. Even Chanil had limited vision now.

She came up to walk beside one of the men. She stood at his left side, breathing softly. He stopped suddenly, his eyes narrowing. Chanil's knife caught his throat before he could yell. Then she pulled him down and tossed his body to the side as she leapt at his companion. He screamed and tried strike out at her, landing a weak punch against her face. She just laughed maniacally and stabbed him repeatedly in the face and neck.

She heard rustling sounds approaching her, and she took off, melting into the night and circling around to attack the front of the group. By the time she got there, she found three more bodies. She heard panicked footsteps. It sounded like a pair of men running wild through the jungle. She heard heavy breathing.

A soft cooing sounded nearby, and Chanil returned Eztli's call with a light tweet that identified her.

"I think they're all gone," Chanil whispered. It was so dark now that she wasn't actually sure if that was true.

Eztli' cooed again, and they found each other in the dark. Then they made their way back toward the road.

When they arrived at the edge of the jungle, Chanil smelled the blood. The moon was nearly full, and it peered over the white road nearly unimpeded by canopy cover. Three bodies lay on the road. Chanil looked at Eztli' questioningly as the girl came up beside her. Eztli's evil grin told Chanil everything she needed to know about who was responsible for the bodies.

Chanil sniffed the air and picked up the scent of smoke. A fire. She gestured, and Eztli' and her jogged back up the road toward the camp. Chanil could see a crowd of her warriors around the entrance. Tents and lean-tos burned within the camp. Chanil saw Nimaq towering over a pair of captured Invaders.

"Puma," he said in his respectful growl as she approached.

"Report," she said.

"We captured these two. The rest are dead." His voice was heavy with the recent violence, and she saw the wild look in his eyes that he always carried after a battle.

Chanil looked back at the camp, the fires burning there. "And the fires?"

Nimaq shrugged. "Apparently people resent being taken as slaves," he said, grinning. The expression didn't quite fit his stoic face, and it was unnerving. "Some of their captives joined us in the fight, and they decided to burn the place down."

Eztli' came up to Chanil then, Ch'akanel breathing heavy beside her. "Found this one," she said, gesturing.

Chanil smiled at them both but especially Ch'akanel. Then she turned back to Nimaq. "Have they said anything?"

She found herself wondering if maybe they should have spared Translator. She hadn't killed him or seen his body. Maybe he was one of the ones who had fled in the jungle. City boy, Chanil thought wryly, realizing he would probably die out there if he scared that easily in the darkness.

Nimaq shook his head. "Can't understand them," he said simply. Chanil nodded.

"We take them back with us. Someone will be able to talk to them. Maybe they can tell us where the next attack is coming from."

Nimaq inclined his head. "Yes, Great Puma." Then he barked some orders to the nearby warriors, and the two Invaders were tied together and made ready for capture.

Chanil looked around her. The camp burned, but it looked like all her warriors had survived. She felt her stomach unclench, and the deep pit of guilt finally leaving her. The villages would be safe. The Waxtek would not starve. At least, not today.

Battle Lines

Never underestimate what a powerful reputation can do.
Fear is the ultimate weapon against your enemies.

—the Book of Queen Snake Lady

ITZA' WATCHED AS CHANIL PACKED her supplies. Her older sister's calloused hands moved deftly over her things, selecting and rejecting. Itza' watched the dark brown fingers hesitate as they glided over the familiar threads of Chanil's childhood blanket. The thick strands clung to her skin for a second as though asking to go with. But Chanil decided against it, and Itza' saw the fingers move on to the next item.

"I wish you could stay," Itza' said, leaning against the wall in her sister's private room. "Feels like you just got back."

Chanil stopped what she was doing to smirk at Itza'. Her younger sister smiled back, but Chanil couldn't help but notice how that smile was not as bright as it had once been. Itza's eyes were somehow darker and deeper than they had been in childhood, and with the weight of years of war, they sparkled less than Chanil remembered.

"That's because I've barely seen you these past two winals," Chanil teased back. "Where have you been sneaking off to, little one?"

Two winals, Itza' thought. Fourteen days, half a moon. Had Chanil really been back that long? Had it really been that long since Itza's foolish plan to save the Waxtek villages had failed and Chanil had to rescue the situation with her usual risky strategies?

Itza' didn't voice her feelings of guilt or sadness over her plan nearly ruining everything. She didn't say anything about the gnawing guilt she felt in her stomach at what might have happened to Chanil had she been killed in that enemy camp or how the villagers would have suffered or how the raids might have continued without end until the Yaxchilan forces arrived.

Instead, she shrugged and said, "The usual. Strolling through the markets and playing dice."

Chanil laughed. "I bet Xok hates that you still do that."

Xok, not Mom, Itza' thought. It hadn't been 'Mom' for a long time now, and Chanil seemed much happier with that. The bond between her and Night Star had never been stronger.

Itza' grinned and crossed to sit in the hammock near where Chanil sat on the floor organizing supplies to take with her for the next battle. "She does, but it helps to get to know people."

"Is it true you sent one of your aides to Lord Chehn's court last time we sent some workers there?" Chanil checked some of her weapons, seeing which ones needed cleaning and which ones might be useful to bring.

Itza' nodded. "A helpful face to speak on our behalf." That, of course, was just the cover story. Itza' had sent her newest aide, a girl named Zayla, to join the mob of workers, builders, servants, and other vassals that Yaxchilan sent to continue helping Lord Chehn maintain his large river fortifications. Zayla would serve the lord in court during this time, a helpful gift. But, in reality, Zayla was a spy. Itza' had recruited her personally, like all her special aides. And then, she had sent her to Chehn's court because Zayla spoke the language and could take care of herself. Itza' felt guilty about that, too, and she missed Zayla terribly.

Itza' shook her head to try and clear the mess of feelings piling up there inside her heart. Most of all, Itza' felt guilty for living in a large palace while warriors like her sister went out and did the real work of defending the kingdom.

"You okay, Itz?" Chanil asked, and Itza' realized she had just been staring off into space.

She nodded. "Just . . . feel useless, I guess. Here you are going off to fight our enemies again, and what am I doing? Sitting in a palace playing spy."

Chanil shook her head. "You help plan our strategy, sis. *And* you're the one who learned how to speak the Invader's language. Without that, we wouldn't have even known this attack was coming."

Itza' scrunched her face. "It's not like I cracked a secret code. I just found someone who could teach it to me."

"Sounds good enough to me," Chanil said with a shrug. "All that time spent playing dice helps out is all I'm saying."

Itza' tried to accept the words. It was true. She had found a traveler in the markets once who could speak the Invader's language, and she had offered him a job teaching it to her and the other members of the family and translating. Because of that, the family had been able to interrogate Chanil's captives and learn of a large attack Tlapallo himself was leading into the mountain passes of the Waxtek lands.

But Itza' didn't see that as anything special. Anyone could have gotten that information. It's not like she interrogated the prisoners herself. She had a sudden mental image of tiny, little Lady Itza' standing before two giant warriors. In her mind, the little girl pointed an angry finger and demanded answers from the huge men. But her words came out like a baby's, and they just laughed.

Itza' laughed out loud herself. Chanil gave her a funny look. She grinned. "I was just imagining what it would be like for me to be the one out there instead of you. The terrifying little girl. Maybe I could talk our enemies to death."

Chanil laughed, but she scooted over to her little sister and grasped her hands. "You're more than that, Itz. How many times have you given me an idea or helped me figure something out? Sure, I can cut off heads. But I can't see politics like you. I can't just know if this person is lying or scheming because I already figured out everything that's going on. It takes both of us, yeah?"

Then Chanil leaned in close and whispered, "For as long as there are days . . ."

Itza' rolled her eyes, but she couldn't help but smile. "As long as there is light," she finished the refrain. Chanil's words definitely made her feel better. But still, Itza' felt small and inadequate. She needed to do something more.

"Puma!" Lord 5-Thunder's loud voice carried over the clamor of men and women shouting as the two shield walls crashed together, of boots grating against the rocky ground, of shields being smashed.

"We're here!" Chanil's voice called out from the front ranks of the Yaxchilan warriors. She sounded gleeful. Front and center. It was her favorite position. Even from where he stood at the rear of the mass of warriors there on the field, Lord 5-Thunder could hear his eldest daughter's maniacal laugh as she engaged the enemy.

Lord 5-Thunder smiled to himself. "Push!" His voice boomed out, and the warriors surged forward against the shields of their enemies. Looking past the mass of Yaxchilan warriors, Lord 5-Thunder saw a sea of snarling beasts. Some would have called them men, but 5-Thunder knew better. His enemies were no longer Tlaxcala warriors of the Great Army. They were beasts and monsters come to try and ravage the Waxtek lands that lay between Coyolapan's and Yaxchilan's realms.

Further out, past the mass of snarling western warriors that assailed Chanil's shield wall, Lord 5-Thunder saw his counterpart. Lord Tlapallo's giant headdress reached almost to the sky, and

5-Thunder could see the long quetzal feathers quivering in anger and anticipation as Chanil and the other Yaxchilan warriors held the ground against his onslaught.

Tlapallo had tried to march an army along the southern edge of Waxtek lands, where the mountains reached up toward the sky. But Lord 5-Thunder had been waiting for him. And now, along the rocky foothills of the mountains where Waxtek miners labored to bring forth the very obsidian stones that lined the weapons of each side in this conflict, the two armies met.

And Tlapallo was stuck.

The Yaxchilan warriors had worked with the Waxtek to block the roads, which had forced Tlapallo's army down a narrower path through the mountains. And they had dug traps in the surrounding jungle so they couldn't be outmaneuvered. So even though Tlapallo technically had a larger force, Chanil and the other warriors were able to stop their march with a careful choice of where to strike.

Lord 5-Thunder thought he caught Tlapallo's gaze across the battlefield. The Yaxchilan warriors were positioned on higher ground along a hill, and he could look down on his former friend and ally as their two armies crashed together. 5-Thunder clenched his jaw in anger as he thought about the friendship lost here, about how Tlapallo's realm had become a vassal state of the Great Army over the past several years and how they were marching further east now.

"Push!" he bellowed out again, and he heard the crash of swords on shields as his warriors moved to respond.

In a quiet growl, 5-Thunder said, "Come on, old friend. Give up ... Give up."

But he knew it was pointless. Tlapallo was stubborn and proud, and Lord 5-Thunder knew it could take several more hours of this pointless shoving match before his former friend would consider talking. The Yaxchilan warriors would have to hold for a while before there was any chance of victory here.

Nevertheless, Lord 5-Thunder stared across the battlefield

at Tlapallo, bored into the distant figure with his fiery eyes, and willed the man to give the signal for his warriors to hold back. He still hoped talking might become an option.

Next to Lord 5-Thunder, a roughened rasp said, "Do you think he will, Great Ajaw? Give up, that is."

5-Thunder glanced at the man. The tall figure was cloaked in bright armor that had the sharp, angular patterns of the Waxtek nobility embroidered onto it. 5-Thunder shook his head.

"Not exactly the easy victory we were hoping for when we asked for your help, then, Great Lord 5-Thunder," the raspy voice grated against the ground angrily.

"Victory against Tlapallo will never be easy, Lord Chehn," he replied in his own violent growl. "But we won't budge from this spot, and he will realize, eventually, there's no chance of victory."

Lord Chehn made a sour face. His wide cheeks scrunched up, and his oval brown eyes narrowed to mere slits. "We are trusting much on your assessment, good sir."

They both knew it was true. But what choice did Chehn have? The Waxtek kingdom was smaller than either Yaxchilan's or Coyolapan's realms. And, worse for them, they were caught between the two larger realms.

From the front rank of the Yaxchilan shield wall, Chanil grunted and heaved an enemy warrior back. Underneath her bright, woven armor, her body was drenched in sweat from the unending shoving match taking place. The long blade of her knife found a gap in the enemy's armor as he tried to regain his footing and his position.

Another of Tlapallo's warriors replaced him immediately. On and on, it had gone like that all day. The Yaxchilan warriors had a good position, but their enemy was unending—a seemingly infinite number of warriors that kept coming like some immortal beast. When one was killed, another simply replaced it.

To her right, she could see the massive form of Tlapallo's son, Itzcoyotl. The giant mountain of a man rose nearly a head above the warriors on either side of him, and he was doing a good job of disrupting her shield wall at his location. His powerful strikes were like thunderclaps, and the Yaxchilan warriors there were having trouble keeping him back. A bloody tangle of bodies were mounting up at Itzcoyotl's feet. Chanil had to do something, think of something, or the mountain might break through.

"Hey, Little Coyote," she called out in a taunting voice. Itzcoyotl's name meant something like Obsidian Coyote, and Chanil knew that. "Here, little coyote. Here, little doggy."

She didn't look at him. She couldn't, of course. Her eyes had to stay focused on whatever nameless monster attacked her from across the line of warriors. She had to dodge and block. She had to slam her weapon down on the shield of the Coyolapan warrior in front of her so that the Yaxchilan warrior to her left could stab or slice him. But in every pause, at every beat when she could spare a breath, she called out a taunt to Itzcoyotl.

"Here, doggy, doggy."

"Little coyote looks hungry! They not feeding him!"

Soon, the warriors in the rank behind the front took up the work of throwing taunts as well. A whole chorus of voices lashed out at Itzcoyotl, calling him a little doggy, telling him to find his master, he needed to eat.

Chanil wasn't sure, at first, if it would work, but she had to try. And, after a while, she could tell he was getting irritated. His movements weren't as quick. His return insults carried more and more frustration. When he called Chanil the most used up whore in Yaxchilan, she could hear the bitterness in his voice. He meant it.

So Chanil offered him a chance to get what he wanted. "Come and fight me, little coyote! I tired of killing your puppies, little doggy. Come and fight this little girl who killing all your men!"

She heard a loud and vicious roar from the mountain of a man. The volcano had erupted, and Chanil smiled at the same moment as her knife blade found the face of the man in front of her.

But just then, a loud and long trumpet sounded from behind the enemy's lines. And then another one, this one even longer than before. The Coyolapan warriors slammed their shields together, and in near perfect unison, they stepped backwards.

"Hold!" Chanil shouted.

An instant later, Lord 5-Thunder's command came, echoing the same strategy. "Hold!"

The Yaxchilan warriors stayed put. Their enemies backed off. Two paces. Three. Four. When there was a narrow gulf of several paces between the two walls, they stopped. Warriors exchanged glances. The Yaxchilan warriors didn't know why the other side had sounded a partial retreat. Maybe to call for negotiation? Maybe to reassess? Or maybe they were getting ready to concede and leave the area?

Looking across the gap, Chanil saw Itzcoyotl's eyes boring into her. She wondered if he knew why his warriors had been called to move back. But he didn't seem concerned with anything other than casting a look of pure hatred at Chanil.

She returned his stare, smirked, and then let out several loud barking sounds to taunt him. The warriors around her all laughed. Itzcoyotl's eyes burned under the brim of his woven coyote helmet. In an instant, he had shoved aside the shield of the man next to him and taken a step forward into the gap.

"Come on, Puma! It's your chance now, little kitten!" He hurled the words at Chanil. Her heart pounded in her chest, but she threw a smile on her face. She would never let Itzcoyotl see her fear.

She turned her head slightly to shout over her shoulder. "Little doggy needs his mommy!" The warriors laughed, and Chanil slowly stepped forward into the gap.

It was a strange feeling walking into the space between the two walls. Chanil was very aware of the way the ground felt, how much rockier it was than the jungle earth around Yaxchilan. She was also aware of the sheer number of eyes on her. Every warrior on both sides would be watching what happened between her and Itzcoyotl. Despite how many people there were, there was an eerie silence in the gulf separating the two armies.

"I'm here, little doggy!" she yelled out, trying to sound confident. But in reality, she felt terrified. Itzcoyotl was half a head taller than her and built like a mountain. Chanil hadn't known exactly what she expected by taunting him. Her only thought had been to try and get under his skin so he would have a harder time focusing. She knew weakening their strongest warrior would help her army get closer to breaking up their shield wall.

But now, here she was, staring across the narrow gulf at the prince of Coyolapan, and every fiber of her being screamed at her to run away. What had she been thinking? She'd fought in the shield wall for many years now, ever since she had earned her name in the north with Night Star. Ever since the Great Army had finished absorbing Tlapallo's kingdom and their raiders had started their relentless onslaught on the border of Yaxchilan and the Waxtek kingdom.

She had never called someone out into single combat though. Not in the middle of a battle. It did happen, though. She had seen it. Usually before the shield walls collided, some warriors would throw out challenges, and sometimes someone would respond. There were rumors that the result of some battles were decided that way.

"You sound scared, little girl." Itzcoyotl's deep voice brought Chanil back to the present moment. The large warrior was moving forward. He had a single-handed sword in one hand, and his large shield in the other.

Chanil looked at the ranks of her own warriors and called out to them, "Single-handed one!"

A sword emerged within seconds, and Chanil took it in her hand, sheathing the long knife warriors used in the tight shield wall formations. She banged it against her shield. "Mommy's waiting, little doggy!"

Inside, though, she thought, What am I doing? And why did they pull back?

But she wouldn't get a chance to find out the answer to either question. Itzcoyotl came at her like a hurricane, swinging his large sword in a vicious arc aimed at her head. She brought up her shield to block. The crash was as loud as thunder, and it felt like an earthquake had shaken her whole body.

The warriors erupted in that instant, shouting and cheering. Chanil was vaguely aware of the sound of her father's voice calling out to her. She thought she heard him telling her to stop. But that wasn't really an option since Itzcoyotl was swinging again. This time, his weapon came down hard and perfectly vertically. Chanil knew the larger man would be hoping to crash through her shield completely. She remembered how that had happened in her very first battle, and her shoulder remembered the days and days of pain that had followed from her enemy's blade slicing her arm.

She had learned more tricks since then, though.

Itzcoyotl was attacking in anger. His eyes were burning fires of rage, and he had fallen completely for Chanil's little taunts. His moves were exaggerated, and that made it easier for Chanil to deflect the vertical strike. She stepped offline as she raised her shield at an angle, the top tilted toward her. Itzcoyotl's powerful strike still clapped loudly against her shield, but this time it ran like water off a roof.

Chanil used the momentum of his strike to push his blade downward even further as it passed along her shield. For an instant, Chanil had Itzcoyotl's weapon pinned into the ground, and she brought her blade down hard against his arm.

He didn't make a sound. She had to give him that. But she felt the impact—the way his arm bone gave in slightly as the weight of her blades crashed down onto his armor. Then she felt the blades of her weapon bite into his protective covering, and she yanked the weapon back, pushing down as she retracted her arm.

She couldn't tell if she had cut into his flesh, but she doubted it. The bite of her blades hadn't felt deep enough. Itzcoyotl brought his weapon up in a wide arc, and Chanil jumped back to avoid the swinging blade. But she saw the slowness of it, how it was just a bit less powerful than his previous strikes. Itzcoyotl righted himself, and the two warriors stood facing each other. Chanil caught the look in his eyes and recognized it immediately. He was in pain.

"Stop!" A loud voice, commanding, flew over the scene. Chanil didn't recognize it at first, but the Coyolapan warriors seemed to. They stiffened. Lord Tlapallo appeared at the front of his army.

His gaze went to Chanil then to his son. His expression was unreadable under the black paint on his face. But the feathers in his headdress quivered like a rage held just beneath the surface.

"What are you doing?" He yelled the words out in a disgusted tone. "Get back here. Now!"

He barked the command at Itzcoyotl, who hesitated. His eyes were still locked on Chanil, and she could see the anger was rising there again. But the pain had made him hesitate. And now his king was ordering him to fall back in line.

Chanil smirked. She could have returned to her own line of warriors or said something gracious. But, instead, she looked at Itzcoyotl and said, "Mommy will see you later, little doggy."

Itzcoyotl fumed and took a step forward. But Tlapallo's voice whipped him back. "I said stop!"

Then he said something Chanil could not understand. But, whatever it was, Itzcoyotl turned back toward his father suddenly, a look of disbelief on his face. Tlapallo repeated the phrase, slower and with more intensity. Itzcoyotl turned back to Chanil for a second and spit on the ground at her feet. Then he whirled and disappeared with his father into the ranks of Coyolapan warriors.

A moment later, someone on the Yaxchilan side shouted, "Puma!" She turned to see Nimaq beckoning to her.

"Negotiations," he growled in disgust. Chanil nodded and folded herself back into the safety of the ranks of her brothers and sisters in arms.

A tent was erected for the negotiations. Mats were brought in, and servants even prepared cacao beverages in anticipation of the talks. Lord 5-Thunder and Lord Tlapallo sat opposite one another, their feathered headdresses competing to see which would reach the heavens first. Lord Chehn sat next to 5-Thunder. After all, it was his kingdom under attack. He needed to at least be present, didn't he? Chanil sat down on the other side of her father. Opposite her, Itzcoyotl glared angrily, his one arm wrapped heavily in a thick bone cast. Chanil had tried not to look too smug when she saw that.

Lord Chehn lit a large pipe. It had an intricately carved inscription on one side that told of how Lord Chehn's father had once been lost in the jungle and saved by a shape-shifting trickster. A complementary illustration of the story adorned the other side of the pipe.

Lord Chehn took a long drag from the pipe. His gaunt features were intense. The sharp lines of his painted face contrasted with the wide, muscular bulk of 5-Thunder and Tlapallo. Nevertheless, Lord Chehn had a violent intensity to his movements that suggested his reputation for seizing power was well deserved.

He exhaled the smoke from the pipe, his rough voice following close behind the sharp-smelling cloud. "The Great Tlapallo wants to speak, eh?"

Lord Tlapallo stirred. He looked carefully at Chehn and then turned his attention to Lord 5-Thunder. "I wanted to give you a chance to end this before more bloodshed occurs."

Chehn scoffed. 5-Thunder smirked mercilessly. "Afraid of losing, old friend? You know you won't get past us."

"I don't need to get past you, Ajaw," Tlapallo began. Chanil heard nothing in his voice to indicate the length of time he had known her father, the battles they had fought together, the times spent camping out in the jungle.

"We can simply grind your warriors into dust over time," he finished.

Lord Chehn pulled his lips back—an expression of disgust made more frightening by the gems in his teeth. "You western kings are too confident."

"Go home, Tlapallo," Lord 5-Thunder said coldly. "You know I won't give in."

"I have more than twice your number, Ajaw. And more can be called here."

Chanil saw her father smirk then. His wolfish, boyish grin. He covered his mouth with his fingers and looked at Chanil. She saw the glint of mischief in his eyes.

"That may be, old friend. And maybe you could overwhelm us . . . eventually. But how many would it cost you? You wouldn't even have enough warriors left over to continue your march."

It was Itzcoyotl's turn to speak. "You cannot stop us, you know that. We'll break through eventually."

Lord 5-Thunder looked at the young man as though seeing him for the first time. He raised his eyebrows in a smug expression. "How's the arm, my boy? Looks like a nasty break."

Chanil couldn't hold back her smile. Her full lips spread in a wicked grin, and she met Itzcoyotl's gaze as he glared at her.

"This battle isn't over," Itzcoyotl growled, clearly meaning both the larger battle and the one between him and Chanil.

"Then let's get back to it." Chanil's declaration was flat and loud. She turned to Lord Tlapallo. "You called your warriors back so we could talk. What do you have to offer? Anything? No? Then let's go back and finish this."

Tlapallo narrowed his eyes at her. "Don't be foolish, girl. My army is still bigger than yours."

Chanil laughed. "But it's getting smaller, Great Lord. Your son won't be able to fight. Who will stand in front now? You?"

Tlapallo looked pointedly at Lord 5-Thunder, who just raised one of his arms. "My heir is eager to bleed your warriors, old friend. Fortunately for you, I'm not as blood thirsty. So, what's your offer?"

"Half." Tlapallo said, the words matter-of-fact.

Lord Chehn was incredulous. "Back to the wall!" He shouted loud enough for the gathered warriors, observers, servants, and noble rulers. "Half! You are crazy!"

Itzcoyotl attempted a shrug. "Half your kingdom to save the other half."

"I give you half now, and you'll take the rest within a moon. I'd rather take my chances on the battlefield."

Lord Tlapallo's opening offer had been ridiculous. But Chanil knew that was how it went. He had to act confident and smug. He represented the largest empire in the west and commanded a huge force. He had to act like he had nothing to lose. Chanil knew better, though. There was a reason Tlapallo had spent more time attacking the Waxtek over the past year rather than going straight for Yaxchilan. He wasn't as confident that he could take Yaxchilan in one strike as he portrayed. But undoubtedly, the western kings demanded some sort of victory from him.

He had seen Lord Chehn's smaller realm as an easy path to appeasing his new masters. But Lord Chehn had convinced her father to provide support. And so now, Tlapallo and 5-Thunder played out their war in their neighbor's lands. It made them both act more confident than they otherwise would have been. Any land that was lost was not really theirs to begin with.

So, the negotiations dragged on. Tlapallo and Itzcoyotl wanted land. Lord 5-Thunder cautioned Chehn to not yield land. They could pay Tlapallo to leave, but letting them settle would only set a dangerous precedent. Chanil agreed. Her father was no idiot when it came to strategy. If the Great Army got any inroads into Waxtek lands, then they would just use that to grow stronger, launch more raids, recruit more warriors.

But Tlapallo was insistent, immobile, and uncompromising. "We have riches, good sirs. We don't need your paltry jewels. We need farmland."

Chanil had heard this before. The expansion of the New Alliance was driven by the food shortage, just as much as their ambition. It made her nervous. A starving enemy was unpredictable. They could do anything.

"Twenty measures," Lord Chehn finally offered. Lord 5-Thunder shook his head. Tlapallo and Itzcoyotl smiled.

"You can't be serious," Chanil shouted. Chehn gave her an icy look but did not acknowledge her words.

"Let me fight for it," Chanil added suddenly. Everyone looked at her. She looked only at Itzcoyotl, however. "It isn't over, right, little doggy? Let's settle this ourselves. You and me."

Itzcoyotl laughed. "You should keep your daughter in check, good sir," he said to Lord 5-Thunder. "Before she gets herself hurt."

"Tell that to your arm, little doggy," Chanil tossed back at him.

Lord Chehn spoke up. "Silence, Lady Chanil. It is my kingdom we are discussing, and *I* will decide what happens."

No one really had an argument for that, no matter how stupid of a choice Chanil and her father thought Chehn was making. Tlapallo knew it, too. He smiled, smug. In the end, Lord Chehn and Lord Tlapallo agreed on a swathe of land in the south of the Waxtek kingdom. It had cornfields, and it had obsidian mines. And, of course, Chehn would have to pay Tlapallo to leave his lands.

He's given them food and supplies to make more weapons, Chanil thought bitterly as she watched Tlapallo and Itzcoyotl march back into the west with their army. And paid him as well.

She turned to her father. They stood atop a short hill that was still stained with blood and littered with bodies, where weapons and fallen banners were strewn like a child's playthings on the ground. They watched their enemies leaving, knowing it was only temporary. Chanil had fought right here on this hill, and for what? Tlapallo and his son would return, probably with more warriors and probably with a better strategy next time.

"He's paying for the very weapons that will kill him, Father," Chanil said, looking up at Lord 5-Thunder. His jaw was tight, the snake-like scar there looking like a caged python.

5-Thunder nodded angrily. Then he turned around and started off. "I know, little one," he said over his shoulder. "I know."

Chanil watched her father go one way and Tlapallo another. She stood on top of the hill between them. She knew, in her heart, this had not gone the right way. She knew something had to be done to stop the Great Army. Before all of Lord Chehn's lands were theirs and Yaxchilan found itself surrounded.

The room was lit with only a single candle casting dim light around Chanil's private tent. She saw the light from the flickering flame through closed eyelids as she lay on the large cot. She smiled, feeling Ch'akanel's fingertip gently tracing the outside of her thick thigh. She looked down, watching his dark hands open up to squeeze the inside of her thigh, and she bit her lip.

"I'm glad you didn't get hurt today, Chan." His voice was like the softest beating of a slit drum. She could see his dark brown eyes clinging to her body, the way his gaze outlined her curves along with his hands.

"Did I worry you, love?" Chanil asked. She lay naked on the cot, one hand behind her head.

"Worried? That such a small army would pose any threat to you? Never." He scoffed. Chanil smirked at him.

"It's good to know you have so much faith in your future queen," Chanil teased. Ch'akanel bent down and kissed her stomach.

"I'll be your most loyal advisor, my love."

"You'll be more than that," she said, sitting up and lifting his chin with her fingertip. Ch'akanel shook his head.

"We both know better than that, Chan. You can't make me a king."

Chanil clenched her jaw for a second then shook her head again, saying, "You know, if I were a man, I could bed whomever I choose, and no one would care."

"I'd care," Ch'akanel replied with wry grin.

"That's not what I meant, and you know it. I just . . ."

"Hate secrets," he finished for her, and she nodded. "Especially family ones."

Abruptly, she leaned forward and kissed him hard. "It doesn't matter. Once I'm queen, I can do what I want. I'll make the rules."

"And maybe you'll decide to sit behind the warriors, then, instead of up front, eh?" Ch'akanel whispered in her ear.

"Not likely," she said, grinning.

"You should consider it, Chan. Today was hard. I could not bear to lose—" he started to say, but Chanil silenced him with a kiss.

"It's over, love. I am still alive." She kissed him again, her mind already leaving the battle and the politics behind to focus on other things.

"But what if anything were to happen to . . ." he started, his hand involuntarily reaching out toward her stomach.

"Do not worry, my love. It's over. We are unharmed. The battle is won."

Ch'akanel still felt the echoes of pain that had shot through him when he had heard about what Chanil had done. He felt guilt for having been positioned so far away. But as Chanil continued to press her body against his, he felt all other thoughts vanish as he gave in to the passionate fire Chanil stoked within him.

Counting Moons

All actions have consequences. We may not know it at the time, but everything we do impacts the course of life all around us. Even the simplest of choices might be the one to bring down an empire.

—*letters from A Queen in Exile*

NIGHT STAR SIGHED HEAVILY and looked over Chanil's head at the mural behind her daughter. The mural showed an image of a skull hanging from a calabash tree, like fruit. A young woman held out her hand to the hanging skull, and the mural showed droplets of spit traveling from the skull to land in the woman's outstretched palm. Night Star knew the mural depicted a very old story among the Winaq. The skull that had impregnated a daughter of the underworld with the twins that would become heroes of legend and myth. Night Star loved the story and its layers of meaning.

But today, sitting across from her own daughter, she felt annoyed at the irony of the imagery. She set her full lips in a tight line of frustration.

"I told you this could happen, Chan," she said softly, her exasperation apparent.

"I know, Mom. It wasn't intentional."

"Haven't you been counting your moons?" Night Star asked. Chanil sat on a mat opposite her, a loose tunic of woven armor around her torso. Night Star tried to see if she could visually discern any signs of what Chanil had revealed to her that night and decided she couldn't. That, at least, was good.

Chanil nodded, eyes somewhat downcast. "I thought I had been." She exhaled sharply and puffed out her cheeks, just like she used to when she was a kid about to get in trouble. "There's been so much fighting lately—we've been on the road so much. I—I must have lost track at some point."

Night Star shot her a fiery look. "You can't afford to lose track, Chan. You are the heir. I've told you it was dangerous to be involved with the merchant's son."

"He's not dangerous. And you're sounding like Xok." Chanil's voice took on a harsh tone.

But Night Star was not having it. "You know that's not what I'm saying. Don't even pretend. But this could shame your father badly—and the other kingdoms are already looking to see if he is strong enough to win this war."

"We'll win with or without them." Chanil tried to sound defiant and confident, but she didn't feel it. She really only felt nauseous.

Night Star shook her head. "The other kings still might be holding out hope for an alliance with us at some point. If you marry Ch'akanel, they could see that as an insult—us choosing a common warrior over their noble sons."

Chanil knew intellectually that her mother was right. But her insides burned hearing the words. It was her choice who she bed and who she married and who—

She couldn't finish the thought.

"We aren't getting married, Mom, it's still a secret," she said.

Night Star pointed at Chanil's stomach. "Oh, so you're just going to have this baby with no husband? That won't go over any better. For anyone."

Chanil swallowed hard. Her kneecaps tingled, and her clavicles felt slimy. She felt guilt, too. Had she done it again? Made another reckless choice that was going to cost her people?

"I—I . . . don't know what to do, Mom." She hadn't meant for her voice to crack at the end, but it did. And Night Star's heart cracked with it, hearing the pleading in her baby girl's tone. She crossed to her daughter and pressed her forehead against Chanil's.

"My sweet shining star," she said to her daughter. "I know it's hard. Believe me—if anyone knows how hard these stupid, political games can be, it's me."

Chanil nodded and felt tears running down her cheeks. She reached out and grabbed onto her mom. She felt her entire body let go as Night Star took her into her massive arms and wrapped her up tightly in the safety of those big branches. Chanil sobbed.

In between sobs, words flooded out.

"I messed up again, didn't I?"

"First Itzcoyotl and then this . . . what was I thinking?"

"I don't want anyone else to suffer for my mistakes."

Night Star rode out the storm with her daughter. She held them both afloat as Chanil's tough, broad frame shook like a giant canoe in a hurricane. As the shaking subsided and Chanil started to breathe again, Night Star pulled back a bit and looked at her daughter.

"It's going to be okay, Chan. I promise you—we'll figure this out, yeah?" Her mother's words were intense but also gentle, caring, and commanding. Just what Chanil needed.

She nodded.

"It's time for tough choices, little one," Night Star said, cupping Chanil's face in her hands. She gave her daughter a comforting smile. "But we'll make them together, okay?"

Chanil nodded again. She wanted to disappear under the branches of the giant ceiba tree that was her mother, but she couldn't. For the sake of her family, of the war, of the unborn baby growing inside her, she had to act. She had to decide.

"Do you want the baby, Chan?" That was Night Star's first question. And Chanil realized she hadn't even considered that. Chanil wasn't like Itza'. She didn't think of every single possibility and then analyze all the consequences of each choice and then reassess and reanalyze and then come up with the overall best solution and then move forward. Chanil just moved. She just decided.

In her mind, she was pregnant. That was it. How she felt about it didn't really matter because that was the truth of the situation. At first, she found herself wondering if Ch'akanel would make a good father, but she instantly knew that he would. She also knew he wanted kids, lots of them. Probably more than Chanil would ever have the patience to push out.

"I want a family," she said to Night Star. The older woman's eyes glinted with tears, and she nodded.

"The family you didn't have," Night Star said. It made her heart break to think of how she hadn't been able to really be a mother to Chanil. It had taken everything in Night Star to be able to live with that pain for so many years.

"I don't want to lose my child or for her to lose her mother," Chanil said, clenching her jaw to quell the pain in her heart. She didn't exactly blame Night Star as much anymore, but she still resented the choices the family had made.

Night Star sat back and sighed heavily again. Her expression was sterner now, more serious. "Then this is going to be a difficult choice."

"What are you thinking?" Chanil asked intently.

Night Star looked into her daughter's eyes. "I think you have to hide the pregnancy."

Chanil felt her heart drop. She had wondered if her mother would say that.

"How can I do that while we have a war going on?"

Night Star stood up and crossed to the window. She looked out at the jungle in the distance. "I mean, it's not like you can fight anyway. How far along do you think you are?"

Chanil bit her lip nervously. She hesitated. Then, realizing she didn't want to lie, she said, "Three . . . maybe four moons?"

Her mom turned a wide-eyed stare on Chanil from the window. "You've been fighting with a baby inside you for three moons?"

Chanil got up, too, and stared at her mom. "I should have asked Tlapallo if he would put his plans on hold for a while maybe? See if we could just relax for a bit until I give birth?"

Night Star put up her arms. "I know. I know. I can't say I didn't do something similar. Guess it feels different when it's your own daughter. But still, you won't be able to fight safely anymore. Or fit in your armor."

Chanil was getting the picture now. She would start showing soon. More than she could hide by just loosening the armor she always wore. She couldn't really think of how she could keep her physical changes secret.

Unless . . .

"You're thinking I should go into hiding, aren't you?" she asked in disbelief. And Night Star nodded.

"It's the only way to keep it secret until we can figure out what to say to people about the baby."

"We are at war, Mom. I can't just abandon my people and my warriors like some coward!"

"Which is why I told you to be more careful." Night Star's reply was blunt, and it stung. "But you said you wanted this baby, yeah? So, this is where we are."

Chanil swallowed and looked at the floor. She felt dizzy, and nausea visited her in violent waves. The consequences were sinking in, and she didn't like them. To be away from the army, from her family, for what? Five moons? How would things change in that time? What would the state of the war be like?

"I have a cousin on the Island," Night Star was saying. "She's a good person—and she owes me a favor or two. It's dangerous, but if you can get to her, she'll hide you and Ch'akanel until the birth."

Chanil's head was spinning now. *A cousin . . . on the Island . . .*

"She has a daughter, actually, about your age—Yahíma is her name. Might even have kids of her own at this point," Night Star continued.

Chanil felt her heart pounding in her chest. She looked across the room at Night Star. "Mom?"

Night Star heard the tone of desperation in her daughter's voice and strode over to Chanil. She embraced her again. "I know, my shining star. But it's going to be okay. I'll tell you what to say and who to ask for, yeah? You just have to get there."

Chanil tried to nod and act like this was fine. Like everything was fine. But her heart raced, and her blood ran cold, and her knees didn't feel nearly as steady as they usually did. She would be leaving. She would have to travel all the way to the Island to find a cousin she had never met and—what? Wait out the rest of the pregnancy in hiding? Maybe that would have been nice if things were different. But she was filled with worry over what would happen while she was gone. And Chanil had never been so far from home for so long.

A thought struck her. "But how can I explain having to leave for so long?"

Night Star smiled. "You'll see at the meeting tomorrow morning. The family has come to believe that we are spread too thin in this war and need to start seeking out alliances. Xok and your father were planning on discussing sending you and Itza' to different kingdoms to secure some friendships to aid in the war."

"Okay, so I can go ask some of the other ajaw for help and then sneak off to the Island when I'm done." Chanil didn't like the idea of hiding, but at least it would be partly in service to their family.

"Exactly."

Chanil narrowed her eyes. "I haven't heard about this idea of seeking alliances."

Night Star shrugged. "We haven't talked about it much, but I think it will come out tomorrow. And when it does, I'll make sure you and Ch'akanel will have an excuse to go away for a while, yeah?"

A sharp exhale escaped Chanil's throat. Then she nodded. The decision was made. Her feelings were coming under control as she accepted the new plan. "So, where am I being sent then?"

"I'm not sure. We'll see tomorrow. But for now, I need to tell you what to bring and what to say when you go and visit our family."

Separate Ways

How many roads to peace? How many roads to war? Does it matter?
The real trick is telling the roads apart.

—collected sayings from the Book of Itza'

IXCANUL WALKED AROUND THE TABLE, filling each person's glass with a richly spiced and warm cacao beverage. She wore the ornate jade necklace that was now common for Itza's attendings. Itza' had commissioned the pieces and wore a matching one herself. Itza' watched Ixcanul's delicate movements, the young girl's nimble fingers and wrists gracefully moving to lift each cup and pour into it the contents of the large drinking container she carried. Her hands moved quickly but softly, never spilling a drop as she filled each cup to the brim. Her footsteps were equally light and nimble. She was every bit the demure and docile servant.

No one would ever suspect that she learned such delicate movements with a knife, Itza' thought.

"May I fill your cup, my Lady?" Ixcanul asked as she came over to Itza', who nodded and lifted her cup. As the two hands met in the passing of the cup, Itza' used one of her fingertips to tap Ixcanul's hand gently but quickly two times, a slight pause, and then twice more in rapid succession.

Pay attention, but say nothing, the taps said. *Observe—invisibly.* Ixcanul filled the cup and then moved herself to a quiet position of observation against one wall.

"We are very glad you made it back. All of you," Lady Night Star said, looking at Chanil as she sipped her beverage.

Itza' felt similarly. She had heard about Chanil's fight with Itzcoyotl, and the thought of her older sister having been cut down by that brute terrified her. "I can't believe you took on Itzcoyotl one-on-one like that."

Chanil grinned. "It wasn't a long fight. I would have won, too, but that Lord Chehn wanted to *negotiate*."

She practically spat out the word 'negotiate' as though it were a personal insult.

"And now that he has given some of his lands to Tlapallo, we need to reassess," Lady Xok said. She sat next to Lord 5-Thunder around the family's meeting table in the room atop one of the tall buildings in the city center. Night Star and Q'anchi' sat roughly opposite them around the circular table. Itza' was opposite Chanil.

"I think we need to reassess our understanding of the Great Army," Itza' said, cradling her cup in both hands, letting the bittersweet aroma carried by the drink's steam rise up and into her nostrils. She breathed in and felt the comfort of the drink, the reminders of home and family that came with it.

"There's nothing to understand," Chanil scoffed. "They're monsters."

But Itza' disagreed. "The New Alliance didn't just decide, one day, to spread. And we all know why Tlapallo joined them—his people were starving. His trade options were cut off. And what did they want from the Waxtek? Land to farm."

"They wanted the obsidian mines," Chanil countered. "The farms were a bonus. They know we trade for that obsidian to make our weapons."

Itza' nodded. "Yes, okay, so it's not just food. All I'm saying is we can't keep up an endless war. We need to think of a way to leverage our enemies, and to do that we have to understand them."

"There's always a reason for an empire to spread," Q'anchi' intoned, his deep voice sliding across the table.

Lady Xok nodded. "Our warriors are being taxed greatly between defending our western border and constantly fighting alongside the Waxtek."

"If we could figure out what they want—" Itza' began.

But Chanil's hand slammed down on the table. "They want our land! They want us dead! You two aren't out there, you haven't seen the bodies. And I don't mean the warriors. You haven't seen the villages raided and pillaged—or heard the screams of the women they take. The bodies of the children they burn—"

She cut herself off, looking away. She thought suddenly of the child she had seen who had been burned alive years ago—the very first time she had seen a body like that. Or smelled one. She could still recall the smell of burnt hair. Sometimes when they cooked certain meats in the markets, she thought she smelled the child again, but she had to remind herself that it was only a street vendor.

And what about her own child? She couldn't let her baby go through something like that. She wanted to end this threat before her child was born. But that didn't seem possible anymore.

"They're monsters," Chanil whispered. "You're wasting your time, Itz. There's nothing there to understand."

Itza' could feel her sister's rage. And though it was true that she hadn't been in combat herself, she did understand why people hated the west. But Itza' saw it differently, and she didn't like the prejudice coming from Chanil.

"It's not that simple," she protested. "A third of our people have family in the west, many in Coyolapan." She gestured to indicate the whole realm of Yaxchilan. "They are us. And we are them. You don't see the reports, Chan, or hear the way people in the markets are talking about this war. We're spreading ourselves too thin against a larger enemy to just keep fighting an endless war. Not without more allies."

Chanil looked across the table at Itza'. Her eyes blazed as she met the deep obsidian stare of her younger sister. She tried to hold that gaze, though something inside her screamed to look away. And before she knew it, a knot of wild panic was growing in her chest as though she were surrounded by four hundred of Itzcoyotl's best. Chanil wasn't sure where that panicked feeling came from, but she was certain it had something to do with Itza's eyes.

"Enough!" Lord 5-Thunder's voice rumbled over the war council. Itza' broke her stare to look up at their father. Chanil's feeling of panic vanished.

"You're both wrong—and you're both right. Tlapallo isn't going to stop, no matter if we understand him or not. We don't have enough leverage to change his mind. At the same time, it is true that we are spread too thin. So—we do need allies."

"It is a pity the Red City will not join us in defending our lands," Q'anchi' said. The Red City was the largest kingdom in the east and almost as powerful as Yaxchilan.

Lord 5-Thunder grunted. "I suspect Lord Jaguar Paw is playing a longer game. He's vowed neutrality in this conflict in order to preserve trade."

"So he says," Itza' pointed out. She had been suspicious of Jaguar Paw for a while now. So much so that she had even sent one of her aides to serve in his court as a gift to his son. Though, she hadn't exactly told anyone that.

Xok pursed her lips. "The Red City controls trade for nearly the entire region. Jaguar Paw might not be able to afford to take a side. And he might be influential enough to be able to force the west to accept that decision."

"Perhaps we should just ask Jaguar Paw what he is doing?" The sudden suggestion from Q'anchi' was both a wonderfully absurd and practical idea.

5-Thunder smiled. "It could be useful—to hear what lie he might tell."

"I could do it," Itza' said suddenly. The group looked at her.

"Thinking of sending one of your spies?" Chanil joked.

"What makes you think I haven't already?" Itza' shot back. "But no, I mean me. Send me with a small delegation—peace talks or some such. And I can try to learn what Jaguar Paw's plans are."

Lady Xok and 5-Thunder traded glances. A silent conversation passed between them, and Itza' wondered what they were thinking. But Q'anchi' spoke first. "It might be possible to . . . purchase . . . an alliance from the Red City."

This was news to Itza'. The truth was that the aide she had sent as a gift was, effectively, a spy. But she rarely heard from her, and the information she got was limited. She had begun to fear the spy was turned or perhaps had been killed. Either way, she did not know what Q'anchi' meant by buying an alliance.

"What kind of purchase, Q'an?" Itza' asked. The others murmured their interest as well.

"I have heard rumors Lord Jaguar Paw is looking for swords and spears," the old man said, his eyes ablaze as they darted around to each member of the council while he spoke. "We could offer him warriors in exchange for alliance."

Itza' swallowed. That is a risky business, she thought.

"If he is looking for warriors, why has he not asked us before?" Lady Night Star asked, also skeptical of the suggestion.

Q'anchi' merely shrugged. "He may not want to be in Yaxchilan's debt. But if we make our price clear . . ."

5-Thunder clenched his jaw, clearly unhappy with the situation. "We need more information before we decide. Too much mystery surrounds Jaguar Paw. Even among his own courtly visitors."

"Then perhaps we do have to send someone to speak with him," Night Star offered loudly.

"So, how long do I have to make preparations before I leave?" Itza' asked. "It's about time I did more than just hide in the palace while other people risk their skins, eh?"

Lord 5-Thunder and Lady Xok exchanged a long glance.

"You won't be going," the Ajaw said flatly, his tone indicating there would be no discussion. Itza' looked at her father and saw the resolve in his eyes.

Why is he so adamant? she wondered.

Chanil voiced Itza's thoughts for her. "But Itza' would be perfect for this."

There was an extended pause, and then the Queen explained. "Ah . . . yes . . . she would. But Lord 5-Thunder and I have been talking . . . and we believe we need Itza' for something else. We . . . need someone to go to Sprouting Earth. They're one of the most powerful kingdoms in the area, and they have many alliances, already, within the Peninsula."

Itza' felt goosebumps run along her legs. Snake Lady! she thought, recalling the woman whose actions still haunted her dreams. The queen with cavernous, black eyes and answers to questions Itza' had held in secret for years. Her family wanted to send her to speak with Snake Lady.

She could barely contain her excitement.

"I will need to know more about our history with them," she ventured, seeing an opportunity to finally uncover the reasons for the animosity between the two kingdoms and the two families. But Lady Xok saw through her daughter's schemes.

"You will deal with their Ajaw, the young Lord Chak Mol. He rules now that his father has passed. I doubt he knows any more about our old disagreements than you do. It is him you must convince and assess. But do not worry, my daughter, I will make sure you are prepared with everything you need to know."

"And what of the Red City and Lord Jaguar Paw?" Chanil asked.

Lady Night Star spoke up. "If it is warriors he is seeking, then perhaps we should send him one of our best?"

Chanil and Itza' looked at each other, understanding the implications behind Night Star's words. Itza' suddenly felt fearful for her sister.

"Chanil just got back, and you want to send her out again?"

"It is a diplomatic mission, Itz'," Chanil countered. "I won't be fighting. Besides, it's important."

"We will send strong delegations to accompany each of you," Lord 5-Thunder stated, the matter already settled in his mind. "This will not be a battle mission. But we will not risk your lives on it either."

"It could take some time to convince Jaguar Paw to accept our offer," Chanil ventured awkwardly.

"Take what time you need," Lady Night Star said quickly. "We will send many gifts with you to help with this purchase of friendship."

Take what time you need . . . Itza' found Night Star's phrasing curious. The journey to the Red City was not that far, and how long would it really take to find out if Jaguar Paw would agree to help or not? But the matter seemed to be settled among the others. Itza' could sense the meeting coming to a close.

I will need to review these things with Ixcanul and see what the young lady picked up on, she thought.

"Then we are settled?" Q'anchi' asked. "Chanil will visit the Red City. Itza' will go make peace with the Snake Dynasty . . ."

"And, in the meantime, we will continue to defend our borders from Lord Tlapallo's incursions," Night Star finished.

They all agreed. The two sisters had preparations to make.

Part Three:
Puma Shatters the Sky

Lord Jaguar Paw

Wars are won as much by economics and trade as by the bravery of warriors.

—*letters from A Queen in Exile*

LORD JAGUAR PAW'S GUARDS led Chanil and her retinue through the wide avenues of the Red City. The place was even larger and more opulent than Chanil remembered. Every building seemed newly made. Every ball-court was painted in the brightest colors. And even the poorest of Jaguar Paw's people seemed wealthy and well-fed.

In some ways, Jaguar Paw's immense wealth and success made sense. The Red City was vital to trade and commerce for the whole region. Winaq and Tlaxcala alike came to buy and sell. As did the other western peoples, like the Mexica, the ones who had formed the empire now known as the New Alliance.

Still, it struck her as odd that the Red City would be thriving while places like Yaxchilan and Coyolapan faced trade issues and starvation during the war. Jaguar Paw seemed to be growing richer while nations like the Waxtek were on the verge of collapse.

How had Jaguar Paw managed this?

She heard chatter from her warriors behind her. It seemed her own people were noticing the same things.

"All the buildings look new here," one aide marveled.

"I've never seen so many finely dressed women," a warrior whispered.

"That's because *these* women haven't been scared off by your stench yet," another replied.

"How is Jaguar Paw doing so well, and we're at war?" Ch'akanel mused.

Chanil recalled an early lesson from Lady Night Star and quoted it aloud. "Some men suffer during war while others profit from it."

Chanil caught some glances from Jaguar Paw's guards that had been sent to guide them. Even though the languages of Yaxchilan and the Red City were different, they were similar enough that translators were rarely needed. At the same time, the influence from the west was clear throughout the city—even in the language. Their vendors sold more foods from the west, wore clothes in their style, and the pictures of gods and goddesses on stone and wooden buildings alike seemed to be a blend of Winaq, Mexica, and Tlaxcala. Compared to Chanil's childhood memories of the place, the Red City she saw now looked more like Coyolapan than it did a kingdom of the Winaq.

She had a feeling that Jaguar Paw's continued success and his proclivities for all things western were related.

Jaguar Paw had Chanil's group come to the central plaza. They would meet out in the open. Chanil marched toward the plaza in her full regalia—large puma headdress, corona of feathers, armbands won in combat. She carried a large, ornately decorated spear as well. Ch'akanel strode beside her, similarly decorated in a noble warrior's dress and sporting large eagle feathers in his headdress. His piercings and armbands glinted in the sunlight as he marched alongside the woman he loved. Behind them, a contingent of about a dozen of Chanil's most trusted warriors followed closely in step with their leader. These were men and women Chanil had handpicked for this mission because their loyalty was beyond question. They would sooner die than disobey or endanger the Great Honored Puma. In addition to the warriors, a small group of aides walked with them.

At one end of the central plaza of the Red City, stone steps led up to a large, raised platform that was shielded from the sun by a broad canopy.

Approaching the canopy, Chanil could see Jaguar Paw seated there on his throne bench, a giant piece of stone that had been carved and painted and decked out in jewels to indicate his wealth. The Ajaw sat there cross-legged, watching them approach.

Chanil was acutely aware that she and her warriors were noticeably outnumbered. Lord Jaguar Paw was a man who favored intimidation as a negotiation tactic, which partially explained the unnecessarily large number of warriors he had positioned around the plaza area where they met.

But such a tactic merely made Chanil smile. In the back of her mind, she heard the voice of Lady Xok chiding her for letting such an arrogant smirk cross her face, but she could not help it. Chanil knew that if Jaguar Paw murdered Chanil, all of Yaxchilan would go to war against him. And she knew he was not foolish enough to risk that.

He shows me exactly how impotent he fears himself to be, she thought, still smiling as she signaled for her retinue to halt a respectful distance from the raised platform where Jaguar Paw and his contingent watched.

Ch'akanel took a half step forward and bowed low, kneeling and allowing his head to almost touch the sandy ground of the plaza. When he arose, he called out loudly for all to hear.

"Great and Honored Lord, Divine Ajaw Jaguar Paw! This—" he indicated Chanil standing proudly beside him. "—is the Great Honored Puma! This is Lady Chanil of the Sky, Daughter of Lord 5-Thunder and Daughter of Yaxchilan!" To his credit, Ch'akanel had used a term for 'Lady' that strongly implied Chanil would take the throne of Yaxchilan following her father.

On his throne, Jaguar Paw pursed his lips. Chanil could see he was no less decorated than his royal seat. His headdress was impossibly complicated. His face was pierced, his ears gauged, and every single jewel in his kingdom seemed to reside in either his face, his teeth, or was wrapped around his arms and hands.

Jaguar Paw sat a bit more upright hearing Ch'akanel introduce Chanil, but he did not rise. Since Chanil was not a queen, he was not compelled to stand for her. It was a technicality, but acting on it was a deliberate choice.

Instead, he stared at her and she returned his stare confidently. She had grown up around Itza's intense and piercing gaze. In comparison to that, Chanil had found very few who could intimidate her.

"Greetings Lady Chanil," Jaguar Paw said from his seated position. "I welcome you and your companions to the Red City."

Chanil could not help but notice that Jaguar Paw chose a different word for 'Lady' to address Chanil, one that implied only a woman of royal blood regardless of station. She could tell from the murmurs behind her that some of her warriors had caught the potential slight as well. With a gesture, she signaled for them to quiet down.

"This may be a long day," she whispered to Ch'akanel. Then she bellowed out to Jaguar Paw, "Greetings, Divine Ajaw Jaguar Paw. I have come from Yaxchilan to speak with you, Lord, about the war that rages around our two kingdoms." She used the term, 'Divine Ajaw' because she knew that the Red City still used divine kinship alone to decide succession.

Jaguar Paw tapped the end of his scepter against the throne repeatedly. His face twisted and his lips pursed. He gestured with the scepter outward, indicating the whole area around them.

"As you can see, daughter of Yaxchilan, there is no war here."

As he spoke, Jaguar Paw rose up, finally deciding to stand and remove himself from his throne. "Unless you have brought the war with you, that is," he called out, and Chanil heard a hint of violence in the man's voice. She wondered what was really going on with Jaguar Paw.

Ignoring the veiled threats and posturing, Chanil simply replied, "We bring only an opportunity that could benefit both our kingdoms, Lord Jaguar Paw."

At that, he smiled, his jeweled teeth glinting in the growing sun of the day. He moved down the stone steps, crossing toward Chanil and her entourage. In response, a portion of his guards started to move to flank their ruler and accompany him down to the open square of the plaza. Chanil heard a familiar grunt from behind her.

"A bit slow, those guards, eh Puma?" Nimaq spoke. Chanil nodded discretely. She had seen it as well. Jaguar Paw had given no signal to his guards, and those that moved in to accompany him had been scattered in a disorganized fashion around the canopied area. Chanil thought the guards looked and moved more like hired mercenaries than a cohesive unit that consistently trained together. But how could Jaguar Paw ever trust hired thugs with his life?

Chanil found herself glad that Itza' did have a spy in Jaguar Paw's court. Chanil had gotten a name and a way of contacting them, though Itza' had cautioned her that she believed the spy was either dead or turned.

Jaguar Paw walked toward Chanil's position, showing no signs of stopping at a safe distance. Chanil could see his guards becoming somewhat nervous. Chanil inclined her head at his approach and said, "Divine Ajaw, please allow my warriors to disarm so you may approach unbothered."

Jaguar Paw sneered and did not stop. He brought himself about two paces from Chanil and stared into her eyes. "I do not fear you or your fighters," he said quietly, though his eyes told Chanil he felt less safe than he let on.

Then, louder, he said "You say you bring an opportunity?" He dragged out the last word strangely, lengthening the vowels and twisting it into something new.

"That's right," Chanil said flatly.

"Well then, Daughter of Lord 5-Thunder, let us drink!"

He smiled, his lips curling away from his face to reveal the myriad of jewels arrayed around the edges of his teeth. His guards relaxed noticeably, though Chanil could see no reason to relax at this distance. Then he whirled around and headed back up the stone steps toward the canopy.

"Come, Noble Lady!" he called over his shoulder. "Leave your weapons and come drink . . . and tell us about this glorious *opportunity*!"

"You know, Great Puma, I think that turd is still in range of a spear throw." Nimaq grunted. Even the accompanying aides smiled.

Chanil turned to face her group. She handed Nimaq her weapon. "Don't lose it, old man," she said. "Maybe one day you'll get your wish, and it'll end up in that turd's back, yeah?" The group laughed.

"Ch'akanel, give up your blade too, you're coming up there with me."

"Yes, my Lady."

"The rest of you will just have to make do without us for a while," Chanil teased. She knew full well her warriors would be watching every move on the platform just in case.

Chanil was about to turn around and head up to the platform when a thought struck her. She moved past the group of warriors to stand before the collection of aides that accompanied them. Even though Chanil knew each of them well, she realized she probably did not know at least one of them as well as she thought she did.

"Which one of you was sent by my sister?" she asked. There was nervous and confused movement among the aides at first, with several of them exchanging glances as if rooting out a spy in their midst. But one girl did not flinch. She stepped forward confidently.

"I was, my Lady."

Chanil smiled and nodded. I should have known, she thought. K'utalik had been Itza's aide for a while before being given over to Chanil. She realized, in that moment, that had not really been a coincidence after all.

"Thank you for your honesty, K'utalik. You're coming up there too. I may need someone with your skills."

"Yes, my Lady," K'utalik responded, smiling wide.

The Popol Nah

Every kingdom of Winaq is different. From the languages spoken to the customs that are followed. There are many similarities, though. From these, some have argued we were once all united. But that has always been difficult to believe. We argue too much.

—*the Book of Queen Snake Lady*

"LADY ITZA' OF YAXCHILAN, youngest daughter of Ajaw 5-Thunder, we welcome you!" Lord Chak Mol let his voice carry out over Itza's head and over the crowd around them. The feathers in his headdress shook from the power in his odd voice. Itza' bowed low in return.

Chak Mol was the new ruler of Sprouting Earth, the eldest son of Queen Snake Lady and the late Lord Shield Skull. His father had died in the battles that rid their lands of the last remnants of the foreign Invaders who now burned villages and raided all around Yaxchilan and the Waxtek realm.

"We are honored to be welcomed here in the great city of Sprouting Earth, Lord Chak Mol," Itza' replied formally, bowing low in deference to the man's higher status. Coming out of the bow, she looked up to the raised stone patio where Chak Mol stood surrounded by the ruling nobles of Sprouting Earth.

The raised patio sat in front of a richly decorated and brightly painted, low stone building with three doorways. The whole area was engulfed in a haze of incense smoke from large burners distributed throughout the raised area. Every important ruler of Sprouting Earth seemed to stand up there on that patio.

And there, next to Chak Mol, was the woman who haunted Itza's dreams. Snake Lady, the Queen of Sprouting Earth.

Snake Lady's dark hair was braided in a complex pattern around her head. Her sleeveless wraparound dress was woven in a shimmering and dizzying snakeskin design. And her long and toned arms were decorated with twin snake armbands running from the caps of her shoulders down to the top of her hands, the animal figures crusted in jewels and each sporting bright gems for eyes. The armbands sparkled in the morning sun, and Itza' found her gaze drawn to their jeweled eyes. Itza' remembered the story Grandmother had told her about how Lady Xok had broken Snake Lady's curse. About the snake that had crawled from her mother's belly. A snake with jewels for eyes.

Itza' looked up at the Queen. And Snake Lady stared down at her—her gaze was as cold and impassive as Itza' remembered from childhood, and her eyes were as dark as obsidian. Itza' recognized the color as similar to her own, but whereas Itza's had a shine to them, Snake Lady's were like deep caverns that revealed nothing. They made the Queen's expression nearly impossible to read. Itza' felt her skin crawl and her heart began racing. She had wanted to speak to this woman for so long, and now here she was.

"Please, daughter of Lady Xok, come and join us," Snake Lady ordered. Her voice was strong and commanding with a slight rasp. "Your guards may wait below, but feel free to bring what aides you require."

"Thank you, Honored Queen" Itza' replied, doing her best to put aside the feeling of discomfort Snake Lady's stare and jeweled armbands had given her.

Itza' signaled for her guards to remain but stay alert. She took three aides up with her: Ixcanul, of course, and two older aides sent by Lady Night Star, who were really bodyguards disguised as attendings.

The four women joined the rulers of Sprouting Earth, and Lord Chak Mol led the entire assembly in a long ceremony of greeting and welcoming. He offered many gifts to Itza' and her people—quetzal feathers, jewelry of jade and gems, obsidian mirrors, weavings and pottery, and a wealth of food items found nowhere in Yaxchilan. Itza', in turn, had come laden with numerous similar gifts for the Snake Dynasty and the people of Sprouting Earth. In exchanging gifts, the two parties continued a long tradition among the Winaq that taught them it was better to begin with offerings—by giving as opposed to trying to take or demand.

The process took many hours. Exchange of gifts followed by performance of songs and dance. Itza' was fascinated by the performances and the similarities and differences between her realm and Chak Mol's kingdom.

The sun was low in the sky by the time the ceremonies had ended, and the gathered rulers could begin to talk about why their visitors had come. To start the process, aides brought mats for the nobles, and it was there that they would sit in the open porch area in front of the Council House to discuss politics with Itza'. They were served cacao beverages spiced with chili peppers, and though they gave Itza' space to gather her words, she could tell that many were anxious, if not suspicious, about what this visitor from Yaxchilan might have to offer them.

"Please, Great Lady Itza'," Chak Mol said when they were all seated and ready to begin. "We are excited to hear what you have to say."

Itza' inclined her head. Chak Mol's voice was powerful but nasal and raspy. He was of slender build and darker skin, with somewhat strangely colored eyes that glowed like dark jade in the light. His face was long and narrow, his nose hooked and thin. The long septum piercing that he sported had intricately carved, ancient glyphs. His chin was pierced as well, his teeth inlaid with jade, and his ears were gauged and decorated. And when he smiled at Itza', the widening of his grin seemed impossibly broad, his bright, white teeth merging with the long septum piercing, creating a surreal effect.

Truthfully, Itza' was not sure where to begin her plea for an alliance. The past few hours had revealed much about the inner workings of Sprouting Earth to her, but that had only left her with more questions. Did Chak Mol really rule here? Political power seemed spread over many regional governors and representatives. And Snake Lady clearly still held great influence. Would Itza' need to convince them all? Or just the ajaw?

"Lord Chak Mol," Itza' began, pitching her voice and choosing her words so as to suggest confidence but not arrogance. "Great Snake Lady. Honored council rulers of Sprouting Earth. I am here because my kingdom, and each of our kingdoms in turn, are in danger. Yaxchilan continues to fend off incursions from the Great Army and its Invader allies. But we are only one nation."

"A large nation, though . . ." Snake Lady murmured, but somehow her voice slid perfectly into the pause between Itza's words.

Itza' tried to ignore the interruption and continued. She subtly switched the pacing and tempo of her words to resemble the rhythms and patterns in the epic literature of the Winaq.

"We have seen how smart,
    how clever,
        how effective
your Great Ajaw,
your Great Lord Shield Skull's
plans against the Invaders were.

We have seen how
he made friends

and formed alliances,

    to crush his enemies,

        and uplift his companions."

Itza' paused for a beat, and Snake Lady, again, filled the gap. "You have *seen* much it seems . . ." The words were almost a hiss. But they also managed to imply that Yaxchilan had seen much but done nothing.

Itza' did not respond directly but used the momentum to shift back to what she wanted to say. "We have seen. We have learned. And we have come here to do the same. We have come here to suggest an alliance—"

"Yaxchilan has never been our friend before," Snake Lady interrupted, the soft tones of her voice gone, replaced by the stony walls of a ruler used to being obeyed.

Itza' did not like where this was going. She had hoped to at least be heard, but it seemed the Queen had no intention of taking Itza's words seriously.

It was Chak Mol who chimed in, however. "We will hear our visitor and listen to this offer from a neighbor."

Itza' noticed there were murmurs of agreement from many members of the council, and Itza' hoped they, a least, could see Snake Lady was being unreasonable.

"Please, Lady Itza', continue," Chak Mol said, the timbre of his nasal voice scratching through the air.

"My Lord," Itza' inclined her head. "I have come to offer an alliance between our two kingdoms to face the threats of the Great Army and the Invaders together."

The group erupted in grunts and murmurs. It was not clear to Itza' whether much of it was in favor or not. It seemed to be more a reaction to the incredulity of these two particular kingdoms becoming allies. Comments and questions began at once. The voices flitted around the circle, but it seemed like the questions were not directed at Itza' yet.

"What does Yaxchilan offer for this alliance?"

"Why do they choose now to suggest this?"

"We already dealt with the Invaders. We don't need another war."

It went on for some time, but eventually Chak Mol held up his hand and motioned for silence from the group. However, it was Snake Lady who spoke up to ask her question directly.

"Why should we wish to ally with Yaxchilan?" Her voice carried out across the circle for all to hear. The tone fell on Itza's ears like a slap. Snake Lady somehow managed to make even the name 'Yaxchilan' sound like a curse.

"We have many friends already. We have driven the Invaders from our lands without your help."

Itza' tried to push down the buzzing nervousness in her toes. She tried to look Snake Lady in the eye but found it difficult to hold the woman's gaze.

In response, she said, "You have done much to drive the Invaders away. And as your allies, we would help you continue to face such threats. Surely, however, you can see that if Yaxchilan falls or is captured by the Great Army, our enemies will have a foothold in the eastern lands and a gateway to the mountains in the south."

If Itza's words had any effect on her, Snake Lady did not show it. She simply stared at Itza' with that intense, impassive look in her eyes. Itza' felt more unhinged and uncomfortable under that stare than she was used to feeling. Itza' was used to her gaze causing that feeling in others, but she had no experience in feeling it herself. She didn't like it.

"Perhaps we will drive off the Western Armies as we have driven off the foreign plague," Snake Lady countered.

Itza' felt herself getting off her rhythm because of the Queen. And not just because she had wanted to talk to her for so long. Something about Snake Lady's stare was unnerving. Itza' felt—something . . . uncomfortable in her chest. And she knew she was also getting irritated at the woman's unrelenting antagonism.

"Or perhaps the Great Army would use Yaxchilan as a central

base from which to launch their attacks," Itza' shot back, trying to not let it show that Snake Lady was getting to her.

Another noble spoke up, a younger man who represented some of the businesses and merchants in Sprouting Earth. He was short and stocky, with a rounded face and a quick smile. Itza' had spoken to him earlier and liked the man for his honesty and directness, as well as his love for food.

"How can we be sure Yaxchilan will even be able to fend off this army?" the nobleman said. "Lord Jaguar Paw of the Red City still favors neutrality. Perhaps Yaxchilan should do the same."

But Itza' knew that this would never be an option for Yaxchilan. "We will not give one ear of corn to the New Alliance," she said, her voice loud enough to carry the weight of her authority and pride in her people. "We can only hope the Red City does not become a vine of the spreading gourd that is the Great Army."

"Your words are sharp, daughter of Lady Xok," Snake Lady's voice slithered its way along the ground to where Itza' sat. "But Sprouting Earth will not ally itself with Yaxchilan."

Chak Mol finally spoke up, his nasal voice sneaking into the conversation behind his mother's words. "Respectfully, Mother, I have not yet decided. My father helped our people by proving the value in alliances. We should not ignore his example."

Itza' felt a glimmer of hope. Chak Mol might be open to the idea. How many might follow? From the glances and murmurs, Itza' estimated that less than half the gathered nobles would automatically side with Lord Chak Mol's decision. It was a sad assessment.

"You will rule as you must, Great Ajaw," Snake Lady said, unfazed and as impassive as ever. Her eyes never left Itza', however, and the young lady was beginning to feel a sharp tightness in her chest as she returned her gaze. It felt like some heavy weight was winding around her ribs, gripping them slowly until it threatened to break them. Itza' had to fight not to gasp out loud from the pain.

Snake Lady cast her gaze over the gathered nobility and proclaimed loudly, "But I will never support an alliance with *them*."

Itza's pain vanished the instant Snake Lady looked away. With the pain gone, Itza' was freer to look around and assess the impact of Snake Lady's statement. She compared their reactions to their earlier reaction to Chak Mol, and her heart fell. It was clear to Itza' whose lead they would follow in the way their body language deferred to Snake Lady. If Itza' had any doubts about who really ruled Sprouting Earth, they were dispelled in that moment.

Chak Mol's words broke through Itza's reflections. "As you can see, Lady Itza', this is not an easy decision for us."

Itza' sensed the potential for a double meaning to Chak Mol's statement. Perhaps he needed more time to change her mind. He was her son, after all.

"Of course, my Lord," Itza' said slowly. "It is not a quick decision, and it has been a long day. Perhaps we should speak on it again tomorrow."

The other nobles seemed in favor of this suggestion, as did Chak Mol. Snake Lady seemed unimpressed, but her eyes had softened somewhat and no longer made Itza' feel so uncomfortable.

Itza' decided to add a final thought. "Yaxchilan is a kingdom with plenty, good sirs and ladies. Please let us know if there is anything we might offer that could help prove our value to you as allies."

"You dismiss her offer too easily, Mother," Chak Mol said.

The two were in Snake Lady's private room at the top of the main temple in the city. Snake Lady was sitting on an ornate, stone bed. She reflected on the fact that she had spent many long nights arguing with Chak Mol's father about matters of state in this very chamber.

In fact, both of our sons were made in this room after such arguments, she thought.

"You do not know them as I do," she said intently. "We should sooner slit our own throats than be their allies." Her voice was pure venom—she made no effort to hide her hatred for Yaxchilan. Chak Mol straightened himself in the wooden chair at one end of the room.

"I do not know because you and Father would never tell me, because all records of the reasons for your bitterness are sealed." His voice grew louder as he spoke. He hated the secrets surrounding the feud, and he hated how his mother still acted as if she ruled the kingdom.

"And for good reasons, my son. Trust me on this."

"You know she is right about the Great Army. We may have pushed the Invaders back, but they simply returned to their masters in the west. We only shifted the frontlines of the war to kingdoms like Yaxchilan."

Snake Lady's eyes glinted in the bright light of the partial moon that made its way into the high room. They were a fierce black with sparks of red and yellow as she turned an angry look to her son.

"Your father and I did what we had to in order to protect our people," she shot out at him. Chak Mol saw the anger but did not care. He did not fear upsetting his mother, as many did.

Nevertheless, he found her fury at this visit from Yaxchilan frustrating. And her insistence that she had helped his father turn the tide in their war with the Invaders was puzzling. Chak Mol knew his mother had opposed his father's plans to make alliances. What part had she really played in the war?

"You and Father fought to protect our people," he said, forcing a diplomacy he did not feel. "And now you must let me do the same to keep our people from facing an even greater enemy. My warriors have told me much of the Great Army's evils and its strength. They must be stopped. And we must maintain friendships to do this . . . Mother, I am going to rule in favor of an alliance."

Snake Lady crossed her legs and leaned forward. She pointed one finger at her son, and the jeweled snake on her arm sparkled in the moonlight. "You do not rule alone here. And you have not yet proven yourself to the other earthen kingdoms."

Chak Mol stiffened hearing her words. His mother referred

to the central alliance between Sprouting Earth and the smaller neighboring kingdoms, which also carried Earth in their title: K'an Kab, Chak Kab, and Sak Kab. Together, with Sprouting Earth, Yellow, Red, and White Earth comprised a set of closely affiliated nations that had maintained tight political connections. Sprouting Earth was the largest among them, and they looked to its ruler for stability in the region. They had followed Lord Shield Skull during his reign, but Chak Mol knew that they were still assessing how to react to the change in leadership.

"The earthen kingdoms follow us because they remain loyal to *me*," Snake Lady continued, her finger driving home the point of her words. It seemed the snake head on her hand was threatening to leap out and bite at Chak Mol if he did not heed her message. "Without my support, those alliances could be severely weakened."

Chak Mol was incredulous. "You cannot jeopardize our whole kingdom over this feud between you and Lady Xok!" He slammed a fist on the table beside the chair he was using. Snake Lady remembered how often his father had done the same thing.

Infuriated by his mother's stubborn refusal to let go of the past, Chak Mol got up and walked over to one of the open windows. The moon was not yet full, but it was bright, and the silvery light shone over all of Sprouting Earth from his vantage point. Chak Mol thought about his people down there below, about the citizens who were his children and what their fate might be if kingdoms like Yaxchilan fell to the Great Army. He felt a terrible sadness at what such a future might bring for them.

Snake Lady remained seated on her bed. Despite her external anger, inside she was relatively calm. She knew, of course, that she could never risk their alliances with the earthen kingdoms just to spite her son. But she wanted to make sure he did not forget how much her words and decisions influenced the course of events in their realm.

What she was really interested in was Lady Itza', this strange daughter of Lady Xok that had been sent on what seemed an impossible mission. The girl had stood up to the pressure of Snake Lady's fierce gaze, which was almost unheard of. She had kept her cool under the Queen's pressure.

And she had the eyes, Snake Lady saw, recognizing at once the source of the nearly black irises Itza' possessed and what that might mean. But did Lady Xok's daughter know what that meant? Or what power she possessed?

Based on what she had seen, Snake Lady doubted it.

It seemed her son's mind was also turned toward the young Lady from Yaxchilan. Looking over his shoulder, he said, "Besides, I trust the words of their messenger. Lady Itza' is . . . intelligent and convincing."

Snake Lady smirked. She was not surprised at her son's reaction.

"Perhaps that is why they sent her to us," she said. "They knew she would catch your eye, my son, and make you receptive to her words." Though the Queen also wondered if Yaxchilan was trying to hint at a different way to cement an alliance between them by sending Lord 5-Thunder's youngest unmarried daughter.

She had to admit that a more permanent alliance might heal the rift between their two kingdoms. The Queen found herself reflecting on the implications, a set of possibilities forming in her mind.

"I think they sent her because they knew you would have tried to kill Lady Xok or Lord 5-Thunder," Chak Mol said in response.

Snake Lady smiled. "Anything is possible."

Snake Lady saw in Itza' the potential for a powerful ally or a horrible enemy to contend with. And to be an ally, she would need something to anchor that alliance. Snake Lady reached her decision almost instantly. She needed time with Itza', time to learn who the girl really was and to decide what to do with her.

"We cannot rush this decision, my son," Snake Lady said.

"Then let us invite them to stay," he offered, which was exactly what Snake Lady wanted. "Give Lady Itza' time to change your mind, eh?"

Snake Lady nodded in agreement. Let us see if Lady Xok's daughter is what I believe she is . . . and whether she can survive my tests.

A Bitter Drink

No one knows where I came from. One day, I just appeared. The silent killer of men. I am like the shadow that haunts your dreams. The woman on whom all things are blamed. I am the ash grey face of death.

—Xelaq'am's Songs

"I MUST ADMIT, GREAT PUMA, I find your offer surprising," Lord Jaguar Paw said as he sipped his beverage. He sat opposite Chanil and Ch'akanel in the center of the canopied area. Other members of his court milled about or stood and watched the meeting between the trio. Chanil and Ch'akanel sat on simple wooden chairs, and Jaguar Paw ordered for drinks to be poured for everyone. And then, to Chanil's continued annoyance, for over an hour, they listened to the man deny any connection to the war around him.

"And why should we not be closer allies, Lord?" Chanil asked. She was tired of the political banter and insincere tones. She asked the question flatly and directly, looking Jaguar Paw in his eyes and never touching her drink.

"Allies for what purpose, Lady?" the Ajaw asked, his tone perpetually locked in feigned ignorance, as though they had not spent hours talking already, as though he had only just learned that there was some strange conflict going on around him. His eyes continued to dart around as he spoke.

"We trade openly with Yaxchilan—and all others!" He made a point of saying the last part loud enough for all to hear. "And we will continue to do so. Our exchanges have always been most . . . profitable."

Chanil gritted her teeth. Something about Jaguar Paw's tone made her skin crawl. And she had noticed how his eyes lingered on her aide, K'utalik, as the man had said 'profitable.'

"Lord Jaguar Paw," Chanil began slowly, forcing her voice into a calm state. "We are talking about the continued incursions of the Great Army. They threaten our borders and our people. Surely, your kingdom would be safer if we stood together to hold this enemy back."

The Ajaw took a long sip of his drink, pursing his lips and twisting his face when he finished. "There are no incursions here," he said flatly.

Chanil shook her head. "I know you have vowed neutrality, but the Great Army continues to raid and pillage—"

"There are *no* incursions here, my Lady," Jaguar Paw interrupted, his voice oddly cold.

Ch'akanel could sense the tension bubbling between the two leaders and opted to jump in before Chanil could say anything.

"Hmmm!" he exclaimed loudly, looking at his cup intently. "I must say, Lord, the drinks here are . . . delicious. I don't think I've ever tasted one quite like this."

Instantly, Jaguar Paw's face changed, his smile returned, and his posture softened. Chanil saw, however, that the anger in his eyes never really went away.

"An excellent observation, general!" Jaguar Paw exclaimed. "You must have quite the discerning palette. Perhaps *you* can explain it to them, my dear?"

Jaguar Paw directed that last part at K'utalik, and he had indicated that with an unnecessarily condescending gesture. Chanil and Ch'akanel traded confused glances, but K'utalik simply smiled and bowed her head.

"Of course, my Lord. It is an ancient recipe from my grandmother's village . . . they are the only ones who still make it this way."

Jaguar Paw beamed at her, and Chanil felt sick. His grin was like a mask of death painted over brutal anger. "I knew it! I can always tell . . . when someone is from there."

"My Lord has a discerning eye," K'utalik said without missing a beat. The smile on her face seemed absolutely genuine, though Chanil doubted any woman's smile could be genuine with Lord Jaguar Paw.

"I can always tell," Jaguar Paw repeated, this time more slowly. "The women there roast their cacao beans in a particular way," he began explaining the drink himself, despite having asked K'utalik to do it.

"And they cultivate the most flavorful chiles in the whole region. And the powder from these chiles is what makes the drink, wouldn't you say, girl?"

"You have studied much about our traditions, my Lord," K'utalik replied. "I am happy our drink pleases you." Of course, she could tell Jaguar Paw really had no idea how her people made the drink. But she also knew that he would hear in her words exactly what he already wanted to hear.

"I have been fortunate to have some servants, from time to time, from that village," Jaguar Paw said, looking at Chanil. "They really do make the best cacao. Ixtux! Come forward!"

Within seconds, a young lady appeared. She inclined her head to the gathered royals but did not speak. She had a demure and submissive posture, but Chanil thought the girl might be acting.

"This is my servant, I call her Ixtux. She is from your village, girl," Jaguar Paw said to K'utalik. "Perhaps you know each other?"

"I know her family, my Lord," K'utalik said, bowing her head.

"I knew it! Please—go and talk together. Perhaps you can make this wonderful drink for your Lady here one day."

"Thank you, my Lord," K'utalik said, and the two aides moved off to the side, just out of ear shot.

"I know they miss their homes terribly," Jaguar Paw said as they left. "I want to make sure Ixtux is happy here. Now—" Jaguar Paw took a long gulp and finished his drink, "—you were offering me your skills as a warrior in exchange for helping to protect Yaxchilan, is that right?"

Ch'akanel was about to speak, but Chanil held up a hand. "No, good sir," she said bluntly. "We are here to help build an alliance between our kingdoms to help hold back the Great Army."

"But I have no quarrel with the Great Army—or anyone," Jaguar Paw said, his voice perfectly innocent. "We are at peace here in the Red City. We are neutral."

"And yet you would like to employ our services as warriors, as you said, Lord," Ch'akanel offered.

Jaguar Paw smiled his death grimace again. "Well, there are always . . . security issues in a large trading area such as this. We can always use some helpful sword hands. We would lend some of our own to Yaxchilan as well, of course. To help put down whatever small issues you are having."

It was a pointless offer. Chanil laughed, and everyone could see Jaguar Paw did not like being laughed at.

"Yaxchilan does not need unskilled thugs," Chanil shot back, looking pointedly at the security guards around Jaguar Paw. Jaguar Paw opened his mouth, but Chanil would not let him speak.

"You have seen the Great Army—you have heard what they do to the towns and kingdoms they take over. Yaxchilan will never meet that fate."

Chanil stood up, stepping forward to stand tall over Jaguar Paw. Before he could rise up, she clapped her hand down on his shoulder, smiling in mock friendship. She felt him try to stand, but her force was too powerful for him to be able to even budge.

"Tell me, Great Ajaw," Chanil whispered so only Jaguar Paw could hear her. "How much is the New Alliance paying you for your supposed neutrality?"

Chanil removed her hand, and Jaguar Paw sprang to his feet.

The two stood face-to-face. Jaguar Paw's eyes burned with a raging fire that told Chanil, in no uncertain terms, that the man would have killed her if he could. In contrast, Chanil's face was a calm mask of confidence. She smirked and handed Jaguar Paw her still-full cup.

"Enjoy this drink while you can!" She turned as she spoke, shouting out for all those gathered to hear.

"This drink comes from our lands!" She pointed at the full cup in Jaguar Paw's hands as she carved a circle around the space to face each of those gathered around them.

"It comes from the villages of Yaxchilan. It is ancient knowledge! If the Great Army comes through our realm, they will leave none alive who remembers how to make it!" She turned back to face Jaguar Paw.

"They will leave you with nothing of your history or the teachings of your elders. They will kill your leaders and burn your books. Your language will be outlawed, and your children taken as slaves!"

The crowd was unsettled and unsure of how to react to Chanil's words. "So, drink up, good sir," she said, pointing at the cup. "There may not be many sips left of it for you."

Chanil left with Ch'akanel and K'utalik before Jaguar Paw could respond.

The group made their way out of the Red City. They wound through the streets and avenues and out past the defensive wall of the inner city. Almost everyone was nervous, except Chanil.

"Relax, friends. No need to hurry. If they kill us, all of Yaxchilan goes to war," she told them as she strode through the broad avenues with calm and deliberate steps.

"I think it's only if they kill *you*, Puma, that Yaxchilan goes to war," Ch'akanel pointed out. "The rest of us are expendable."

"Not to me you're not," Chanil said. "To kill any of you, they'll have to kill me, yeah?"

Still, the group made an efficient path out of the city. It was late morning when they reached the edge of the outer stretches of the Red City. From there, they made their way to the docks and bought passage on a large ferry traveling downriver to the Great Lake. The Lake was a way station for anyone and everyone traveling across the eastern lands. From there, a person could go anywhere.

The Lake was its own city, in a way. No ajaw or kingdom ruled those waters. There were ferries that took people to all corners of their world. The routes to the pilgrimage sites on the Peninsula were especially popular. Large, floating barges were anchored throughout the Lake, providing travelers with overnight lodging and unique markets.

The ferry holding Chanil and her group took them to shore along the easternmost embankment of the Lake. There, the group travelled farther inland just as darkness descended upon them. They made camp just off a main road heading east, away from the Lake.

Chanil waited until nearly everyone was asleep to pull Nimaq and K'utalik aside and speak to them privately. K'utalik's soft eyes were wide with concern. Nimaq grumbled sleepily and leaned against a tall tree.

Chanil handed K'utalik a piece of paper. The young girl took it with a puzzled expression. "What is it, my Lady?"

"Instructions. It's signed so that the warriors will know it's genuine. And Nimaq here will be able to say he heard it himself."

Nimaq grunted. "Why do I get the impression I'm not going to like what's coming, Puma?

Chanil grinned. "Because you're no fool, old man. Did Night Star give you any instructions when she ordered you to come with me on this mission?"

He nodded slowly and twisted his face. "I should have guessed something was up. She said to follow your lead no matter how strange or odd your directions might be, my Lady."

"Good," Chanil said flatly. Then she turned to K'utalik. "Did you really recognize the girl that Jaguar Paw made you speak to?"

"I did, my Lady," she replied gently. "She is another of your sister's spies."

Chanil's eyes went wide for only a moment. "She is the one my sister told me about, then."

"Yes, my Lady. But we have not heard from her in some time. I would have arranged a meeting between you two but . . . well . . ."

"But I cut our visit a bit short, eh?" Chanil laughed, and K'utalik smiled.

"She and I did not get to talk as long as I had hoped, no."

Chanil realized then that she might have missed out on a valuable chance to learn whatever information Itza's spy had gathered during her time in the Red City.

Perhaps I should have kept a cooler head, Chanil thought, though she doubted she would have been able to stomach Lord Jaguar Paw much longer. She added it to the list of things in her life that her big mouth had interfered with.

"Nimaq, I need you to guide everyone back to Yaxchilan. Those are my orders."

He sighed heavily. "And why would you not be guiding them yourself, Great Puma?"

"Because I have to continue on with a different mission. But that's all I can say."

Nimaq growled and nodded. Chanil could tell he didn't like it, but he had already committed to obeying. K'utalik, on the other hand, seemed excited.

"Where are we going, my Lady?"

Chanil shook her head. "I need you to go with Nimaq and the others."

She held up a hand when K'utalik started to speak. "You were there at the Red City, and you, alone, spoke with my sister's spy. I need you to tell Itza' what happened. Give her whatever information you can."

K'utalik bowed her head. "My Lady, wherever you are going, I can help you."

"Don't bother, little one," Nimaq said roughly. "I know that look. Puma has made up her mind."

Feeling a wave of sharp sadness suddenly grip her, Chanil crossed to Nimaq and embraced him tightly. He seemed stunned for a second and unsure of what to do with his hands. Then Chanil pulled back and looked at him.

"You've never let me down before, old man," she said, pushing down the tears that wanted to come through. "Make sure everyone gets back safe to my sister, okay ?"

"I wish I were going with you, Great Puma. But if you need a babysitter, I'll happily play the part."

She gave K'utalik a hug, too. "Tell Itza' everything, little one. You've been so much help."

"I will, my Lady. We will see each other again soon, I promise!"

Chanil ordered them back to the camp then. She felt tears stinging her eyes as she watched them leave, a wave of guilt washing over her for what she was about to do. She knew Nimaq would deliver her orders, and K'utalik had her instructions. But she felt like a coward sneaking away in the night and abandoning her people during a time of war.

She placed a hand on her stomach and thought of the little one growing there. She had to protect her baby no matter what. But to leave her home? To sneak off in the dark like some thief? Without intending to, she fell to her knees. Her body shook, and she choked back the sobs that suddenly gripped her.

She felt the heavy weight of all her decisions in that moment. Of all the times she had pissed people off or thrown herself into dangerous situations. Of all the battles she had fought knowing a baby grew inside her. And now, leaving her kingdom at this moment because she couldn't risk her stupid choices impacting their family's chances for alliance or her father looking weaker when he needed to win a war.

She felt her stomach heave, and she threw up. She gripped the jungle floor tightly and tried to puke out all the stupid things she had ever done. When it was over, she wiped her mouth and forced herself back to her feet.

Her mother had told her it was the time for difficult choices. And she had been right. But Chanil reminded herself that this was the path they had decided on. There was no turning back now. By now, she knew, Ch'akanel would be waiting by the road. Chanil needed to get her shit together, walk out onto that road, and find a boat to take them to the Island. That was her mission now. Protect her baby.

She took one last look at the bright fires from the camp where her warriors and aides were sleeping. She said a silent prayer for them and for Yaxchilan. Then she turned toward the road and walked off. She knew it would be a long time before she saw any of her friends or her lands again.

Inside the Ts'onot

Kneel at the water's edge. Look down into that clear pool. What do you see? A reflection of your face, a poor imitation? Sometimes I wonder if that is the real me. And this life I live, maybe this is the reflection, the imitation.

—collected sayings from the Book of Itza'

SNAKE LADY OBSERVED ITZA' and her delegation for multiple moons. She saw how the young lady from Yaxchilan maneuvered through political and social landscapes, how she changed her tone and words to make her suggestions more appealing to whomever she spoke to, and how the girl dove into the documents and histories Snake Lady had given her access to.

Snake Lady particularly noted that Itza' would spend the end of each day with the common people. She watched Itza's group walk through the markets again from her vantage point on top of one of the central temples of her kingdom.

Snake Lady sniffed the air and thought she could separate the scents of her own people from those that Itza' had brought from Yaxchilan. The visitors came from farther west. Their lands were slightly drier and the soil less inundated by limestone. All these facts left traces on their boots that Snake Lady had detected during their long council meetings.

Itza' and her people also lived in places with different fruit trees and different ways of preparing cacao and chiles. It impacted the way they smelled, how they tasted the foods here, and what they bought and rejected at the markets.

Snake Lady watched it all, assessing everything. She was certain that Itza' was intent on making the people here love her.

Snake Lady surmised that the people of Sprouting Earth had good reason to like this newcomer from Yaxchilan, too. Itza' made a point of helping families out, of using her wealth and power in ways that benefited the community, even helping to settle local disputes when incidents happened.

Snake Lady wondered about Itza's fool of a father and whether he realized what potential his youngest daughter held. She saw in Itza' the possibility of a powerful queen—if only she weren't the second born. Watching the people below, Snake Lady smiled to herself at that thought. Yaxchilan's loss would be her gain.

She thought of the plan she had in mind. A plan to benefit her own kingdom and ensure her son had a stable legacy after she was gone. Snake Lady was going to arrange a marriage between her son and Lady Itza' in exchange for supporting the alliance with Yaxchilan.

A scuffing sound reached the Queen's ears. It came from behind her, from one of the doorways that led up to the top of the temple on which she stood. From the patterns in the footfalls that approached her, Snake Lady knew it was her son, Chak Mol, no doubt coming to check on her. From the mix of smells, she could tell he carried two drinks for them and that he had recently exerted himself.

"Still spying I see." Chak Mol's odd voice scratched across the stones to reach Snake Lady's ears.

She half turned and said, "If I had spies, you would never know . . . a fact I think this young noble who visits us is aware of."

Chak Mol came to stand beside his mother and handed her

a cup filled with their favorite evening drink—cacao mixed with honey and flower petals. The Queen took it gently from her son's hand, but never looked away from the metropolis below.

That evening, Snake Lady wore a skintight wraparound dress that left her shoulders and arms bare. It was patterned in ancient symbols that she doubted anyone else could read anymore, besides the priests. Uncharacteristically, her jeweled snake armbands were absent. Apparently, the creatures had been sent off on some secret mission, and Snake Lady was left without their protection in that moment.

"You think Itza' knows you spy on her?" Chak Mol asked, trying to figure out his mother's earlier comment.

"I think she may be the one who sent spies to infiltrate our court over the past few years," Snake Lady answered. She took a small sip of the liquid, letting the sweet aroma of the honey float across her nostrils. For a moment, the intensity of it was enough to block out the torrent of smells from the city below. But, only for a moment.

Chak Mol made a dismissive gesture. "You would blame Lady Itza' for the sun not rising if you could, Honored Queen." His tone was unmistakably bitter. He had grown tired of his mother's constant prodding and antagonism against their visitors.

Snake Lady chuckled. "Her lineage is powerful . . . perhaps she *can* cause an eclipse!"

"Mother," he began, "It is clear to me that you have good intentions. I know you love our people and want what is best for them. But is anything that Lady Itza' has said these past few winals untrue? She is right about the threat of the Great Army and the need to hold positions like Yaxchilan from them."

Snake Lady eyed her son over the brim of her cup. Her black, obsidian eyes flashed with streaks of yellow and white, like distant lightning seen through a storm cloud. Chak Mol swallowed, feeling the tightness in his chest that accompanied that look from his mother. But he did not stop himself from speaking. He was the Ajaw after all. He ruled here, not Snake Lady.

"And look at what she has done since being here," Chak Mol continued, looking away from his mother and out over the city, gesturing with his arms as he spoke. "She supports our merchants, learns our language, helps our people . . . she plays every bit the part of friend and good relative, Mother. You must see this."

Snake Lady took a slightly longer sip than usual. "I see that she appeals to you, my son."

"Not this again."

It was Snake Lady's turn for a dismissive gesture. "There is no harm in it, my son. She has great beauty. But you cannot let it blind you."

Chak Mol turned fully to face his mother and look her in the eye. Although he stood nearly a head taller than her and was adorned with a giant headdress, Chak Mol still felt as if he were facing a legion of deadly warriors from the underworld as he forced himself to stare into the glossy, black caverns of Snake Lady's eyes.

"Perhaps it is *you* who are blinded—blinded by this ancient feud that no longer matters—"

"It matters to me," she said flatly.

"The war matters more. The future of all our peoples depends on what we do here. And I will not have the pride of one ruler rob us of an opportunity to safeguard our future on these lands!"

To his surprise, Snake Lady actually smiled. "Your kingdom will need more of that fire, my son, if we are to survive this conflict."

Did she mean the war or the conflict surrounding the decision to ally with Yaxchilan? Chak Mol decided his mother probably meant both. It was not an easy thing for the Winaq to form alliances. His father, Ajaw Shield Skull, had been adamant about it, and it had proved successful. But many were still weary of permanent alliances. It was a fact that their enemies constantly leveraged to pit different kingdoms against each other.

". . . But I still do not trust her," Snake Lady said, turning back to look out over the city. She saw that Itza' and her group had disappeared.

Chak Mol grunted in frustration. "You are immovable, Great Queen. Lady Itza' is a good person. We will need allies like that."

Snake Lady did not respond but was secretly pleased. Her plan was moving as she had hoped. Her son had become a man who wanted to assert his power but had not yet decided how best to do so. Positioning herself in opposition to Lady Itza' would only serve to make the girl more attractive to her son, who wanted to be rid of the overwhelming power his mother still held in the kingdom. If she drove him into Itza's arms, he would never realize he simply traded one mother for another.

"You might be right, my son," Snake Lady said before finishing her drink abruptly. She turned to head back down the temple. "Perhaps I should go and speak with Lady Itza' alone and resolve this conflict between us."

Snake Lady slipped into the growing shadows of the night, leaving her son to puzzle over his mother's true intentions.

The Winaq called them ts'onot—underground caverns and rivers that ran beneath the surface of the limestone bedrock that formed the Peninsula. Yaxchilan had few of them. But Sprouting Earth lay at the southern edge of the Peninsula and had many within its realm. Snake Lady brought Itza' to one at the outskirts of the city that night.

Itza' could hear the dripping of water, the way sounds echoed off the smooth walls. The ts'onot were sacred to her people. They provided water, yes, but they also connected to the underworld realm, to the lands of the dead and the lords of death. Ts'onot were both givers of life and powerful connections to death.

Snake Lady stood beside Itza' at the edge of the underground lake inside the ts'onot. Torches lit the area, casting chaotic shadows.

"Why did you bring me here, Great Queen?" Itza' asked. She had been given no reason for the summons by Snake Lady's messenger. So far, the two had passed their time in awkward silence.

Snake Lady grinned and turned toward Itza'. As she stared into the stormy depths of Snake Lady's eyes, Itza' felt a curious sensation. A tingling started somewhere deep and low in her spine, near where it curved from her back to her hips. And then the sensation radiated outward. It grew stronger as it spread, climbing and growing. It was a damp and heavy weight. Then it came, coiling and wrapping around her torso as it wound its way upward toward her chest. As it reached the level of her lungs, she felt a sudden urge to cough and had to fight against the demands of her body to suppress the impulse.

Snake Lady saw the effort, the small involuntary twitches of Itza's throat and chest. Itza' was captured by the look in the older woman's eyes. She felt as though she could not tear her gaze away from them even if she had wanted to. The tightening feeling in her chest grew, and now, Itza' felt it rising upward to her throat. A heavy, crushing tightness worked its way around the young girl's windpipe, and she found she could no longer swallow. Breathing became more difficult.

Itza' wanted to run or to cry out in pain. She wanted to flee from Snake Lady. Her body screamed at her to leave the underground ts'onot, to climb the damp and slippery stone steps back up to the surface, gather her friends and warriors, and run all the way back home to Yaxchilan.

But something told her that would be a mistake, that she had to endure this strange test. Pushing aside every instinct to escape, Itza' stayed there. She did her best to return the impassive stare and ride out the tempest brewing in the black eyes that held Itza' captive. Even as she felt her windpipe close to a mere slit, barely enough room remaining to sustain her breathing, Itza' forced herself to return her own cold, dark stare.

Itza' saw a gentle smile finally cross the older woman's face. Snake Lady blinked for, what Itza' realized, might be the first time since they had come into the ts'onot, and Itza' felt the last of the tightness vanish. She gasped and took a deep inhale. The pain that had gripped her slithered away into a nothingness, as sudden and as strange as its initial arrival.

"Tell me, daughter of Lady Xok," Snake Lady broke the silence as she knelt over the underground pool. "Do you understand the powers you possess?"

Itza' was not entirely sure she knew which powers Snake Lady referred to, but she sensed the older woman did not mean the political power afforded by her lineage. "You mean the effect my gaze can have on people? The way yours seems to also . . ."

Snake Lady rose up to stand and face the younger woman. "You cannot control it yet."

Itza' just nodded. She felt vulnerable in that moment and despised the feeling. She had waited for so long to speak to Snake Lady, and so far, their interactions had been disappointing to say the least. The woman was arrogant, stubborn, and fearsome all at once. But as much as she wanted to scream every time the Queen ripped apart her arguments for an alliance in court, Itza' couldn't help but admire her.

Snake Lady leaned forward and held her lips a hair's breadth from Itza's ear.

"I couldn't control it either, little one . . . at first," she whispered.

Then Snake Lady pulled away and sat herself down on a large, flat rock nearby. She gazed out over the water of the ts'onot. The twin snake arm bands, returned from their secret missions, glistened as they reflected the water's light along their wearer's arms. Itza' found herself wondering what to make of Snake Lady.

"I may not be able to control it as you can, Honored Queen," Itza' began formally, "But I have learned to use them, to leverage my skills—"

Snake Lady held up a dismissive hand. "Save the speeches for court," she said flatly. Turning her gaze toward Itza', she commanded, "Tell me about the time when you first used your power."

Itza' knew from her time at Sprouting Earth that Snake Lady was used to being obeyed and feared when she issued commands. But Itza' was still unsure what game was being played out here between the two women.

"I am not yours to command, Noble Lady."

"Hmmmmmmm," Snake Lady hummed, and it seemed like the stones caught her tone and vibrated in return. A low echo flowed throughout the underground chamber in response.

"And all that scheming in Yaxchilan has blinded you from recognizing friend from foe, little one, eh? Not sure who you can even trust anymore..."

"Are you my friend, Snake Lady? Or my foe? Your ajaw never visits, and I know you distrust my mother."

"Hah!" The sudden cackle echoed loudly off the cavernous, stone walls. "You know *nothing* of Lady Xok and I's history. Perhaps in time...but not here. Tell me, little one, have you ever met anyone else with your eyes? Or mine?"

Itza' wondered, again, what game was being played here. She realized she would never find out unless she played along. She decided on an honest response to Snake Lady's question.

"Once—a visitor from the southern highlands—"

"A woman?" Snake Lady interrupted abruptly.

Itza' shifted slightly. "Yes—an older woman. A noble from one of the kingdoms deep in the south."

"And did you speak to her, little one? Did you gaze into her eyes as you have gazed into mine?"

Itza' pondered the question for a moment. She had not thought back to that old woman in a long time. The memory of the strange, noble visitor from the highlands was faded and dusty, covered by more recent memories of war and scheming, and the fog of childhood.

"I...don't remember," she said. "I was very young. I just remember they were like yours—black and shimmering and intense. She radiated power, that old woman. I think even my father feared her."

Snake Lady smiled at that. "Your father fears more things than he lets on, little one."

Itza's eyes shot up at Snake Lady. "You know my father, don't you?"

"Mmmm," was all the response Snake Lady gave, but she nodded her head in confirmation. "Now, little one, will you tell me about the first time you used your powers?"

Itza' paused for a moment. And then relented. "I was seven years old," she began. "My father had sent me to study with the priests in one of our temples. He wanted me to learn the old writing system so that I could read our ancient texts."

Itza' used a phrase for the writing system in her language that indicated the ancient, religious writing system that was rich in metaphors and hidden meanings that took years to learn. The Queen nodded solemnly.

"A good thing for a young lady to know," she said softly.

Itza' nodded in return. "I have always found it useful. One day, a priest refused to let me see some text—he said it wasn't appropriate for a young girl. Maybe he was right. But I was young and stubborn, and I hated secrets. I stared at him and asked him to let me see it. Again, he refused. I felt . . . annoyed. But also, something else. Something . . ."

"Like a storm underneath your skin?" Snake Lady offered.

"I—yes . . . I think so, maybe. Something inside that wanted to come out. I just stared at the man, letting that deep, strange feeling take over. It felt like a giant shadow—no, like a deep, black cloak covering me, giving me a confidence no seven-year-old should have. I didn't say anything, but the priest couldn't turn away. Eventually, he surrendered. He gave me the paper and muttered something as he walked away."

"And after that?" Snake Lady prompted.

Itza' was lost in the memory now, retracing the steps her younger self had taken, as if reliving the experience again for the first time.

"After that . . . he was different with me. He never quite looked at me the same way. But I don't think he ever said anything to the others or to my father."

Snake Lady cackled again in the echoey chamber. "And let them all know that a little girl had terrified him? I should think not."

Itza' felt guilty suddenly. "Terrified him? Is that what you think I did?"

"Men in power are particularly . . . vulnerable to this kind of thing. You shamed him, certainly."

"That wasn't my intention," Itza' replied softly.

Snake Lady caught the tone of guilt in the young woman's voice.

"You were a child, little one. You did nothing to feel guilty over. It would have been better if someone had taught you about these things at that age. Still, your strength now is . . . surprising, given you had no teachers."

"And who were your teachers, Great Queen?" Itza's tone had more than a hint of sarcasm to it. The older lady smirked but did not rise to the barb.

"I was taught by an old woman . . . She took pity on me and showed me how to use my powers. She saved my life by doing so."

"And are you offering to be my teacher now, Great Snake Lady?" Itza' asked eagerly.

Snake Lady stood and crossed over to stand before Itza'. "Would you be a worthy student, I wonder? And how would empowering the daughter of Lady Xok impact my own kingdom later on?"

Itza' felt her jaw clench at the mention of her mother. She was used to people having nothing but respect—or at least a healthy fear—of her family and the power of Yaxchilan. But in the mouth of Snake Lady, her mother's name became almost a curse. It stirred a powerful, impulsive anger within Itza'.

"I am not your enemy, Honored Queen," Itza' spoke the words slowly and deliberately, doing her best to not show the anger.

Snake Lady simply smiled. "So now you can recognize friend from foe, eh?"

"I have come all this way to seek an alliance with you. Why would I do that if I were your enemy?"

Snake Lady eyed the younger woman carefully. She found herself growing to like this younger daughter of Lady Xok, despite her best efforts. Perhaps she could be the one to heal the rift between the two kingdoms.

"Very well, daughter of Lady Xok," Snake Lady said, her mind cementing the plan that would serve both Sprouting Earth and Yaxchilan. "I will teach you of your powers, and I will judge your proposed alliance based on how you are as my student."

Itza' scoffed. "You would decide the fate of an entire kingdom based on how I study?"

"You were sent here to build an alliance, no? You, *alone*, were sent. Clearly, your family believes I should weigh this alliance based solely on your words and actions, then, eh?"

Itza' could not find a way around that logic. "And what must I do, then, to secure this alliance? Master my powers?"

Snake Lady smiled strangely, an almost menacing grimace spreading across her features. Her black eyes sparkled again in the dim chamber. "If only that were all I required of you, little one," she said, laughing. And the cackles echoed off the rocky walls of the ts'onot.

The Island

The first time I stepped onto the Island, I knew I had come home. Not like Yaxchilan wasn't home, too. But something had always been missing, I guess? Incomplete, maybe. When we crossed the Sea and came to the lands of your grandmother, little one, I finally understood what my spirit had been searching for all these years.

—*excerpt from the alleged Diary of Lady Chanil*

THE WOMAN EYED CHANIL with an expression that somehow conveyed both deep suspicion and utter disdain. She leaned one arm across the doorway of the hut, blocking the entrance. Her generous lips were pursed as she looked Chanil over carefully.

Chanil sighed in frustration.

"Please, good lady," she said for what felt like the four thousandth time. "I am your cousin. My mother is Lady Night Star."

Just like every other time she had said this, Chanil didn't see any reaction from the old woman at Night Star's name. Chanil was doing her best to speak the language of the Ayiti, but she gathered she wasn't doing a good job of it. The old woman mumbled something under her breath, but Chanil could barely make out any distinct sounds, let alone understand the words.

Chanil looked back over her shoulder at Ch'akanel behind her. He shrugged. They had been standing in front of this hut for what felt like hours without progress. Chanil's attempts at conversation were getting nowhere.

"Maybe this isn't the right place?" he offered. Chanil sighed again, realizing there was probably only one way to find out.

So, even though it was a risk if this wasn't the right home, she reached into her bag and pulled out the blanket. The one she had been wrapped up in as a baby. The one Night Star had given her. She held it up for the old woman in the doorway.

The woman's face changed instantly. A huge, bright smile lit up her features. Her eyes went wide, and she looked at Chanil as though Chanil had just materialized in front of her in that moment.

"It can't be! I don't believe it." The old woman touched the blanket lightly, gingerly. Then she frowned again and pointed.

"Flip it over," she said tersely. Then, when Chanil look confused, she repeated her words more slowly and gestured.

"Flip . . . it . . . over."

Chanil obliged. The woman ruffled through the folds, eyeing Chanil suspiciously the whole time. Clearly she was looking for something, but what it was, Chanil had no idea. Then the woman stopped at one corner of the blanket, where a spiral design had been embroidered with lettering between the lines of the spiral. Chanil had no idea what that spiral signified, but the woman's eyes got wider seeing it.

"It is you!" She smiled again and pulled on Chanil's arm. "Get in here before somebody see you!"

That was how Chanil met her mother's cousin—her cousin. The one who was supposedly going to keep them safe until Chanil gave birth.

In the two-room hut, the woman sat Chanil down at the table in the center of the main room. She made a big show of wiping off the table and the stool before guiding Chanil to her seat. Then the woman smiled and patted Chanil's large baby bump. It was definitely not something Chanil could hide anymore. She brought another stool for Ch'akanel.

Then the woman sat down opposite Chanil and slumped her head into her hand. She smiled. "Let me see that blanket again."

Chanil grinned and handed it over. She also showed the woman the necklace Night Star had given her on her first menstrual cycle. The old woman almost fainted seeing that. She held it up to the light and rubbed the smooth edges. She looked at it as though expecting it to transform into a poisonous snake at any moment before she seemed to finally decide that everything Chanil had brought her was genuine and that, therefore, Chanil was her kin.

The woman slapped her hands on the table. "Who is your mother, girl?"

Chanil looked at Ch'akanel. His expression clearly told her that he was relying on her to steer them through this. But she could barely understand the words the older woman was saying. Chanil sighed and decided to answer honestly. "Lady Night Star," she said in her best attempt at speaking the language of the Ayiti as her mother had taught her.

The old woman narrowed her eyes and leaned in. "Who is your mother?"

Chanil realized her mistake. "Koeia," she said flatly. And the old woman nodded.

"You are lucky that you look just like her. That accent—we will work on that." And the old woman laughed.

"Now, do you know who I am, hm?" Her tone was playful and intense at the same time. Her voice was deep but almost musical. Even though Chanil had learned some of the Ayiti's language from Night Star, the woman in the hut was hard to understand. She spoke so fast, and her words seemed to melt together until Chanil heard nothing but a jumble of vaguely familiar sounds. Could these really be her people too?

Chanil remembered what Night Star had told her to say. "Koeia's favorite cousin?"

"Ha!" The laugh was sharp and short.

Just then, the door to the hut swung open, and a young woman with a baby bump even larger than Chanil's waddled in. Chanil was struck by how beautiful the woman was. She had a long face and wide cheekbones with full lips and a broad nose. Her eyes were an intense, light brown, and they were fixed on Chanil and Ch'akanel with that same suspicious expression the older woman's had held.

The newcomer launched into a conversation with the older woman, and Chanil was hopelessly lost. She couldn't follow any of it. They went back and forth, interrupting each other. Gestures came and went. Chanil—her belly—the blanket—the sky. It went on for some time.

Then, abruptly, it ended, and the newcomer plopped down next to Ch'akanel. She looked him up and down and then turned to Chanil. In words that must have seemed painfully slow to her, she said, "You are Koeia's daughter?"

Chanil nodded.

The woman made a gesture Chanil had never seen then pointed emphatically at herself. "I'm Yahíma. We cousins."

She leaned back and rubbed her belly. She smiled, and Chanil wondered if everyone in the family had big smiles. "Our babies be cousins too, eh?"

Chanil smiled back. Even though she was far from the lands she knew and the language she was used to, somehow, she felt better than she had in a long time. For no reason she could explain, these two women felt like family. Even if she had never met them before.

"Well, are you going to tell us *your* name, girl?" the older woman said in that intense but playful tone. Chanil thought she looked to be about a similar age as Night Star. Yahíma was probably a few years younger than Chanil.

"Did you even tell her your name? Or you just play games?"

Yahíma shot back. She turned to Chanil. "Momma Afua always be playing, eh?"

Afua looked to the sky and put up both her hands in exasperation. "What horrible thing I do to raise such a disrespectful child, eh? Can't even introduce her own momma properly."

Yahíma made a dismissive gesture and then looked at Ch'akanel.

"You the father, then, eh?" she asked. His face suggested he didn't really understand. Yahíma turned to Chanil and pointed at Ch'akanel with her thumb. "Where did you get this man, eh? He is too pretty."

Chanil laughed out loud. Her cousin kept going. Yahíma turned to Ch'akanel. "Can you cook? Do you clean? Can you do anything other than look beautiful, hm?"

Before he could respond, Yahíma made a dismissive gesture with her hand. "Hmph. You should get yourself an ugly one, cousin. They work harder, eh?"

Yahíma laughed and so did Afua, and Ch'akanel could only shake his head at the bits he understood. Chanil's cheeks hurt, she was smiling so much.

"Did she feed you yet, cousin?" Yahíma asked, getting up and looking pointedly at her mother.

Afua looked at the heavens again and shook her head. "She haven't even told me why she here yet."

Chanil opened and closed her mouth a couple times. Yahíma grinned. "How she gonna tell us anything, no food in her stomach, eh? She's eating for two, Momma."

Yahíma and Afua worked to get Chanil and Ch'akanel some food while Chanil did her best to explain why she had come. She told them what Night Star had said she should—which mostly involved telling the truth but leaving out some of the political details. It took a while for Chanil to get the story across because they couldn't always understand her accent.

In the end, Chanil managed to get them to understand her situation. Yahíma took Chanil's hand in her own and said, "You are family, Lady Sky. We do everything we can for you—and the little one." Then she eyed Ch'akanel with a menacing grin. "And maybe the pretty one, too, eh?"

They laughed some more, and Chanil realized she might actually like being out here with this new family.

After two moons had passed, Chanil practically felt at home. It didn't take her long to realize that Night Star must have spoken to her in the Ayiti's language as a child, because it didn't so much feel like she was learning the words but remembering them from some distant, almost forgotten part of her memory.

Life with her cousins suited Chanil. She certainly enjoyed the simpler, quieter pace of things around the hut over the demands of courtly proceedings back in Yaxchilan. Chanil wasn't used to sitting around, though, so she stayed as active as she could, which Afua approved of.

"Don't want a lazy baby, eh?" she would say.

"You move as much as you want, Sky. Don't listen to nobody tell you different, okay?" They called her Sky because that was what her name meant, more or less.

Ch'akanel stayed busy too. Despite Yahíma's initial concerns, Ch'akanel proved he was more than just a pretty face. Chanil had known that his grandparents were farmers, but she had never actually seen him working in the field. He was good at it. She found their simple life appealed to her.

She only wished she could do more to help out as the pregnancy went on.

And on. And on. And on.

Chanil did not like being pregnant. For one thing, her baby—who everyone was convinced would be a girl—liked to kick. And that made Chanil nauseous. Which only seemed to make the baby kick more. It was a vicious cycle. She wasn't even born yet and was already trying to battle the Great Puma Warrior.

Fortunately, Yahíma was a medicine woman and she had cures for everything. She made tonics and pastes and had all sorts of concoctions she could whip up for her cousin's nausea or when her feet ached or she got hot flashes. The list went on.

Chanil was immensely grateful for Afua taking them in. But it was Yahíma who she really bonded with. They were close in age, and both were pregnant. But it was more than that. Yahíma was sarcastic and blunt and didn't ever let anyone push her around. Chanil respected that. She was also smart and caring. A lot of the villagers came to her for advice on what plants to use to cure their illnesses or to ward off some curse that such-and-such had thrown their way. Yahíma helped everybody.

"What you gonna name her, eh?" Yahíma asked Chanil for the four thousandth time. They were sitting outside in some reclining chairs Ch'akanel had made for the two of them. Chanil had her feet wrapped up in some leaves, which held a paste that Yahíma promised would end her painful swelling once and for all.

"You don't know it be a girl, cousin," Chanil said, evading the question.

Yahíma gave her a look. "I know."

They turned as Ch'akanel emerged from the road that led up to the hut. He carried two large sacks on his shoulders. Chanil guessed they were supplies from the market.

"You bring those leaves I ask for, old man?" Yahíma shot out playfully as Ch'akanel hauled the heavy loads toward their home.

"I can never be one let you down," he said, breathing heavy. His language skills were getting better, but there was still work to be done.

Yahíma put up two fingers for Chanil to see. "Twice now I tell your old man. He forgets every time."

Ch'akanel put the sacks down by the door and crossed to lean over Chanil. He kissed her forehead. "How's my queen?"

Yahíma scoffed. "You know we all royalty here, eh? Momma Afua's a queen. I'm a queen. Little Sky a queen, too."

"You *were* a queen," Chanil teased back. "Until Afua give up that royal title, eh? And why she do that?"

A loud groan came from inside the hut. "Mm! Mm! You know why!"

A moment later, Afua appeared in the doorway, a fierce expression on her face and a finger leveled right at Yahíma. "I give up all my power. All this land could be mine. Why I'm going to give that up? I tell you. For my little girl. So she don't get killed by my own cousin. Imagine that!"

Afua eyed Yahíma intently, effortlessly slinging one of the sacks Ch'akanel had brought over her shoulder. Afua turned to take the pack into the kitchen. She smiled at Chanil and winked. "It was worth it. Ha!"

Then she disappeared. Ch'akanel followed her with the other bag. Yahíma was smiling, but Chanil didn't know how they could be so accepting of the situation. She had gathered that every one of Night Star's cousins had been forced to make a deal with the former king, the Cacique. Night Star had fled to Yaxchilan, but the others had not had that option. Afua had given up all her rights to land and inheritance, effectively given up all political power, and accepted a type of exile. Chanil wasn't sure what each of the other cousins had done.

But Chanil was beginning to understand how intensely the family had feared the former cacique, and that made it easier for her to understand why Night Star had thought Chanil might be in danger and hidden her true lineage. Afua had implied, many times, that the only way Yahíma could have been kept safe was for Afua to accept exile and disappear.

"Tribute time coming, cousin," Yahíma said, interrupting Chanil's thoughts. There was something odd in her tone.

Yahíma heaved herself out of the chair with difficulty. She checked the wraps around Chanil's feet, nodded, and then headed inside. She patted Chanil's shoulder as she passed her and said, "Tribute time coming. We'll have to hide you."

Chanil had no idea what she meant.

The men came one morning without warning. There were nine of them. Seven wore armor and carried weapons. Two had fancy robes and a confident air that suggested they had nothing but disdain for the small hut they visited and their time would have been better spent elsewhere.

Chanil was in the back room of the hut, sitting on the wide hammock she slept on, when she heard the group approaching. Yahíma was outside in her chair, and Chanil heard her cousin speaking to the strangers. A moment later, as Chanil was standing up, Afua rushed into the room and put a hand over Chanil's mouth.

"Cacique's men," Afua whispered. Her eyes were wide, and her tone carried more fear than Chanil had seen the woman ever show. "You not here, eh?"

Chanil nodded and swallowed. Night Star had prepared her for this. The current cacique, who was another of Chanil's cousins, could not know she was there or who she was. The current king was the son of the former cacique—the one who had forced Night Star and the others to flee or give up their political power. His son, though not as brutal as his father, was still an unknown factor. And anything he learned about Chanil could only work to their detriment. At least, that was what Night Star had told Chanil.

They heard Yahíma yelling, and a second later, heavy boots stomped into the hut. A trio of armed men marched into the kitchen area. Afua stood in the doorway to the small bedroom where Chanil had been resting. Chanil could tell that the older woman was trying to hide her from view, but it was pointless. The armed warriors had already seen Chanil, and they stomped up to Afua in the doorway.

Chanil stood up as Afua and the warriors exchanged words. They spoke quickly and angrily, but Chanil caught the gist. They wanted to know who Chanil was. And Afua didn't have any answers they deemed good enough. Spoken words turned into yelling, and one of the warriors tried to shove Afua aside.

"Stop!" Chanil bellowed out in the language of the Ayiti. It wasn't the voice of a young girl. It was Puma's voice, the one that carried over the din of battle and commanded men and women. The warriors eyed her intently.

Chanil stepped forward. "Leave this poor woman alone," she said in her commanding tone. She gently pushed passed Afua and through the trio of men. They made room for her reflexively. Her commanding presence and her large baby belly triggered their sensibilities.

She turned to face the trio of men, clustered by the doorway now. "Why are you here?"

"Who are you?" one of the men said. His eyes were suspicious. Chanil knew she still had something of an accent, and she could never hope to lie about being from the Island.

She stepped confidently toward the man. Her belly pressed into his armor. "Who am I? You barge in here and hurt my friend and make demands of *me*? You're lucky I don't report you!"

Chanil tried to move and act like a royal lady. She imagined how Lady Xok might have reacted and moved and spoke, and she did her best to imitate that. She pointed her finger angrily at the warrior and then turned toward all of them.

"This old woman has been helping me! I have half a mind to report all of you to the nearest ca . . . caci—whatever he's called!"

"The Cacique, my Lady?" another of the warriors asked, his tone growing humbler as he realized this pregnant woman facing him was probably a noble lady.

"Whatever the word is!" Chanil said with a dismissive hand gesture she had seen Xok use. "Now, if you men are done intruding on the affairs of women, you may step outside and at least allow us to make ourselves presentable."

The trio of men looked at each other, clearly embarrassed, and then retreated toward the entrance of the hut. But a powerful voice stopped them. "Wait!"

Standing in the doorway to the hut, a tall man in fine robes eyed Chanil carefully. He was middle-aged, probably in his fourth or fifth decade. He stepped carefully into the hut toward Chanil.

"We serve the Cacique, good lady," he said slowly. "We are here to collect tribute from this family."

"It's right here! Big man didn't even take it," Yahíma's voice called out from behind the tall figure in fine robes. Chanil looked past Fine-Robes and saw four more warriors standing around Yahíma.

"It sounds like your tribute is there waiting for you, good sir," Chanil said.

Fine-Robes kept his gaze locked on Chanil, however. "Who are you?"

He pointed a ragged finger at her. "You look familiar."

Chanil swallowed. She pulled her face into an arrogant mask. "I am the Princess Yellow Flower of the Mexica Empire, good sir."

Fine-Robes narrowed his eyes in suspicion, but Chanil kept going. "This woman has been helping me ever since I got lost in your—your—well, your rather impassable jungle."

Chanil tried to take on the same mannerisms and halting speech patterns she remembered from Lady Xok in childhood. She wasn't sure how good a job she was doing. Certainly, everyone around her looked confused. Whether that was because it was working or because her accent made it difficult for them to understand her, she wasn't sure.

Fine-Robes opened his mouth to speak, but then a crashing tumult sounded from outside. Chanil heard the familiar roar of Ch'akanel, and she rolled her eyes. Looking past Fine-Robes, she saw Ch'akanel crash violently into one of the warriors outside. Inside, one of the warriors drew his weapon. Chanil dropped her act and moved reflexively. In an eye blink, her knife was drawn, and she had buried it in the warrior's arm. She twisted hard, and he dropped his weapon.

Then she yanked the blade out and kicked the man into the wall. At the same time, she turned, ducked under the attack of the closest warrior, and cut him along the groin. As he fell forward, she sliced into his leg, dragging the cut all along his inner thigh. She felt her blade sink into bone and catch.

She released the knife immediately, stepping back as the man bled out. Crashing sounds could be heard outside as Ch'akanel wrestled with the last remaining warrior on the patio. Chanil heard Yahíma yell from outside as the third man in the hut charged toward Chanil.

Chanil grimaced as her lower back spasmed. But she gritted her teeth against the pain and leapt to one side as the man thrust his spear in her direction. She wrapped a hand around one of his wrists and quickly disarmed him. Then she sucker punched him in the solar plexus and gave him a vicious uppercut elbow as he doubled over.

The man fell to the ground. Chanil waddled over to the spear on the floor, picked it up, and quickly finished the warrior off. The last warrior—the one she had started the fight with, stabbed in the arm, and kicked into the wall—was crouched on the ground, a look of fear in his eyes.

Chanil breathed heavily, feeling the awkwardness of having to move quickly while carrying a child. She turned toward the doorway where Fine-Robes still stood. His eyes were wide as Ch'akanel pushed him forward and entered the hut.

Fine-Robes fell to his knees and put his forehead to the floor. "Great Lady!" he cried out. Then he lifted his torso up to look at her. "You are the daughter of Koeia!"

It was Chanil's turn to go wide-eyed. Fine-Robes was nodding to himself intently. He turned to Afua. "She looks just like her!"

Afua had a fierce look on her face and pursed her lips as she eyed the man.

"Puma?" Ch'akanel asked, wanting to know what Chanil was going to do.

But Fine-Robes spoke up. "Your mother is the true cacique, Great Lady!"

"Shut your mouth, old man!" the warrior on the floor suddenly spat out. He jumped up to his feet, a knife in his hand and death in his eyes as he looked at Fine-Robes. Chanil moved forward instinctively, thrust out her spear, and drove the point into the man's chest. He gurgled, and blood dripped from his mouth as he sagged to the floor.

Chanil looked around them. Afua was leaning against one wall, her face full of concern. Ch'akanel still hovered over Fine-Robes, uncertain what to do with the old man. Yahíma entered the hut and gasped seeing the bloody scene. She put one hand on her belly and the other over her mouth. Then she looked at Chanil, still holding the blood-stained spear, as though seeing a stranger.

Fine-Robes put up his hands but stayed kneeling. "Please, Great Lady. Allow me to help."

Chanil narrowed her eyes and looked at Afua. "Who is this man?"

Afua made a dismissive gesture. "The cacique's man."

"I am Mabó," Fine-Robes said quickly. "We are all under the cacique. But I was there—before. When his father ruled. I knew your mother, Great Lady. I knew Koeia. She would have been a great cacique, and all knew it."

Chanil saw the earnestness in the man's eyes and wondered if he was telling the truth. She looked at Afua again. "Is that possible?"

She nodded. "Oh yeah. Koeia should have been cacique. Everybody know that. Don't change nothing."

Chanil looked at Ch'akanel. "The others outside?"

"He's the only one left, Puma," Ch'akanel said flatly.

Yahíma crossed to Chanil, her back to the group, and whispered in her ear. "If we kill him, others will come looking, cousin. Bad enough you killed them all. The Cacique will wonder what happened here."

Mabó looked up at Chanil. "I can help you get rid of these bodies, Great Lady. And I can tell the Cacique there was some accident. Bandits on the road. Only I survived."

Chanil handed her spear to Yahíma, who took it as though she had never seen such a thing in her life. Then Chanil knelt in front of Mabó. "Why you help us? Help me?"

He lowered his eyes. "Your grandmother saved my life."

"Bah!" Afua scoffed loudly.

"It's true! When the invasion happened, she kept me and my family safe. And Koeia fought alongside my sons, Great Lady. What the old cacique did—" His face twisted, and Chanil saw the anger there. The deep hatred. "I owe your mother and your grandmother."

"Then why you come here looking for us? Demanding extra tribute?" Afua asked pointedly.

"I didn't know who lived here. I was only told to come here and make sure there weren't any outsiders living in this place."

Chanil stood back up. She looked at Afua. The woman tilted her head in an expression that told Chanil she might believe the man.

"Very well, good sir," Chanil said. "Help us with these bodies, and I will spare your life. But I want your help in return."

Mabó touched his forehead to the floor again. "Anything, my Lady, for the daughter of Koeia."

A Calculated Offer

Second chances can sometimes be even worse than the first time around.

—*the Book of Queen Snake Lady*

"HAVE YOU ALWAYS USED THE COUNCIL MAT in the court of Sprouting Earth?"

Itza' tossed the question over her shoulder at Snake Lady while her eyes scanned the long codex on the wooden table in front of her. It was especially old, written in the almost code-like language of the priests. But interestingly, she found the old language here at Sprouting Earth to be more similar to the ancient texts in Yaxchilan than their present-day languages were. She wondered if all of the Winaq had once been united by a single language.

Snake Lady watched Itza' carefully for a while, noticing how the girl became less guarded while studying. As if she had heard the thought, Itza' stopped reading and stood upright. She half turned to face Snake Lady, who sat on an ornate wooden chair on the opposite side of the room.

"Well . . . have you?" Itza' said flatly. Snake Lady smiled, but her eyes remained intense and somewhat removed.

"We once had a system more like what you use in Yaxchilan . . ." Itza' heard the effort it took for Snake Lady to utter the name of her city and realm without venom in her voice. ". . . But that was long ago. The council mat is . . . more fitting for us here."

Itza' looked at Snake Lady. Despite the intensity of her eyes, Snake Lady's body seemed completely relaxed. She leaned casually into the ornate chair as though she had been draped over it, the colors and images on her dress blending with those on the furniture.

"Perhaps one day Yaxchilan will also come to build a Council House, then, and hold our meetings there," Itza' offered. She found that she liked the system used at Sprouting Earth—in which authority was more spread out among different council members as opposed to being concentrated in a single king, or queen, as it was in Yaxchilan.

"It certainly has advantages," Snake Lady mused. "Especially for making sure *our* voices are heard, eh?"

Itza' caught the meaning in Snake Lady's words. She knew that her father, Lord 5-Thunder, was unusually open to listening to his advisors and, most especially, to both his wives. But he could just as easily have been a ruler who shut out the advice of women and those with whom he disagreed.

"The council seems particularly swayed by *your* voice, Honored Queen," Itza' said, letting a youthful smile cross her face.

Snake Lady ignored the subtle barb and changed the subject. "So, tell me, what have you learned from your studies of our history, little one?" She pointed with her lips at the pages that lay behind Itza'. "And spare me any denials—I know you spend hours studying in the temples every day."

Itza' inclined her head formally and responded mischievously, "I would never attempt to deceive you, Honored Queen, Great Snake of Sky and Earth."

Snake Lady smiled at the wordplay Itza' employed to make her name glide poetically into the words for sky and earth. She thought about what a joy it would have been to watch the neurotic Lady Xok deal with such a mischievous child. In response to Itza's passive-aggressiveness, Snake Lady merely gestured with her hands for the girl to continue.

In reality, Itza' had learned a lot. Probably much more than Snake Lady had intended or wanted, since Itza' had noticed that she had only been given access to areas with very old, historical records. Nevertheless, Itza' had studied records since she was a young child. She could read between the lines of the differences she found between here and the Yaxchilan records.

"It is written in some of your old texts that the Invaders came here before," Itza' began. "I've never heard of this."

Snake Lady nodded. "It was a long time ago . . . they—or ones like them—came to the northern part of the Peninsula that juts out toward the Island."

Itza' was somewhat surprised that such information had never reached Yaxchilan, but the northern kingdoms of the Peninsula were somewhat isolated from ones farther west, such as Yaxchilan or the Red City.

"And what happened?" Itza' asked.

"You're the one who read the accounts," Snake Lady retorted.

"Your histories say they brought a great sickness with them— that it nearly wiped out the Winaq."

Snake Lady nodded. "We were nearly destroyed by that first invasion attempt. But fortunately, the lands and waters protected us, and our would-be conquerors fared no better. They were forced to return home."

"Are these new Invaders a second attempt then? Are they from the same kingdoms on the other side of the Sea?"

"Hmmmm . . ." Snake Lady pursed her lips. "That I cannot say."

Itza' heard more in her tone, however, and asked, "But you suspect?"

"I do. But many do not. And either way, we must still deal with the enemy before us." Itza' wondered if Snake Lady was referring to Itza' herself when she spoke of the enemy before her.

"It would take a long time to learn all that is written here at Sprouting Earth," Itza' offered.

"Longer than your visit will last, eh?" Snake lady teased.

"Is that your way of saying you're kicking me out?" Itza' replied with a small smile.

"If I intended to banish you, why would I have let you stay so long?"

"And why have you let me stay so long, Honored Queen? You did not really want to train me so badly. Nor to ally yourself with Yaxchilan."

And there it was.

The direct question.

Snake Lady decided it was finally time to address it.

"In fact, I would like you to stay *longer*, little one," she said flatly.

Itza' eyed the older woman suspiciously. A death threat? But Itza' shrugged that idea off. Snake Lady was not a warrior and not one prone to using violence to get what she wanted. She could just order Itza' to leave and never have to shed any blood.

Something else more permanent, then—and Itza' realized the implications before she could finish the thought. The endless attacks, the ongoing appraisals and tests, and the veiled hints that Yaxchilan might have meant something more by sending Itza' than she was telling. Had Snake Lady intended a marriage from the beginning? Or had she been appraising Itza' and now, somehow, decided Itza' passed her tests?

"Are you suggesting . . . me and your son . . . but then our kingdoms—"

"Yes, little one," Snake Lady hummed, looking Itza' directly in the eyes. "I am offering you marriage to my son in exchange for supporting an alliance with Yaxchilan."

Itza's mind was racing. In the back of her head, she realized she also did not quite have the authority to really decide on this counteroffer. She suddenly had a mental image of their family having sent Chanil here instead and Itza' to the Red City. She almost laughed thinking how different Chanil's reaction would have been.

But Itza' was not Chanil. She didn't rage against the idea of a political marriage. It didn't really bother Itza' that she didn't know much about Chak Mol or didn't really find him that attractive. She saw what Snake Lady saw, what Xok would have seen—the consequences for their kingdoms, their people. And Itza' saw a chance to make a difference instead of sitting on the sidelines.

Itza' intuitively understood Snake Lady's reasons and did not feel powerless because of the offer. Itza' knew she was the youngest, unmarried daughter of an ajaw. She was a logical candidate for marriage to secure a political benefit. And she had been sent here to Sprouting Earth for a political reason.

She also knew that Chak Mol was not a strong leader, and Snake Lady would not live forever. In Itza', Snake Lady would have an apprentice, an ideal mix of political strength but also youthful inexperience that Snake Lady would, Itza' had no doubt, try to mold into the queen she thought Itza' should be. And, while that constant game of political cat and mouse with Snake Lady might be annoying, Itza' found herself warming to the idea of marriage for one very simple reason.

Chanil would rule Yaxchilan.

If Itza' married Chak Mol, then Chanil, effectively, would rule Sprouting Earth. And that just might create an alliance strong enough to beat Tlapallo and the Great Army. Together, the Twin Panthers might command an area with enough power and resources to preserve the eastern lands and save the Winaq.

Watching Itza' process all of this, Snake Lady smiled menacingly. She said, "I assume you see the reasons."

Itza' replied, "I do. But I must speak to my family."

Snake Lady cackled loudly. "Your father will grit his teeth and yell. Lady Xok will pout and pace. But both will ask you what you saw here and what you think is best."

Itza' swallowed hard. Snake Lady was right.

"I'm open to accepting your proposition, Great Queen," Itza' began slowly. "But there are things we should discuss first."

Snake Lady cackled again. "Out with it, child. I'm not getting any younger."

Itza' pursed her lips. "Fine. I assume that by now we both know that I know that you cursed my mother. And that you did so to prevent her from having children. I need to know why."

Snake Lady's eyes took on that glossy texture of the silent rage she sometimes had. She paused, taking in Itza's revelation but not revealing her surprise at it. Instead, she said calmly, "You *want* to know why."

Itza' shook her head. "No, Great Queen. I *need* to know. How can I be queen here if we don't trust each other? How can I lead if I'm always plagued with doubts about your motives?"

It was Snake Lady's turn to purse her lips. She had to admit, the girl had a point. But Snake Lady didn't want to share the story. She felt her whole being rebel against the idea of doing so.

"You are powerful enough to rule here regardless, little one," Snake Lady hissed. "You have all the power you would ever need right there."

Then she pointed at Itza', right in her face. At her eyes, Itza' realized.

"You mean *your* power—the power you gave me, Great Snake?" Itza' used an odd word pairing to refer to Snake Lady, which implied a strong connection with a particular snake god from their mythology—a creator and destroyer figure.

Snake Lady smiled knowingly. "Yes . . . and no."

"It was your curse that shaped the day of my birth. Your snake power that gave me my eyes, eh?" Itza' felt her anger boiling over in her words.

"Yes . . . and no, little one," Snake Lady repeated. She got up suddenly and walked to a small table against one wall with a large drinking gourd set on top of it. From it, she poured a cup for her and Itza'. The smell of warm, frothed cacao wafted through the air, carrying with it a complex mix of spices and something almost metallic underneath.

Itza' sniffed the air and wondered if it was blood she smelled in the drink.

Snake Lady brought Itza' the cup. She took it but eyed the contents suspiciously. She was wary of strange drinks in strange cups delivered by older women.

"Do you know where I come from, little one?" Snake Lady asked as she sat back down in her comfortable chair.

"No," Itza' replied, trying to force her frustrations aside. "Your origins seem a closely guarded secret, even within your own courtly records."

Snake Lady smiled again. "Hmmm . . . I was not fortunate, like you, to be born in civilization, little one. I was born at the edges of our world during a time of extreme violence. My childhood was filled with tortuous pain."

Though Snake Lady was looking directly at Itza', her black eyes seemed distant and far off. It was as though she was dreaming.

Sensing a double meaning to Snake Lady's words, Itza' asked, "You mean pain from the violence around you?"

She shook her head. "I mean the snake inside me," she said. Her raspy voice lowered into a deeper register, and she twisted one of her arms seductively. The jeweled snake armband caught the light from the candles in the room and reflected it back along the walls in small, irregularly shaped rainbows.

"The snake inside me was pain," she continued, and Itza' crossed the room to settle slowly into a chair next to her. "The pain that calls us into service when we are off our path, eh? Trust me, little one, *you* have undoubtedly never known this pain . . ."

Itza' barely registered the last part though, as she was still fixated on the words Snake Lady had used. *The snake inside her . . .* The words echoed in her mind. She thought she knew what Snake Lady meant—the pain that came to those who were destined to be seers and day-keepers.

Normally, such individuals were identified early and trained appropriately so that they did not experience the terrible pains that were said to afflict those who had fallen off their path—the road of their life. Certainly, in that regard, Snake Lady was right about Itza'. As a royal daughter, she had been trained as a day-keeper beginning in childhood, and so, her path had always been followed according to their traditions. She had never felt the pains of being away from her duties to her people.

But Snake Lady did, Itza' thought. How was that possible for a royal child?

She did not have time to ask, however, because Snake Lady kept talking. Her voice was slow, and its raspy quality grated against the stone floor as her words filled the room. Her eyes were strangely soft, at least for her, and she gazed into the fire of a candle before her, on the table between the two women.

"It poisoned. That snake. It lit my blood on fire and burned through my veins like a lightning storm inside me. It gave my body horrible pains, and I could not eat for days. More than once, I tried to kill myself to end the pain ..."

She trailed off for a moment, then her eyes lifted to meet Itza's. For the first time since she had met Snake Lady, Itza' saw something other than an angry fire in those eyes. Something almost loving.

". . . But then someone helped me," Snake Lady finished. The words escaped her throat, and the warmth in her eyes left with them.

But Itza' could see that there was more to this story, that finally, Snake Lady was giving her answers. And Itza' was not about to let that opportunity pass by. She had looked for answers her whole life.

"Someone?" Itza' prompted.

Snake Lady shrugged and twisted her face ambiguously. "Hmmmm," she hummed in her odd way, flicking her arm out in a dismissive gesture. "An old woman, an aunt of sorts. She took me in and taught me how to use the power you see in my eyes. She helped me to find my path and end the pain."

Itza' felt goosebumps run along her arms, and she wondered at the identity of this strange old woman. But then she realized Snake Lady was probably just trying to divert her attention away with veiled secrets and avoid giving Itza' any real answers.

"You're not telling me how this connects to my own power and winning this war. Do you expect me to feel sorry for you? The woman who cursed my mother and hates my father? And I know it was your magic that threw the Invaders off your lands and put the frontlines of this war on my kingdom." For some reason, Itza' felt real frustration thinking about that last fact. She forced herself to quiet down, clenching her jaw reflexively to keep her words under control.

But Snake Lady eyed her as impassively as ever. Then a smirk crossed her face, and she said, "Your father clenches his jaw the same way when he is angry. Did you know you do that, little one?"

Itza' opened her mouth to say something sarcastic. But then she stopped. An image of her father's jaw passed through her mind. The chiseled line of his jawbone and the muscles rippling beneath the surface. And the strange snake-like scar along his jaw that moved and slithered whenever he clenched his teeth.

"The scar?" Itza' asked, her voice high and intense. She felt more revelations coming.

Snake Lady nodded slowly, and Itza' rose out of her chair, slamming down the drink Snake Lady had given her.

"You cursed my father too, didn't you?"

Looking down at the older woman, Itza's eyes glinted wildly, jagged cracks of red and yellow showing in her black irises.

"Is that why he has that scar? Is that why he is sick so often?"

Snake Lady looked up at the younger woman standing over her and her mouth trembled.

"I never hurt your father, little one. I—" Then she pulled back again, the steel veil of impassivity returning to her eyes, and she swallowed hard as she pushed down the words threatening to come out.

"You what?" Itza' pleaded. "You won't tell me why you cursed my mother. You won't reveal the secrets of our dark power to me. And now you hide what you know about my father. Some mentor you would be!"

A sudden cackle escaped Snake Lady. But Itza' saw a sadness in her eyes. Snake Lady closed her eyes for a long moment and then opened them after a time to take another long sip of her drink.

"A terrible one," she admitted at last. "But I have never lied to you. I did not cause your father's illness, I promise you that."

"But you know more than you are saying, Great Queen. Help me understand my past. Be a *good* mentor, and help me learn how to use these powers and defeat our enemies."

Snake Lady eyed the younger woman for a moment. She realized Itza' might not be able to rule or move past her doubts without knowing.

"To use our powers requires understanding where they come from and who we are. Ah—" Snake lady held up a hand as Itza' began to interject. "—There is a way for you to gain what you seek here. A ritual—an old ceremony. It comes from the ancient ones, and it will begin to unlock your powers."

Itza' looked at Snake Lady with a mixture of suspicion and wonder. "And the secrets of my past? What ritual will help me learn those?"

Snake Lady swallowed hard again, realizing what she had to do. "There is no ritual for that, little one . . . Only a very long story—if you are ready to hear it."

Itza' stepped back and sat down again in the chair next to Snake Lady. She eyed the older woman intently. "Great Queen, I have been ready all my life."

"Very well, Daughter of Xok, here is the story you have been waiting for. Here is the reason your mother was cursed and the order of things that shaped the face of your day . . ."

Xelha'

Never kill your friends. That's my only rule. I've tried to live by it.
But sometimes the line between friend and foe becomes blurry and hard to see.

—*Xelaq'am's Songs*

"THE STORY BEGINS RIGHT HERE, *with this young girl born on the Eastern Shores of the Peninsula during a particularly fearsome red moon. The blood-colored moons always mark the moment of a sacred but dangerous eclipse, and in normal days, being born at such a time would have been considered a terrible omen.*

"*But the danger of the eclipse that was present on her birthday paled in comparison to the dangerous violence all around her. The Eastern Shores were at war—a terrible and bloody conflict that had persisted for many years. It was in the midst of that terrible war that the young girl came to lose her father and her mother and began to experience the bone-splitting pains in her body that made her early life nearly unbearable . . .*

The young girl rolled away from the bright light of the candle near her hammock and pretended not to hear the two women talking nearby. The young girl's wrists ached beneath the bandages from where she had tried, unsuccessfully, to cut into the rivers of blood. Her stomach twisted and turned in nauseating knots from the tonics and medicines she had been given. Her bones still held the memories of the horrible pains that plagued her daily and made her want to end her life. She was numb from the weight of everything, and she just wanted to close her eyes and drift away, to leave behind the smells of incense and sweat and herbs that filled the room, to discard the bright and overwhelming light from the candles in every corner, and erase the sounds of the women's voices by the doorway as the they tried to decide what to do with her.

"This isn't the first time," one of the women whispered, but the girl could hear her clearly. A grunt followed as the sole response from the second woman.

"She is the daughter of an ajaw. We have to help her," the first woman continued.

"The ajaw is dead, and his kingdom is about to fall," the second woman replied tersely, her harsh and raspy voice cutting brutally through the air.

"All the more reason to help her. She has nowhere to go. And her misery is—"

The second woman cackled, a grating and sudden sound. "Ha! It is not misery, little one. She is sick—can you not see? Her spirit is sick, and her heart is broken—and that is another type of sickness. . . The pains come from this."

A bit of shuffling in the doorway, and the young girl lying in the hammock picked up the scent of a third person. She guessed it was another old woman by the crinkles in the smells. But the newcomer did not speak.

"You know why she has these pains?" the first woman spoke again.

"Hmph," the second woman responded. "Have you seen her eyes, little one? I know *exactly* where her pains come from."

"Then can you help her?" the first woman asked, her voice pleading.

Another grunt came as the response. Then more shuffling and a long silence. Finally, the young girl heard the second woman's harsh voice return to the conversation.

"Fine. I will take her—I'm sure none of you will know any better what to do with her."

More shuffling from the doorway, and eventually, the young girl heard the three adults leave. She shut her eyes tighter and tried to sleep. The smells of the three women lingered in her nostrils for a long time before she finally dozed off.

"Before they had died, the girl's parents had named her Xelha', after the beautiful waters of her homeland. Her father's kingdom had been a great port city on the Eastern Coasts, and the girl had been born in the waters of the ocean—at least that was how the story went. But Xelha's fate was not to remain near the waters of her home. The war raged on, her parents were killed, and her pains continued. But everything changed when the old woman took Xelha' in.

"Xelha' was told to call the old woman her auntie. She was the only family Xelha' had now. Auntie taught her about the pains that wracked her body and where they came from—the sickness she had that made her muscles burn like lightning storms raging inside her and her bones feel like they might break with every step . . ."

"But how do you *know*, Auntie?" Xelha's voice was soft and floated like incense in the air. But it also carried an impatient quality that she had been chided for more than once.

"I have learned to listen, little one," was all that her aunt would say in explanation. It was a familiar refrain. But she went over the lesson again—and again—and again. She was teaching the young girl how to be a day-keeper, an ajk'ij—one who knew how to divine the future and the meaning of visions.

"And learning how to listen will keep the pain away, Auntie?" Xelha' couldn't keep the sadness out of her voice.

Her aunt nodded and took the young girl's chin in her hand. She looked at the girl, who could not have been more than twelve or thirteen years old, and smiled. Although her aunt could be harsh, and her demeanor was rough and cold most of the time, her smiles were still full of love. Usually.

The older woman looked down at Xelha' and studied the girl's eyes. They were very dark—but not yet as dark as the old woman's. Auntie's eyes were as jet-black as Xelha's hair or the darkest cave. Or obsidian stone, Xelha' always thought when she tried to place the color and the texture, the way those black irises could reflect different colors or shades sometimes.

Xelha's eyes were not obsidian colored—not yet. That would come with time . . . and healing, Auntie knew. Nevertheless, the girl had eyes darker than most others, and they sparked with an intensity and sadness that many found hard to look at directly for too long.

"There is a snake inside you, little one," her aunt said. She rarely answered Xelha's questions directly.

Xelha' made a rancid face. She did not like snakes. They scared her. She had seen how a bite from a snake could bring down even the strongest warrior.

Auntie saw the look of revulsion. "Hate them all you like, little girl. But you only hate them because you don't yet understand them. Your ignorance has cost you plenty already, eh?"

The pains that had plagued her had gotten much better since her aunt had started teaching her how to understand their world. But she still felt the quivers and tremors in her body, the biting venom of something alive moving around inside her muscles and joints. It terrified her.

"Can you take the snake out, Auntie?"

Her aunt cackled suddenly. The harsh sounds reverberated

off the walls of the small, pole and thatch roof hut they lived in. She turned from Xelha' and sat down on the floor a few feet away, in front of the divining bundle on the flat table in the center of the room. The table was where Xelha's lessons usually took place. She was learning to count the days and read the messages in the sacred beans that the Winaq used to converse with the spirits around them when they had questions.

But this time, Auntie cleared all the objects off the table and beckoned for Xelha' to sit across from her. As the girl obeyed, her aunt took out a piece of paper and some drawing supplies from under the table. She unfolded the raw fig bark paper and began tracing a long black line. The line curved and undulated almost like the bends in a river but followed a more regular pattern. The deep black of the ink glistened slightly, catching the light and creating the illusion of small patterns in her aunt's brush strokes, almost like scales.

"The snake is like a river, little one," Auntie said as she gently brushed the black ink onto the paper.

"The snake gives life . . . but it has terrible power and can take life as well. Just like the waters . . . The snake is both creator and destroyer . . ."

Her aunt stopped drawing for a moment to ignite the small incense dishes at opposite ends of the low table. As the smoke swirled upward, Xelha' tasted the sweet aroma of the resin burning in the dishes. She felt the heavy blanket of the smoke begin to wrap around her as her aunt continued the lesson.

"The snake sheds it skin with each new cycle, little one. Like the world around us, it is reborn and renewed . . . with each destruction comes new creation . . ."

Xelha' felt her body swaying slightly with her aunt's words now. She was caught up in the rhythms of the sounds. She felt the smoke passing into her body and, looking down, thought she could see little flashes of lightning running along her thighs and her bare arms.

"The snake in the sky will rise," Auntie continued. "It carries the stars and sun and moon across their paths each day and night. The snake gives us our power, little one."

With the last part, Xelha' felt a thump in her heart, and for the first time in her life, every sensation in her body suddenly ceased. The pains that wracked her, the achy bruises they had left behind, the beating of her heart and the blood in her chest, the sounds and the smells of the world around her. Everything disappeared, and all she felt was a strange, blissful—nothing. Her eyes closed. Her world was wrapped in utter blackness. She felt her body relax in a way she had never dreamed possible.

And then she heard it.

A low hissing sound seemed to come from everywhere all at once. Her eyes shot open reflexively, but to her surprise, all she saw was dense, grey-black fog from the incense smoke. The hissing grew louder and louder, surrounding her, confusing her. Then the smoke began to writhe and quiver. The grey-black fog squirmed and unraveled itself, slowly revealing the image of a large black snake hidden in the smoke.

The snake's head turned toward Xelha', and she felt a terrible fear rising up in her chest. She felt her heart beating wildly under the prison of her ribs, and she tried desperately to rise up and run away. But she could not move. She was paralyzed.

The snake faced Xelha', and at the same time, she felt the smoke of the incense coil tightly around her body. It squeezed against her, and she began to feel a heavy, wet, crushing sensation as the smoke tightened and tightened against her. She opened her mouth to scream, to call for help, but nothing came out. Instead, more incense smoke rushed in, filling her with its strange sensation like lightning striking her from the inside.

The snake brought its face right up to Xelha's, and she could see its eyes were brilliant, bright gems—jewels that sparkled like a rainbow of colors cast through clear raindrops. It flicked its tongue several times, and Xelha' could feel the push of air against her throat from the quick pulsing movements of its tongue so close. Then the snake opened its mouth, a cavernous maw of the deepest black. The only light within that murderous cave came from the two long fangs within the serpent's jaws—jeweled and brilliant, just like the eyes. Xelha' squeezed her eyes closed in fear of the monstrous creature.

"Open your eyes, little one!" She heard the angry rasp of her aunt's voice, seeming to come from deep within the open jaws of the snake.

"You must look, girl! You must learn to see!" Auntie was nearly shouting, the grating rasp of her voice like jagged pebbles being ground together.

Xelha' forced herself to open her eyes. And then she gasped.

"It is time for you to meet the snake inside you, girl," Auntie said from somewhere around her. "It is time for you to start to regain your power, little one!"

Xelha' stared into the ever-growing chasm of the snake's mouth, shocked into silence. The sound of her aunt's cackles filled the air around her.

"I cannot tell you how much everything changed for the little girl after that first vision, little one. She began to learn about her power and how to harness it. Her road began that night; she took her first steps toward accepting the snake within her. For years, she and her aunt lived humbly, moving south from the Eastern Coasts toward the great river that marks the southern border of the Peninsula. Her aunt was a powerful day-keeper, and people sought her advice everywhere they went—ajaw and peasant alike.

"The young girl learned how to divine the days and interpret visions, much better than she would have had she been raised as the noble lady her lineage made her. She learned about the powerful spells and magic that some day-keepers could bring—spells to cure diseases, others to bring the rain for crops, and others to ward off enemies and bad omens.

"But after several years of travel, her aunt eventually brought *the young girl to a kingdom by the river, ruled by one branch of the family of the famous Snake Dynasty lords. Her aunt secured herself a position advising their ajaw, and the young girl was officially made her courtly apprentice. For the first time, the young girl was treated as the noble lady her birthright demanded.*

"She learned the politics of her ajaw's kingdom, the aspirations of the Snake Dynasty family, and she worked with her aunt to advise the king on the best strategy to achieve his aims. The young girl met with rulers from other kingdoms and learned about the tentative alliance her ajaw was trying to strengthen with some of his neighboring kingdoms.

"And, most importantly, she learned that one of those neighboring kingdoms was not to be trusted. She was told of a great feud between their kingdom and the one that had now taken her in, and how everyone who ruled that other kingdom was treacherous and could not be trusted at their word. When their ajaw came with his two sons, Xelha' was told to watch the men closely, for the whole family was nothing but liars and deceivers.

"But the girl was still young, and like all young girls, she was susceptible to the fatal illness that afflicts all youth—lust. Her romance with the youngest son of the treacherous ajaw began slowly at first—traded glances, prolonged conversations. But before long, the two were deeply in love . . ."

The boy and the girl met in secret at their usual spot. It was late evening at the end of the dry season, and the evening heat hung in the air like a blanket of warmth thrown over the loose jungle on the city outskirts. The two met near a small stone building, which had a hidden alcove built into a cul-de-sac along one of its tall and curved walls. They embraced tightly in the shadows, hiding from the gaze of the silvery half-moon in the sky above. Their bodies pressed against each other as they kissed again and again. When they spoke, it was in hushed whispers, filled with the overtones of youthful passion.

"I thought you might have been killed," she said between rough kisses, her intense eyes watery with tears. "I heard what happened in the battle."

The boy smirked confidently. His own eyes blazed with an intense fire and passion that nearly equaled the girl's. His hair was a jet-black tangle of loose curls falling across half his face. His jaw was chiseled and strong despite his youth, and he pulled her in tightly with his powerful arms. She moved her own hands up the curve of his biceps as they kissed again.

Then he placed his lips by her ear, and his low voice came out in a baritone register, "You know I cannot die, little flower." And he smirked again.

The girl smiled back. She liked the boy's confidence and stubborn attitude, though she did not know how much she believed the legend about him and his brother's supposed invulnerability. Still, she found his assuredness immensely appealing, and she bit her lip as she looked up at him.

The boy looked down at her in return. Her face was long and oval shaped. Her black eyebrows framed her intense and dark eyes, leading his eyes down the steep angle of her nose as it broadened widely at the base and the tip hooked downward. Her lips, still caught in a half-smirk of their shared passion, were wide and full, two deep red rivers the boy wanted to swim through over and over again.

"I'm not a little flower, good sir, hmmm?" the girl said teasingly. She sometimes finished her sentences with an odd humming sound that the boy had never heard anyone make before. She had told him, once, it was a nervous habit.

"But that is what the villagers call you, no?" the boy teased back.

"My parents named me Xelha', good sir," said the girl, leaning forward to whisper the last part in his ear and smell the sweat along his neck. She felt her body pull involuntarily closer as she picked up the scent of his pheromones in the air. Then she pulled back and looked at the boy in mock anger, casting her eyes into an intense glare that sent shivers down his spine.

". . . And you will call me by my proper name, Great Blood-Letter, for I am just. As. Noble. As. You."

The boy met her gaze with his own intense, fire-brown stare and did his best to maintain the confident look he usually sported. He was the youngest son of the Ajaw, and already becoming a famed warrior. He had no reason to feel intimidated by the look of a young girl. And yet, Xelha' was no ordinary girl. Her eyes were filled with secret power, and her face was the most beautiful he had ever seen. And when she used his warrior title, he felt that weakening in his knees that could incapacitate even the most powerful of men before a woman they love.

So he relented, letting his gaze soften and wander over the curves of her face and her body. He said, simply, "Whatever you wish, my love, my sweet Xelha'. Whatever will keep you here with me."

"If you want to stay with me, perhaps you should stop throwing yourself so recklessly into battle then, eh?"

"How else is a young prince to earn his reputation?" he countered in his low voice, already deeper than one would expect for his age. "I must prove myself a brave man for my people."

"Hmmm," Xelha' hummed again in response. She knew this was the way warriors thought, but it had never sat well with her. She had seen violence all throughout her childhood, and she doubted much good could come from more of it.

Impulsively, she let her hands slide down to the belt around Blood-Letter's waist and curled her fingers slowly and deliberately around his waist band. The boy swallowed hard as he felt her fingers sliding against his skin, along the lines of his lower abdomen beneath his clothes.

"How long do we have?" she said, looking up at him as her lips formed the words slowly.

He swallowed again, hearing the gentle rasp of her voice. "My father thinks I am celebrating with the other warriors. I have all night." He flashed her a mischievous grin full of boyish promises he wondered if he could keep.

The girl leaned in and smelled him again, letting her face glide a hair's breadth from his neck so he could only feel the warmth of her breath along his skin. She pulled him close by his belt and ran her long tongue along his ear before whispering, "My aunt is away tonight. But she'll be back by dawn."

In one quick and fluid motion, the boy moved her hands aside forcefully and lifted the girl up by her thighs. She opened them around him as he wrapped her around his waist. He pinned her against the smooth stone wall, and she gasped suddenly. Her dark eyes locked onto his.

"Then I don't have to be quick this time, my love," he whispered quietly into her ear as he lifted the skirt of her dress.

"But we must be quiet, good sir," she gasped as her lover's lips skirted along her neck, sending goosebumps down her body.

"I'm always quiet," the boy returned, though both knew that was not true.

Xelha' smirked. "If your family finds out—"

"They won't—" Blood-Letter assured her as their bodies melted together.

The girl's eyes looked hard into his, a veil of sadness and worry crossing her face as she said, "They'd never accept someone from my lands—"

But the boy was shaking his head. "One day, they will. They will have no choice—when you are my wife."

Then he kissed her again, and Xelha' felt her body give in to the moment.

"You can't be serious," Itza' stared at Snake Lady sitting across from her, her eyes filled with a burning intensity. Her blood felt cold, and she couldn't bring herself to trust what she was telling her.

"Is it so hard to believe?" Snake Lady said flatly, sipping her drink.

Itza' clenched her jaw again but said nothing. It was obvious to her that the young girl, Xelha', was the woman Snake Lady had been before becoming Queen of Sprouting Earth.

Which made Sprouting Earth the kingdom she settled in with her mysterious aunt . . . And their treacherous neighbors . . .

But she didn't want to believe it. She didn't want to accept that the treacherous ajaw that Snake Lady was describing was Itza's paternal grandfather—one of the greatest rulers in Yaxchilan's history. And she certainly didn't want to believe the other part—that Snake Lady had been in love with the ajaw's youngest son . . .

"You . . . and my father . . . " Itza' breathed the words out slowly. But then something else occurred to her.

"So, this is why you cursed them? Some jealous revenge for a teenage romance? You're—"

Snake Lady put up a hand to stop Itza' from continuing. "So much like your mother, always assuming the wrong motives . . ." She shook her head and eyed the younger woman with a grim look.

"I told you, little one, I never cursed your father. We were in love . . . once, when I was a foolish little girl, and he was a cocky, impulsive, young warrior. But he was something else in those days too, my dear."

"What? What else was he, oh Great Queen of Snakes?" Itza' asked intently.

"I told you it was a long story. Sip your drink, Great Lady, and listen closely . . ."

Blood dripped from the young man's mouth, and Xelha' did her best to wipe it off. Another bout of coughing seized the young warrior, and she felt him shake like an earthquake in her arms. The sounds crashed like thunder against the wooden poles of the small hut at the foot of the mountain, blending with the sounds of the rainy tempest raging outside. Heavy *plops* of rain could be heard banging against the thatched roof. The rainy season had started somewhat later that year, but it was no less intense.

Blood-Letter's head lay in Xelha's lap. His large torso and legs lay across the pelt-draped bench underneath them. Xelha' could not help but wonder how a man so big and strong managed to escape death on the battlefield at every turn yet grew sicker and sicker each rainy season.

It doesn't make sense, she thought, stroking the tired warrior's chiseled jaw as he rested his eyes in the warm comfort of her lap. He insists he and his brother are invincible . . . yet here he is, sick again.

As if reading her mind, Blood-Letter opened his eyes and grunted. "You're wondering how I can be so fortunate on the battle-field and so sick the rest of the year, I bet."

Xelha' nodded, looking down at the man she loved with her intense gaze. Blood-Letter felt like her eyes grew darker and glassier each time he saw her lately. Her voice had become a husky rasp as well.

"You say there's a prophesy in Yaxchilan—that the day-keepers said you are invincible—"

"Hey now," he grunted in interruption, squirming in her lap. "That's not quite right. My father's greatest advisor and day-keeper had a vision on the night my mother got pregnant with my older brother."

Xelha' raised her eyebrow. "And how does he know it was that night exactly, hmmmm?"

Blood-Letter smirked at his lover's strange humming sound. "Never mind that—it's all part of the legend."

"And you do like having a legend about you, eh?" Her sensuous, raspy voice slid along the side of his neck and danced over his ears. Then another cough seized the large warrior, but he pushed it down, feeling some of his strength returning.

"I'm merely trying to tell you what happened, my love, my heart, the future queen of all that is mine—"

Xelha' raised a hand to stop him. "Okay, okay, great warrior . . . don't strain yourself. I'm listening."

They looked into each other's eyes and smiled warmly. "And this day-keeper, my friend, he is. He's called Q'anchi—"

"An interesting name," Xelha' muttered, wondering how many people in Yaxchilan were still named after snakes these days.

"Isn't it? Anyway, my friend—he saw a vision that day. And because of that, he learned that neither I nor my brother would ever fall on the battlefield and that no man's deeds would ever cause my death."

"Hmmmm," Xelha' let out her long humming sound. "I agree—that isn't the same as being invincible at all."

Blood-Letter just shrugged. "So far—so good."

Xelha' rolled her eyes, but her lover was already resting his own again and didn't see the expression. The two sat in silence for a while longer, listening to the downpour and thunder outside. They would have to wait out the storm before they could travel again, back to their respective kingdoms. Xelha' guessed it would be too late by the time the rains stopped anyway, and they would end up sleeping in the hut that night.

After a while, she said, "Your sickness is getting worse, isn't it?"

Blood-Letter just mumbled something sleepily under his breath in response. But Xelha' could see, even if she had been there only a few years so far. She could tell that his bouts of coughing grew worse and worse with each rainy season. And now he was coughing up blood sometimes.

If he doesn't get help soon . . . But she didn't want to finish the thought. Surely, the priests in Yaxchilan can see what is happening . . . he's cursed.

But Xelha' had noticed that many of the priests trained in the cities were not as adept at sniffing out curses and magic as Xelha' and her aunt. They didn't want to see the curse sometimes or deal with the political ramifications. Or they waited until they had more evidence than they ever actually needed before finally admitting to what should have been obvious. Xelha' had seen it many times in the court of Sprouting Earth, where she resided now. She had seen men ignore the words of her aunt because it was not fitting to have a peasant woman see something before a noble priest.

Something has to be done for him, she thought. Her heart ached and was heavy with worry for Blood-Letter. She watched him sleep for hours, listening to the rain die down outside as night took over, and the sounds of the jungle animals began to return. She started to drift off, her head propped against the poles in the corner of the hut where the bench lay. She woke, at some point, to a gentle *swish-swish* sound along the floor. She opened her eyes and then heard the unmistakable *hissss* of a snake. As she watched sleepily, a dark and slender form writhed and undulated its way across the floor of the hut by the bench.

Xelha' should have been alarmed, but she felt so inescapably tired in that moment. Her eyes could only stay half open to watch the serpent move along the floor. In its wake, the wind picked up for a moment, and she thought she heard a soft voice whisper in her ear.

Help him, the voice said. Cure him, it whispered. Xelha's eyes were already closed again.

"It took nearly a whole year for the girl to find the way to cure her lover. In the end, she learned the missing piece of the puzzle by accident. Her aunt was called to come help a village on the outskirts of Sprouting Earth, along the border of the realm Yaxchilan ruled. The girl went with her to find that many of the children in the village were terribly ill. For days, curers from both Yaxchilan and Sprouting Earth worked with day-keepers and medicine men from all over to try and figure out what could be done for the children.

"But the curers from Yaxchilan did not trust the curers from Sprouting Earth, nor the other way around. It made the work slow going as members of each rival kingdom accused the other of being untrustworthy or incompetent. But eventually, an old woman helped. She was very old—an ancient creature with a sun-etched face and a smile that beamed like the sun. Her laugh came easily, and she used

her jokes and teasing to bring down the tension in the village as the children were getting worse, and some had died already. She was special, and Xelha' noticed that everyone called her Grandmother with that particular accent that made the word somehow a title.

" 'What can we do, Grandmother?' everyone asked this ancient woman. But it was not until Xelha' came to her with a small gift of blue flowers she had found by the river that the oldest of women seemed to have an answer.

" 'She knows,' was all that Grandmother said. 'She knows . . . '

"And then the ancient one gathered all the other curers and medicine men together, and the whole group worked all night. In the morning, they came to the area with the sick children. Each of them held some sort of tonic, and Xelha's Aunt said it had been made using the flowers Xelha' had found.

"The group lit the incense and said the words for healing, and they gave the children the special tonic that had taken all night to prepare. By dawn on the third day, all the remaining children were cured. And Xelha' knew what her missing ingredient was to save Blood-Letter . . ."

Xelha' slithered through the shadows of the great palace building in Yaxchilan. She clung to the dark corners and climbed the walls to hide in the rafters when she needed to avoid the guards on their patrols. Days before, she had bribed two of the guards into extinguishing some of the wall torches at certain places so she would have more cover for her approach.

She arrived at the prince's bedchamber, where Blood-Letter had been taken after falling ill just as the rains started. Through the connections she had made in the Yaxchilan priesthood, word had reached her that her lover had been struck by a particularly vicious bout of his illness. He was bedridden and could not move—could barely eat or drink. Though his illness was kept secret from the populous, Xelha' had heard that some of the priests did not think

Blood-Letter would survive.

It was late in the night by the time she stood over Blood-Letter's bed. In his sleep, the young warrior grunted and moaned with pain, and Xelha' could see the blood-stained cloths left on the bedside table by the curers who had been watching him during the day.

She wasted no time.

Xelha' pulled out the medicine bundle from the pouch at her waist and got to work. There was already incense burning, but she swapped out the herbs for a special resin she had made. Then she placed the hand-made candles, which she herself had fashioned, at each corner of the room. She pulled out a few pieces of red chord and loosely tied strands to one of his wrists and ankles. She moved about the room and began to pray, letting the words flow from her lips like the rushing waters of a desperate river. She tried to clear her mind of negative thoughts and feelings and let only her love imbue the words with meaning and power.

When it was time to deliver the tonic that she had made, she stood carefully at Blood-Letter's side with the small gourd. She placed the gourd beside him, unsealed the top to expose the liquid inside, and pulled out a short stingray needle from a tiny pouch she always carried with her. Deftly, having practiced the move many times over the years, she used the needle to draw a small amount of blood from different parts on her body. She pricked her tongue, her breast over the heart, her abdomen, one thigh, and a foot. Each time, she added a bit of her blood from the area into the tonic.

Inside the gourd, some of the flowers Xelha' had learned were powerful medicine still lay whole. She had added them as protection for the mixture. She watched as a drop of her blood slid along one of the brightly colored petals, the light blue mixing with the deep red from the rivers inside her.

After she had let her own blood, she did the same to Blood-Letter. She pricked him, making small cuts on his chest, his thigh, a wrist, along his jaw on one side, and his right ear. She collected a few drops of blood from each spot in the gourd. Then, she sealed the gourd that contained both their blood and gently mixed the tonic in her hand, praying intently as she did so.

After a few moments of her mixing, the winds in the room changed. The air became wetter and hotter, and the incense smoke swirled and writhed in new directions. From this, Xelha' knew it was time.

She unsealed the gourd and, with painful caution, placed the lip of the sacred cup against the pale lips of her lover. She tilted the container and let some of the medicine slide into his mouth, over his tongue, and drip down into his throat. The man twisted suddenly in bed but did not wake. A few drops spilled along his chin and his cheek, seeping into the cut along his jaw where Xelha' had drawn his blood. Xelha' waited until he had calmed down again and then gave him more of the drink.

Now we wait, she thought, sealing up the gourd and placing it back in her pouch. She did not have to wait long.

In less than an hour, the prince was convulsing. His body shook violently. Xelha' tried to hold him down, but he was too big and his movements too erratic. His head tilted back, and an odd humming sound began emanating from deep in his throat, as if a large creature were growling from inside the cave of his esophagus. His eyes opened, but his pupils had rolled back in his head, and soon, he was bleeding from his mouth as the strange growling got louder and louder.

Xelha' panicked. She did not know what to do or what was happening. She tried to hold on to the man she loved as his giant body writhed and squirmed in her small hands. His arms and legs kicked and jerked as if lightning were striking him over and over again. His head shook as if seizing, and air escaped his throat as the low growl turned to an odd, windswept sound, like hot air blowing through a cave.

Eventually, though, the shaking and convulsing subsided. Blood-Letter's body calmed down, and his breathing became normal once more. As he slowly woke up, Xelha' looked him over. He seemed different, somehow. His skin was darker, perhaps, or maybe smoother. The veins in his arms and thighs seemed to pop out more.

Then Xelha' looked at his face and saw the scar. Right there, where she had pricked him with the stingray needle along his jaw, Blood-Letter now had a strange scar he had not had before. It was long and thin, a dark black wave that undulated irregularly against his chiseled, perfectly straight jawbone.

Like the black snake my aunt drew . . . Xelha' realized suddenly, and felt goosebumps run along the back of her left leg. She traced a finger lightly against the scar, puzzled and entranced.

Blood-Letter's hand reached out and grabbed hers. He looked up at her, slowly waking up and registering the world around him.

"Xelha'? What are you doing here?" His voice was hoarse from days spent coughing.

Xelha' smiled warmly. "I came to see you, love. I heard you were sick."

Blood-Letter shook his head. "If they catch you here . . ."

She put a finger to his lips. "It's okay, my love. I bribed the guards days ago. I had to come . . . to help."

Blood-Letter felt confused. Bribed the guards? Help with what?

He started to sit up, brushing off her attempts to stop him. He forced himself up into a seated position despite the pain and difficulty and looked Xelha' in the eyes. They were bright and full of excitement. His mind was clearing, but he still felt a dense fog surrounding all his thinking. He still felt as if he were half dreaming.

"To help with what, Xelha'? You know I don't trust the magic your mentor does." He looked around him cautiously. He sniffed the air.

"What incense is that? What are those candles in the corners?" Then he looked at Xelha' intently, the fog clearing more and more with each second. The realization of why she must have snuck in there dawning on him.

"What have you done?" The hoarseness did not hide his alarm or frustration.

She shook her head. "It's okay, my love," she said softly, taking his face in her hands. Her intense dark eyes were wide with love and relief. "You're cured."

Blood-Letter eyed her suspiciously for a prolonged moment, then said, "How? What did you do, Xelha'?"

She had not expected this. "It's just medicine, my love," she said softly. "Same as any curer would do."

Blood-Letter's eyes narrowed. "What kind of medicine?"

"I . . . I made it. From the blue flowers that grow along the river. I saw them cure a whole village of sick children! So, I knew it could help you too."

"What are you saying?" Blood-Letter's voice was low, like a feral growl. "Those flowers are poison!"

Xelha' put up her hands in protest. "They don't have to be! Don't you see? That's what I figured out. It took—so much time. But I figured out how to do it. How to change them. For you, my love."

Her voice trailed off softly as she called him 'my love.' The words didn't feel quite right in that moment. Blood-Letter was barely looking at her anymore. His eyes only got more and more full of rage as she spoke. His breathing was jagged and shallow.

"Magic . . ." His voice was a low growl, and the word sounded like a curse on his lips. "The meddling magic of witches has cost my family enough."

Xelha' swallowed hard. He had never used that word to describe her before, and it sunk a barb deep into her heart. "I am not a witch, good sir, hmmmm," she said, her voice shaky with sadness. "I help people—and I have helped you. Look at you! You already look better!"

But the angry warrior just shook his head. His jaw clenched reflexively as he leveled the fierce gaze in his eyes at her. The snake-like scar writhed with his tensing muscles, and he became aware of the feeling of its presence on his face. But no matter his feelings, he couldn't match the intensity of her black-eyed gaze, and eventually, he looked away.

"But at what cost, Xelha'? What will your magic cost me?"

She scrunched her face. "What are you talking about? It's just medicine."

Blood-Letter grabbed her hand and slid one of her fingers along the snake-like scar on his jaw. "This—this doesn't *feel* like just medicine! Do you even know what you have brought by doing this here? These things always have a cost! Believe me!"

He was having trouble keeping his voice down, and she worried someone might hear them and come inside to check on the prince.

"I—" Xelha' started but found her voice faltering. "I—just wanted to help you. I—love you."

The warrior's eyes softened but only for a moment. The hour was late, and both knew that the castle would soon be buzzing with early morning aides and staff.

"I know you were trying to help, but I do not *need* that kind of help. We do not suffer witches in Yaxchilan, and your magic is unpredictable. You have to find out what the cost is—before things get worse."

Xelha' was taken aback, but he gave her no time to speak. He grabbed her arm and started guiding her off the bed.

"I want you to go. I need to think this over and . . . you need to figure out what you've done."

Her heart ached at the strange turn in the man's demeanor. And with that pain, her sadness started to turn to anger. The moons spent studying and listening, the sleepless nights spent gathering herbs and sap and all manner of things to figure out a way to break an unknown curse. And after all that she had done—she was just a witch to him after all.

She felt her eyes welling up with tears and, for the first time, felt ashamed to cry in front of him. She shook her head as she stepped away from the bed. The warrior looked up at her, but she noticed he could not totally meet her gaze.

"I hope you are well, great warrior. And that your future is better for it." Her voice was impassive. In one motion, she turned her back on Blood-Letter and left. Xelha' snuck her way out of the palace and away from Yaxchilan.

Itza' took a long and slow drag from the tobacco pipe in her hand before passing it to Snake Lady. She still had not touched the drink Snake Lady had given her before the start of the story, but she had, instead, brought out her own tobacco bundle and paraphernalia during the tale. She wanted to have something she knew and trusted close at hand while listening.

"So . . . the harsh and obdurate Snake Queen was once a tender, loving girl?" Itza' breathed the words out along with the smoke in her lungs. The skepticism in her voice was obvious. She stared at Snake Lady and, for the first time since their initial meeting, she studied the woman's eyes as closely as she could.

Snake Lady's irises were as black as a cave. Itza' tried to imagine those eyes becoming darker and glassier over time and with age. As far as Itza' knew, her own eyes had been black since birth, but she also recalled how they had changed as she learned more about the history and magic of the Winaq from the priests. How knowledge about their world had made them deeper and darker in a way that she had never been able to explain to others.

"It is hard to imagine you and this young Xelha' being the same person," Itza' purred, feeling the tobacco smoke run its course within and along her body. She curled her legs up into the chair in a distinctly pantherine gesture.

"A snake sheds its skin, little one," Snake Lady replied, handing the pipe back to Itza'. "We all began as something else . . ." she muttered, looking off at the hundreds of books shelved within the small room where the two women sat.

Itza' scrunched her face. "I knew my father didn't trust women with magic, but I never heard him sound like that in my lifetime."

The Great Snake Queen made a dismissive gesture. "He was young and arrogant then. A courageous but reckless warrior. I'm sure your mother tempered his attitude considerably."

Snake Lady smiled knowingly at the last part then added, "The feud between the kingdoms was old by the time I got there. The prejudices ran deep, and I'm certain, looking back, that was part of why he reacted so strongly."

It was an unusually balanced and empathetic appraisal, delivered in a somewhat softer tone. It made Itza' wonder if maybe this tale really was true after all, and Snake Lady had loved Itza's father.

"His reaction must have hurt you deeply then, Great Queen," Itza' spoke softly. She took another drag from the pipe.

Snake Lady nodded. "At the time, hmmmmm."

Itza' handed the pipe back to Snake Lady, saying, "No wonder you wanted to curse my mother then, and have her suffer as you suffered, eh?"

A soft laugh came from the Great Snake as she took the pipe, then more headshaking. "Foolish girl..." she muttered, taking a short hit.

"Your father's words did hurt me, and I was angry," she continued. "But I am not a jealous person. I was not upset that he married your mother, and I harbored no hatred for her."

"Then why, Honored-Mother-of-This-Fertile-Soil-Here, did. You. Curse. Her?" Itza' growled. Snake Lady handed the pipe back to Itza'.

"Take a long inhale of that, little one... you're going to need it..."

"In truth, it wasn't just Blood-Letter that was angry at the girl. Her aunt also raged when she found out what little Xelha' had done. She yelled at the girl, saying much the same as the ungrateful young warrior had said. Her aunt told Xelha' that she had no business trying such magic, that she wasn't ready for it, that it did, indeed, have a price, and that such things were far from just simple medicine.

"Little Xelha' wept and wept. A river of tears flowed from her as if the torrents of the rainy season emanated from her body, itself. She could not sleep for worry about what the price of her magic might be. She pleaded with her aunt to tell her what that price was, but the

old woman could not. She said it would require a long journey to find out. Her aunt left the kingdom. She went away to try and find the answers—just in case the price was something terrible for them all.

"Left alone in Sprouting Earth, little Xelha' took over her mentor's duties at court. She advised the ajaw and earned his favor, and she heard more of the news from other kingdoms—including Yaxchilan. It was in that way that she heard of the terrible flooding the rains had brought to their lands that season. How the water that poured from the sky had been too much and had flooded the plains and the terraced hills where they planted their crops. The soil had been inundated, and the crops had failed over a huge portion of their realm. A food shortage had gripped Yaxchilan—famine was spreading in many of the villages and smaller towns.

"Xelha' knew, at once, the floods and the famine were her fault. This had to be the price of the cure. Through her informants at Yaxchilan, she also knew that Blood-Letter was no longer sick. She put two and two together and realized that her work to heal their prince had cost the people of Yaxchilan their health and their lives. Xelha' wept even more. She blamed herself for everything going on in Yaxchilan. And worse still, Blood-Letter blamed her, too . . .

The letter arrived in secret, delivered by messengers from Yaxchilan by way of other messengers from another of the earthen kingdoms. It was given to a guard, who passed it to an aide, who slipped it into Xelha's hands while they passed each other in the market.

Xelha' had to wait until her duties at court were finished for the day to read it. She didn't get to open the parchment until after nightfall. The letter was surprisingly short, written in Blood-Letter's own hand using a simple script for personal writings—not the elegant and painstaking glyphic system carved onto stone monuments and painted on the great codices. This was a simpler system, used between lovers or spies, for passing more personal messages. And, apparently, for delivering heartbreaking news as well.

Do you see what your meddling has brought? Horrible rains, and now the crops have failed! Our people are starving. I told you everything has a cost. You should have told me your plan from the beginning. Then I would have told you not to bring your witchcraft into my life. I've had enough of witches! They have attacked our family too many times. They bring nothing but pain and death to those they touch. My own brother was nearly killed trying to save villagers from drowning!

I do not know what spell you put on me or if you truly cured my illness. If you did, then I should thank you. But I would rather have died than let my people suffer as they do now! And who knows what you have actually done or tried to do? Perhaps this is simply some other scheme. To bind me to you or force me to marry you out of obligation. Whatever it is, I will not have it in my life! Or my kingdom. Our paths are no longer one, good lady. Your road will not end with me. Whatever dangers your powers and your magic bring, I will not have them anywhere near my kingdom or my people.

At first, Xelha' was angry. She raged against the foolish brute who could not even see what she had tried to do for him. She hated the ingratitude and arrogance of men like him who could never see the value in what she and her aunt did and were capable of. But eventually, the anger faded. And her broken heart stabbed itself into the spaces between her ribs, and she rocked herself to sleep in tears each night for days on end.

Until her aunt finally returned.

The old woman was there at court one morning as if nothing had ever happened. They went through the day as if no time had passed since her departure and as if Xelha's entire life had not been turned upside down. And then, that evening in her aunt's pole and thatch hut at the edge of town, when no one else was around, she stood opposite her aunt across the small cooking fire.

"I should never have learned these things! I ruined everything, Auntie! I killed those people!"

Her aunt did not look up from the pot she was stirring. The fire crackled across the logs, and smoke danced around her ancient features.

"I'm a witch! Do you not see! This evil has been inside me for so long I can't even see it anymore!"

"Humph," was the only response from the raspy lump of human sitting by the pot.

Xelha' was furious. "Do you even care, old woman? Are you even listening to me?"

In anger, she threw a bowl of water at the fire. Her aunt stuck out a short broom head reflexively. It blocked most of the liquid, but some droplets still managed to get through. In response, the flames hissed and hissed as the water fell on the fire, like four thousand tiny snakes had just been set loose inside the hut.

Finally, Auntie looked up at Xelha'. The fire lit her face and blended with her sun-etched skin, but it only made her eyes seem darker and more cavernous.

"So . . . you think it was a mistake to cure the boy, eh?"

Xelha' nearly screamed. "Ugh! Are you not listening? It cost their kingdom so much!"

The woman's eyes lifted slightly. "So . . . you think you caused the rain, eh?"

"I—" Xelha' felt dumbfounded. "You said yourself these things have a cost—Blood-Letter said the same."

"Foolish boy," Auntie spat, turning back to the pot. "How would he know? Very interesting that—"

But Xelha' wasn't listening. "I killed those people . . ." She remembered the times she had tried to end her life as a young girl. She thought hard about how to be successful the next time.

"Foolish boy," Auntie repeated. "Foolish *girl* . . . Only a fool would think such magic would cause a flood."

Xelha' stopped, suddenly. She stared intently at her aunt. Her eyes grew so intense, she thought she could hear the heartbeat of the old woman in her ears.

"Are you saying I didn't cause the floods? Did I cause the famine, Auntie?"

Her aunt shook her head. "No, my dear. Stop listening to the words of foolish men, little one. You had nothing to do with the rains."

Xelha' was so relieved that she laughed out loud. She plopped down onto a stool in the hut and felt tears well up in her eyes again. Only this time, they were tears of relief and joy.

Maybe she can tell Blood-Letter this, and he will forgive me? she thought excitedly.

"So, you *did* find out the truth on your journey, Auntie? You found out my magic didn't cause this awful thing?"

Her aunt nodded again, almost smiling. She grabbed some bowls with one hand and filled them with soup from the pot with the other. She handed one to Xelha' and then found them both some spoons. The young girl dug deep into her meal. The relief from her guilt had made her realize just how hungry she was. It was as if she had not eaten since getting Blood-Letter's message.

"Of course I found out," her aunt said as she chewed the roots in her soup. "Your cure would never cause a flood, little one."

Auntie's tone struck Xelha' as odd. She sounded as if she had stopped mid-sentence but was taking another gulp of her concoction. Xelha' felt the wind change in the hut suddenly, and a cold breeze brought goosebumps along the younger woman's bare arms.

"No, little one . . . the price for *your* magic will be much steeper than a single bad harvest . . ."

Xelha's blood ran cold as she looked at her aunt who still sipped her broth casually as ever.

"Auntie . . . what is it? You have to tell me!"

Her aunt put down her bowl and looked Xelha' in the face. "I told you not to meddle with these things until you were ready . . .

Ey-ya! Fine—let's be done with it. The price is simply this: the cost for your prince's future health is the future of his lineage."

Her tone was flat and impassive. Her eyes were cold and unnerving. But Xelha' did not fully understand the woman's words.

"The future of his lineage? What does that mean, Auntie?"

"Hmph," the old, familiar reply came. Then came the simple explanation that would shape the fate of things to come for many years. "You stupid little girl. It means that your cure is not perfect, little one, it is not permanent. It will last—but! Only so long as the man you love has no future lineage—only so long as he does not have children!"

Xelha' screamed. Her heart sank, shattered, and broke into four thousand pieces all over again.

"I should never have done this, Auntie! I should never have learned these things or come with you. I can't do this anymore—I won't do this anymore. I won't use our magic any longer. Blood-Letter was right. It causes nothing but pain and misery."

But her aunt just cackled loudly. She stared Xelha' in the eyes, and a terrifying grimace gripped her face as she said, "Oh no, little one. You cannot give up now. In fact, girl, I happen to know that your work has only just begun."

"I don't believe you. I don't believe any of it!" Itza' hurled the words across the table at Snake Lady and rose up out of the chair. She moved toward the older woman and, for a moment, considered pulling out her concealed knife and ending the reign of the merciless Snake Queen right then and there. But, instead, she moved past her, threw open the door to the small room, and stormed out. She walked out into the fading light of the day, her footsteps barely audible to Snake Lady as she listened to the young woman leave. In Itza's absence, Snake Lady closed her eyes tightly and let her tears run down her cheeks.

The Puma's Roar

Peace was never my goal. I only wanted to make the world tremble at the sound of my name.

—*Xelaq'am's Songs*

THE MOUNTAIN TREMBLED from the deafening roars that filled the night sky. The moon, full and bright, looked down on the cave at the base of the mountain. From deep inside, she heard another roar. And another. It had been going on for hours now.

But eventually, the roars subsided. And then the moon picked up on another sound. A faint gurgle. And then, an eruption. The loud, wild cries of a newborn baby greeting the world for the first time. The cries were almost as loud as the roars that had preceded the infant's arrival.

Inside the cave, Afua handed the baby to Chanil, who wrapped up her newborn daughter in the same blanket Chanil had been given by Night Star as a baby. Chanil leaned back, breathing heavy, and beamed down at her child.

"What did I tell you, cousin," Yahíma laughed loudly, sitting nearby with her own baby nursing in her lap.

Afua smiled. "A healthy baby girl, Lady Sky."

"A girl," Chanil breathed out. Her voice trembled. Her whole body felt weak and depleted after so many hours of pushing. The labor had been a difficult one, and Afua had seemed prepared for the worst at one point.

But none of that seemed to matter now. Her daughter was here. Chanil held the small baby—so tiny. The infant gurgled and fussed, but her crying was over for now. Her eyes were mere slits, and she looked as tired as Chanil felt.

"Will you get in here already, old man?" Yahíma yelled out. "Your baby girl waiting for you."

A rustle of sounds near the cave entrance and then Ch'akanel appeared. He had a wide grin on his face as he rushed over to Chanil's side. His long locs were pulled back and tied away from his face. Tears welled up in his eyes as he cradled Chanil with one arm and felt his daughter's little fingers, checking to make sure all her toes were there.

"We did it," he whispered.

Chanil nodded. "We did it, my love."

Afua moved around the two parents and the newborn, saying words Chanil could barely understand. But she got the gist. There were always important ceremonies following birth. And even though this birth had to remain a secret, they still had to do everything they could to make sure the girl was welcomed into the world properly.

After Afua had finished her blessings, she sat down and beamed at the baby. She giggled and spoke to the newborn like an excited grandmother, which, Chanil figured, she basically was. Afua seemed delighted at having two grandchildren now—Chanil's baby girl and Yahíma's newborn boy.

"When you are ready, Sky," Afua said, sliding over to Yahíma's baby. "I will take you to the spot where your mother's placenta is buried, eh? And we will bury this new one's there too, yeah?"

Chanil smiled. She had wondered recently about her own

placenta. She had always been told it was buried in Yaxchilan alongside Itza's and Lady Xok's. But had Night Star stolen away to bury it on the Island?

"Is it dangerous?" Ch'akanel asked. "Won't the Cacique's men be guarding that place?"

"Maybe Mabó can sneak us in," Chanil said, referring to the man she had spared and who had sworn his loyalty to her mother and grandmother.

Afua made a face. "He turned out to be okay, hm."

Yahíma shook her head. "It isn't a guarded place. It's a secret. Every family here keeps the spot for these things a secret from anybody else."

Chanil nodded in understanding. She had learned more about her people's ways during her stay on the Island. "So they can't try any funny business with your spirit, eh?"

Yahíma pursed her lips and nodded. Afua made an affirmative gesture. "The secret keep all them curses away. It protects us."

Ch'akanel turned to Chanil. "Mabó told me there is a regular ferry every moon that can take us back to the mainland whenever we want. He'll arrange it for us when we need to return."

Yahíma went wide-eyed. "You just got here and already gonna leave?"

Chanil looked at her pointedly. "Five moons not just getting here, eh? Besides, I have a war to win, remember?"

Her cousin made a sour face but said nothing.

"Tell Mabó to arrange for me to go back with the next ferry," Chanil said, but Ch'akanel heard the command in her voice and knew it was the Puma who was speaking.

"You mean *us* to go back, don't you?" he asked, already knowing he wouldn't like the answer.

Chanil shook her head. "I go back alone. Just at first. I have to know where the family stands and what's happened with the war. It could be too dangerous to bring our girl home right now. I need you to stay with her."

Yahíma laughed and slapped her thigh. "You stuck here with me, old man, a little while longer!"

Afua grinned and dismissed all other conversation. "You going to tell us what her name is? I need to know what to call my granddaughter while you gone, big warrior."

Chanil laughed. "That part is easy, Momma Afua. Just call her your 'shining star' like you did with my mother."

Chanil tucked the blanket around her daughter. The girl was awake, looking up at her mother intently. She gurgled and cooed. Chanil felt her heart reach out, and all she wanted to do was lift up that baby girl and never let her go.

But she had to. At least for now.

"Don't look at me like that, little one," Chanil said, adjusting the blanket. "I'll be back as soon as I can."

A strong arm wrapped around Chanil's waist and pulled her in tight. "Not soon enough," Ch'akanel whispered, kissing her cheek.

The baby's eyes opened even wider as her father looked down at her, and Ch'akanel whistled.

"That's going to take some getting used to," he said, having trouble meeting his daughter's gaze.

Chanil laughed. Her daughter's eyes were wide, and though she had been slow to open them, now they seemed to never close. The baby took everything in.

The eyes were also intense, almost frighteningly so. Afua and Yahíma had both commented on it. Afua had even said to not bring the baby into the market because her eyes would be noticed and then rumors would start. Yahíma had gasped the first time seeing those eyes. She had looked at Chanil as though something were wrong, but Chanil had shaken her head and brushed it off.

Chanil had seen eyes like this before. She had grown up with a pair just like them in many ways.

"You should have seen Itza's as a baby," Chanil teased. "Hers were all black, like obsidian stones. It was unnerving."

Chanil looked down into her daughter's fierce gaze. The infant reached out, and Chanil picked her up and folded her into her strong arms. She held the infant's head up and returned the intense look.

"I like the grey," Chanil said. Her daughter's eyes were not black like Itza's. They were ash grey, like smoke or very dark storm clouds. And they had wisps of black running through them.

Ch'akanel shook his head. "I've never seen eyes like that. Even your sister's aren't like this. They really do look like . . . like an ash cloud, don't you think?"

Chanil rubbed her nose against her daughter's, and the baby laughed. "You daddy silly, eh? You just a baby. You just my shining star."

Chanil felt Ch'akanel's warm lips wandering along her neck. "Do you have to go?"

Chanil grinned. "Not until the morning," she said knowingly. "But I've been gone too long already. I have to find out how our family is doing. For all I know, the war is over . . ."

She swallowed, unable to finish the thought. Unable to face the idea that things could have gotten much worse for Yaxchilan in her absence, and it would all be her fault. That worry terrified her more than anything else. She loved her daughter. But Yahíma and Ch'akanel would keep the baby safe. Chanil had an ally in the cacique's court here. This place was safe.

She had to find out if Yaxchilan was still safe as well.

At the Edge

*I have said before that my eyes are not truly black. My aunt explained it once to
me. She said, "Your power comes from the rivers, little one." But I was young and
confused. "Water is life," she told me. "What you see in your eyes is a reflection of the
water that runs through our world and sustains our world." I protested that my eyes
were black, not clear like water. "Do not be fooled by the color, foolish girl," she said
slowly. "Your eyes are many things. They hold our secrets, little one, and that is why
they appear black: to hide the power you possess from those who would do us harm."*

—*the Book of Queen Snake Lady.*

THE WOMAN FOUND LITTLE ITZA' SITTING at the edge of the
small ts'onot. Itza' dangled her feet over the edge of the limestone
rim that had been built around the cavernous opening of the giant
well. This particular ts'onot was just a deep hole that went straight
down into its underground pool, eventually connecting to the system
of rivers and caves that ran beneath the surface of their world on the
Peninsula. The people in this region had built a sturdy fortification of
stones to secure the rim, and a pulley system to retrieve water from
the sacred well. Although Itza' knew it might be dangerous to sit on
the edge of the stone rim for long, she did not care. In fact, part of her
wondered if she should just fling herself down and be done with it.

Snake Lady said quietly, "Your mother would have my head if you fell in, little one."

Something about the simple caring in her voice made Itza' turn, and she looked up at the older woman standing next to her. Snake Lady saw the pain there. She was reminded of her own pains as a younger woman. Then Itza' looked back down into the well of the ts'onot.

She must get through this, Snake Lady thought.

Itza's mind was racing, her brain putting together connection after connection. The pieces of the puzzle of her life were falling together. And they came together so fast, their implications so clear, that she couldn't bear it. For the first time in her life, she almost wished she had stayed ignorant.

"You cursed my mother . . ." Her voice was soft and full of jagged edges where the pain lay bare and open. ". . . to save my father."

Snake Lady nodded gravely, pushing down the tears that threatened to break through her wall of impassivity. "You must have so many questions, little one," she breathed out.

But, surprisingly, Itza' shook her head. She gathered up what strength she had left and turned her body around. She looked up at Snake Lady and said, "I only have one question, Great Queen."

Snake Lady raised her eyebrows in response. "Hmmmm?"

"Have we killed our father? Did Chanil's and my births seal his fate somehow?" Her voice cracked, and tears fell from her eyes, but she would not look away from the Snake Queen, who seemed to hold all the answers to her life.

Snake Lady knelt down in front of Itza' and took her hands in her own. "It was not your fault, little one. It was not your fault."

Itza' had tears running down her face. Snake Lady felt her own tears threaten to pour out like rivers. But she held them back and continued. "There were so many things that I should have done or could have done over the years. Your father, too. But no child is to blame for what happened. And you have a father, remember that, little one. You have him there to guide you and hold you and love you in his way. And I know him—better than most. I know there is nothing he wouldn't trade for the moments with you and your sister."

Itza' nodded, wiping her eyes. "You must be getting old, Great Queen. You're getting sentimental."

The two of them laughed. It was the first time Itza' had heard Snake Lady do so.

"There must be something I can do," Itza' said after a while. Her tone was desperate, pleading.

Snake Lady stood tall and let go of Itza'. "I tried that. Without knowing the source of the curse . . . these things are delicate."

Four hundred possibilities ran through Itza's mind. But given how much her father hated magic, and that he already knew about his curse, she didn't really see any possibility that was fundamentally different from what Snake Lady had tried when they were younger.

Without knowing the source of the curse . . .

Itza' remembered her visit, years ago, to the ancient temple on the outskirts of Yaxchilan. Grandmother had drugged her and told her the story of how her mother had broken the curse. In the end, Grandmother had said that Itza' would meet Snake Lady and find the answers. And she had said that when that happened, Itza' might come to hate the old woman as much as her father did. The words had not made sense then, but now they made Itza' wonder.

"Was it *her*?" Itza' asked. Snake Lady caught the tone around the word 'her' and knew, at once, who Itza' meant.

She looked down into the ts'onot. "I've wondered that as well, little one. It could be why he hates her."

Itza' sighed. "So, we have no answers. Again."

Then, more cautiously, she whispered, "How long does my father have?"

Snake Lady took her hand gently. "I honestly don't know. I'm surprised he has lasted this long."

"It's been getting worse every rainy season," Itza' said somberly.

"Then he might not have long at all, little one."

And Itza' could see the glint in Snake Lady' eyes. The tears held back for a man she had once loved and who now despised her.

Itza' squeezed her mentor's hands tightly. "I have to go back. I—don't even know what to tell them or what I'll do when I get back. But I need to see my family. To prepare."

Snake Lady nodded. "Of course. My proposal can wait."

Itza' let out a small chuckle. "I think we both know it makes sense."

"Then go home, little one. Tell them of the proposal and say what you need to. I'll be here, waiting for you when you come back."

Coming Home

The ground trembled with the march of the Great Army. Their footsteps shook the land like an earthquake and toppled our temples and our trees. They tore out our roots and left us homeless in our own lands.

—collected writings of the Occupation

THE SOUND OF LORD 5-THUNDER'S COUGHS filled the room. It echoed off the painted stone walls and shook Itza's bones as she lay on the cot by her father's side. They were alone in his bedchamber. He had sent everyone else away in anger. Itza' patted his forehead with the towel and willed Q'anchi's strange tonic to cure her father of the mysterious curse that had plagued him all his life. But Itza' felt a deep despair as she crouched over him and wiped his fevered brow.

She knew it was hopeless. So much had changed since she had left. She had been back for only a winal now, just seven days, but it seemed like the whole world was different.

Chanil nowhere to be found.

The Waxtek realm conquered.

Her father, dying.

Itza', a queen? A bride? That was still unclear. Because their scouts had given them horrible news recently. And everything else was being put on hold.

"Tell me again—" her father began, but more coughing wracked his body. "—the messengers," he spat out hoarsely.

"You should rest, Papa," Itza' said quietly. Her voice cracked, and she felt her heart breaking. Where was Chanil? Why wasn't she here to sit by their father? He was dying, and she was just gone.

5-Thunder turned an angry look on Itza'. His eyes blazed, and his chiseled jaw was clenched tight. Itza' saw the snake-like scar there, and her eyes welled up with tears. All that work Snake Lady had done had been for nothing. He was still dying.

And it was all her fault. Her birth, Chanil's birth—that had killed him. And they hadn't even known because they were just babies.

"Tell me," her father croaked out again.

She relented. "Tlapallo is coming. A huge force backed by many Invaders. They're massing, and now that Lord Chehn has lost his realm, we can be sure they are coming for us."

5-Thunder nodded and looked up at the ceiling. Itza' could see the rage in his eyes and the tension in his shoulders. He was the king, the most powerful man in the most powerful kingdom of the Winaq. And he could do nothing to help his people.

A terrible battle was coming, and he could only lie here. Itza' knew how much her father would have given anything to change his fate.

Itza' bit back her tears. Where was Chanil now that Itza' needed her most?

When Itza' returned from her time with Snake Lady several days prior, her first surprise had not been Chanil's absence. It had been the return of her aide, Zayla, who she had sent to Lord Chehn's court in the Waxtek realm many moons ago. Itza' had not expected Zayla's homecoming to hit her so hard, but she had been overjoyed to see her.

Zayla brought terrible news—the first of many, Itza' would discover.

"The Waxtek are all but fallen," Zayla had told the council. Lord 5-Thunder had banged his fist on the table. Lady Xok had pressed for details. And Night Star was quiet.

"Lord Chehn is losing support among the other nobles," Zayla had explained. "They plot against him. Tlapallo and the Great Army are bribing them, I'm sure, promising land and riches in exchange for loyalty. The Waxtek realm will fall—and soon."

"The mines," Night Star had whispered.

"Our entire western border," Xok had said.

Itza' felt a crack sprout in her heart.

Later that night, Zayla had come to visit Itza' in her room. The two women had thrown their arms around each other and laughed and cried and spent hours remembering each other's bodies. Itza' could see a new hardness in Zayla's beautiful, blocky face. And Zayla could see the lines of worry etching themselves into Itza's youthful expressions.

After their passions were spent and they tangled up together in Itza's bed, Zayla asked, "Did Snake Lady really ask you to marry her son?"

"She's very calculating. I think it makes sense," Itza' said. Then, seeing the sadness grow in Zayla's eyes, she added, "It's just politics. It would bring our two realms together and make it easier to stand against the Great Army."

Zayla nodded slowly and changed the subject. "Any word about Lady Chanil?"

Itza' shook her head. Chanil still hadn't returned. But her warriors had. And so had K'utalik. Itza' had to speak to her as soon as possible. She guessed the young girl had answers that Itza' would not like to hear.

❋

Still no word from Chanil.

K'utalik had given Itza' a report on everything. But that hadn't told them much other than that Chanil had gone off to some unknown location.

It took Itza' a while to figure it out. Itza' could only guess as to where Chanil was. But she had been an idiot not to realize sooner that Chanil had left with many aides specifically chosen by Night Star. And K'utalik had relayed the meeting between Chanil, her, and Nimaq. The one that clearly implied Nimaq had received special orders from Night Star.

It was late in the evening when Itza' barged into Night Star's private study without so much as a word or a knock on the door. The older woman looked up upon the young girl's entrance and stood.

"Can you get word to her?" Itza' hurled the question at her mentor.

Night Star saw the fierce intensity in Itza's eyes. They were even darker and deeper than they had been before she went to Sprouting Earth, and Night Star felt a twinge of panic in her chest looking into those caverns.

She nodded solemnly. "I already did. I'm waiting to hear back."

Itza' was angry, and she didn't care to hide it. "I can't believe you! Our father is dying, and you knew where Chanil was this whole time, and you did nothing!"

Night Star could see the pain in Itza's face. She crossed over to the young girl she had trained since childhood and knelt down before her, feeling Itza's terrifying gaze cast down on her.

"I understand why you're angry, my Lady. I would be too. I sent word as soon as your father turned ill."

Itza' listened carefully to Night Star's tone, but her anger seethed, getting the better of her.

"You need to tell me what's going on," Itza' demanded. "You knew Chanil was going to disappear. Why? And why keep it secret?"

Night Star kept her face calm. She loved Itza' like her own daughter in many ways. But her loyalties were to Chanil first, and she had no qualms about that. "She had another mission to—"

Itza' held up a hand to silence Night Star. She realized it wasn't a normal gesture for her, but one she had picked up from her time with Snake Lady. Itza' had picked up other tricks from the Snake Queen, too. She could hear the shifting tones in Night Star's voice. She could detect a small change in Night Star's scent. Itza' didn't know how she could do this, or why now, but it made her distrust what she was being told.

"You're lying," Itza' said flatly. "Or at least hiding so much it might as well be a lie."

A chill scampered along Night Star's spine. Itza' sounded so sure. As if she knew, not just suspected. Night Star decided that it would only hurt their relationship further if she kept trying to be evasive.

"You're right, little one. I am being cautious—very cautious here. But I promise you that I love Chanil and our family and would never do anything to risk our safety or this war. Chanil will get my messages, and she will return. I'm sure of it."

Itza' narrowed her eyes. She heard double meanings in Night Star's words, heard the real pain in her tone of voice, saw the sweat on her hairline.

"What could possibly warrant Chanil disappearing during a war? You say you love our family—"

Itza' saw Night Star's right eye twitch just a bit when Itza' said the word 'family.' The change in her scent grew more intense. Family. That was the key word. Itza' wondered why. Maybe she was just being paranoid. Maybe all those moons of scheming in Snake Lady's court and trying to gauge political relationships had made her a little crazy. Night Star was Chanil's mother. Even if she couldn't acknowledge that publicly, even if she had to hide it, she was still Chanil's family—

Then Itza's blood ran cold. Her eyes widened, and her stomach flipped over.

"Family," she breathed. She turned her fierce gaze on Night Star. She saw the warrior woman blink and wince. Itza' heard Night Star's heartbeat thumping in her ears, and it took Itza' a few moments to realize that she was hurting Night Star.

She looked away. The warrior gasped.

"Itza' . . ." Night Star couldn't finish the sentence.

Itza' shook her head. "I—I'm sorry. I can't control it yet."

Night Star looked at her with a mix of fear and worry. "What did you learn during all that time at Sprouting Earth?"

Itza' didn't want to tell her. And besides, everyone was keeping secrets apparently, so why shouldn't she?

"Not enough," was her sarcastic reply. "But I can tell you what I just learned now, watching you. Family. That means everything to you."

"Of course," Night Star said honestly."

"It means enough to lie—like when you lied about being Chanil's mother. And it means enough for you to risk losing a war. Like when you sent Chanil to hide away. I'm guessing to the Island, yeah? To your *family* there. And I'm guessing that the only reason Chanil would do that is the same thing—family."

Night Star said nothing. She couldn't. But she knew her silence revealed just as much.

"Chanil is pregnant, isn't she?" Itza' asked, and she felt tears threatening to pour out. It was bittersweet. Because Itza' could intuitively see the political reasons why Chanil having a baby with Ch'akanel—who else would it be?—would be disastrous during this time of war.

Accepting Night Star's silence as an admission, Itza' continued. "And now, with our father, the king—dying—we need Chanil back here more than ever. A healthy, definitely not pregnant or secretly married, Chanil. To rule and lead our warriors when Tlapallo comes."

Night Star nodded at that. "We need her back," she agreed.

"So, tell me, old friend, how long ago did you send that message? And how far along was my sister when she left?"

Twin Panthers Reunited

A moment always comes when one must finally decide. That single moment then divides our existence into two. There is everything that led up to this decision. And there is everything that followed it.

—the Book of Queen Snake Lady

"I FAILED YOU, PAPA." Chanil's words were barely a whisper in the catacombs underneath their family's temple in the central plaza. Then, louder, she shouted, "I failed you, old man!"

The words reverberated off the stones, and Itza' flinched involuntarily. The two daughters stood side by side, looking over the body of Lord 5-Thunder. The giant who had ruled Yaxchilan for decades, who had held them in his massive arms as children—now a cold corpse. A healthy warrior's body besieged by an unknown illness that had taken him just before his kingdom needed him most.

Chanil felt a terrible rage fill her. She wrung her hands against the scepter in her right hand. She had come home to a funeral. She had come home to questions and whispers, anger and joy. But none of that had mattered because her father had been dead by the time she returned. Then they made her queen.

Yaxchilan was at war. Yaxchilan needed a leader.

"I wasn't here in time to say goodbye, Dad," Chanil said. Her voice cracked.

Itza' felt tears sliding down her cheek. "I failed him, too, Chan. I couldn't save him."

"Your father would never have thought of either one of you as a failure." The soft voice of Lady Xok glided across their ears. The former queen was cloaked in shadows along one wall, darkness hiding her mask of grief. But they all heard the strain in her voice, the pain there.

"He was proud of you—both of you," Xok continued. "And he loved you very much."

Chanil clenched her jaw. "I'm such an idiot," she said. "I should have just stayed."

The secrets were out by now. Chanil hadn't really seen much reason for hiding them from the family anymore now that she was queen. There was no joy in that honesty, though.

"You didn't know what was going to happen, Chan," Night Star said. The warrior stood as tall as ever beside Chanil. She put one hand on her daughter's shoulder, but Chanil shrugged it off.

"I should have just trusted," Chanil said bitterly. "My stupid choices and my big fucking mouth—"

"Chan!" Xok reflexively called out the unladylike behavior. But Chanil was queen now, and she could do as she pleased.

"This is all of our faults!" Chanil said, whirling around. She looked at Xok and Night Star in turn. "All these damn secrets! And for what? My dad is dead, so who cares if he's embarrassed that I love someone who isn't a king? My daughter is in hiding so my cousin or whatever doesn't find out about her. Meanwhile, Itza' here has to go to another kingdom to find out about our father's curse?"

Itza' bit her lip. "Chanil's right. Our secrets are killing us."

Chanil tapped her scepter loudly against their father's tomb. "No more. My orders. My decision. No more secrets. You hear?"

Itza' turned to look at her mother in the shadows. Itza' knew there were layers to secrets, that total honesty was dangerous. But she also knew Chanil was grieving and venting her own feelings of guilt.

Still, Chanil would need to know what was happening in her own realm if she were to rule effectively. But Itza' didn't see how knowing about Snake Lady's attempted cure would help Chanil right now. How would Chanil react knowing it was their births that had made their father's sickness flare up again? Itza' herself could barely stand knowing, and she didn't have a kingdom to rule or a war to win.

So, Itza' said nothing. Even though she felt like she was betraying her sister. But it wasn't permanent, she told herself. She would tell Chanil after they defeated Tlapallo.

She wondered if she was making the same rationalizations their family had made years before when they'd hidden the truth. Was that what growing up meant? Rationalizing when you lied and when you spoke the truth? No wonder Chanil hated it.

"Tlapallo is coming," Itza' said, pushing her thoughts aside. "That is the truth. We have a battle to win, and with the Waxtek realm practically theirs already, we are all that stands between the Great Army and the Winaq. We have to win."

Chanil nodded. "Well said, little one. I've called the war council. I want you all there—even you, Itz. We need all of us together to figure out how to kill that coward and his brutish son."

They all agreed. They said their goodbyes to Lord 5-Thunder for the day—though each would return every day for many moons to speak to the spirit of the man who had led them and looked out for them for so long.

Chanil and Night Star climbed out of the tomb quickly to make ready for the war council. Itza' stayed behind with Lady Xok, who lingered over her late husband's body.

Itza' clasped her mom's hand and squeezed it tightly. She felt her smooth, uncalloused palms and smelled the familiar scent of flowers on her mom's skin. Lady Xok squeezed back.

"I miss him," Xok said softly. Her body shook in an exhale of grief, and she choked back tears.

"I do, too, Mom."

"I know—we should head back up and plan out this war. I just—I can't leave him. He was my world and—I was never good at war anyway, yeah?"

Itza' understood. She could see the defeat in her mom's shoulders. The resignation. Itza' had a feeling that this war council wasn't the only one her mom would be sitting out from. She was going to pull back more and more now, Itza' guessed.

Chanil was queen. Night Star would be her primary advisor. Itza' doubted Lady Xok would feel like she had much of a place anymore. It made Itza' sad, and she resolved to make sure her mother got whatever she needed in her grief.

But for now, Itza' had something else she needed her mother to know.

"I know about the curse, Mom," Itza' said.

Xok was confused. "We all know about the curse now, Itza'."

Itza' shook her head. "No—I know about *your* curse, Mom."

Xok went wide-eyed. Her breath stopped, and she looked at Itza' with an expression of pure terror. But Itza' wasn't done.

"I've known for years. Ever since Snake Lady visited. Well—a little after. But I know she cursed you to have a barren womb and that you broke that curse."

"Itza'. . ." Lady Xok croaked, her voice a panicked whisper. "Itza', listen to me—"

But Itza' held up her hand to silence the former queen. Xok stiffened seeing the gesture—the familiar mannerism from Snake Lady.

"I'm not mad."

"You're not?"

Itza' shook her head and felt tears coming. She had cried so much lately, and she was sick of it.

"No. I'm not mad. I'm sad! My dad is dead. And we have to get ready for this terrible battle without him. And—I'm heartbroken.

Because I know the truth now, Mom. I know about Snake Lady and Dad. About their relationship when they were younger."

Lady Xok made a face that suggested this was only getting worse for her.

"And I know about Snake Lady trying to cure Dad—how that gave him the scar. How the price of that magic meant Dad would only be healthy if he didn't have children."

Now Itza's voice was cracking, and she realized she missed Snake Lady in that moment. She missed having someone there who understood the depths of the pain of all these decisions.

"Wait—what cure?" Xok's voice cut through Itza's sadness.

"The cure Snake Lady tried to give Dad. The one that wasn't totally right. So, he was fine—until he had kids. That was the price."

"That was the price . . ." Xok's voice was barely a whisper, and her eyes were far away.

"You didn't know . . ." Itza' said, the understanding dawning on her.

Xok shook her head. "Your father never told me about how he got his scar. But—you're right. He wasn't sick until about a year after Chanil was born. He told me it was an old illness returned. But we didn't know why."

Itza' looked up at her mother, and the two shared a long conversation in the silence that followed. Then Xok wrapped her arms around her daughter and squeezed tight.

"Oh, my poor baby girl," Xok said through tears. "And you've been blaming yourself this whole time. My poor baby."

"It was awful, Mom," Itza' admitted. Then she pulled back and looked up at her mother. "But I get it now. I get why you lied about Chanil's lineage and held things back. Because as awful as this truth is—I can't tell Chanil. Not yet. Not while she's grieving over Dad and planning a war."

Lady Xok nodded. She saw the pain in her daughter's eyes. Xok cupped Itza's hands in her palms.

"My little girl—all grown up."

"I hate lying to her, Mom. Just until the battle is over, yeah?"

Xok nodded. "I'm glad you told me. I had no idea. And neither does Night Star. After the battle, maybe you should tell us all what you learned from Snake Lady, okay?"

Itza' agreed.

Then, with genuine curiosity, Xok asked, "How did you ever manage to get Snake Lady to reveal all that to you?"

Itza' made a face. "Eh—let's just say I kind of folded it into the bride price, yeah?"

The war council was brief. At least, considering the immensity of the problem before them. But Chanil didn't see battle plans as complicated. And she didn't waste time on many words.

"They're massing in the south, right?" Chanil asked the scouts and spies who had been sent to peer across the border.

"Yes, Great Queen," they all replied.

"The mountain passes," Nimaq grumbled.

"They could come along the western border, too," Ch'ojal offered. He was the oldest general in Yaxchilan. "But I doubt it."

Night Star agreed. "Too long of a march. If they're gathering in the south, then we know what roads they'll take."

Itza' spoke up then. "So, then we know what roads to block."

The council chuckled. But not because it was a bad idea. Just the opposite. It was exactly the kind of strategy they knew worked well against the huge forces Tlapallo liked to use.

"What about the Invaders, Great Queen?" another general asked. "Their explosive weapons can destroy anything."

Chanil scoffed. "*Rifles-ob*," she spat out the foreign word they had learned for the explosive weapons. "They always miss," Chanil said confidently. "And if it rains, they will be useless."

That settled the matter for Chanil.

"So, we block the roads and force them through the mountains?" Night Star said, collecting the consensus thoughts so far and giving them back to the group for re-evaluation.

"I think we should meet them at the base of our mountain," Itza' offered. There was only one mountain she could mean. It was at the southernmost edge of Yaxchilan territory. It would be where Tlapallo's warriors would cross into their realm if they attacked from the south.

"Why the base, Itza'?" Chanil asked.

"We block the roads soon—while it's still raining, but not so early they can do anything about it. Then we funnel them across the mountain roads, and we can harass them and ambush them the whole time they're passing through."

Chanil grinned, seeing the whole plan. "And when they finally emerge, they'll have to face our whole army on that open ground there."

"Exactly," Itza' beamed.

The other warriors agreed. The plan needed to be polished, but it was a good strategy. The roads would be blocked, and they would know exactly where Tlapallo was at all times.

"You ready to get your hands dirty then, sis?" Chanil said with a wicked grin.

"Me?"

"We'll need everyone we can get in those ambush parties. The sneakier the better. And I can't think of anyone sneakier than you, little sister."

Itza' smiled. She would get the chance to do more than strategize for once.

Itza' came to visit her sister in the evening. As queen, Chanil didn't have a special room yet, so she was still using her old bed chamber that she'd had since moving into a room away from Itza'.

"Hey, Chan," Itza' said as she slid into the bed chamber.

"Hey, Itz," Chanil returned with a grin.

Chanil was sitting on a mat on the floor, looking over some reports from the borderlands. Itza' sat across from her and peered at the papers. They were the most recent reports on how large a force Tlapallo was massing. Itza' had read them a while ago.

"Looks like he's using a lot of the Invaders," Chanil said casually.

Itza' nodded. "His way of keeping his own losses down."

Chanil looked at her. "You had good insight today, Itz. I'll miss your sharp mind."

Itza' looked at her with a puzzled expression, and Chanil said, "You know—marriage to Chak Mol and all? Queen of Sprouting Earth. That whole thing, yeah?"

Itza' opened and closed her mouth. "Right."

She had almost forgotten.

Chanil chuckled. "It'll be good to have that alliance though, right? I mean, that's why I'm assuming you agreed so easily."

"Yeah," Itza' said softly. "That's why . . . Definitely not the Ajaw. He's so weird."

She laughed, and Chanil laughed too. "Well, you know I couldn't do it. Obviously. But as long as you're okay with this decision, I'll support you."

"I am," Itza' said timidly. Then, realizing it was actually true, she repeated, "I am. I'll have Sprouting Earth, and you'll have Yaxchilan, and maybe together we have a chance, eh?"

"Always, little sis," Chanil said. "As long as there are days . . ."

"For as long as there is light," Itza' finished. Then she scrunched up her face and took a big breath. "So, now all we have to do is beat an enormous enemy, hold the border, I go get married and rule a kingdom, and you get your baby and your husband back from under the nose of your evil cousin?"

Chanil grinned. "Sounds easy enough, doesn't it?"

Itza' smiled, but she felt the sadness underneath it. The bittersweet feeling of having Chanil back but having lost their dad. Of having the family finally more united and honest but also preparing to split ways and leave for another kingdom. But she shook her head to clear all that away. They had to focus on the needs of the present.

"Speaking of Sprouting Earth, I'd like to send Snake Lady a message asking for warriors. She might be willing to send some troops in anticipation of our future alliance."

Chanil whistled. "Wouldn't that be something? Sprouting Earth fighting right alongside Yaxchilan?"

"It's worth a shot," Itza' offered.

"Go for it," Chanil said. "Couldn't hurt to have more warriors on our side. That why you came to bother me tonight, little one?"

Itza' cast her a vicious look. "I'm not your little one anymore now, am I?"

A sad expression skirted over Chanil's face for a second as she thought of the huge distance between her and her infant daughter. But she tried to push that aside as she remembered her daughter's beautiful face instead.

"You're going to love her, Itz," Chanil said, and there was no hiding the joy in her tone. "She has your eyes."

Itza' felt a chill run along her spine hearing that. Chanil's baby had the same eyes as her . . . and Snake Lady? Why? And what did that mean?

But it was obvious to Itza' that Chanil didn't think of this as more than something the infant shared with her auntie. So, Itza' filed her questions away for later, put a big smile on her face and said, "Tell me all about my little niece, Chan. I can't wait to meet her!"

Chaak is Summoned

Chaak brings the rains.
The torrential floods announce his arrival.
The clap of thunder is his heartbeat.
The lightning that streaks across the sky is his footprint.
He is here. Chaak has arrived.
Nothing can stand against him.

—Xelaq'am's Songs

THICK DROPS OF BLOOD FELL off the jagged edges of Itza's blade as she slid the knife out from the space behind the man's clavicle. He flopped forward, his face burying itself in the soil. Apart from the gurgling of the man's last breaths, a thick silence hung in the darkness before the dawn. Itza' and her group were staked out in the jungle, waiting to ambush those on the road nearby.

Itza's face was painted black, a dark shadow that blended with her obsidian eyes and the darkness of the jungle. Her woven helmet was shaped as the maw of a ferocious and darkly colored panther, and in that moment, she felt every bit the black jaguar that her outward appearance was modeled after.

She listened to the sounds of the jungle around them, searching for any sign that her group had been heard or that others were coming. Nothing. Only the normal sounds of animals passing through the mountain.

She heard Nimaq growl. He crossed over to her, and something approaching a smile crossed his face. "Not bad, my Lady. Not bad at all," he said gruffly.

Itza' smiled. Her heart was pounding in her chest, and she could feel the adrenaline coursing through her veins like hot rain. But she wasn't scared. She had trained all her life, and she found that once the darkness set in and she let the angry fire inside her spark, her fear melted away. And all that remained was a stalking jaguar in the hunt. It had surprised her at first. But now she was lost in a battle joy of sorts, in the thrill of hunting and stalking her enemy.

She knew the real battle would take place below, in the open field where Chanil was assembling all the warriors right now. But Itza' still had her part to play. And every enemy she killed was one less that her sister had to worry about.

Nimaq grunted and motioned for the ambush party to move on to their next victims.

"Tighten those boots, old man."

"Don't worry, little one, Ixta' would never let me live it down if you don't get back in time for your daughter's birthday."

Chanil, Puma-Strikes-First, looked over the warriors before her. Her fingers and arms glinted with rings and jeweled armbands. Her helmet was a grisly war puma, its giant maw open to devour the enemy. Inside it, her face was painted in the mask of a death god. She walked the ranks, checking her warriors' armor and their weapons but more so looking each one in the eye and letting them know that she was there, that she knew who they were, and that she was proud to stand with them. She moved warriors around when she needed to, and she made sure everyone saw that their leader was confident and calm before the battle ahead.

"We are with you, Great Puma!" one of the warriors she had passed called out.

She turned toward the man.

"And I am with *you*. With *all* of you!" She roared the last part, and the warriors whooped in response.

She had begun her walk in the front ranks and finished in the rear. This was where many leaders stayed during their battles, in the safety of the back ranks. From there, they could observe and call out orders to their commanders in the front lines. But Chanil was not that kind of leader. She would make her way back to the front and take her place in the center, where Puma-Strikes-First could show the meaning behind her battle name once more.

The general, Ch'ojal, stayed in the back. He was her second-in-command here and would be in charge of observing and calling out orders.

"All is ready, Honored Puma," Ch'ojal intoned as Chanil approached him.

"Any word from Night Star's warriors?" Chanil asked. He gestured with his chin in the direction where the second part of the Yaxchilan army was waiting. "They're in position at the other attack site. The last scouts said the enemy was almost upon them already."

Chanil nodded. Chanil's forces would meet the main body of Tlapallo's army at the base of the mountain. But the enemy was massive, and Night Star was commanding a large group of warriors at a different battlefield down the road where scouts had also reported seeing the enemy moving.

"Then we should expect the same here soon, general."

"Yes, Great Puma."

Just then, a voice from one of the lookouts called out, "Great Puma!"

Chanil turned in the direction of the voice. "Smoke!" the man cried out, and murmurs could be heard moving through the crowd as everyone looked up to see the gray plume high in the sky.

The smoke was from the first set of signal fires. It indicated that Tlapallo's army was marching and had reached the first lookouts on the mountain.

Battle was coming. Chanil's toes tingled in anticipation.

"I must return to the front, General," Chanil said, moving away from Ch'ojal to join the front ranks.

The second signal fire was beginning to smoke by the time Chanil took her position in the center of the front rank. The sun was climbing high in the sky, partially hidden by clouds. Chanil guessed their enemy would arrive at the base of the mountain before long.

She and the other warriors stood ready in the field. Before them, the tall expanse of the mountain loomed upward, its roads and pathways hidden by rocky terrain and dense jungle as it reached up toward the sky. There were only a handful of paths that emerged from the mountain and led onto the field, and the warriors could see them all.

The main force of Yaxchilan warriors waited a modest distance away. When the last signal fire was lit, Chanil would order them to begin moving forward to close the distance and remove the space for their enemy to fan out. In case something unexpected happened before then, Chanil wanted the option of changing formation.

In the jungle, all around the edges of the battlefield and up into the foothills around the roads and paths snaking down the mountain, archers and hidden warriors lay waiting. Those hidden forces were there to provide harassing attacks and take the enemy's attention while the enemy tried to move down the mountain.

Chanil thought of Itza', her little sister, who she knew was somewhere out there in the jungle with her ambush party. It made her happy to know her sister was defending their people and becoming a great warrior in her own right.

One of the lookouts called out again, and Chanil looked up to see the next signal fire smoking. The enemy was moving quickly. Chanil realized this could be a good sign that they were running scared. She also knew it could mean that they were moving unbothered and unopposed. But she left no room in her mind for pessimism or attitudes of defeat.

"Brave warriors!" she called out, the Great Puma roaring upwards toward the sky.

"Brave fighters
  Pumas and jaguars
  Eagles and coyotes

My squadron
    Of Death-dealers
        Blood-letters
            Bone-crushers

They are coming!
    The pirates
        Pillagers
            Marauders
                Killers

The would-be conquerors
And failed farmers

They want our lands
But they
    Do not know our lands

They think
    They have come to conquer

We will show them
They have come
        Only to die!"

The warriors of Yaxchilan whooped and cheered, roaring out as Chanil saw the last signal fire starting to smoke over the top of the mountain. She began beating her shield with her blade, a low and steady rhythm. The warriors next to her joined her, followed by the other ranks and then, eventually, followed by all those gathered there in the open field.

"For years now," Chanil roared out, her voice carrying above the din. "The Great Lord Tlapallo and his foreign plague have tried to end our ways of life. It is finally time. For us to end *them*!"

More roars and shouts from the warriors-turned-animals around her. Chanil moved forward, and the entire army moved with her. They stomped toward the base of the mountain, their footsteps echoing in the banging of their shields. They let out a low grunt with each step, a strong "Hooh-hooh-hooh," as the large force marched across the field.

As they neared the base of the mountain, Chanil saw the jungle quiver. She could smell the air change and knew her enemies were there, hidden just behind the cover of the trees. Her excitement grew. And her rage. She poured every ounce of her grief for her father, for her guilt over the choices she had made, into that rage, into the shield and blade in her hand.

There was a shift in the jungle cover, and then the first of Tlapallo's forces began to appear on the footpaths.

Chanil could smell their fear and sweat. She heard them shouting and saw some rushing forward to claim the narrow space at the bottom of the mountain. The ones in front were clearly the foreign Invaders, the mercenaries that Tlapallo preferred to use as disposable shock troops. Many carried large rifles, and they quickly loaded them and leveled them at the oncoming wall of warriors marching relentlessly toward them.

Puma heard the deafening, concussive bangs and explosions as the rifles went off—some from the men at the base of the mountain, some from those still hidden by the trees. She heard most of the shots miss, but some struck, and cries of pain could be heard among the Yaxchilan warriors.

Then Chanil heard sounds of screams and yells in the jungle, and she knew that their friends there were attacking—with rocks and knives and anything else they could.

She also heard the *whiz* of arrows as the archers in the jungle near the tree line emptied their sharp, winged-obsidian tips onto the enemy. The arrows would most likely not kill, but they would lower heads and make it harder for the enemy to organize or shoot their rifles.

Seeing the warriors coming together, Chanil opened her gaping maw and let loose a fierce battle cry, the roar so long and loud and intense that it reached upward toward the sky. Some would say later that the mountain itself had trembled in response.

Another barrage of rifle shots went off but noticeably fewer this time. More misses, some hits, and more screams from the chaos developing inside the jungle. Tlapallo's forces were fanning out now, dozens reaching the base of the mountain to try and arrange themselves into formation.

Chanil's warriors continued moving forward, almost close enough to where the rifles would no longer matter.

Chanil, the Great Puma-Strikes-First, opened her mouth again, showing her fangs as the cavernous maw of death widened to strike fear into her enemies. She intended to let loose another great roar that would shake the earth and sky before the two armies collided.

But at the exact moment she felt her voice rush from her throat, a giant thunderclap ripped across the sky, one so loud it drowned out all other sounds. It seemed as if the thunder had come from the Puma herself.

The Yaxchilan warriors knew, then, that the gods had heard Chanil's first roar, and they had answered her. A second thunderclap sounded within seconds, almost as loud as the first, and then all gathered heard the crash of heavy rain beginning in the mountain. The warriors whooped and cheered in response. The stench of the enemy's fear grew stronger in the wet air.

"Ts'o'ok u taal Chaak!" Chanil heard a warrior yell.

She laughed. Yes, brave warrior, she thought. The rain god had arrived. Their prayers had been answered.

As the rains began to fall, the full force of Tlapallo's army came. Like a swarm of angry hornets, they poured from the mountain paths and out of the jungle. They raced down onto the field to assemble. More arrows fell down on them, mixing with the heavy pounding of the rain drops that followed as the storm arrived over the battlefield.

They snarled and hurled curses at the Yaxchilan warriors, their gods, and the land itself.

Chanil saw one man in particular. More than a man, really. A giant, mountainous figure with rippling muscles and a huge head-dress. Itzcoyotl. He stalked forward into the front ranks of his warriors as they assembled their shield wall.

Chanil felt her blood boil. She roared again and surged forward.

"Our work begins!" she called out. As the two walls of shields collided, another thunderclap filled the air.

Itza' heard the *smack-thud* of her body hitting the ground hard. Her head began spinning, and her vision blurred. She had only a moment to register the bright, clear sky peeking through the canopy directly above her before her attacker was on top of her.

His eyes blazed with hatred as he loomed over Itza's body. The stench of his fear and his anger filled her nostrils, and streams of sweat flowed down from his helmet and his curly beard and poured onto Itza's face. It stung against the cut along her cheek. Itza' felt the warm rivulets of blood worming down her lips from her bleeding nose. As the man raised his arms to strike, she sat up and punched the man's face then shoved him with her shin.

He fell back, and Itza' pounced. She reached down to the man's waist and drew his knife. With the short blade, she stabbed into a gap in his armor between his chest and arm. His arm went limp, and he howled like a wounded animal.

Itza' began to stand up just as another enemy warrior swung his sword out at her. She instinctively crouched into a lunge and sprung at him. Her arms wrapped around the back of his thighs while her shoulder slammed into his waist, and she pivoted as she drove her new attacker back, turning him and lifting one of his legs hard to dump the man on the ground.

He squirmed and tried to lift his body, but it was too late. The black jaguar found her kill swiftly, leaving a bloody trail along the Tlaxcala's woven armor as she slid herself along his body after burying her borrowed blade in the man's face.

Itza' stood up once more and tried to take in the scene. Her group's final ambush had not gone as planned. The enemy had heard them before they were in position, and the two groups had collided in a messy and chaotic brawl, half exposed along the road, half fighting in the jungle.

She saw Nimaq struggling against two Invaders just inside the tree line, and she rushed forward to help him. At almost the same moment, Itza' heard a series of violent explosions in the distance and realized they might be the sounds of the Invaders' rifles. She was vaguely aware that this probably meant the battle had begun.

She crashed into one of the men assailing Nimaq, throwing him deeper into the jungle. He stumbled slightly from the blow but recovered quickly. Itza' saw Nimaq launch himself forward at his remaining opponent out of the corner of her eye.

The man facing Itza' was tall, almost as tall as Lady Night Star. His face was young, and his eyes—a mix of light browns and greens—were wide-eyed in utter terror. Behind her woven jaguar cap and darkly painted face, her black, obsidian eyes stared at him with a fiery intensity. Her armor was covered in red stains from all those she had killed that day, and she knew her killing was not yet over.

The man took a couple of steps back as Itza' advanced. He reached behind himself awkwardly, intently pulling at something around his waist. Before Itza' could see what it was, the man tripped on a vine and fell hard to the ground. Itza' rushed forward just as the man finally pulled out the thing he had been searching for. It had a curved, wooden handle and a long snout that looked like the Invaders' rifles, only smaller.

He leveled the thing at Itza'. The explosion was loud and long and left the air ringing and a cloud of smoke around him. The pistol trembled in his hand as he struggled to his feet, never lowering the weapon from where it still pointed at the space where Itza' had been.

A wind rushed through the jungle, and the smoke began to clear. Where Itza' had been, there was nothing. The man looked around nervously. His heart pounded hard in his chest as he searched. He looked behind himself, whirling quickly, but found only a thin tree. He dared to hope for a moment. He dared to breathe a little easier.

Composing himself, he knelt to reload the small pistol. And that was when Itza's blade found his throat and slit it.

She rushed back to the road to find the rest of their enemies dead as well. Nimaq was still alive, but several of their warriors had been killed.

"The rifles, my Lady," Nimaq said, handing Itza' back her long blade.

"I know—it's begun."

And just then, they heard a loud crack of thunder in the sky. It was a tremendous thunderclap, one that shook the mountain and drowned out all sound for a few moments. Then came another, a second explosion almost as loud as the first. The sky filled with clouds, and they heard the heavy fall of rain beginning.

"It worked!" one of the Yaxchilan warriors cried out. Others whooped in response.

"The gods have heard us!" Itza' called out, knowing the rain would make the Invader's explosive weapons less reliable.

"What now, Honored Jaguar?" one of the warriors asked. And Itza' realized it was the first time the warriors had turned to her for leadership.

"Now we descend. The battle has started! It's time we joined with the others." And the company of warriors moved quickly down the mountain to find Chanil and her troops.

The rains beat hard against the two armies battling at the base of the mountain. It soaked the Invaders' rifles and made them useless. But it also softened the ground, and soon, the field was a slippery mess of brown and black and red. Blood pooled in the footprints left by boots and ran along troughs and furrows carved by walls of warriors pushing into the ground as they shoved against each other's shields. Thunder clapped, and lightning streaked across the sky that had been clear just hours before.

In front of Chanil, an unending horde of ravenous monsters clawed at her and her warriors. The stench of their sweat and blood filled the air, along with the insults they hurled. Chanil could see the whites of their eyes, the terror and the hatred there, as they struck out against her shield and tried to bury their blades in her heart.

A bolt of lightning flashed bright in the cloudy sky, striking a tree near the battlefield and igniting it. The loud cracking of the tree's trunk echoed off the mountain and blended with the thunderclap that followed. The Tlaxcala warrior in front of Chanil flinched at the sound, and Chanil laughed. Her voice filled the air as the thunderclap subsided, the powerful roar of a hunter in mid-hunt, hungry and searching for its kill.

"They're afraid!" she called out to her troops, and many roared back.

The man hacked at Chanil in response, but she caught the attack on her shield and shoved him back. He stumbled in the mud, and a long downward cut from the Yaxchilan warrior next to Chanil ended him.

Another Tlaxcala warrior took his place immediately, stabbing and thrusting his weapon wildly. Chanil moved back, letting the man think his attack was working. He took the bait, overstepping far too much and falling within reach of the Yaxchilan warriors. They pulled him into their ranks, and Chanil passed him into the warriors behind her who made quick work of the man.

He was replaced again, and the battle raged on. Chanil felt her battle joy take over, and she slashed and hacked away at Tlapallo's warriors and the ugly, pale Invaders they had allied with.

On the other side of the shield wall, Chanil could see the massive form of Itzcoyotl. He was not directly opposite her, but he was close by, also occupying the front ranks. Chanil could see his tall form moving quickly and deftly to hold back the onslaught of Yaxchilan warriors.

She called out her taunt to him. "Here, doggy, doggy."

The other Yaxchilan warriors took up the call, and a small chorus of barks and taunts assailed Itzcoyotl. But Itzcoyotl did not respond. He just smashed his shield harder into the warrior in front of him. He cut deeper with his knife, and in every moment after a successful kill, he turned one eye to Chanil as if to say, There, I killed another of your children, girl. There—now what will you do?

Chanil's blood boiled in rage.

The storm kept pounding them with rain. Arrows flew from the margins of the jungle tree line to harass the flanks of Tlapallo's army. Screams and yells sounded from the jungle on the mountain slope where Yaxchilan and Coyolapan warriors played their deadly cat and mouse games.

Chanil fell into the endless rhythm of the shield wall. Block, counter, kill. Block, counter, kill. The bright colors of the woven armor on Tlapallo's forces became a blur as warrior after warrior jumped into the gaps left in the wake of Puma's blade.

It seemed to go on for hours. The two walls shoved each other. Screams and grunts filled the air. Chanil's nose was inundated with the smells of blood, of flint and obsidian sparks, or fear and excitement. Her body was drenched in sweat, and her own maniacal laughter seemed like a distant echo of some horrible monster.

She was lost in the battle.

But she was also moving forward. Despite Tlapallo's greater numbers, the Yaxchilan warriors prevented the full force of their army from being able to descend from the mountain, all because of their careful choice of where to fight. And she could feel their enemies wilting. They were getting tired, and they were getting frustrated.

"Push!" she heard herself call out. Her warriors heaved forward, slamming into the Tlaxcala shields. Chanil knew they could defeat the enemy if they only stayed strong. All they had to do was break their lines, and Tlapallo's forces would start to crumble. They would turn and run, heading back up into the mountain passes, and the Yaxchilan warriors could hunt them like deer in the retreat.

"Push!" Chanil roared again.

She felt a hard pressure against her ankles and saw one of the Invaders to her left trying to cut down at her foot. He realized too late that her boots were reinforced. She laughed and severed his arms with a quick hack and slit his throat a moment later.

The lines pushed forward, driven by Chanil as she slammed her shield violently into the enemy in front of her, knocking him back half a step. The enemy's second rank would push him back into position, of course, Chanil knew this. She went low as he came forward—she raised her shield and pummeled his groin hard, and then she cut upward to meet his face as he doubled over.

His body slumped forward, partially falling onto her, and she shoved the bloody corpse aside. At the same time, from the enemy's second rank, a lightning-fast blade thrust outward at the Yaxchilan warrior next to Chanil. It caught the warrior by surprise, the razor-sharp point slicing through the man's armor to find his belly. The Invader twisted the blade as he pulled it back, ripping open the warrior's insides. The warrior fell, convulsing to the ground in front of Chanil.

She hacked out violently as she roared in anger, catching two Tlaxcala warriors with her wild strikes. "Push!" she roared again, and the lines pressed forward.

She felt a shifting then on the enemy side. A lessening of the resistance against her and then a faltering in the organization of Tlapallo's warriors in her area. A moment later, she could feel the lines collapsing in front of her.

"They're breaking!" she called out. "With me!"

Chanil stepped into the gap being created as Tlapallo's warriors fled. She saw fear in their eyes as many of them turned or backed away. She felt the forward surge as Yaxchilan warriors broke their own formation to start chasing some of the fleeing enemies.

"Puma!" A loud roar. A deep rumble that carried over the whole din of the storm and the battle.

She turned toward the sound and saw Itzcoyotl approaching her fast, his weapon pointing at her. His coyote headdress snarled at her. His woven armor was streaked with Yaxchilan blood, and Chanil felt her rage growing at the sight of him.

"Come and fight me, Puma!" he yelled, his voice like the eruption of a volcano.

Chanil did not wait for him to get closer. She leapt forward, but at an angle. His downward strike just barely missed her, slashing through the air where she had been an instant before. In unison, they turned toward each other. Their shields collided with each other's swords, and the bang was like a loud thunderclap.

Chanil grinned. "Your army's running, little doggy. You should run home, too."

Itzcoyotl just laughed. "This is only the beginning, Puma. It doesn't matter if you win here or not. We'll just keep coming."

Itzcoyotl heaved suddenly and slashed out with his sword, but Chanil was already gone. She had learned from her previous fights with Itzcoyotl that he was too powerful for her to just meet force with force. She moved off at an angle, crouching as she skirted around his giant form.

She dodged around his massive thighs like a stalking cat and slashed at his hamstrings.

He howled in pain as one of the blades of Chanil's weapon got caught in his thigh and broke off there.

He whirled around and the impact of his strike against her shield slammed Chanil to the ground, her feet slipping out from under her on the mud. She landed on her back, tasting blood and dirt in her mouth. Itzcoyotl was standing over her in a second, his foot stomping toward her face.

She rolled her hips over and kicked his stomach. It took the power out of his foot stomp and gave her time to rise back to her feet. She blocked another strike and roared.

"That all you got, little doggy?" She laughed and leaped back just out of range of Itzcoyotl's next slicing attack.

Itzcoyotl breathed heavily and glared at her. "You never learn, Puma."

"I've learned how to beat you and your father," Chanil shot back. "I've learned how to keep my people safe."

Itzcoyotl's laugh was short and jagged. "You have no idea what path you closed. This—"

He gestured at the chaos around them—the breaking lines of each army, the screams as warriors hacked each other to pieces, the ground soaked in rain and blood. "This didn't have to go this way."

"Oh, spare me," Chanil called out. "We were your friends! You betrayed us! You're a butcher!"

She didn't wait for his next words. She lunged forward, chopping down at his shield and upper arm, driving him backwards in the slippery mud. But the attacks were a diversion. Her real goal was to find his ankle. She took a step forward and felt his foot against hers. She hooked her foot behind his ankle and drove his body forward while pulling his foot back.

He fell hard and covered his body with his shield. Chanil raised her sword high and smashed it down on that wooden shield with all her strength. Again and again, the Puma attacked and roared. A clap of thunder sounded above them, and splinters of wood flew out in all directions as she shattered Itzcoyotl's shield with her massive blows.

"You're dead, little doggy! You'll pay for every kid you burned, every village you sacked!"

Then she felt a sharp pain along her own thigh. She whirled and found another Tlaxcala warrior facing her. No—this wasn't one of Tlapallo's. This was an Invader dressed in Tlaxcala armor. He held a long knife in one hand, and his face was smeared in blood.

Itzcoyotl was on his feet an instant later. Chanil saw him discard the broken remnants of his shield and draw a long knife from a sheath at his thigh.

"Your army's fleeing," Chanil shouted.

Itzcoyotl shook his head. "It's not as bad as it looks. And either way, you're not leaving this field alive."

Chanil clenched her jaw and gritted her teeth. She looked back and forth between the two opponents. She saw murder on both their faces, and she knew there was no getting through to the Prince of Coyolapan.

She feinted toward Itzcoyotl but then launched herself at the Invader. The man was unprepared for her speed. He thrust out with his knife, but she deflected the blow against her shield, wrapping herself around him and slicing the skin around his neck as she moved in a circle.

She returned to face Itzcoyotl as the Invader dropped to the ground next to her. Chanil smirked. She was aware of the pain in her thigh from the Invader's cut, but she ignored it. Itzcoyotl was also injured. He didn't seem to care.

"I can't be stopped, little doggy," Chanil said smugly. "And my people will never do what you and your father did. We will never sell ourselves out to the empire!"

The two warriors launched at each other again.

Chanil was not a small figure, but everyone looked small compared to Itzcoyotl. She had to fight with that in mind. She moved rapidly and used her agility to dodge around him, to keep him constantly guessing about where her next attack would come from. She gave him small cuts, tried to attack his unshielded joints, to break bone and separate flesh from muscle.

But Itzcoyotl was no fool. He understood her strategy. He knew how to use his smaller dagger to catch and pull her shield away so he could slash at her with his sword. In one fluid movement, he did just that, sliding away her protection and cutting along Chanil's face so fast she never even saw the blade. Chanil felt blood rushing down her cheeks. She felt another cut along her arm where his knife found a gap in her wrist protections.

"You're dead, Puma," Itzcoyotl shouted, his eyes holding a smug expression. "Whatever happens to me—you're dead now."

She ignored his words and lunged toward him, paying him back for every cut, and her own blade dripped with Itzcoyotl's blood. Chanil felt her breathing become heavier and heavier, though. And she was aware of slowing down somewhat, of having to block more. Her mind was not quite as sharp as it had just been.

Poisoned blade.

The words echoed in her mind. She recalled that Night Star had once said that Itzcoyotl might poison his blades. That seemed like a lifetime ago now. Chanil shook her head to push away the dragging numbness of the poison and the doubts threatening to fester in her heart at that moment.

She was vaguely aware of other figures encircling her and Itzcoyotl. A mob of Invaders surrounded the two of them now, and she had to leap at multiple opponents just to stay safe.

Itzcoyotl let loose a loud, cackling laugh and grinned madly at her. She forced herself to grin back as she ducked under the sword of one Invader and drove her knife into the man's groin. At some point, she had lost her own shield, she realized. She couldn't remember that happening. She only had a long knife and her one-handed sword now.

Chanil danced around the Invaders, keeping them between her and Itzcoyotl. She taunted him as she cut each one down. She felt her breath coming in ragged gasps as the poison worked its way around her system. But she didn't care. She had to keep going.

"Your friends ain't helping, doggy!"

"Come and fight me yourself, doggy!"

When there was only one Invader left, she moved as though to launch at him. Itzcoyotl had expected this and leaped toward where Chanil would have been had she actually attacked the Invader. But Chanil wasn't there. Her movements had been a feint. Instead, she had pulled back and around, and she could see Itzcoyotl's back now. But her vision was blurring, and her mind was playing tricks on her. For a moment, it wasn't Itzcoyotl, but Ch'akanel. And he wasn't holding a weapon, but a baby. Chanil's baby.

"No!" she roared out, shaking the vision from her mind. She leaped at Itzcoyotl's exposed backside and stabbed at his thigh with her knife, turning the blade as she pulled it out. Itzcoyotl cried out in pain and lurched backwards. Blood poured out of his leg. She stabbed his side between the ribs. At the same moment, Chanil felt a sharp pain in her own arm, which made her drop her sword. But her knife was still there, in the other hand, and she sliced at Itzcoyotl's arm.

He turned toward her—the two were tangled up now. Knives shot out and were deflected. Arms twisted. Chanil felt her blade bite along his arm and rip through the armor. Just as fast, she felt a stab in her abdomen, and she clamped down hard on Itzcoyotl's arm there. She stopped him from being able to pull the weapon out and stabbed at the arm that he was using to hold the knife inside her. He let go, cradling his arm. He slipped, and Chanil heard a distant laugh that sounded like her own as she watched him go down.

"It's done, doggy. It's done."

She felt a sick pain in her stomach. Her vision was black at the edges, but she could see Itzcoyotl there on the ground. She thought she heard him mumble something, but she couldn't make out the words.

She saw him lying there, his face a mask of pain, his body spasming. He was clutching his arm and his side. Chanil moved slowly toward him, each step a challenge. He had no weapon now. His knife was buried in her stomach. Hers was still in her hand.

"It's done," she whispered.

She stabbed at him. Mud. Dirt—she had missed. Her vision was so blurry that she couldn't tell if he was still in front of her.

Pain radiated all over her body. But she couldn't stop. No matter how tired she felt. She had to kill Itzcoyotl.

The Puma strikes first, her mind screamed at her, and she could swear it was Night Star's voice and not her own.

Another sharp pain shocked her mind back into focus as a blade bit through her armor and carved a trench along her left arm. Where had that come from? She couldn't tell. Her body reacted on impulse, leaping and whirling to face whatever attacker had just come for her.

She turned toward the attacker, her blade moving quickly along the line of his follow-up attack. The move let her block his strike and cut at his face at the same time. But she could tell that her left arm was useless. It flopped around, and she could no longer control it.

This is it, the Puma thought, resolving herself to her fate. She would not cry or buckle. No matter what, she would keep going until the enemy cut her down or the enemy was no more.

Another sharp cut—Chanil felt blood rushing down her whole torso. She heard a snarling creature nearby and knew that its claws had cut deeply into her chest. She wobbled but refused to fall.

Keep going, little one! It was Night Star's voice, echoing off stone walls in the plaza where she trained Chanil as a young girl.

But I'm tired! My arms can barely move. The child's voice was young, and Chanil recognized she must have been only six or seven at the time.

Why do we fight, Chan? Lady Night Star let the question hang in the air. The child, tired and somewhat arrogant, had scrunched her face but knew the answer.

"We fight to protect our people, our relatives, our land!" Chanil shouted the response aloud.

You must have a purpose for why you fight. You have to fight for something greater than yourself. Otherwise, eventually, when you run into something stronger and tougher than you, it can make you quit if you don't have that inner purpose to keep you going.

Night Star's words echoed in Chanil's mind.

Suddenly, a horde of snarling monsters surrounded her. They grabbed at her, but they could not hold her. Even as her vision blurred, she shoved and bit and clawed with everything she had left. She would not let them see her fall or show weakness in her movements. Any monster that approached was struck as soon as it fell within range.

The Puma always strikes first.

Why do we fight, Chan? Lady Night Star's voice, full of love and patience, echoed in Chanil's mind as her vision turned to black.

Itza' stumbled hard. Her footing gave way, and she dropped to one knee. She reached out for a tree to support her, but there wasn't one.

What is this? her mind wondered. She felt a panic in her heart, as if a sudden poison had entered her blood, and her legs would not work.

I don't slip, she thought. And it was true, Itza' almost never lost her balance or tripped. She had too many years of climbing walls and balancing on tree branches as a child. A fall could have meant serious damage.

Why did I slip?

She was in the jungle, moving with her group toward the battle at the base of the mountain. There had been no enemies around, no sudden sounds or attacks. There had been no reason for her to lose her footing.

And yet, she had.

As if someone had suddenly taken the wind out of her lungs and the blood out of her veins, she had dropped. As if her legs were simply gone.

The panic in her heart was growing into a deep pain that almost made it hard to breathe.

What is this? she wondered again.

"Come on, my Lady" Nimaq's gruff voice intruded her thoughts. She felt the old man pulling her up. His grip was strong and his arms powerful as they lifted Itza's relatively light frame.

"We have to hurry!" she shouted to the other warriors, not even thanking Nimaq as she sprinted off toward the battle. Her heart felt like they had to get there as soon as possible.

"Honored Lady." The Yaxchilan warrior knelt on the blood-stained ground of the battlefield in front of Itza'.

His head was bowed low, and in his arms, he lifted a large, bladed weapon toward Itza'. She knew the weapon well—it was her sister's favorite for close combat. The wood came from the villages around Yaxchilan, and it had been carved with glyphs and images to protect the blade and its user.

Looking down at it, all Itza' could think about was how so many of its blades were cracked and broken, how the deep cuts in its wooden frame were caked with blood and the leather wrap around its handle had started to come undone.

She placed one hand on the weapon but did not take it. She could not bring herself to take up the weapon of her sister, to wield it as Chanil had, to fill her older sister's boots.

"Keep it," she said with a wave of her hand.

She left the man wide-eyed as she moved forward, walking slowly through the battlefield. The ground was red with blood, and bodies were everywhere. Screams and yells could still be heard as the Yaxchilan forces dispatched fleeing enemies.

But Itza' wasn't really paying attention. She was looking for her sister's body. It did not take long to find it. Every warrior who was not off killing enemies seemed to be gathered in that spot. The Warrior Queen of Yaxchilan lay in a blood-soaked pit, her body surrounded by more dead Invaders and Tlaxcala than Itza' could even count. The story was clear, even in the confusion of battle and death.

Itza' could see she had died as the great warrior. Itza' knew that Chanil would have preferred that.

The crowd parted and gave Lady Itza' space to enter the scene of death. Itza' crouched over Chanil's corpse. The tears flowed from Itza's eyes, and the saltwater streamed across Chanil's face, cleaning some of the blood and paint from it. Words from their childhood echoed painfully in Itza's mind.

For as long as there are days, Itz . . . She heard Chanil's voice as if the woman were standing there beside her.

"For as long as there is light, Chan," Itza' whispered, her voice breaking as she spoke to her sister for the last time.

Then she tilted her head back, her body gripped by a terrible, painful grief. The younger sister of the Great Puma opened her jaguar maw toward the sky—the sky that had heard Chanil's battle cries and let loose a torrent of rain and thunder to scare their enemies—and she let out her own giant roar. The young jaguar roared and roared until the heavens echoed with distant thunderclaps to let her know that they had heard her.

Lady Night Star wrapped her arms around Itza' and held her so tight that Itza' thought her bones might break.

"I should have been there," Night Star said, sobbing.

The two women looked down at the spot where Chanil had died. The Great Puma's body had been wrapped and made ready for burial. Warriors lined up to have the honor of carrying Lady Chanil's corpse back to Yaxchilan.

But Night Star wanted to see the spot herself. To feel what had happened by standing there where her daughter had given her life to help bring them victory.

"We needed you to fight Tlapallo," Itza' offered softly. She wiped the tears from her eyes, smearing dirt and blood over her painted face.

Night Star shook her head. "Anyone could have killed that old fool. I should have been here. With her. Protecting her."

"My Lady," Nimaq's rough voice sounded as he came up beside Night Star. "I—I—"

He couldn't finish his words, and Night Star wrapped an arm around his shoulder.

Itza' looked up at the sky. The warriors had told her about Chanil's battle roar—the one that had summoned the storm.

"We won!" she shouted the words at the sky. Then, softer, "We won, Chan. Tlapallo is dead—thank your mom for that. The Invaders are crushed. The Great Army won't be coming back for some time. Not if I have anything to say about it."

The last part was spoken through clenched teeth. Itza' felt sadness, yes, but also a huge anger at the insane violence all around her and what it had cost her people, her family. Her father was dead. Her sister was dead. Her niece was far away on the Island. She knew the family would make her queen now. It was the only hope for continuity at this time.

She hated the idea of that. She hated everything about this war.

Nimaq cleared his throat. "Chanil's mother?"

Itza' nodded. She hadn't meant to reveal that. But now that she had, she realized it was the right thing to do. So, before Night Star could say anything, Itza' turned to them both, her eyes blazing with a fierce anger, and said, "That's right. Night Star is Chanil's mother."

"Itza'," Night Star said, a concerned look on her face.

"No—We're done with secrets. Chanil was right, we don't need them. And . . . Well, with everyone else gone, your options for a queen are limited right now, eh? So, since I'm your best bet for now, I make the rules. We are done hiding the truth of my sister. In fact, I'm going to make sure her story is written in every book and monument from here to the southern highlands!"

Night Star swallowed, recognizing the grief that moved Itza's words. But she nodded and bowed her head. Nimaq did the same.

"Great Queen," they both intoned.

Itza' clenched her jaw, feeling the weight of an entire kingdom suddenly press itself on her shoulders.

"I'm going to make sure the whole world remembers what Chanil did here. And maybe, just maybe, that will help us get her daughter back home safe."

Nimaq's eyes went wide. "Daughter?"

Itza' pulled Night Star and Nimaq along with her as she walked toward the road. "I'll explain everything, general. We have a lot of work to do."

Epilogue: Xbalam

Don't believe everything you hear about me. They say I can kill a man with just a look. They say my spirit prowls the city at night, looking for evildoers to slay. They say my womb is barren and I massacre men to prevent anyone else from having a family. Who can say what's true—if I never leave any survivors?

—*Xelaq'am's Songs*

ITZA' DIDN'T WANT TO BE QUEEN. She didn't want anything. Her father was dead. Her sister was dead. And they hadn't been able to locate her niece yet either. She wanted to give up and run away.

But Itza' took the crown anyway. Her people needed her. Tlapallo was defeated. The Invaders were crushed. But Itzcoyotl—somehow—had survived. He would come back—one day. The war wasn't over.

Itza' climbed the steps. She was seated on the throne. She held the manikin scepter that her father had held, that Chanil had held, however briefly. She crossed her legs and tucked her feet beneath her and let them call her Queen of Yaxchilan.

Snake Lady had forgiven her for reneging on their deal. Itza' wasn't ready to rule two kingdoms, was she? Victory had cost Yaxchilan nearly everything. She had to stay home and rebuild.

Snake Lady had understood. Mostly.

What else could she do?

The breeze was gentle in the apiary. The smell of flowers reached Itza's nostrils and reminded her that there were still sweet things in this world. She kept her eyes closed against the bright morning sun.

Her body still shook from the ceremony. She felt weak from not sleeping and not eating. She hadn't meant to give so much blood. It had just come out.

Flashes of cold memories played out behind her closed eyelids. The fire. The smell of incense. The sweat and excitement of the priests. Q'anchi's eyes, blazing like uncontrolled flames as he had made the cuts.

She had made cuts, too. There was so much blood. Why had she given so much blood? That wasn't normal.

Had she wanted to die?

A silence followed. Something like death.

And then the visitor arrived.

It happened just like her father had said it would. She followed the ritual, she fell into a trance, and then—the visitor came.

She had almost laughed.

It made sense. She couldn't really say goodbye to Chanil. Itza' didn't feel like a queen herself. She was just a placeholder until Chanil came back from the dead and took up her rightful position as the Hero of Yaxchilan.

No—that wasn't right. Itza' shook her head and opened her eyes.

She was still in the apiary. It was daytime. The sun was bright, and it burned her eyes, and the pain reminded her that she was alive, and Chanil was dead.

And Itza' was queen.

She remembered the ceremony. That was last night. She hadn't slept. That was part of the process. She had fasted and stayed awake and bled and taken the sacred herbs.

And she had taken in the spirit whose sad job it would be to guide her as queen of the realm so that now all would fear her.

Little Itza'.

They were supposed to fear her. To call her by the spirit's name. Ixkiaqkoj. The Red Puma. That was her fate. The Puma had come to her. She had almost laughed.

She was certain it was Chanil. Or, at least, a part of her. She could live with that. For now.

Itza' really only had two things to do. Hold off the Great Army and find her niece. She would let the Red Puma do the rest.

She would let the Red Puma rule. It was as close to having Chanil there as she could get. Let the Red Puma rule. She felt sorry for her enemies already.

She smiled. The sun felt good on her skin.

The Queen of Yaxchilan, Xajaw Ixkiaqkoj, the Red Puma—once Lady Itza'—made the difficult climb up the decaying, crumbling steps of the ancient temple. The night air whipped her cloak in all directions as she clung to jagged, rocky surfaces to steady herself. The darkness was deep that night; the moon hid its face from the earth below, and clouds covered the stars.

But Itza' could still see.

Her black eyes took in every small bit of light and reflected it back out onto her world. She gripped the vines and roots that had grown over the ancient steps and used them to pull herself up. She dug her claws into the rocky slope of the temple steps where the staircase had eroded, over generations, into nothing.

When Itza' finally reached the top of the temple, she saw only an empty room. She blinked in disbelief. Had the old woman left? Had Yaxchilan's ancient Grandmother finally passed?

She rubbed her eyes. And then she saw it. A single candle sitting on a long workbench. Itza' took a step toward the doorway. A fierce gust of wind flew around her, whipping in all directions. She pulled her thick cloak tighter against her body. Her obsidian eyes were locked on the candle in the room.

The flame was still.

Despite the strong gusts outside that pulled and pushed the young queen and threatened to throw her off the mountainous height of the ancient temple, the candle's flame never moved.

Itza' crossed the threshold.

A few torches were lit now. They cast long shadows and bright triangles of light in the large chamber. Itza' smelled a cooking fire nearby and warm corn dough.

"Come around the back, little one." A familiar voice. Old and wizened, raspy with an unmistakable smile.

Itza' followed the sound of the voice and the cooking fire. It led her to the right, around the giant circle carved into the floor, past incense burners and stools. Past the open window that looked over the jungle, and over to the far corner of the room, where Grandmother sat in front of a large cooking fire with three big stones.

"You can sit, little one," the raspy voice said. Grandmother's attention was fixed on the fire. She poked it erratically with a large stick.

Itza' sat down next to the old woman. Grandmother handed her a cup immediately. Itza' sniffed the concoction suspiciously. She gave the old woman a stern look.

"It's just tea, Great Queen," Grandmother said, chuckling. "Truly, this time."

Itza' smelled it again and tried to decide whether or not to risk it. In the meantime, she brought out a large bundle from beneath her cloak.

"I need your help, Grandmother," Itza' said, handing the bundle to the old woman. Grandmother took it gently and set it in her lap.

"So, you don't hate me after all?"

Itza' took the smallest of sips from the cup and said, "Is that your way of saying you cursed my father?"

The old woman prodded the fire, and a small shower of crackling embers danced in the air. "You know better than that, I think, Great Queen."

"Snake Lady still sees it as a mystery. So does my mother, I believe."

Grandmother smiled and turned toward Itza'. "But you figured out who it was, didn't you?"

Itza' eyed her over the brim of her cup, eyes glinting with mischief. "Who else? My father's debts were always paid."

Grandmother's eyes sparkled intently. "I knew there was a reason I liked you."

"This isn't what I need your help with, Grandmother."

The old woman nodded somberly. "But I can't help you with the other thing."

Grandmother turned back to the fire and took a deep breath. It was like someone had been choking her and suddenly let go, and her lungs opened up to take in as much air as possible. Itza' saw the smoke from the fire enter her open mouth and then the small flashes of lightning along her bare arms and lower legs.

The old woman's body shuddered, and she hunched over, staring deeply into the fire and stirring the embers with her stick. "I can't help you with the other thing," she repeated, but now her voice seemed far away, her tone quieter but more intense.

Itza' swallowed. "I need your help finding my niece, Grandmother. We haven't been able to locate her."

Grandmother did not look at her. She tilted her head as though listening to something. "The gift is not enough."

Itza' looked at the gift bundle she had brought the old woman. It had fallen to the floor when Grandmother hunched forward. "I will bring you more, whatever I can for as long as I live. I just need your help."

But Grandmother wasn't listening it seemed. "All our gifts are not enough," she said in a low groan.

Itza' felt goosebumps on her arms and an anxious feeling in her spine. The old woman almost seemed like she was dreaming now. But her eyes were still open, fixated intently on the fire before her.

"Where are you, little one?" Grandmother whispered toward the flames.

Itza' went wide-eyed. "That's what I need to know, Grandmother. Where is my niece? Why can't we find her on the Island? She should be there. Her father should be there."

Grandmother shook her head and poked the fire. She grumbled, and Itza' thought she was whispering to herself for a moment, but she couldn't make out the words.

"Grandmother, I'm going to look for her either way," Itza' said. "I have to find her. No matter what it takes."

"You can try," Grandmother said in an oddly deep voice. A low laugh crawled from her throat.

Itza' felt that odd chill again. The old woman's voice hadn't sounded normal, as though someone else spoke through her.

Itza' eyed the old woman cautiously. "What does that mean, Grandmother?"

Then Grandmother smiled. Her eyes vanished in the wrinkles of her face. But she never looked away from the fire. "It means that times are changing, little one. A powerful force is coming."

Then, as though speaking to herself, she added, "The snake will decide."

"Decide what? What is coming, Grandmother? The Great Army?"

"Hm? Oh—what? No, no, no. Not what, my dear. Who." Grandmother raised her eyebrows for emphasis. She tilted her head and nodded as though someone had said something to her.

"Who? Who is it, Grandmother?"

"*Her*," Grandmother said, pointing with her stick into the fire as though the answers were right there in front of Itza', and how could she not see?

"She is coming," Grandmother said, finally turning to look Itza' in the eyes. The intensity of her stare sent chills down Itza's spine as the old woman's eyes bored into her.

"*She* is coming, Great Queen. The jaguar is coming."

Chanil's spirit slipped in the muddy ground of the steep hill. She caught herself, landing on all fours. Her unbound hair fell down in front of her face, and she breathed heavily.

She felt an odd pain in her stomach. Her back. She felt warm blood dripping down her arms and her neck. The droplets fell from her clavicles onto the muddy ground below and she watched the little red pools forming.

Get up! her mind screamed.

Standing, she saw she was on a muddy path leading down a steep hill into utter darkness. And there, in the middle of the road before her, was the giant yellow jaguar. She recognized its blocky head and bright eyes. The irises sparkled like sunlight, and the old jaguar had a gentle calm about it as it watched her.

Chanil swallowed hard. Her bare feet curled into the ground, and she felt the cool mud squeeze between her toes.

She crossed slowly to the jaguar, taking deliberate steps so that she would not fall again. Her body ached, and she felt blood seeping from four hundred different cuts. But she pressed forward, relentless.

Her body went cold. She felt a chill and dropped to her knees before the large jaguar.

"I can't stand," she whispered, barely able to hold her head up.

The jaguar made a snuffling sound and moved forward. She smelled the warm, earthy scent of the animal, the tinge of blood in the air. She felt the jaguar press its large head against the side of her neck and nuzzle against her.

"It's time." Chanil had no idea where the words came from. She felt her eyelids closing as she leaned into the soft warmth of the jaguar's body.

"Am I dead?" Chanil heard herself say. The jaguar pressed harder into her, and Chanil knew that meant yes.

"My baby . . ." She could barely get the words out. Her voice cracked, and the tears flowed out and mixed with the growing pool of blood on the ground.

"She will need you." The voice was harsh, raspy. But also, familiar somehow. It jolted Chanil up and she pulled away from the jaguar, her eyes wide.

"She will need you," the voice repeated. "Follow me, brave warrior."

Then the jaguar turned and walked down the hill into the inky blackness below. Chanil suddenly found herself able to stand again. Her body didn't ache as much anymore. It felt almost light, airy. As she forced herself to move down the hill and follow the jaguar's path, she felt lighter and lighter with every step, until all her pains eventually faded away and she slipped into the darkness.

Acknowledgments

This book would not have been possible without the support and hard work of so many people. I would like to thank my family and friends for being so supportive of me. In particular, I would like to thank Tohfa, Maya, and Nicole for putting up with the endless hours of listening to ideas and new drafts and then final drafts of a story that ended up very far from where it originated. Without their constant support, patience, feedback, and, most of all, enthusiasm, I would not have had the courage to keep going and finish this book.

I would like to thank the entire publishing team at Fifth Avenue Press. Erin and Emily for their continued guidance throughout the publication process. Nate for helping design the cover. And, of course, my wonderful editor, Gabriella Jones-Monserrate, without whom nothing in this book would be the same. She worked many long hours with me to help craft Chanil's story, the way it was intended to be. I also give a huge thanks to Raúl Cruz for his tireless work on the cover and map.

I would like to thank Victor Montejo, the Guatemalan scholar, philosopher, poet, and so much more, whose work has always inspired me throughout my life and whose published version of El Q'anil was one of the initial inspirations for this novel in its original form. I give thanks to my uncle, Quetzil, for teaching me about

Mayan languages and providing endless resources on all things related to the Maya region. I would not have been able to navigate the linguistic elements of this novel without that knowledge.

I also give thanks to my Guatemalan (Ixim Ulew) and Puerto Rican (Boriken) ancestors, for the knowledge and stories they have passed on directly and indirectly, through dreams and visions and late-night conversations. The Indigenous communities of Guatemala and Puerto Rico, and indeed, everywhere in the world, continue to endure, persists, resist, and thrive even as power structures around them seek to degrade their very existence. In recognition of the contributions of some of these fights, all profits from the sale of this book will be invested in Indigenous-led and operated organizations in Guatemala that seek to empower Indigenous communities and support their struggles.

Thank you to anyone I have overlooked. The fault is entirely mine. I appreciate every comment, word of support I have ever received. Big thank you to all the coffee shops and bookstores where parts of this book may have been written or conceived.

Milton Keynes UK
Ingram Content Group UK Ltd.
UKHW031947281024
450365UK00008B/501